QUILLIFER THE KNIGHT

QUILLIFER

———

BOOK TWO

WALTER JON WILLIAMS

QUILLIFER
THE KNIGHT

WITHDRAWN

SAGA PRESS

LONDON SYDNEY **NEW YORK** TORONTO NEW DELHI

SAGA PRESS
AN IMPRINT OF SIMON & SCHUSTER, INC.

1230 AVENUE OF THE AMERICAS, NEW YORK, NEW YORK 10020

For Kathy Hedges

COLDWATER

WEST MOSS

GLENFIRTH

STEDLAW

MINNITH PEAKS

BLACKSYKES

HYTHE ORDIC

R. SAELLE

ABERUVON

ALLINGHAM

KINGSMERE

MOSSTHORPE

INNISMORE

FORNLAND

SELFORD

THE TOPPINGS

INCHMADEN

Sea of Duisland
(Mare Postremum)

WHELARGID

WEST RANGE

NEWTON LINN

USKMORE

R. OSTRA

ETHLEBIGHT

AMBERSTONE

GANNET COVE

PENARTHAR

MUTTON
ISLAND

REALM OF DUISLAND

CHAPTER ONE

You were born at Winecourt, on that blessed sun-struck coast of southern Bonille, where the vineyards line the river valley and produce vintages famous throughout the world. You disappointed me when you told me the origin of your city's name, for instead of a word pairing that evokes a land devoted to delight and song and the inspiration of the grape, it's merely the capital of some old Sea-King named Winefrith, who gave his name to the place and died.

A disappointment that history may have been, but it was the only time you have disappointed me. For I delight in you, in the sweet caress of your lips, in the scent of myrrh that hangs in your masses of black hair, in the little freckles that cross the bridge of your nose, the freckles that embarrass you but each of which I would kiss if I could.

I find your forbearance a wonder. You know my faults better than anyone—you have, to a degree, indulged them—and you forgive me more easily than I forgive myself. You know how badly I have compromised myself, and you forgave me ahead of time.

It is well that we league so well together, so that in each other's company we form a kind of single organism. How else would I dare to commit such treason as we have planned? Were I alone in the world, I would quail before the enormity of the crime. Yet as we are together, united in heart and united in thought, I find myself ready to topple lords from their seats, kings from their thrones, and the gods themselves from their aery realms.

It is not treason if we prevail.

Well, enough of that. We are committed to our emprise, and it's far too late for second thoughts. There is no point in worrying now. Let me kiss you and see if your lips provide the inspiration for another subject.

Ah, indeed. Yesterday you asked me about the crooked little finger on my left hand and were surprised when I told you it was a result of a shipwreck. I had not the time to tell you of that voyage yesterday, but if you will join me on my couch, pillow your head on my shoulder, and spread your warm, soft hair on my breast, I will don my noble-hero face and relate the story, though I may intermingle it with kisses or caresses as the fancy takes me.

Winecourt is a port city, and of course you are familiar with the ships that sail in and out of the harbor. Even the blessed climate of southern Bonille can be subject to storms, as I know from having looked down at the Races from my house at Dunnock and seen the water foam white through those famous fang-toothed rocks deadly to ships. You account yourself a good sailor and thrived on that winter voyage we shared to Balfoy, in northern Loretto.

Yet that voyage was paltry compared to the roaring wind that blew *Royal Stilwell* onto the iron shore of Fornland. For five days we had taken no sight of the sun, or seen a single star, and we knew not where on the great ocean we were.

I was half-owner of the ship, which I had helped capture in the late war, and *Royal Stilwell* was homeward bound from far Tabarzam, laden with fine silks, spices, incense, fragrant cedarwood, ivory, and that rare wine made from sweet grapes raisinated on straw. The cargo was worth more than the ship, and I was in a mad terror lest I lose it all—and that was not my only concern, for though the cargo was insured, my life was not, and all other things being equal, I preferred to preserve myself. Yet my captain, a seasoned skipper named Gaunt, had seen the mare's tails curling high in the sky as they blew in from the northwest and knew that a storm would follow. We had taken all precautions, the upper masts struck down, canvas shortened, the guns double-breeched and the wheels blocked, the cargo roped and wedged into immobility, and safety lines and nets rigged over the decks. The bonaventure-mizzen, our fourth mast, had proved vulnerable to weather in the past, and so it was struck below.

Yet the storm, when it came, overwhelmed all our preparation. We saw it coming across the night horizon, a long, silent, ominous line of lightning flashes advancing toward us like a skirmish-line of ghosts. The wind nearly died away, and then, in a great lightning-flare, we saw the great wave the storm pushed ahead of it, a black onrushing shadow with a foam-flecked crest like the slaver of a hungry animal.

"Hold fast!" cried Gaunt. "Hold fast, my rampallions!"

He was a sturdy man of great strength, with enormous fists like kegs at the ends of his arms, and he latched onto the bulwark with both his powerful hands. I had time to seize the fife rail, and then the wave broke over our larboard quarter and swept us to the stem. I am a big, strong fellow, as you know, but I felt my arms almost pulled from their sockets by the force of the sea. I was underwater for I know not how long, and I felt the deck tilt beneath my feet, a list so severe that my feet flew out from under me; and then I was surrounded by foam, and the ship slowly righted, and I found myself on my knees with my arms still holding the rail. All was noise and shrieking—not just the cries of the seamen who had been swept overboard or into the safety nets or piled in a vast struggling mass of arms and legs and broken heads at the break of the forecastle, but the wail of the storm-wind in the rigging, from the deep bass tones of the backstays, to the tenor cries of the shrouds, to the treble screams of the running rigging, a hellish chorus that drowned the voices of the mortal men who fought for their lives amid the wrack.

Royal Stilwell staggered upright as the great weight of water poured off the decks. "Up with the helm!" shouted Captain Gaunt, barely heard over the hurly-burly of the storm. "We must not be rolled under!"

The timoneers picked themselves from the deck and hurled themselves against the whipstaff, fighting the great weight of the rudder and the force of the water that drove against it. Thanks to the captain's swift action, we managed not to slew broadside to the wind, which would have been the end of us, but instead ran before the storm. And though we had set only the spritsail and a reefed foresail, with such a wind behind us we ran like the swiftest courser in the royal stable.

Yet there was one being in the salt sea faster than we, for I saw it come gliding down the front of a wave as it loomed above our poop—a great ocean serpent, vivid green striped with yellow and a great horned head with a thick viridescent mane that might have been hair, or might have been seaweed. Though the night was black, I saw it perfectly well, for, like many of our supernatural visitors from the Land of Chimerae, it seemed to glow with its own shimmering light. As our stern lifted beneath the rising swell, I raised a hand to shield my eyes against the blaze of the sea-drake, for such beings are difficult to look at for anyone from this mortal world. Though the worm was bearing right down on us, and large enough to damage the ship, and though that great snarling head was filled with teeth that could have engulfed a sheep with ease, I was too struck with wonder to feel fear.

The monster soared down the face of the wave and loomed over the poop, bright as a beacon, and I held my breath and clutched the fife rail in anticipation of a collision; but at the last second the creature twisted its serpentine body and surged up along our larboard side. I had a glimpse of one great golden eye, and somehow sensed amusement glimmering there, as if the sea-drake relished the storm and its unlikely encounter with a ship and the surprised officer who stared from the quarterdeck. And then wave and foam spilled over the ship, and when the poop rose again from the water, the beast was gone.

We found it difficult sailing, for *Royal Stilwell* was a high-charged galleon, with large fore- and aftercastles, and the wind caught these tall structures and tried to blow us broadside to the waves, which would have rolled us under in an instant. We could only preserve ourselves by constant attention to the finer points of sailing. Every wave smashed with its great weight against the rudder, and so exhausting was the battle to hold our course that we had to relieve the men at the whipstaff every half hour. The ship's timbers worked so heavily that the caulking was squeezed from between the planks, allowing water to jet into the vessel, and the carpenter and his mates had to wade through frigid water in the bilges and hammer the oakum back into place. We all grew aware, as we never had before, that there was only a handsbreadth of wood between us and our instantaneous doom.

For two days we ran before the wind. The days were nearly as dark as the nights, and the sun was never visible behind the dense storm-cloud. The sea formed great, scudding, heaving mountains of foam, and foam blew in long salt streamers over the decks. The pumps were at work all the day long. The ship was so wet that we could never sleep dry, and our only meals were cold biscuit and cheese chased with small beer. We had no meat, for if we tried to steep the salt beef, the fresh water would have rolled right out of the tubs. My body was sore with being thrown against bulkheads or pinrails or the capstan, and I'd had but little sleep.

Our voyage to Tabarzam and back had taken eleven months, during which time I had worked at learning the sea-officer's craft, and Captain Gaunt judged that I was qualified to stand a watch. This was lucky, as one of the mates suffered a broken leg in the storm's first onset, and another was overcome by terror, ran weeping to his cabin, and refused to come out. So I stood a watch, though Gaunt ordered the boatswain to stand the watch with me, and prevent me from making a fatal error. I made no such error, though I was grateful for the bosun's support. Nor did I confine myself to an officer's duties, but helped to mend, splice, and secure along with the ordinary seamen.

Our compass was worth but little, though it suggested that the wind was backing from northwest to southwest. We had every right to believe Fornland was below our lee, and I expected at any moment to see the cliffs of Penarthar rear up right before our bows. Captain Gaunt was as concerned by this prospect as I, and when it was clear the wind was continuing its shift to the south, he decided to stop flying before the wind and heave the ship to.

Royal Stilwell would ride quite naturally without a single sail aloft, for so tall was our sterncastle that it would act like a wind-vane and keep the bow pointed directly into the oncoming sea. Yet the timing of the evolution would be difficult, for we would have to turn the ship about in a neat half-circle and not be caught broadside by a wave in the middle of the maneuver.

Captain Gaunt called the officers onto the poop to best consider how to perform our evolution. We clung there to lines or rails and shouted over the shrieking wind as spume rattled like hailshot into our faces.

"We must snap her right round," said Gaunt. He was pale with exhaustion, and his great hands were torn and bloody. "The spritsail must be doused in an instant, and the lateen put right to weather."

"We will not be able to hear you," said the chief mate. "And it may be too dark to see any signal. Can you use a lantern?"

"We may not be able to keep it alight. Can you hear whistles, do you think?"

"We would be lucky to hear a cannon!"

I was puzzling how to snap the bow around, and it occurred to me to drop a mast overboard. This was the sort of inspiration only exhaustion could produce, for cutting down one of our own masts was a mad idea, and though it would drag alongside and spin the ship around, it would have to be cut free at exactly the right instant, or *Royal Stilwell* would keep going in circles till she foundered. Yet there were other things we could throw in the water.

"Can we put out a sea-anchor?" I asked. "Snub off the hawser at the right moment, it may tug us into the wind."

This was debated for a while, and in the end the debate was ended by exhaustion, for no one had a better idea.

"Pray Pastas this may serve!" said the captain.

"May the Netweaver give us strength," the chief mate said piously, and then we dispersed to our tasks. As the sea-anchor had been my idea, I was put in charge of it, and so I took a party to rouse out some old canvas from the sail-locker, then brought up one of the smaller hawsers from the cable tier and lashed one to the other. I put some cannon shot in the roll of canvas to make sure the old sail got in the water promptly and did not float on top. I soon had everything ready atop the larboard forecastle, and I reported to the captain on the quarterdeck.

Gaunt sheltered beneath the break of the poop deck, with the whipstaff and the binnacle before him, and the miserable timoneers holding our course against the brute strength of the storm. He had two lanterns to signal with, and a whistle, and his own great voice. He had been waiting only for me to report, for my errand had taken the longest to prepare, and the other officers were already at their stations. He explained how he planned to signal, and I shouted into his ear that I understood.

"But I do not know if I will see those lanterns, or hear the whistle," said I. "The storm is so black, and the spray so dense, that I can find my way only by feel."

"You will have to judge by the movement of the vessel," said Gaunt.

I went forward, clinging to bulwarks and lines as the sea burst over me. The lantern-light faded behind me as I groped my way over the streaming deck. I was in doubtful mind, uncertain whether I was experienced enough to know when or how to do my duty.

I took my station on the forecastle, and clung to the shrouds while gazing aft in hopes of seeing the lantern-signal through spray and foam and bursting waves. It was at that moment that I remembered the opening words of *The Art of Navigation*, a book I'd borrowed from the captain to further my study, written some decades earlier by Antonio de Wivara, a veteran sea-captain of Varcellos.

> Do no one enter the sea by choice but out of necessity, but because the man who sails, if it were not for the relieving of his conscience, to defend his honor or to protect lives, I say and affirm that such a person is a fool, or bored, or completely crazy.

It occurred to me that I had fair claim to be all three.

Royal Stilwell lifted as water boiled under our larboard quarter; then timbers groaned and the ship rolled as a wave hurled itself against us. I ducked my head as salt water sluiced over me, and I sensed the ship rising atop the great mountain of water. As the crest of the wave passed beneath us, I felt the galleon's motion change. I strained my senses as I peered aft, but I saw no lights, heard no whistle. The wind still keened through the rigging, and the ship still sped through the water.

Captain Gaunt, I knew, would not throw the rudder hard over: The great wooden blade would then act as a brake, and the ship would lose way and wallow in the wave-trough. The helm had to be put up gently, the spritsail and foresail braced round to keep as much way on her as possible.

Spray stung my face, and the howling wind seemed to snatch the breath from my lungs. The wind was definitely shifting forward, and from this I knew the turn had begun. Dimly I sensed men bustling around me, sailors who belonged to another party who tended the spritsail sheets and braces.

"Ready the sea-anchor!" I cried. "Stand clear of the cable!"

My party of sailors heaved the old sail to their shoulders and carried it to the bulwark. The canvas had to be thrown cleanly into the water, threading it between the highly organized tangles of line that were shrouds, stays, and the running rigging. Not only was the rigging an obstacle, but the storm-wind was trying to blow the sea-anchor back in our faces, or to tangle it on the flukes of the bower anchor lashed to the forecastle just below the level of the deck.

I could feel the wind shift forward. Suddenly there was slatting and banging overhead, a vast thunder like a cannonade, and fire stitched along my worn nerves. The foresail had gone aback, the wind now lifting and whipping the canvas instead of filling it. The chief mate hadn't braced the sail around fast enough, and if he didn't correct the mistake soon, the sail would take the wind in front and act as a giant brake, stopping our way and even sending us stern-first through the water. In the present circumstance this could only mean disaster.

At the crashing and booming overhead my mind chattered madly, and I felt an overwhelming impulse to do *something*, anything, to retrieve the situation. I resisted the impulse to order the sea-anchor over the side. I looked aft again for a signal or command, and again saw nothing.

Royal Stilwell rocked as the force of the wind lessened. We were in the trough between two waves, and the oncoming wave was to a degree blocking the wind. Yet so far as I could tell, we were still making way through the water, and the flogging foresail hadn't yet put a stop to our movement. As the wind's scream faded slightly, I could hear the chief mate's commands: *"Haul taut!—Brace up!"* And suddenly, with a great shivering roar, the foresail filled, and *Royal Stilwell* surged ahead.

"Let go the lee sheet and halliards! Clew down!" Another voice boomed out of the darkness, surprisingly near where I stood on the forecastle. It was the second mate, and he was dousing the spritsail, because we had run so far up into the wind he could no longer keep it full. "Let go the weather sheet! Clew up!"

The foresail over my head began to rattle again. I assumed it was braced around as far as it would go, and that the chief mate would douse it at once before it went aback. That foresail was our last bit of canvas, and after this the ship would lose way quickly. I felt the bow lift and the wind freshen on my face. "Let go the sea-anchor!" I said. "Get it into the water!"

The seamen hurled the roll of canvas into the water, and I rushed forward to make sure it cleared the bower anchor and other obstacles. I could see nothing and received a face full of ice-cold seawater for my pains. But I groped for the hawser and felt it shooting over the bulwark, nearly scorching my fingers, and I knew the canvas had found its way into the sea.

Royal Stilwell was losing way and beginning to stagger in the face of the oncoming wave. I tried to judge how much cable had flown out—ten fathoms? fifteen?—and then reasoned that I could always let out more of the hawser if I needed to.

The hawser had been allowed to run out between the uprights of a stanchion, so that a crewman could draw it against the stanchion if necessary and provide a check on its speed. "Belay the cable!" I said, and the crewman threw a loop of the hawser over one of the stanchion's uprights, and the line snapped taut with a sudden deep bass *thrum*.

The ship was wallowing now, and I sensed that it had lost all momentum and was stumbling back along the slope of the wave, the fore- and aftercastles buffeted by the wind. Spray pelted the deck. I divined the crest of the wave gathering over us, and I knew that we had failed, and that only luck could save the ship.

"Hold fast!" I cried, and wrapped my arms around a pair of shrouds. Then there was a cracking noise from the stanchion, and I felt the hawser snap against my waist like a great iron bar. It knocked me to one side, and then the entire ship tossed as the bow lunged to windward. In an instant the wave was crashing into us, tons of water thundering over the larboard bow and pouring like a cold river onto the forecastle. I locked my arms around the shrouds and was buried in black water, blind and hopeless, conscious only of my own failure and the lives that would be lost to my mistake.

Then I felt *Royal Stilwell* lift again, and suddenly there was a blast of wind in my face, and the ship was shrugging off the water like a great whale breaching from the sea. Through my oilskins I felt the cable still hard against my side, the ship's beak was angling down again as we followed the curve of the wave, and we were no longer careening headlong before the storm, but moving in a staid, stately way with the wind howling over our larboard bow. . . . The sea-anchor had worked and brought the bow around at the very last second.

I sagged against the shrouds with relief, my knees grown weak. As soon as I had caught my breath, I began assembling my party again to better secure the cable. I was afraid the power of the wind and waves would tear the stanchion clean off the deck and take the cable with it, so I carried the tail of the hawser around the foremast and snugged it tight so the mast would take the weight rather than the stanchion. By the time I'd accomplished this task, another wave rose white-crested over the ship and broke over the forecastle. But this time we weren't buried in water but in spray and foam, and I realized that we were now riding almost easily under bare poles, with the storm pushing the sterncastle downwind, and the sea-anchor off-setting us just a few points, so that the bow didn't bury itself in an oncoming wave, but lifted gently toward the crest.

I reported to the captain, and once the ship had ridden a few more waves and he was satisfied, he dismissed everyone but the men on watch.

We were riding so much more easily that the cooks were able to start their fires and were able to keep the fresh water in the steeping tubs, so soon we were served a pottage made with dried peas and onions, followed by salt beef, cheese, and a plum duff filled with currants and raisins and drenched in molasses. Those of us in the officers' berth were also treated to a hot brandy punch, and this sent me to my boxlike bed with my head spinning and my skin aglow with warmth. I slept soundly till my watch was called. The ship was riding well enough that I had little to do except keep my eyes peeled for the horrid specter of land looming up under our lee.

This possibility disturbed the captain as well, and he had a hawser rove out of the starboard hawsehole and fixed to the starboard bower anchor, just in case cliffs loomed up in our path and we had to drop an anchor and pray it would hold.

After my watch I had another hot meal and slept dreamlessly for eight hours. When I rose, I found myself so hobbled by pain and bruises that I could barely manage to don my oilskins. I had some cheese, biscuit, salt pork, and, for warmth, a cup of mulled wine, then dragged myself onto the quarterdeck.

The storm raged like a fury for another day, then began to diminish. The sky was gray rather than black, and the waves, though steep, no longer loomed over the ship like a toppling tower. The foam did not cover the whole sea, but lay in white streaks on the water. *Royal Stilwell* rode more placidly on the waves, and the crew were able to rest and to have regular hot meals.

I invited Captain Gaunt and the others to dinner on the morning of the fifth day. I issued the invitations not in the character of a junior officer, but rather that of the ship's owner, and had them to dine in my own splendid cabin under the poop, with food from my own pantry. I served a pottage of vegetables and bacon, followed by pick-led oysters and anchovy, ham, spiced Varcellos sausages, fresh-baked white manchet-bread, and lastly a cake sweetened with dried fruit. This with wine and brandy, and I brought out my guitar, and we sang a few songs, "Old Captain Jermain" and other favorites.

It was the best meal we'd enjoyed since we'd left land, and the best sauce was that we had escaped from deadly danger and now had every chance of coming safe into port and selling our cargo for a great profit.

"Thank the Compassionate Pilgrim," said Gaunt as he sipped from the wine-cup in his vast fist. "He has given us the wisdom to endure the storm."

"Was it the Pilgrim, or rather Pastas Netweaver?" asked I. "For I heard you call upon the god when we were in danger."

Gaunt flushed, for he was a most thorough champion of the Pilgrim's philosophy and quite learnèd in his own way. He was com-pletely self-taught and mingled the Pilgrim's thought with his own hard-earned wisdom. He had made strenuous efforts to convert me to the Pilgrim's path, and we'd had many discussions during the long night watches, in which he urged me to abandon the old gods, who he maintained did not exist, and view the Pilgrim himself as divine.

I had my own reasons for crediting the existence of gods, which I did not share with him; but it was for the joy of argument that I opposed the captain's opinion, and many and fine and eloquent were our debates as we paced the deck beneath the stars.

But now it seemed I'd caught him out, calling upon one of the gods he maintained did not exist.

"Though the Compassionate Pilgrim knew the minds of men," Gaunt finally said, "I have not heard that the Pilgrim knew aught of the sea, and so when I have time for reflection, I follow the Pilgrim's teachings. But in a storm I pray to Pastas, like a sailor."

"That is pragmatic philosophy," I said, "and I cannot gainsay it." I raised a glass, on the verge of toasting the captain and his accommodation with divinity. But at that moment there was a great thunder of feet on the planks above our heads, followed in seconds by a pounding on my cabin door. The boatswain entered in dripping oilskins and spoke the words that froze our blood.

"Land!" he cried. "Land right under our lee!"

CHAPTER TWO

Perhaps you would refill my wine-cup? It is thirsty work to relive that storm, to feel again my fear and my bruises, and to remember the taste of salt spray on my tongue.

Now we are engaged in something just as hazardous. If I am not so afraid now, it is because you are with me.

Tomorrow we shall be traitors, but until then we are free to consider only pleasure. Therefore I will rest my head in your lap and continue my tale. It seems that tonight I am far more comfortable speaking of my past than reflecting upon my future.

On hearing the boatswain's despairing cry, we abandoned our feast and dashed up on deck, and through the surge and spray we saw black, jagged cliffs lining the northern horizon, four or five miles distant. The wind was from the south and blowing us right down on the land.

"We shall have to put sail on her," said Captain Gaunt. His great fists fastened on the taffrail as if he would tear it clean away. "Call up all hands."

While the pipes shrilled down the hatches, we returned to our rooms to don our oilskins. I looked about the remains of my abandoned feast, and wondered if I should ever see that cabin again. I reflected that if I were to die, it were best to die with a belly full of good food and wine, and so I quickly pledged myself with another cup and ate a piece of cake, and then I ran up to the deck and awaited orders. Now I was no longer the owner of the ship, but rather the most junior officer on the quarterdeck.

The sea-anchor put the wind on our larboard bow, and thus when we made sail, we would be on the larboard tack. Gaunt's orders came fast and were emphasized by flailing arms and fists, as if he were engaged in a boxing-match with some invisible foe.

"Lay aloft and loose the foresail! Lay aloft, the afterguard! Loose the mainsail! Stand by—let fall! Down from aloft! Man tacks and sheets! Clear away the rigging—haul aboard!"

The ship heeled mightily as the sails filled, even though they were thrice-reefed, and I gazed at the sea in alarm as the deck seemed to fall away beneath me. Sea-foam boiled over the lee bulwark, and the taut canvas was hard as iron. The sea-anchor, which had so well preserved us in the worst of the storm, was cut free. The timoneers fought to hold *Royal Stilwell*'s course as the spritsail and lateen were set. Even under these few sails, we surged through the water with the sea hissing beneath our keel, spray crashing over the bows, fast as a shining carbonero. My heart leaped at the way the galleon took to the sea, and I found myself grinning as the spray dotted my face. Truly, I thought, it was good to be young, and alive, and engaged in a contest with the elements. But soon enough my smile began to fade.

To explain why, I must make a digression, and for that I beg your pardon. In your girlhood in Winecourt you saw ships, and were no doubt familiar with their ways, but you have not conned a ship in a storm, or had to cope with clawing to windward off a lee shore.

Royal Stilwell was, you remember, a high-charged galleon, with tall fore- and aftercastles that caught the wind. The wind's pressure on the hull, masts, and rigging drove the ship to leeward, a motion the ship resisted with its deep keel, which is why a ship heels as the wind tries to push its upper works over, and the keel resists. But the keel cannot hold the ship still, and as long as the wind blows, the ship will scud to leeward, whatever its attitude toward the wind. This constant downwind movement is called "leeway" and is always present.

Stilwell's fastest point of sailing was with the wind on either quarter, or behind, but she could not sail into the wind, or anywhere near it. We could lay our course about a point into the wind and no more, and that was with the lateen pushing the stern down as far as it could, and the timoneer leaning on the whipstaff with all his weight. If we pinched up any closer, we would begin to lose way and soon be in irons.

A point into the wind should have been enough to keep clear of the land, but not in a great storm. For the vast force of the storm-wind overcame the resistance of the keel, and heeled the ship far over and drove it toward the land faster than we could make up the distance by sailing. Thus, even though we sped fairly through the water with the sea boiling beneath our hull, we grew ever closer to that iron shore, and it soon became clear to all of us that we would be wrecked if we stayed on the larboard tack.

Yet we could not put her about. We could not tack across the wind, because the storm would blast us back and drive us stern-first upon the land, most likely with our masts tumbling about our ears. And we could not wear the ship around, for we had not the sea-room and would go directly on the shore.

"Can we not drop another sea-anchor?" I asked the captain. "Off the starboard side, so that it puts us on the starboard tack?"

Gaunt wiped spray from his face and turned to me the hollow, weary eyes of despair. "We have not time to make one."

"Have we not the bower anchor ready?"

Gaunt was silent for a moment as the idea moved visibly across his face, and then kindled a light in his eyes. "By Pastas," he said, "I will do it."

I grinned at him. "Do you not mean 'by the Pilgrim'?"

There came no answer, for he was already shouting orders. "Leadsmen to the forepeak! Muster the crew on the main deck!"

The leadsmen began to cast their leads, to determine the depth of the water, and found no bottom. This was worrying for, looking at the land, I could see black, stony cliffs rising sharp from the great boiling mass of white surf-spray, and I knew that the land above the sea often reflected what was beneath it. If the land gently shelved down to the sea, then it very likely shelved into the water as well. Likewise, if the land dropped suddenly into the ocean, there was very likely deep water just offshore.

If the anchor found no bottom, then we were surely doomed.

The crew was mustered before the break of the quarterdeck, a wet, dispirited mob huddled in their gleaming oilskins and facing the certainty of their own death. I looked down at their faces, upturned and pale like flowers seeking the sun during rainfall, and then Gaunt stepped forward to the quarterdeck rail and spoke.

"I'm going to drop the best bower," he said, "and use it to bring us round on the other tack. You must listen to my orders, my cockerels, and obey instantly. Now take stations for stays, and watch me with care, for if there is a mistake, we are done for."

The hands ran to their stations with hope speeding their steps. Gaunt sent the chief mate forward with an axe party to cut the anchor cable on his signal. And at that moment came a relieved cry from one of the leadsmen.

"By the mark twenty!" And only a few seconds later the other called, "Quarter less twenty!"

Twenty fathoms. Relief flooded me as I knew there was bottom beneath our keel.

"Keep her full!" said Gaunt to the timoneers. "Get a good way on her!"

"Half less twenty!"

"Ease your helm down, my bawcocks!" Gaunt said. "Ease her!" *Royal Stilwell*'s bow began to swing into the wind.

"Silence fore and aft! Stand by the anchor! Stand clear of the cable!"

Royal Stilwell hesitated in the wind, and the mainsail overhead lifted, its canvas trembling.

"Let go the anchor!"

The mainsail thundered overhead as the bower anchor crashed into the water. There was a bright flash forward, from the friction as the cable ran out, and for a second we were lit as if by lightning.

The galleon swung into the wind, and the relentless storm-wind caught us and flung us backward, the canvas all flogging, the ship drifting stern-first toward its destruction. Then the ship came to a shocking halt as the hawser went taut, and I was almost thrown off my feet. There was a great crash from all the gear followed by a babble of wonder from the crew, and then, above the din, the voice of the captain.

"Stop in your wind, now!" he admonished the crew. "Haul all together, my beauties! Haul! Haul!"

The crew bent double as they hauled the great yards around against the force of the wind. Spray burst over the forecastle, but I saw it was shooting up from the starboard bow, not the larboard.

"Cut the cable! Cut!" Gaunt made frantic chopping motions with his hands.

Against the sounds of roaring canvas and the shriek of the wind I didn't hear the axes biting, but very suddenly we were free and falling off the wind. The sails filled, one after the other, with a series of booms that sounded like cannon fire, and the ship heeled far over, as if reaching for the deadly cliffs that awaited us . . . and then we were in motion, foam flying past.

"Helm answers, Captain!"

"Ay. Keep her full, my gaberlunzies, my sweetlings!"

We were flying on the starboard tack, the spray showering over us. The quarterdeck, where I stood, swooped up each of the steep waves, then fell down the other side in a series of sudden drops, each ending in a shivering crash. I ran to the lee rail and tried to judge our heading in relation to the shore, and whether we were winning clear. I stood there for some time in the wind and spray, the sea boiling just beneath me, before I was able to judge that we were clawing off the coast.

I reported the good news to the captain.

"Ay," he said. "If the wind doesn't head us, we may win free."

I went back to the lee shrouds and continued measuring our course, and soon it was clear enough that yard by yard we were leaving the cliffs astern. Again my heart lifted, and again I grinned like a losel at my apparent victory over the elements. And then my grin faded, as, appearing through the mists ahead, I saw a rocky skerry appear, a gray silhouette standing out in a sea of foam like a tall ship plowing its steadfast way into the sea. I could not tell if we would clear its stony prow, and so I ran forward to view it from the forecastle. Again I could not be certain if she stood in our way or not, and so I ran back again to tell Captain Gaunt.

"Take a telescope," said he. "And tell me if you see a place where we may beach the ship. For if we do not clear the island, we may have no choice but to run her aground."

Again I ran forward and scanned both the island and the mainland for anything that looked like a friendly landing-ground. The mainland north and west of us presented nothing but tall cliffs rising from foaming waves, the frowning cliff-faces broken only by feathery, windblown waterfalls pouring off the scarp. The skerry ahead seemed to have a rocky tail of some kind trailing off to the north, but otherwise its cliffs seemed as formidable as those of the mainland.

My survey seemed pointless, however, for by the time I completed it, it seemed clear that we would clear the island, and I saw nothing else ahead of our track but flying scud and the gray, heaving sea. I returned to the quarterdeck and reported this to the captain, and Gaunt gave a laugh and thumped one of his big fists on the quarterdeck rail.

"Ay, we will have stories to tell our sweethearts!" he said. "For tacking with the anchor and the axes may be something no man has done before us. It was something new, and we performed it flawlessly and without scathe."

When I had reminded the captain of the bower anchor, I had intended no such maneuver, but rather anchoring offshore instead of running into the land. But if Gaunt was willing to credit me with the invention of this stratagem, I would be willing to accept the praise.

"Has that maneuver not a name, then?" asked I.

"Not one that I know."

I laughed. "Then I think we may call it 'Quillifer's Haul.'"

He looked at me from beneath one shaggy brow. "*You* may call it that," he said, "but I call it the blessing of the Pilgrim." At that instant was an almighty crack, and we saw directly in front of us the mizzenmast split along its length from the deck right up to the crosstrees. There was a breathless moment in which it seemed all time stopped and our hearts ceased to beat, and then the leeward part of the mast shivered and fell away, and brought all the rest down in ruin. We leaped for our lives as tons of mast and rigging and lateen sail all roared down onto the deck, and then all was frenzy as the crew was summoned to cut all away. The timoneers had run to save themselves with the rest of us, and we had to hack a way to the helm. The binnacle had been ruined, but the whipstaff still stood tall, leaning hard to weather and turning the ship toward the land. The timoneers threw themselves against it to point us up into the wind, but their effort was pointless, and *Royal Stilwell* was doomed.

For with the mizzen we lost the lateen sail, and we needed the lateen to push the stern to leeward and keep the bow into the wind. Now the ship's balance was lost, and even with the helm restored, we were now sailing right onto the skerry, with no hope of clawing our way off. Captain Gaunt ordered the spritsail doused, to keep us as far into the wind as might be, but it made little difference. Now it became of utmost urgency to let the captain know what I had seen in my survey of the coast, and I told him of the towering cliffs and of the little tail on the north end of the skerry.

"I will try to beach her there," Gaunt said. "We may be a little sheltered from the waves behind the island." He also ordered one of the chase guns on the forecastle cleared away and fired every few minutes, to alert anyone in the area to a ship in distress.

Even if they heard us, there was nothing they could do, except perhaps collect our bodies and bury them after the sea gave us up.

Gaunt and I went forward onto the forecastle to better see where we might strand the ship. I was in a strange fey mood—till this moment, even through fear and cold and weariness, I was determined to battle to save my ship and cargo. But now I had lost the ship and the battle, and my fear had fled along with my fierceness. I was but little interested in what might happen next, how ruin and death might come, for it seemed that everything of importance had already happened. I would die ere the day was over, and then someone else—my friends, my partners—would deal with what came next. And as for my ambitions—which I admit are considerable—they would remain unfulfilled. I felt something like satisfaction to let all that top-hamper blow away in the storm-wind and to stand on the rolling deck, to feel my face tingle to the cold spray, and to watch the rocks grow ever nearer.

"I must beg your forgiveness, Sir Quillifer," said Captain Gaunt. Spray rolled down his face like tears. "This is all my fault. The splitting of the mizzenmast was but his vengeance upon me."

I was puzzled. "Whose vengeance?"

"Pastas Netweaver," he said. "For I called upon Pastas to save us, and then gave the credit to the Pilgrim, and the mast split but a second later."

"Gods are quick to anger," said I, and I was right, for I have had some experience in this matter. "But it is foolish to blame a god when we may as well blame the workmen who scarfed that mast together and botched the job, or the storm that has been battering our gear for days, or the deep-hidden faults of one of the crewmen, whose surpassing wickedness some other god has decided to punish, and who has brought us all to this fate."

"I know well enough the wickedness of seamen," Gaunt said, "but in my heart I know the fault is mine." And from the deep sorrow on his face, I knew that at the knowledge of the ship's coming destruction, his great seaman's heart had broken.

"Be at peace," I advised, "save what we can, and perhaps some god will reward us for doing our duty."

"Gods reward worship and flattery, not *duty*," Gaunt snarled, and I recognized the Pilgrim's teachings in his words.

"Then practice your flattery," said I, "and tell the men that you are about to save them, and that they are the best sailors in the world."

He gave me a cynical look, but then he gazed out at the skerry with narrowed eyes and then viewed the island's foam-flecked tail with his telescope. Then he turned back to the break of the forecastle, waved one great fist, and addressed the men.

"You've done everything I've asked you, my cullies!" he said. "You've fought this storm to a standstill, and if it weren't for a bit of ill luck, you'd now be readying yourself for a feast, with beef and mulled wine and fig pudding! But now, my braves, we have one more test—for we must put the ship aground in the safest place I can find, and for that, my bawcocks, I must have your absolute and instantaneous obedience to orders. Now take your stations, and pray to every god you know to bring us safe to land!"

That seemed to hearten the men somewhat, but it was the captain I wished to hearten, and so I stepped forward, waved an arm, and shouted, "Three cheers for Captain Gaunt!" The men raised a cry, and I felt my own spirits rise a little.

As the men went to their stations, I took the telescope and viewed the skerry's tail of rocks, and it seemed to me that I saw more of them than I had before. "I think the tide may be on the ebb," I told the captain.

"Better let me have that telescope."

As I handed the glass to the captain, the signal gun went off, and I nearly jumped out of my oilskins. Gunpowder briefly tainted the air before being swept away. We were come within two cables of the skerry now, and I could see the gray cliffs blackened by rain, the white gannets that nested on the rock, and the few scrub trees on the island's crown.

"Ease up the helm!" Gaunt called. "Handsomely, now." *Royal Stilwell* fell off the wind, her speed growing as the wind filled her sails.

"Amidships!" For now we aimed directly for the island's tail, though the bow's pitching made it impossible for us to keep it fully in view.

Captain Gaunt called out small corrections to the helm, and I had nothing to do but watch. Again the fey spirit descended, and I wondered in a spirit of perfect disinterest what the captain intended. My mind filled with calculations, but they were not calculations for my survival, only a sort of wagering with myself as to the captain's course and the probability of his success.

"Down helm! Hard down!"

We were almost upon the rocks now, laid out across our path like the black, broken tusks of some long-dead monster. The galleon shuddered as the rudder bit the water, and the bow swung up into the wind. There was a grinding noise as we passed close inboard of one of the great tusks, and then we were past it, sailing free amid a sea of foam and sharp, looming stone. Both our remaining sails went aback, but the ship had good way on her, and we sailed on as our starboard bow crashed into one of the great black fangs, and we rebounded into another obstacle. A sea lifted us over the next set of rocks, and then *Royal Stilwell* ground onto hard stone just short of the skerry, and I held on to the forecastle stanchion in order to keep my feet. All way was lost, but a wave lifted us up, and we floated close enough to the island for the jibboom to shatter on the cliffs like a lance, taking with it the little platform that held the sprit topsail. Then the stern swung to larboard and we grounded again. The next wave failed to move us, just lifted us and dropped us again on the rocks. There was a cry from the timoneers as the rudder was flattened by an obstacle, and the whipstaff snapped to larboard.

More waves came, fountains of spray bursting over the bows, and the ship lifted to each wave, but *Royal Stilwell* remained trapped in its pen of stone. We were partly sheltered from the wind by the skerry, and only the fore part of the ship was exposed to the full force of the waves, but still we were grinding on the rocks, and it wasn't long before the carpenter came to tell the captain that the planks were stove in in at least three places, and that the damage was beyond his ability to repair. That handsbreadth of wood that stood between us and the end had failed us, and *Royal Stilwell* was sinking.

The gun went off again, as if to punctuate this final comfortless message. "Bring up food and fresh water to the sterncastle," the captain said. "The poop is high enough that it may remain above the waves. And we'll keep the pumps going as long as we can."

"You can try to turn the lateen into a shelter," I offered, but I was looking at the cliffs just three or four fathoms away and mentally charting the crags and handholds and chimneys that led to the skerry's crown. The strange detachment that had possessed me since the fall of the mizzenmast was beginning to drop away like a discarded cloak, and the wheels of my mind, frozen for a long moment by weariness and pain, were beginning to turn.

But first I turned to Captain Gaunt and embraced him. "You have saved us!" I said. "And now we may spit in Pastas's eye!"

A half hour passed before Captain Gaunt and I had finished our preparations. Canted slightly to starboard, *Royal Stilwell* had settled deep into its rocky den, and the sole reason the main deck was not awash was that the tide was running out and had left the ship stranded. Spray still boiled up over the starboard bulwark with each wave, and a cold rain still pelted down from the sky, and the ship still lifted with every sea. The signal gun had fallen silent, for all the gunpowder had been soaked.

Certain shrouds had been loosened, or cast away, and some stays had been slackened. Other lines had been rigged to the crosstrees and the main yardarm, and axe parties stood by in the waist. Captain Gaunt walked along the tilted deck, touching each line and muttering to himself, his eyes craned aloft to trace each line. As he walked along, he threw lines off the pins and let other crew flake them out on the deck, ready to run.

Finally he judged all ready and took his place on the quarterdeck. I leaned close to him and said, "First thing, send up the strongbox."

"Ay," said he. "I will not forget."

For my strongbox held not only silver but my own private merchant venture, into which I had sunk all my money. The box held as well the ship's papers and the bills of lading, which would be required to claim insurance. I had dealt with maritime insurance before, and I knew that the insurors' caviling was best forestalled through tactical deployment of the proper documents.

Gaunt took his place. "Ready, my rampallions, my madbrain rudesbys, my lass-lorn gangrels!" he cried. "Now cut! Cut and pray!"

Axes thudded down, and shrouds and stays parted. The ship lifted to a wave as spray exploded over the bow, and I saw the mainmast roll a little out of true, its tip scribing a circle against the gray sky. The wedges that held it securely in place had been knocked out. *Royal Stilwell*, and the mast, settled back into place.

Lines parted. Another wave burst over the ship, and the mast rolled again, its tip inscribing a larger circle in the sky.

The third wave pitched the mainmast right over to starboard, and that did the business—the mainmast cracked and popped right above the deck, long splinters flying like hailshot, and then the mast, with its yard and topmast and tackle, fell upon the skerry with a long, rolling series of crashes, like a rockfall.

The trick was not to shake the mast out of the ship—that part was easy and required only the cutting of enough of the mast's supports—but rather to drop the mast exactly where it was wanted, and to that end some of the stays and shrouds were carefully balanced, or loosened, or tightened, to produce just the effect we desired. Gangs of seamen were tailed onto lines in order to haul in, or let go, as needed. But the mast fell too quickly for even a single order to be given, and some lines were torn right out of the men's hands by the great mass of the falling timber.

Yet Captain Gaunt had judged aright, and the mast fell exactly where we had intended, in a kind of channel or flue extending partway up the skerry's cliff-face.

Now came my own part. I removed my oilskins, and a light line was wrapped around my waist. Then I sprang to the ruined mast and began to climb.

I should remark at this point that I am very good at climbing. I have no fear of heights, and I spent many long hours of my boyhood leaping from roof to roof in my home city of Ethlebight. In a failed attempt to save my family, I once climbed my city's walls when the town was attacked by Aekoi reivers, and I once fled across the roofs of Selford to avoid ruffians set upon me by a jealous nobleman.

To go aloft is daunting for landsmen taken aboard a ship, but it was not so with me. When I set myself to learn the seaman's profession, the first time I was taken aloft, I climbed to the masthead without trouble, and was soon skylarking in the rigging like a foretopman. Other aspects of the sailor's profession proved more difficult, such as the trigonometry required for navigation, which is difficult even with an abacus.

I hope you understand that I mention this not to boast, but to explain why it was I who scrambled up the fallen mast, and not some other. The sea roiled below me, ready to swallow me whole, and the mast was so draped in a tangle of shrouds and canvas and lines that the footing was treacherous—though it was also paradoxically safe, because there was so much cordage that if I fell, I could snatch at a line and save myself.

The clifftop was perhaps eighty or ninety feet above the sea, and the canted mast took me up the first thirty feet or so. A pair of seamen followed me carrying the line, so that it wouldn't be tangled in the wreckage. Once I had reached the chute leading upward, I took a careful look at the cliff and began to climb.

The stone was wet and therefore treacherous, and anything resembling a ledge had its own bird's nest, gannets for the most part but also guillemots and kittiwakes. The air reeked of bird droppings. In order to get a firm purchase upon the cliff I was forced to hurl or kick the nests into the sea, along with any unfortunate chicks dwelling there, for I had the lives of a hundred sailors to save, and there were plenty of sea-birds left over. Even when the nests were gone, the rock face was still slimy with droppings. Some of the adult birds defended their posts with vigor, and the slashing beaks soon had my right hand bleeding freely. And all the while the wind blew, and rain poured down the chute in a regular waterfall. I was soaked within minutes.

Despite the obstacles and the opposition of the birds, climbing the flue gave me little trouble. But twenty feet below the crest the flue came to an end, with a kind of overhang at the top that I could not climb over. I would have to leave the relative shelter of the flue and venture upon the open face of the cliff, and as I neared the cap, I studied the rock face with care. Though I had examined the cliff from the ship, the handholds could not be seen from below, and now I took my time and caught my breath while the rainwater sprayed down on my head. I made as complete an examination as I could and decided eventually the more promising path lay on my right.

No sooner had I groped my way out of the channel than a great shrieking gust of wind howled over the rock face and tried to pluck me bodily from the skerry and hurl me into the turmoil of the sea. The blast felt as if I were standing in front of a gun as it was discharged, and I recoiled. As I was blown back, my right hand was torn from the rock face, and my foot nearly slipped. My heart thrashed in my breast as I flailed wildly to regain the flue, and I remained there for a moment gasping for air. Over time I recovered myself, and I looked out again into the wind.

The gust that had nearly killed me had lasted only a few seconds, and there had not been another. But rather than risk that blast again, I decided to venture instead to the left.

I had to drop down the flue another ten feet before I could find a foothold strong enough to make the first attack on the rock face. I kicked away the bird's nest that occupied the ledge and carefully put my foot on the stone. Droppings oozed from beneath my shoe, and the stink of partially digested fish rose in the air. I reached out, found a protrusion that I could seize with my fingertips, and eased myself onto the rock face.

I waited for a long moment, expecting another blast of wind, but it did not come. I reached up with my free foot, discovered a crack that would support my weight, and pushed myself up.

And so I began the climb again, moving from one rain-drenched handhold to the next, fingers and toes straining to hold my weight. I had to take elaborate care that my feet not get tangled in the line I was trailing back to the ship. My arms and shoulders ached, and I felt a freezing cold invade my body where it was spread-eagled against the rock. My hands grew pale with cold, except where they were bloody from cuts. I was losing feeling in my fingers, and I tried stuffing one hand in my doublet to warm it, but my doublet was soaked and no warmer than anything else. I blew warm breath on my fingers and kept climbing.

Then I looked up, blinking in the rain just a few yards below the summit, and I could see no more handholds, just a bare rock face streaming with water, and a little vertical gash in the rock a few inches wide. I reached into the gash in hopes of being able to lodge my fingers, but the bottom of the scrape broke free, and I winced as stone bounced off my face.

I saw what might be a narrow foothold to my left, and I reached my foot toward it, but fell short. It seemed the only way I could reach it would be to take a wild, half-blind leap in that direction, and hope that I might find enough support to prevent me from tumbling into the void. In my current state this seemed not just unlikely, but impossible. Yet the alternative was to stay here until I froze, or try to work my way back down the cliff and into shelter, and both these courses seemed likely to end the same way, with a blind tumbling fall into the gulf below me.

I made my screaming-infant face out of frustration, reached into the little scrape again, and tried to feel the shape of it with my fingers. It was just narrower than my hand, but there was no fingerhold broad enough to hold any weight, just black rock sluiced with water.

I dared not look down and view the heave and scend of the black water that waited for me. Instead I began to try to think of something I could jam into the scrape that could support my weight.

But I had nothing. I carried a small knife for eating, but there was no way to jam it into the little scrape. I considered and rejected items of clothing, which wouldn't be firm enough to hold. And then I thought, lacking else, I might jam my*self* into the gap.

I worked my left hand into the gash, palm outward, and then made a fist, so that my hand pressed hard against the walls of the gap. Then I carefully pulled myself up by my hand and found that my jammed hand would support my weight.

Triumph flashed through my veins and warmed my chilled limbs. I may have laughed out loud. With slow care I regained my footholds, and then unclenched my hand. In order to swing farther to the left, it would have to be my right hand in the narrow gap, not the left.

Again I put in my hand; again I tested it to see if it would take my weight. Nothing crumbled away. With my left hand I reached for the line tied around my waist and snapped it out so that it wouldn't foul my legs. Then I took careful aim at the foothold and swung myself like a pendulum out into the void, supported only by my fist and my wayward hopes.

I scrabbled at the narrow ledge with my foot but failed to find purchase, and I swung back. I scraped the rock, found my old footholds, then took a breath of salt-tainted air and swung again. This time my foot found the ledge, tested it, and found it would support me.

With prudence I pushed upward, rising up the rock face, my left hand groping for a handhold. I found a small crack filled with soaking-wet moss, and I tore the moss away in order to establish a better hold. Now with my left foot and hand supported, I was able to unjam my right hand and venture farther onto the rock face. I replaced my left hand with my right, and then my left foot with my right foot, and then was able to grope farther out onto the rock, and there found a secure foothold, for all that I had to kick away a gannet before finding a reliable lodgment.

From this point it became much easier. The cracks and breaks in the rock were more frequent, and I was able to move upward with rising confidence until the rock face fell away inward—and, gasping for breath and clutching my wounded hands to my breast, I was able to scramble to a summit that seemed capped with snow.

But it was not snow, for the white cap moved. A hundred startled gannets shifted away from me in a kind of tide, dislodging other gannets as they moved. The gannets completely filled their rookery from one end to the other, a muttering mob of seabirds and their young, all hunched against the storm-wind that now struck me with full force, freezing me to the bone. What was not covered with gannets was covered in their droppings, and even the furious sea-wind did not entirely whip away the stench.

A woman stood there, clothed in a black, hooded cloak that did not entirely conceal her pale skin, brilliant green eyes, and streaming red hair.

"Well, Quillifer," said Orlanda. "I see you have returned at last to your homeland, and in much worse shape than when you left."

CHAPTER THREE

I wondered when I would see you," I said.

A cynical smile, or possibly contempt, curled Orlanda's lip. The wind-rippled strands of brilliant red hair blazed like tongues of flame around her face.

"You weren't doing anything amusing till now," she said. "Unless of course I was intended to be entertained by that drear parade of foreign women in your life."

"I didn't find them drear," said I. "Quite the opposite. And I hardly knew you found their exotic nature so offensive."

"No more offensive than their other attributes." Her chin tilted in the vast dark hood, and her green-eyed glance turned thoughtful. "It occurred to me that, as I've promised not to harm anyone you love, you might have been trying to render all womankind immune to my vengeance."

"That's it!" said I. "You've uncovered my secret plot!"

You must understand that while we were having this conversation I was drawing up more line from below, then untying the line from my waist and throwing a loop around a black, rain-slick outcrop of rock. I tied a knot, then tugged on the rope to make certain it was anchored securely.

All simple, ordinary tasks to accompany a conversation that, but for the setting and the black-cloaked woman, might have been the most ordinary in the world. Orlanda's brilliant green eyes followed me from one task to the next.

I went to the edge, flicked the line to send a long wave running down its length to the ship, and waved down to the crew on *Royal Stilwell*. A wave burst over the bow, the spray hurling itself like a white cloak over the half-submerged hull.

When the spray fell and dissolved, I saw arms wave in answer to mine and heard men's cheers over the scream of the wind.

"That broken mizzenmast?" asked I. "That was your doing?"

She offered a self-satisfied smile. "I would not wish your return to be entirely without savor."

I stared down at the black, all-consuming sea. Captain Gaunt had been cudgeling himself over having offended a god and caused the wreck. I had offered as an alternate the notion that the sins of one of the crew might instead be at fault, but I had done so without realizing that that crewman was myself.

"That savor might have killed a hundred men," said I.

"Yet it did not, but instead will provide yet another excuse for you to vaunt your superiority over your fellow mortals. Not," she added, "that you have ever required such an excuse."

I laughed wearily. "Am I then to thank you? But yet," I judged, "a broken mast seems under-subtle, not mischief but malice. Should you not be off whispering calumnies into the ears of the queen and her court?"

"And miss the chance to welcome you home? Did you really think I would fail to notice if you sailed into Selford harbor with a ship full of treasure?"

"I have sailed home before," said I, "and no masts broke."

"I am changeable," said Orlanda. "This you know."

And then she was gone, just as a sailor's head appeared above the crest. I helped him rise into this little isle of gannets, and then helped as well the six young men who followed.

With the line to help them climb and brace their feet against the stone, they had risen to the top of the skerry with good speed, as quickly as they might scramble to the masthead of their ship. I was no longer alone on the rock.

I must pause for a moment, as I see a great many questions reflected in your eyes. I know they have to do with Orlanda, and I would defer the answers, if I may. For that is a long explanation, and it would delay the resolution of my story. Which, you may recall, tells of how I broke my finger.

I tailed onto the line along with the seven sailors, and we hauled up a light hawser. More men came up, including the chief mate, and then the entire party used the hawser to bring up a topgallant yard, which we lashed to the rocky outcrop, so that one end hung out over *Royal Stilwell*. On this we fixed a luff tackle, which is to say a pair of pulleys, one on the end of the yard, and the other down on the ship, and the two connected by a strong line. With this arrangement we could haul up practically anything, and we started by taking up more crewmen. These brought up the oilskins that we had left behind. I was grateful to wear oilskins again, for though I was soaked through, the oilskins at least kept the wind out, and created a kind of waterproof tent that allowed my body's heat to warm the wet clothing now trapped against my skin.

Next up the block and tackle came canvas, which was used to make crude shelters, and barrels of fresh water and crates of biscuit. Then my strongbox arrived, courtesy of Captain Gaunt, and I placed it in one of the shelters. I decided I didn't need to put a guard on it, for it was oak strapped with iron and had a lock that, by a mechanism, shot seven bolts to secure the box. It would take a strong man with an axe to break it open, and that could hardly be done in secret. The key to the lock I kept around my neck on a chain.

More men came up, and with them some of the valuable cargo, the boxes of fragrant spices we had acquired in Tabarzam: long pepper, allspice, cloves, cardamom, nutmeg, and cinnamon. These few dozen boxes I placed in shelter, and then decided to go down to the ship to see what might next be saved.

The gannets made way for us and our cargo grudgingly and packed themselves into a dense white mass on the end of the island. Were we stranded for too long, I supposed we could eat them.

From the skerry I stepped out onto the lower of the two pulleys, took the standing part in one hand to steady myself, and then allowed myself to swoop down to the ship. I alighted on the quarterdeck to the general applause of the crew, and then with the captain went down to the lower deck, which, on account of the falling tide, was no longer awash. We surveyed the hold and decided which of the cargo could be shifted.

I left the captain to direct this work and went to my cabin under the poop. There I changed into dry clothing and added to my array a warm cheviot overcoat I had carried with me since the sack of Ethlebight. Once I'd accomplished this, I noticed the remains of my feast that remained on the table. I poured myself a cup of wine and helped myself to slices of ham, the pickled oysters, and the fine white manchet-bread. I ate till I was past full, and then poured myself more wine and had some cake.

The provender would not be so good as this, I judged, for some time to come.

I donned oilskins and joined the captain where he was rousing the cargo from the hold. Boxes of spices and ivory swayed into the air. The crew were in good cheer, with promise of a little profit in addition to the preservation of their lives. I decided to return to the island, and I stood atop a cedarwood box of nutmegs as it swayed aloft, my right hand holding the standing part just above the tackle.

No one had noticed that the box had been damaged, and when I was fifty feet off the deck, the bottom fell clean out of it. Bags of nutmegs rained down on the sea and the deck, and with the box relieved of its heavy contents, the crew hauling on the line flew backward and sprawled on the deck. The box took a violent lurch and nearly flung me off. I snatched for support with my free hand, and my left hand caught at the tackle just as it shot skyward, and my little finger was caught in the pulley mechanism and very thoroughly broken.

You are very dear, the way you kiss that finger now. In truth, I felt little pain at the time, only a great shock to watch a part of my body caught in the pulley at the exact instant when my life seemed in such peril.

I was lowered to the deck by a gang of careful seamen, and though I held my damaged hand carefully, there was very much to do at that moment, and I managed to do it. The next box was examined more carefully and took me aloft without incident. And then once I was on the skerry, there was more work to do in shifting and stowing the rescued cargo, and though the pain had by that time settled in my hand, it had become a throb like the throb of my heart, of which I was aware only when I chose.

We rescued tons of cargo that day, and as the tide returned and summer brought an end to that long day, we brought up all the crew, even those who had been injured and that one officer who had fled to his cabin and barricaded himself inside. He had not the decency to be embarrassed by his behavior and offered no apology, but was quite regal in his bearing as he came to land, silent, but looking at us all as if we had confirmed his worst suspicions. We were not his shipmates, his attitude suggested, but his servants, and inept servants at that. He was the wise one, and his hiding in his cabin was a choice the wisdom of which was denied to the rest of us.

We also saved the ship's cat and three of her four kittens, all of which had proved more useful than that officer.

We had not the time to puncture the mate's pretensions, for there was more work to do. Eleven months earlier we had left Selford with over a hundred twenty crew, twice the number required to work the ship—we carried the extra in case of trouble, for the sea-road to Tabarzam is infested by pirates and other perils, and we needed enough hands to man the guns. Desertions and disease had reduced the crew by the time the storm struck us, and we lost a handful overboard at the first onset, and so when *Royal Stilwell* was wrecked, there were ninety-seven souls aboard. By the end of the day every one of those men was saved, and each slept safely that night in a snug home walled with boxes of cargo and roofed with canvas.

As night fell and Captain Gaunt, last of all, was brought up by the light of lanterns, the chief mate touched my shoulder and pointed to the northeast. "Sir Quillifer, look you. Lights on shore!"

I looked out and saw, not half a mile away across rolling surf and crashing waves, a series of blazing bonfires. Not on the clifftops, either, but below, on the shore, which told me that there *was* a shore, not just sheer cliffs running down into the water.

If we had managed to get round the skerry, we might have grounded the ship on that shore, in reasonable safety.

"They must have heard our gun," the chief mate went on. "They cannot chance the surf in their boats, but they want us to know that succor is at hand."

"Signal them with our lanterns," I said. Within minutes, torches on the shore were waving back at us, and I felt my heart rise at the presence of those souls, so near, and the hope of rescue.

That night I slept on oilskins laid on the stony ground to make a dry bed, with my good cheviot overcoat as a blanket. The canvas overhead boomed in the wind, and the rain fell with a force that sounded like a hundred tambours. I slept alongside Captain Gaunt and the other officers, for we were packed together so that our bodies might keep warm, and whenever one of us had to turn over, he would call out, and we would all turn. Or so I am told, for I fell instantly to sleep, cradling my injured hand, and even if we turned continually like coneys on a spit, I did not know it, for I did not wake till dawn.

The storm was breaking up, with the royal sun red in the east, turning to scarlet the scudding clouds that flew along the horizon. The wind was reduced to a mild gale, but the great seas continued to thunder white against the shore and prohibited our rescuers from setting out. Squalls flew over the seas like castaways coming to land. And looking at the bay thus revealed by the morning, I recognized it.

Three years ago the previous autumn, as I left Ethlebight for my first visit to the capital of Selford, I had viewed that bay from the cliffs and remarked to myself how perfect a harbor it would make, for it was sheltered by the skerry on one side and a long ness on the other. There was a long, curving shingle beach, now strewn with the wrack of the storm, and grass-strewn soil between the shingles and the cliffs.

"This is Gannet Cove," I told Captain Gaunt. "If we had only been able to weather the skerry, we would have been able to drop anchor in the bay and ride out the storm in peace."

"The god would not have it so," said the captain.

Say rather goddess, I thought darkly, but I put on a smiling, hearty-lad face and said, "Your seamanship has retrieved our fortunes. We will save most of the cargo, and we've saved all the men. As long as we have our lives, we may hope for better days, and better profit."

The captain eyed my injured hand. It had turned purple overnight, and the injured finger was greatly swollen. "We should splint that finger."

"A splint would be too cumbersome," said I, "and prevent me from using the hand. Lash it to the next finger."

The little finger was bound to my ring finger with strips of linen, and then we set about the day's work. The tide had peaked two or three hours after midnight, and though *Royal Stilwell* still lay in its cradle of stone, it was clear that wind and waves had done their work. Part of the forecastle had been torn away, and the bow heavily damaged. Once the forepart of the ship was completely torn open, the seas would sweep through to the stern, and *Royal Stilwell* would not last more than a few days.

So we set to work to bring more cargo to the island, and it was not till midmorning that the sea grew less savage and we saw boats putting out from the shore. I joined Captain Gaunt on the ship to welcome our saviors, who proved to be some of the worthy fishermen of that coast. They brought us bread and goat-cheese and offered us the hospitality of their village, all of which we accepted with joy.

I offered as well to employ them on the rescue of our cargo, and to pay them good silver for the work. This cheered them, for they had expected to rescue destitute mariners entirely at their own expense, and so I went ashore with them to discuss the matter with their entire village.

On shore I found the local squire, who had come down from his house with food, drink, and his servants. I met with the headmen of the village and arranged to pay their people a greater wage than they could ever earn fishing; and I also employed as many of the squire's folk as he was willing to provide.

I returned to *Royal Stilwell* with everything in train, and my strongbox came down from the skerry so that I could make advance payments. Then I, my strongbox, and such of my belongings as could be rescued from my cabin once more took the perilous route to shore. I managed to recover even my guitar.

The squire kindly loaned me his carriage, and I set out for my home city of Ethlebight, a long day's journey to the west. The man who owned *Royal Stilwell* with me lived in Ethlebight, and I hoped to find him at home.

At the same time, the chief mate set out in the opposite direction, to Amberstone, three or four days' journey even by post, in hopes that he could charter a deep-draught vessel to take all our cargo once we had rescued it.

Most travelers on the coast go by sea, and so the coast road is neglected, and now it was full of mud and storm-wrack. Squalls pummeled the coach with brief, fierce showers. The corn in the fields had been beaten down, and the orchards were strewn with wreckage and fallen fruit. Unless the authorities took care to succor the district, there would be famine here come winter.

After a wretched, jolting ride that set pain lancing through my wounded hand, I arrived in Ethlebight after dark and found the gates closed. I had been prepared to bribe my way past the gatehouse, but as soon as the guards heard my name, they opened the gates immediately and welcomed me to my home city.

I am well known in Ethlebight. Three years before the previous autumn, Ethlebight had been sacked by a fleet of Aekoi reivers, and I, eighteen years old and on my first adventure in the wide world, had managed to obtain succor from Her Majesty's government. I had also procured privateering licenses for the city's sea-captains, which allowed them to take their prizes to Ethlebight, and brought money into the devastated city.

Naturally I used some of those privateering licenses myself, and had a share of the profits from the rest, but the city's wealth was increased thereby, and no one in Ethlebight has reproached me—nor should they, for I spent some of my profits in the city, and also in a fund for ransoming the captives.

The carriage passed along darkened streets to Scarcroft Square, that great jewel in the center of town. Even though the fine, many-chimneyed buildings were mere silhouettes in the darkness, and the many windowpanes but a pale shimmer of reflected moonlight, I felt a great contentment settle into me. I had wandered the world, and I was known in the royal capital of Selford and the seat of government in Howel, but Ethlebight was my home.

The carriage drew up at the door of the Spellman home, and I alighted and beat on the door with my good hand. A groom opened the door, recognized me, and brought me into the hall. There, a moment later, my friend Kevin Spellman joined me, and we embraced.

"*Royal Stilwell* is aground in Gannet Cove," said I into his ear. "We have saved the crew, and we now must save the cargo."

He stepped back, and calculation was already reflected in his eyes. "*Able* is in port, thank Pastas. I will send a message to Captain Oakeshott at once. Have you supped?"

"I have not. And I come in a carriage, and the driver, footman, and horses are no doubt hungry as well."

"They will be provided for."

Kevin was a sturdy man my own age, fair of hair and beard, and had been my friend from our school days. In the summer heat, and in the privacy of his own home, he wore only a fine lawn shirt above his trunks and hose, though normally he wore the brilliant fabrics his family imported into the country. He was the son of a wealthy mercer with a mansion on Scarcroft Square who owned, in whole or in part, a small flotilla of ships. Kevin's family had been captured by the Aekoi reivers during the sack of the city, and one of their ships taken and another burned in the port. Thanks to the privateering commissions I had secured and the captures made by his ships, Kevin had been able to recover much of the family's fortune and to ransom his parents, brother, sister, and servants. Since the end of the war, we had been partners in merchant ventures and done well.

"Is your father at home?" I asked.

"He is in Selford."

"You might send word to him, and he can alert the insurors to start gathering great cartloads of silver to pay us. Then, an we rescue some of the cargo, they may be so relieved that they will pay the balance without trouble."

Kevin smiled. "You have a sanguine view of maritime insurance, to be sure."

"Yesterday I survived a shipwreck. If that does not enhance a man's optimism, I know not what will."

A footman brought in a cold supper, along with a bottle of wine from the south coast of Bonille. Kevin busied himself with sending messages and making calculations.

"I will also need a stack of silver," I said, "for I have engaged a small army of salvagers."

"You will have it."

Before I went to bed, I called for hot water for shaving, for I was desperate to crop my whiskers. I keep my hair long, for fair ladies such as yourself like to stroke it, but unlike most men in the kingdom I am clean-shaven. This is not because I hope to set a new fashion, but rather because my beard itches abominably, and I cannot abide the torment when there is a remedy at hand. I had not shaved in all the days since the storm had struck, and my beard had long outlived its welcome.

Relieved of whiskers and their itch, I was given a featherbed for the night, and before undressing and extinguishing the lamp, I took the key from around my neck and opened my strongbox. From it I took out *Royal Stilwell's* most valuable cargo, a chest of teak that held several trays, each lined with plush velvet of a deep violet shade. I took out the trays and viewed the contents—the diamonds, emeralds, and rubies that I had bought in the markets of Sarafsham, now glowing in the soft light of the lantern like fallen fragments of the moon. All of the most excellent quality, all quarried in Sarafsham's fabled mines, then cut and polished by the diamond masters who live in fine homes on the Street of the Shining Stones.

I had bought these with my own silver, not the money reserved for my and Kevin's joint ventures. Each of the stones was held in its own velvet-lined compartment, a precaution to keep the stones from cutting one another. A few had worked out of their proper places in the storm or the juddering carriage ride to the city, and these I returned to their compartments before locking them up again.

If the gems had been lost, I would have been near penniless. But I had been penniless before, and that prospect did not frighten me. I am young still, and should I lose my fortune, there is time to earn another one.

I returned the teak chest to my strongbox and heard the seven bolts clack home as I locked it. I had plans for the stones and would sleep better knowing that they were secure.

Kevin and I breakfasted together the next morning, and then he set out for the port. The vessel *Able*, which we jointly owned, was but an 80-ton pinnace and could carry but a fraction of the cargo in the hold of the 850-ton *Royal Stilwell*. Kevin would have to round up every pinnace, crumster, flyboat, and barge in the port and engage them as our cargo-carriers.

Kevin knew the ships and captains here better than I, and so I was at liberty until *Able* was able to sail, which would not be till the afternoon ebb tide. So I went to my new-built house on Princess Street.

The house in which I was raised had been burned during the sack of the city, and my parents and little sisters killed. When I was able to afford it, I had the house rebuilt, and with an eye for defense. My father's house had a ground floor of brick, but its upper floors were half-timber, and the roof thatch. Determined that my house would not burn should all the Aekoi in the world assault it, I had built the new walls entirely out of brick and capped them with a tile roof. But I had never slept in my new home, for by the time it was completed, I was living in Bonille, and so I leased the house to a young girdler just starting out in the world. She had her shop on the ground floor and lived on the floors above with her growing family—her husband was the mate of a crumster in the coastal trade, and she was now heavy with their third child.

Beyond a few glimpses of the women in the fishing village, I had seen no woman for weeks, and so I very much enjoyed the pleasant half hour I spent with my tenant, talking of nothing in particular while I admired the girdles and belts in the shop, and then bade her good-day and went walking through the town. Much of the damage done by the raid had been repaired, but still there were empty lots where homes had been burned and not replaced, and other houses that stood boarded and empty, still awaiting their owners' return. The fine, rich buildings on Scarcroft Square, made all of the local brick in all its shimmering colors, had been repaired, but I could not help but remember the day of the sack, when the windows had been shattered by wanton corsairs, the square had served to pen thousands of captives, and I had watched the atrocity from my hiding-place, unable to do anything but bear witness to the horror below.

The memory seemed to float before my eyes, suspended between me and the square as if painted on one of those gauzy scrims at the theater. Haunted by this vision, I walked blindly across the square and found myself looking up at a tall, narrow building with a crow-stepped gable. Here, up a narrow stair, I had labored as apprentice to a lawyer named Dacket. He had been taken on the night of the attack, taken along with his family, and had never been seen in Ethlebight again. The tale that had come to Ethlebight was that he had been put on a ship stolen from the harbor, but the Aekoi hadn't known how to properly sail it, and it had separated from the rest during a gale and foundered along with the crew and a hundred or more captives. That story seemed likely, though no one would ever know the truth.

Without Dacket to promote me to the Bar, I had found no one willing to certify me as a lawyer, and so my legal career had died before it had ever begun.

I left the square, walked north, and passed the gatehouse on the Ostra road. Running along the road is the city's necropolis, and there I sought the tomb I had built for my family.

The tomb was a reproduction in miniature of the celebrated round temple of Pastas four leagues up the river, built in the annular style of the old empire. My father had been a passionate partisan of the Netweaver and despised the Compassionate Pilgrim, who had been imposed on the people by Duisland's kings. The night of the attack he had fought, defending the door with his pollaxe, until overcome by the smoke that had also killed my mother and sisters.

And so I honored my father and his faith, and laid him to rest in a temple of a size appropriate to a human, not a god. About the tomb I had scattered the seeds of wildflowers, and so the structure was surrounded by a brilliant carpet of cowslips, harebell, corn cockle, daisies, milkmaids, brilliant red pimpernels, and sweet-scented lady's bedstraw. Above the peak of the portico I had placed a bronze statue of Pastas with his net and trident, and as I approached, I saw that people had made offerings to the god, grain and small coins, and pots of beer and wine, all laid out in front of the tomb's iron door.

I had brought no offerings myself—I had learned, to my cost, the dangers that come with attracting a god's attention—but I knelt on the grass before the tomb, drew into my lungs the morning air scented with flowers, and spoke to my family as if they stood before me in life. I told them of the voyage to Tabarzam, and the storm which I had survived, and my hopes for the rescue of the cargo. Absently I picked the flowers that were before me and made a little nosegay. Before I was done, the tears were running unchecked down my face, and an ache had risen in my chest that made speech nigh impossible.

The flowers tumbled from my fingers to the ground. I rose to my feet and lurched to the door and pressed my cheek to the cold iron. "Forgive me," I said. "Forgive me."

For I had not been home on that night of the attack, but visiting a girl on Mutton Island; and I knew that if I had been in the city, I could have somehow saved my family—if necessary I would have carried my sisters over my shoulders as I fled across the rooftops to safety. Instead, I and a milkmaid had taken our pleasure together in a stable, and I returned hours late. My family had been without me and died in fire, and the best I could offer them now was a splendid tomb.

I clawed the door and wept for what seemed a long bitter hour, and then I fell to my knees and gathered the flowers again. With them in my hand I tottered away, to save what I could of the ship.

Able left Ethlebight on the afternoon tide and threaded its way through the growing salt marsh that separated the city from the sea. Ethlebight was dying long before the Aekoi came, for its bay was filling with silt, and the River Ostra had split into dozens of little channels that wound between tall green rattling reeds on their way to open water. The eighty-ton pinnace *Able* was about the largest vessel able to gain the port, and then only at the peak of the tide, while a ship the size of *Royal Stilwell* had no hope of entering at all.

Able was commanded by my friend Captain Sir Felix Oakeshott, a man in his thirties who looked very piratical with his long black hair and gold earring. During the war, he, I, and Kevin had captured *Royal Stilwell* from Clayborne's rebels, and he had captained our ships in the years since. He was severe in manner but adroit in action, and, commanding a privateer, had done very well out of the war, having won a knighthood and a manor near Bretlynton Head. He and I supped in his cabin that night, and we talked long into the evening. This last voyage had given me stories of the sea that almost matched his own.

Kevin remained in Ethlebight to muster the fleet he was sending to plunder *Royal Stilwell*'s remains.

When *Able* stood into Gannet Cove the next morning, we saw that a great deal had been accomplished on the wreck. Much of the deck had been torn away to expose the cargo, and with a crane made from the foremast and foresail yard, crates and bags were being shifted to the fishing boats that were ferrying it to shore. Once on the beach, the cargo was hauled on driftwood sleds to safety above the tide-line.

Able was the first of a dozen vessels to arrive in the next two days. At the end of that time all were heavy with the most valuable goods, and much of *Stilwell*'s lading was saved.

Some of the spices and incense had been doused in salt water, but were otherwise unspoiled. The ivory survived perfectly well. Some of the wine casks had been started and the wines spoiled, but the wine in other casks remained wholesome. The cedarwood had all been submerged, but cedar was by far the best wood to resist warping after immersion, and I held out much hope.

The silks, I assumed, were ruined, but Captain Oakeshott told me this might not be the case. Silk clothing, he reminded me, should be washed in sweet-water springs, and that there was one of these upriver from Ethlebight. And so the silks were hurried to Ethlebight for their bath.

The cargo having been rescued, *Royal Stilwell* itself was plundered for its treasures, the great bronze cannon, the cabin furniture, the bronze and brass fittings, the cordage, barrels, carpenter's supplies, canvas, and even the ship's bell. The remaining hulk was left for the fisherfolk, who could now improve their driftwood huts with well-founded ship's timbers.

While these operations were in train, I went back and forth from the wreck to the village, and occasionally up the cliffs to view the magnificent sweep of the bay, so well sheltered by the curving ness and the skerry, with its population of gannets. So viewing the bay, I began to conceive a plan that might work to my profit, and perhaps the profit of others as well. But first I asked the villagers if the strand was considered a part of the squire's manor, and I found out that it was not. The villagers held their property, such as it was, in fee simple.

When the laden vessels were beginning to disperse, and the last of the cargo lifted from *Stilwell*'s hold, I spoke to the head men of the village and made them an offer.

"I will pay you not to sell your property to anyone else for ten years."

The fishers looked at each other, and one lean, one-eyed man spoke. "You want to buy our land?"

"Nay," said I. "I wish you *not* to sell. I will pay you to keep your own land and property."

Again they looked at each other. "No one has ever offered to buy our land."

"Nor am I offering. But I will pay you not to sell to anyone else, and I will pay generously."

I had drawn up a contract, but none of them could read, so I asked the squire to review it. He found it puzzling, but told the fishers that I had been truthful as to its contents.

Naturally some felt they were being cheated in some way they could not determine, but in the end simple avarice overcame them, and every property owner in the village made their mark and received the sum of ten crowns, which was probably more than any of them earned in a month; and all any of them had to do to earn it was to keep what they already had.

That day brought the arrival of *Stilwell*'s chief mate with a three-hundred-ton galleon from Amberstone. This enabled us to bring the last of the cargo down from the skerry, and we left the little island to its fleet-winged natives and sailed away.

During all of this business I neglected my broken finger, and so when it set, the finger was crooked. It is no handicap, and it doesn't prevent me from caressing you as you deserve, but it does ache when a storm approaches.

Which is a useful talent for a sailor to possess, you must admit.

CHAPTER FOUR

I see you have grown restless with my tale of sea, salvage, and storm, and are impatient to discover the nature of that green-eyed lady who greeted me on Gannet Isle. I have delayed this revelation not to vex you, but because the tale of my relationship with Orlanda is so far-fetched and fantastical that you might be tempted to view me as a braggart or self-seeker, or perhaps a mere lunatic.

I see that amusement tweaks the corner of your mouth. Yes, perhaps I am after all a self-seeker, but I hope we may agree that I am not yet mad.

You have proved to me many times that you know me better than I know myself, and so I will tell you the plain truth about this lady, and trust you will understand me well enough to know whether or not I embroider the tale.

You have heard, I think, that four years ago I was held for ransom by the brigand Sir Basil of the Heugh, and that I managed to escape with my life and a share of the outlaw's treasure. I have told the story of my escape many times, but any story you might have heard was a plausible fiction. I have never told the truth till now.

We hostages were held in a cliff-walled corrie high in the Toppings and allowed to wander free during the daytime, because there was no escape but by climbing the cliffs, and this could be done only in full view of the guards. At the back of the corrie, behind some woods, I found a fresh, cold spring and a ruined nymphaeum, a monument built by the ancients to honor the spirit of the water. In the remains I found a fallen statue of the goddess herself, all of rosy marble, and set her in the place of honor. I bowed to her and offered her homage and consoled her in her misfortune.

And by and by, I began to see a red-haired lady in the camp, and when I found her playing her mandola in the woods near the nymphaeum, I spoke to her. I fancied I was in love with her and asked her to run away with me, and she consented. She not only guided me away from the camp in the dead of night, but helped me plunder Sir Basil's strong-house, so that I left with the sack of gold, silver, and gems that were the foundation of my fortune. I stole the stolen goods from the man who had stolen them.

Yet once Orlanda guided me from the corrie, she led me to an ancient ring-fort in the Toppings, a place crowned by a great fang of a ruined tower. The air was suffused with a kind of unearthly light, and the music of an invisible orchestra sounded on the air. She said she wished to be my bride, but I would not go, and, with good reason, I suspected something uncanny and questioned her. She is a nymph indeed, powerful and immortal, and because I did not wish to spend a hundred years in her bridal bed, she now follows and persecutes me.

For as you know, I wish to live in the world, and adventure here and make my mark, and I desired not to spend my life on a lascivious couch in fairyland, tended by unseen servants and made the toy of a capricious goddess. What sort of life is that for a man of ambition?

You should not fear for yourself. For I have made Orlanda promise that, though she may toy with me as she desires, she will not harm those I love. And though I know these words of mine may drive her into some reckless, abandoned, jealous act, I do not shame to say it is thee I love, and no other.

CHAPTER FIVE

Six weeks after the wreck I sailed into water-girdled Howel, the winter capital, having come up the Dordelle from my own little manor at Dunnock. The great storm that had reaped a great swath through Fornland, burst the banks of the rivers, ruined the crops, and filled the fields with trash had touched Bonille more lightly, but still some of my tenants had lost their harvest, and I brought enough grain to keep them from hunger.

I had hired a sailing-barge to take me up the river, my horses stood in a pen built on the foredeck, and I had placed on the roundhouse a galley I'd had built at a boatyard at Bretlynton Head. The heat of late summer lay sultry on the vineyards and pastures along the Dordelle, and cicadas cried from the fig-trees and the stately cypress that stood like sentinels on the green hills. The air was scented with sweet flowers.

Along the shore of the lake, between the city and the palace at Ings Magna, I had rented a house from the Count of Rackheath, a noble lately shocked to discover the monumental gambling debts incurred by his son and heir. Covering these debts led to financial embarrassment, and he had been obliged to withdraw from court, along with his wayward son, and travel to his house in the country in order to devote his next several years to recovering his finances. The house came with the staff that the count would otherwise have been obliged to dismiss, and I hoped they would provide fine and discreet service for the young knight-errant who had saved their jobs.

Rackheath's was a fine large home, built of the golden sandstone so common in the city. It stood three storeys tall, with polygonal towers on the corners that faced the lake, and a central gable that rose in gentle, scalloped curves to a pediment. A gilded weathercock shimmered atop the pediment, and elaborately-carved brick chimneys rose along the peak of the roofline. Master Stiver, the steward, met me at the quayside. He was a lean-faced man of middle years, very grandly dressed in black velvet, with a belt of gold links and a long, perfumed beard—and I sensed his disappointment that I was dressed more as a sailor than a lord.

The galley was put in the boathouse next to his lordship's own barge, lodging was found for its crew of sailors, my horses went into the stable under the supervision of my groom Oscar, and my luggage went to my chambers, along with my strongbox.

The steward took me through the house, viewing the great hall with its brilliant silk tapestries that shimmered with golden thread, the reception room with its elaborate boiseries and portraits of ancestors, the game room with its chess and card tables, skittles, billiard table, and dartboard. The count's bedroom boasted a gilded bed in the form of a galley with no less than seven feather mattresses stacked upon one another. Tucked behind the bedroom was the private cabinet with its parquet of rustic scenes, and nearby was found the true treasure-store of the building, the library with its rows of leatherbound volumes. I let my eyes linger along the gilt-edged spines and promised to visit the room soon, and then was taken to the buttery with its casks and bottles, and the treasury for Rackheath's silver plate, which had been removed by the count lest his creditors try to confiscate it. There was a bowling green on the lawn that led down to the river, and a tennis court built along one wall of the building.

I insisted also on visiting those parts of the household that a lord might never see in his lifetime, to wit, the pantry, the brewery, the servants' bath-house, and the kitchen. I wanted to know that these divisions of the household were in working order, and I wanted also to know that the kitchen was clean. I had been to enough feasts in noble houses to know that the food was often shockingly bad, and I wanted the cook and her assistants to know that, as far as I was concerned, tainted meat could not be disguised beneath a sugary sauce.

I was then served a dinner that, for its simplicity and wholesomeness, I suspect had been cooked for the servants, though with it I was served a wine that surpassed anything the servants would ever drink in their lives (assuming they were honest and had not plundered the buttery). After the meal the steward introduced to me the other members of the staff.

In my new household I employed enough souls to crew a pinnace on a voyage to Thurnmark. In addition to the steward, there was a comptroller, an auditor, an usher, a carver and a server, waiters, a cook and her assistants, a clerk of the kitchen to keep track of the kitchen finances, the usher of the hall, the librarian, the yeomen respectively of the buttery, the pantry, the ewer, the wardrobe, the gun room, and the cellar. There was a porter, a baker, a brewer, a coachman, a footman, a great many grooms and maidservants, and a single scullery man, who I imagined must have been greatly overworked.

My modest little manor at Dunnock did not require so vast a staff. I confess I was beginning to feel a little out of my depth.

I should, I thought, ask advice from someone more experienced in the management of great households than I.

There were only two great lords who had ever condescended to speak to me of their own volition, and I decided to write to the Duke and Duchess of Roundsilver that afternoon. And so I went to

Rackheath's cabinet and found paper and quills in the great pigeon-holed desk. I cut a quill with my pen-knife, found a sheet of pinched post, and opened the inkwell, only to find it was dry. In the desk I found the materials for making ink: oak galls, copperas, gum, and a small pitcher meant to hold wine, but which had gone as dry as the inkwell. There was also a mortar for grinding the oak galls, some cheesecloth for straining the ink, and pieces of dark velvet for mopping up the spills.

I called for a groom and asked him to bring me some ink, but it was the steward who brought an inkwell from the buttery, where it was used to keep a tally of the wine.

"Thank you, Master Stiver," said I.

"Does Your Excellency desire me to make you some ink?" he said.

I held out the pitcher. "If you will have this cleaned, and the inkwell, I will make it myself."

"Very good, Sir Quillifer." He took the pitcher and the inkwell, and then hovered a bit by the door to let me know that he had something further to say.

"Yes, Master Stiver?"

"Have you brought a varlet with you, sir? Should I prepare a room for him?"

"I have not yet employed a varlet," said I.

"I will assign a groom, Your Excellency, until you acquire a proper varlet."

I waved a hand in dismissal. "Yes, Stiver, thank you."

I had spent so much time moving from place to place I had never needed a body servant, though now that I was lodged at Howel, I supposed I would. That was something else to consider.

I wrote to Their Graces of Roundsilver with the buttery's ink and begged leave to call upon them. I had my answer, in Her Grace's elegant hand, by the end of the afternoon, in the form of a dinner invitation for the next day.

But in the meantime I made my own ink. I ground the oak galls and soaked them in wine, then added copperas and strained the result. I added gum to thicken the ink to the desired consistency, then, finding it too thick, diluted it with wine. Having tested the result on a scrap of paper, I found the result satisfactory and poured it into the inkwell.

I recalled learning to make ink in my Ethlebight grammar-school, and the great messes we boys made, in part because we didn't use wine to thin the result, but *aqua urina*. The result was disgusting, and resulted in any number of beatings by our beleaguered teacher, but we all thought it a great prank.

And then I wondered how many hours I had spent making ink in my twenty-two years, not only in my school days, but in my years as an apprentice lawyer, and now as a merchant. Surely I had more useful or enjoyable things to do.

I wondered if it were possible to save mankind this labor.

I amused myself by making some preliminary calculations on my bit of paper, but all I managed was to convince myself that I knew nothing.

Well. Ignorance I have found a thing that, once confessed, is soon amended.

I knew more about the ink business by the time I arrived at the Roundsilver palace the next morning. As Roundsilver's country seat was near Ethlebight, the palace was faced with brick, one of my city's great exports. A red facade was ornamented by geometric patterns of colored brick: yellow, sky blue, indigo, and pale green. Brick columns were carved into spirals and fluted pillars; the chimneys were twisted into fantastic shapes and topped with grotesque statues, so that smoke seemed to issue from the nostrils of monsters; and a frieze that ran below the eaves depicted Lord Baldwine, an ancestor of the duke's, in his famed combat with the dragon.

The duke himself was about as far removed from Lord Baldwine as can be imagined, for he was smaller than the average and rather dainty, and wore high-heeled slippers. He was over forty, and his hair and beard were fair, with an admixture of silver. He generally failed to pronounce his *r*'s, not because he had adopted the accent of Bonille, but because he disdained the sound as uninteresting.

His Grace worshipped Beauty in all its forms and surrounded himself with exquisite works of craft: enamels and cameos, paintings and statues, sometimes in a rather extreme passionate style—queens reaching for the poison cup, mythological figures lamenting in their own gore. The subject of each work was unexceptionable, but taken together, they mounted to a kind of aesthetic testament, a monument to the sensibility of the collector.

He had married late, to a young noblewoman about my age, and who might have been a reflection of himself in some kind of ageless, sexless mirror. For she was small and blond and exquisitely formed, with blue eyes both lively and kind.

Their Graces met me in their reception room, with its pillars of emerald-green chrysoprase that held up a barrel ceiling with a fresco of gods welcoming heroes to their banquet. Both duke and duchess glittered with gems, rings on every finger along with brooches, chains, pendants, and chain-link girdles. The duke was dressed in a singular style, in a long tunic of sky-blue watered silk painted with lilies and sewn with freshwater pearls, a turbanlike head-wrapping with fringes that dangled down his forehead like lovelocks, and up-turned slippers with tall heels. His lady, in place of the usual embroidered gown worn over a corset and farthingale, wrapped her slight form in a mantle of shimmering gold satin secured across the front with ropes of frogging and brocade. It was a style that had been devised by the Marchioness of Stayne, an acquaintance of mine, while she was *praegnas,* and had caused a minor scandal at the time. Queen Berlauda had decided to allow the garb at court for any woman carrying a child, but forbade it for anyone else.

But this wasn't court; it was the Roundsilver palace, where costumes should not surprise anyone.

I bowed to the duke and kissed Her Grace's hand, while trying with discretion to view through the gold satin any material proof that the duchess was bearing a child. The results of my survey were inconclusive.

"Your Grace," said I as I straightened. "Is your attire meant to conceal, to enhance, or to astound?" She began to answer, but I continued my exposition. "If to conceal," I said, "your mantle is inadequate, for it fails to obscure the elegant matchlessness of your faultless self. If intended to enhance, it is inadequate, for it is impossible to enhance your beauty beyond what Nature has already furnished. And if intended to astound, it is also inadequate, for your allure and charm have already astounded the world. In short, though your mantle is magnificent, it falls short of the perfection of the lady that wears it."

"If we are to begin with compliments," said the duchess, "I should perhaps first praise your mastery of the language of the courtier."

"But the courtier's language lacks sincerity," I said, "whereas I speak the truth."

The duke offered an indulgent smile. "As the topic stands in danger of over-elaboration, I shall instead answer the question foremost in your mind, and to say that the answer is yes."

I laughed and looked at the duchess. "You are *inciens*? I am delighted."

"I am finding it less delightful than trying," said she. "Though it has spared me attending the queen on her progress, so that is something to be said in its favor."

I felt the duke thoughtful for sparing his wife the rigors of the journey.

"I've invited Master Blackwell to join us," said the duke, "and Mistress Concini from Basilicotto, who composes music, and who has brought to Howel an orchestra of holy sisters. And we have as a houseguest His Highness the Prince Alicio de Ribamar-la-Rose."

The duke's lisp made reference instead to *the pwince* and *Wibamaw-la-Wose*, but I was practiced in deciphering his affectation and knew to install *r*'s at all the proper places.

"I shall be delighted to see them all," said I. "Will I meet *all* the holy sisters, or just Mistress Concini?"

"One nun is sufficient at a feast," said the duke. "And I already feed one orchestra, who I hope will be in tune for us."

A delicate canzona shimmered down from the gallery, where the duke's orchestra had played through dinner. A pair of melodies played against one another in intricate counterpoint, while the bass marched along at a steady pace that put most armies to shame.

"Most of the fine silk was ruined despite the freshwater bath," said I, "though the stronger fabrics, the noils and pongees and gabardines, resisted the sea somewhat better."

"The important thing is that none of your crew were lost," said the duchess.

"Ay. But now I must do them justice with the insurors, for they are paid out of the profit of the voyage."

In fact I was already doing well enough out of the voyage, and so were the crew, for I had sold much of the surviving cargo in Selford, once I had got it there. Despite having to pay others to ship my goods, the profits from the voyage were enough to satisfy any but the most avaricious merchant. Along with Kevin and his father, I had already commissioned a new eight-hundred-ton galleon to replace the one we had lost.

There were less tangible benefits, as well. I now had personal acquaintance with the merchants of Tabarzam and the Candara Coast, as well as those fabulous diamond factors on the Street of the Shining Stones, and that would prove profitable on voyages to come.

"The insurors are proving difficult?" asked the duke.

"Unusually so. I would have expected them to be grateful I hadn't declared a total loss, but they are being most obstinate when it comes to paying out on *Royal Stilwell*."

"Yet the ship was wrecked. How can they dispute it?"

"They claim there have been a spate of ships being deliberately wrecked for the insurance. That *Stilwell* was lost in the greatest storm of the last twelve years, along with at least a dozen other ships, does not in their narrow minds make fraud any less likely."

The duke's eyes darkened. "But surely they must pay out eventually."

"I'm sure they will."

His Grace the duke was something of a mercer himself, as he bought and sold goods, and though he did not own ships, he nevertheless sponsored voyages. He needed profits to support his royal mode of living, and for that reason he was wise to be wary of the manipulations of insurors.

"I'm afraid I have been monopolizing the conversation," I said. "I apologize for going on in this way unchecked."

"I have never heard an account of a shipwreck by one of its castaways," said the duchess. "You have had our complete attention."

"It is all very interesting," said Prince Alicio. "But what is 'monopolize'?"

"It's a new word," said I. "I made it up."

"From *monopolium*," said the duke helpfully. "But a verb transitive."

"Ah," said the prince. "I comprehend." He turned to me. "Your discussion of your business—"

"Your *merchandizing*," said the duchess with a smile.

"This is very new to me," the prince finished. "In Loretto we nobles of course may take part in no business. Should I send a cargo to Tabarzam, or loan money at interest, I would be brought up before a court of honor conducted by the constable, and I would be disgraced."

"But would they let you keep your profits?" I asked, for that sort of disgrace was of little interest to me.

"I would lose my privileges," said the prince, "and I would of course have to pay the tax on my land and buildings, as if I were a commoner."

I decided at that moment to accept no foreign titles. I was already wary of foreign titles generally, if for no other reason than Loretto and other countries were so generous with them.

Except in the far north of Fornland, where they practice the ancient custom of gavelkind, we have in Duisland the law of primogeniture, so only the oldest son of a count becomes a count, or the eldest son of a baronet a baronet, and so on. Only a very few titles are inherited in the female line, by special remainder of the monarch.

But in Loretto all the sons of a duke are dukes, or a prince princes. The daughters as well inherit the distinction and become duchesses and princesses.

In Duisland, a title is rare and valuable coin; but in Loretto titles are so common they may be worth little more than a farthing.

This is made worse by what, in a strange fit of honesty, they call the "minor nobility," who do not have titles but use the "de" in their name, and whose unbearable and bellicose pretensions are matched only by their lack of means.

None of the nobility of Loretto, even those minor lords common as rats in a barnyard, pay taxes, and instead are expected to offer military service to the crown. Because the wealthiest elements in the land avoid taxation, the taxes fall all the more heavily on the commons, and many are impoverished far beyond even the poorest of Duislanders. In Duisland even the needy wear leather shoes of some sort, however worn; but in Loretto wooden shoes are worn even by respectable commoners of the middling sort and many of the poor have not shoes at all.

And as for the military service owed by the nobility, it were better they pay their taxes so that good soldiers can be hired and trained, instead of filling their armies with arrogant nobles all a-quarrel over precedence. (Though as I am a loyal son of Duisland, perhaps I should be pleased that our nearest neighbor and dearest enemy has armies filled with squabbling and inefficiency. Certainly our late King Stilwell was able to use this disorder to advantage.)

So when I travel to Loretto, and I'm approached by some knight or noble with some manner of commercial scheme, I look at the man with extra care to find out if he's what he claims or merely some penniless roiderbanks looking to rob me with a contract and a smile.

Thus also I viewed Prince Alicio with a degree of suspicion, but he gave every indication of being what his title claimed: a gentlemen of demi-royal status. He was dark-complected, with heavy brows and a well-tended goatee, and his hair was dressed in long, flowing curls that wafted a scent of oakmoss. He stood in that fashion adopted by the gentlemen of Loretto, with his breastbone thrust forward and his hips and shoulders drawn back, so that his graceful silhouette was curved like a bow. He wore trunks and a doublet of white samite, embroidered with silver thread and studded with rows of baroque pearls. Gems glittered on his belt, on his fingers, and on the buckles of his shoes, which were white cordovan with red heels. Dressed as he was in white, I had at first thought him a member of the sect called the Retrievers, but as I had never seen Retrievers in Loretto, I thought perhaps the simplest explanation was that the prince happened to own a white suit.

Nor was I the only man in the room to view another with skepticism, as I saw that the prince initially viewed me with a polite but frigid hauteur. I do not think that Prince Alicio had ever dined with someone as low-born as myself, or as disreputable a character as the playwright Blackwell, who, after all, made his living on the stage, and was therefore unsuited for polite company.

Nevertheless the prince warmed to us as the dinner progressed, either in response to my shipwreck tale, or as a result of the wines served, or in response to the six or eight ornate platters that were put before him: a pottage of roe deer and vegetables; rabbit pie served in his honor, with a crust in the form of a heraldic prince's crown; a loin of veal flavored with pomegranates and covered with sweet-meats coated in gold foil; a sturgeon poached in vinegar and covered with powdered ginger; a kid stuffed with ortolans; a jelly in the colors of the prince's arms; a heron roasted with cracked peppercorns and served with a creamy mustard sauce; and lastly a hard cheese carved in the shape of a ship, with masts of marchpane, and a cargo of straw-berries, nuts, and little cakes.

I fancied this was meant to honor me.

Their Graces dined in this elaborate fashion every day, and they and those of us used to their lavish hospitality ate but sparingly—all but Mistress Concini, the musical nun, whose obese outline testified to the size of her appetite. She ate with great fervor, and drank vastly of the wine; and she praised both, as well as the duke's orchestra. At the conclusion of the meal she gave thanks to the Pilgrim, and paused to dab at the gravy she had spilled on her robes.

"I see, mistress, that you wear robes of unbleached wool," said I. "So do the monks and nuns of this country. But when Priscus came to marry our queen, he brought with him clergy from Loretto, and these I saw wore bright colors. Is there some philosophical reason for this difference, or is it mere preference on the part of those con-cerned?"

"I do not know of that," she answered. "But the high clergy of Loretto are very great lords, to be sure."

"The royal family of Loretto esteems the Compassionate Pilgrim," said the prince. "They desire the high clergy to reflect the Pilgrim's glory, and in addition believe that rich clothing will attract the com-mon people, in accordance with the Fiat of Abbot Reynardo."

"I am unfamiliar with this fiat," said I.

"Reynardo stated that as the common people are most attracted by display, by tales and stories, and by promise of reward, then it is permissible to employ these tricks and promises in order to bring them to the Pilgrim's truth."

I was half-amused, and half-astonished. I wondered what Captain Gaunt, that self-taught ambassador of the Pilgrim, would have made of this doctrine?

"So it is permissible," said I, "to lie to people in order to bring them to truth?"

"That was Abbot Reynardo's opinion," said the prince. "For myself, I abhor this teaching, and the striving for riches and display that it has caused among the high ecclesiastics. They have invented and made popular a whole panoply of gods and demigods, along with an afterlife of rewards and punishments, that are not supported in any way by any of the blessed Pilgrim's teachings, and flat contradicted by others. I hold to the teachings of the Pilgrim as the Pilgrim taught them. That is why I have come to Duisland, and joined the sect of the Retrievers."

"There are no Retrievers in Loretto?" asked Blackwell.

"None who proclaim their beliefs openly. For King Henrico believes that the nation should be united in doctrine and practice, and those who disdain our corrupt high clergy do so at risk of their lives."

"And our own country?" I asked, looking about the table. "King Henrico's heir has married our queen—has he imported his father's philosophical conformity?"

The duke considered his answer. "Queen Berlauda has always inclined toward that sect which holds the Pilgrim divine, and those clergy she appoints to her household are of a like opinion. But she does not enforce these doctrines on others, and her husband follows her example."

"Yet did not Her Majesty appoint a Lorettan monk abbot of the Monastery of the Pilgrim's Treasure in Selford?" asked Blackwell.

"She did," said the duke. "But of course that monastery is of royal foundation, and the appointment is part of the royal prerogative. Yet she also appointed Lord Thistlegorm to the office of attorney general, and he is high in the sect of the Retrievers."

"So is Judge Hawthorne of the Siege Royal," said Her Grace. "Surely Her Majesty must repose a great deal of trust in Hawthorne to make him the judge of the treason court."

To me it seemed a simple enough job to find guilty whosoever the queen wanted hanged. I recalled my own time at the Siege Royal, the tall, black candles on the judge's bench that served in the tenebrous gloom only to illuminate the stern pale face of the judge, the blood that had fallen from my person onto the floor, and the knowledge that I was not the first man to shed blood in that court. I had no desire to repeat my visit to the Siege Royal, and so did not speak my thought aloud.

"Poor Scutterfield," said Blackwell.

"This is the marquess?" asked I, for I know of only one Scutterfield, and last I heard he'd been lord great chamberlain, with charge over the House of Burgesses and other public buildings in Howel, along with their staff.

"The late marquess," said Blackwell. His tone was bitter. "Judge Hawthorne sent him to the block last month."

"For treason?" asked I, a little surprised.

"The Siege Royal did not disclose the charges," said the duke, "but only that they were capital."

Blackwell spoke with some heat. "Some tangled, secret doings at court. We are ruled by shadows."

The duke, uncomfortable, shifted in his seat. His dark eyes cast a warning toward Blackwell. "Scutterfield was always at home in a quarrel, and quick to sense a rival. He made unwise accusations, and made them in public. But because of his quarrels, in the end he had too few friends."

"I always found him a gentleman," said Blackwell. "I acted as tutor to his sons, when I was young. And now his sons are disinherited by act of attainder, and have lost both heritage and honor."

The shadows of which Blackwell spoke seemed too thick in the chamber, and I thought I might change the subject. "How fares Lord Hulme?" I asked.

"The chancellor is well," said the duke, "and is preserved in office by Her Majesty, who supports him though he is, as always, unpopular."

"I thought Lord Oldershaw was the chancellor," said Prince Alicio.

Which required a digression to explain that the lord chancellor, who supervised judges and courts, was a different person from the chancellor of the exchequer, who ran the Treasury. Oldershaw was the former, while Lord Hulme was the latter. Hulme was generally disliked at court, first on account of his common birth, but more so because he kept a firm grip on the queen's revenues, and thwarted those officials who wished to buy popularity by flinging Her Majesty's coin to the meiny. That the queen had made him a baron seemed only to make him more offensive to the nobility.

"These offices!" said the prince. "You Duislanders make them so confusing."

"Be thankful," I said, "that you need not distinguish counties from counties-in-themselves, or offices held in serjeantry from offices held in gross."

"For this," said the prince, "will I give thanks daily."

"Sir Keely-Fay," said Prince Alicio, "you fight wars and sail to far countries, build mills and deal in pepper and climb cliffs. What is the purpose of all this activity?"

"The purpose?" asked I. "I know not—I know only that I must occupy myself."

"You spare no time for contemplation?"

I smiled. "On an eleven-month voyage, there's time for contemplation of anything you like."

"What did you contemplate?"

"The sea. The sky. The weather. I read poetry, sang songs, and debated philosophy with the captain."

The prince nodded sagely. "Such contemplation may be the beginning of wisdom, Sir Keely-Fay. May the Pilgrim's thought enlighten you."

"Thank you, Highness," said I.

I should perhaps mention that "Keely-Fay" is the closest anyone from Loretto can come to pronouncing my name, for they have no Q in their alphabet, or in their language the sound the Q represents. Later, when I acquired a degree of infamy in their capital, it was Keely-Fay that was the subject of their execrations.

"I wish to share another fruit of my activity," I said, and reached into my pocket for a small box, which I presented to the duchess. "With the permission of His Grace," I said, "I would like to offer this small thanks for your kindness, your hospitality, and the support which you offered during difficult times."

Her Grace opened the box, and her mouth formed an O. Reflected in her blue eyes I could see the glittering facets of my gift: a blue diamond, pear-shaped, the length of my fingernail. She looked at me with a degree of consternation.

"Quillifer, this is far too generous!"

I affected a shrug and put on my offhand-sailor face. "I brought a chest of gemstones from Tabarzam, and am content to spare one. Though you would do me a favor if you wore this trinket at court, and perhaps mentioned to your friends that you obtained it from me."

The duke was amused. "You turn from sailor to miller to jeweler now? You hope my lady's recommendation will bring you business?"

I made an easy gesture with one hand. "If all I wanted were profit, I could sell the stones to a jeweler. But over the months of the voyage I came to know each stone well, and each now, like a person, seems to have its own character—some tender, some brilliant, some of greater

or lesser quality, some with hidden faults, some with shining, surprising elements within their makeup. Rubies smoldering as if with
hidden fire, smaragds verdant as the spring, diamonds shining like a
knight in armor. . . . It would be pleasing to bestow each upon a lord
or lady, endowing each candidate with a stone that serves their color,
their station, and their personality."

"Much will then rely upon your taste," said the duke, "and the
forbearance of your customers."

I shrugged again. "I am not a jeweler; I seek amusement only, and
to enlarge my acquaintance."

"And profit?" asked Blackwell.

"There are many kinds of profit," said I.

"Well then," said the duke, "as you seek to honor my lady, I will not
stand in the way of her being so honored. Be aware, though, that not
all husbands are as indulgent as I."

"I am all too aware of the dangers represented by husbands," I
said.

Mistress Concini turned to me. "May I call upon you, Sir Keely-
Fay?" she asked. "I should like to see these stones."

I was surprised, but agreed to a meeting. Being chorus-mistress
to a group of nuns, I thought, was a more profitable occupation than
I supposed.

In my mind, I was already beginning to choose the stones that
would suit her.

CHAPTER SIX

he very next day I sold Mistress Concini some gemstones. She maintained they were intended for some
ritual items at her convent, but she listened intently to
my discourse on which gems would best suit her complexion and personality, and bought the stones I recommended—so I
delighted myself with the thought that she has a secret life in which
she wears farthingales, dances the coranto, glitters with jewelry, and
flirts from behind an ostrich-feather fan.

At the end of the following week I was at the tiller of my galley
Dunnock, racing across the lake below Ings Magna. There would be
regattas that autumn, and I planned to take part—and with a crew
of picked men from *Royal Stilwell*, I thought I had a chance to distinguish myself. I'd had the galley built in Bretlynton Head while I was
away, and carried it to Howel on my barge. The hull was white, with
sea-blue trim, and eight stout sailors pulled the oars. I had other crew
as sail-setters and trimmers, but that day I worked with the oarsmen
alone, and the mast rested in its cradle.

I was displaying my arms wherever I could, and had painted my
shield on the fantail of the galley and on the doors of Lord Rackheath's

carriage, and set them waving from the flagpole by the house. I wished to proclaim my presence, for there was no point in my being in water-girdled Howel without being noticed.

My shield is handsome, you must admit: white and blue just like my galley. In the language of the herald, *Azure, a galleon argent a chief fir twigged argent, in chief three pens bendwise sable*.

Which is to say a blue shield with a white ship, and a wide white stripe across the top, with a jagged border resembling in outline the twigs of a fir tree. In the white stripe are three black quills.

Quill-in-fir. The conceit is my own.

I exercised my crew on the lake every day, and had engaged a tutor to teach me tennis. I also continued my explorations into the business of making ink.

The day was fine and bracing, with the first hints of autumn in the cool westerly wind that brought white clouds scudding across the sky. Spray came over *Dunnock*'s starboard bow as we pulled southwest toward Lord Rackheath's boathouse, and spray cooled my face and the bare necks of the oarsmen.

My crew were beginning to tire. A sailor's life is hard, but it rarely requires sustained effort, and the lack of endurance can be a complication when it comes to running or rowing in chase. And so to increase their wind I drilled my men every day, in every weather, in hopes they would be ready when the court arrived and the races began.

The sun glowed on the gold sandstone of the palace, shining above its water gardens. Parts were covered in scaffolding, where repairs or improvements were being made, and a new, very large structure rose behind. I saw horses and wagons on the quay, and took out my spyglass to view batteries of artillery lining up to fire out onto the lake. Though I knew the queen did not care for me, it nevertheless seemed unlikely the guns were forming up to shoot at my boat. The one-o'clock gun had fired some hours ago, and so I assumed that something of moment had occurred, and that there would be a salute. And indeed, as soon as the caissons and limbers of the Guild of Carters and Haulers had placed the guns and withdrawn, I saw powder being ladled down the bronze and iron tubes. Powder, but no cannon balls, and only wads to hold the powder in place. After which the guns were primed, and the cannoneers stood by in groups, as if they had nothing better to do than to await a signal.

I thought I knew why a salute would be fired, for the Queen would soon end her progress from the summer capital of Selford to the winter palace at Howel. She varied the journey every year, and this year had landed at Ferrick, in the north, near the border with her husband's home of Loretto, where he could receive visitors and messages from home. As she traveled she would stay with the local lords, who sometimes bankrupted themselves with the expense of feeding and entertaining the entire court—though of course they all hoped to be repaid with office, which would enable them to enrich themselves with contracts and bribes. Thus the Queen lived off her ambitious subjects' largesse for two months of the year, and had not to spend from her private purse at all.

I drove my oarsmen in a final sprint to shore, let them all share a cask of small beer, and then brought them out onto the lake again in a more leisurely pull toward the palace to see what was toward. The gunners were still at their leisure, and through my glass I recognized one of their number. I moored *Dunnock* twenty yards down the quay from the guns, where burning wads wouldn't fall into the boat if the guns were discharged, and went to greet my friend.

"Captain Lipton," said I, and further words were stopped in my throat as he gave me a ferocious bear hug that set my ribs creaking.

"Well, youngster," Lipton said as he set me back on my feet. "Good it is to see you, sure. I had thought you were lost at sea, and living in an underwater palace with a nymph for your consort and mermaids for your servants."

"I have not been so lucky," said I, though inwardly I winced at the mention of water-nymphs.

I had met Captain Lipton during Clayborne's rebellion, where he had commanded the guns at Exton Scales and been of service both to the army and myself. Afterward he had been a part of the benign conspiracy that resulted in my knighthood. He had a fringe of white hair around a bald pate, and a white beard. He spoke in the sharp, fierce accent of North Fornland, and dressed habitually in worn clothing and a baggy cap that flopped about his ears—but today he wore a trim blue doublet piped with red, a blue-and-gold sash over one shoulder, and, tipped over one eye, a blue velvet bonnet with badge and feather. I regarded this magnificence with surprise.

"Never have I seen you so splendid," I said. "Have you dressed especially to welcome me?"

"Sadly," he said, "this dress is now expected of me. For you no longer address Bill Lipton of the Loyall and Worshipfull Companie of Cannoneers, but the coronel of the Royal Regiment of Artillery."

"Give you joy, Coronel!" said I. "But what is this Royal Regiment?"

"We are now a part of the Queen's Guard," he said. "Along with the Yeoman Archers and the Queen's Own Horse under our friend Lord Barkin."

I looked at the line of demiculverins with their long bronze barrels pointed out at the water. "Why does Her Majesty purpose to guard herself with batteries of great guns?"

"Someone must fire the salutes," said Lipton. "Yet if there is ever riot in the town, we will blast it to bits, sure."

The monarch traditionally was guarded by foot and by horse. On foot were the Yeoman Archers, who no longer carried bows but instead pikes and firelocks; and on horseback were the Gentlemen-at-Arms, more familiarly called the Gendarmes, armored cap-a-pie in the fashion of knights of old. The Gendarmes were the offspring of knightly or noble houses, whereas the Yeoman Archers had less exalted births. During the rebellion, the Gendarmes had risen for the bastard Clayborne, and those who were not killed at Exton Scales were captured, branded on the cheek with a *T* for "treason," and sentenced to ten years' hard labor.

The destruction of the Gendarmes had left a large number of well-born youth with unfulfilled martial dreams, and left Her Majesty without so many of the handsome young gentlemen she so enjoyed about her, and so she had formed a new regiment of demilances—no longer in the antique armor of knights, but modern cavalry in breastplate and burgonet, and armed with pistols and sword. The artillery were added at the same time, to enhance the royal magnificence.

After nearly being unseated by rebellion, Queen Berlauda wanted loyal men in command of the new regiments, and no more-loyal officers could be found than those who had served her at Exton Scales. Lord Barkin, a professional soldier who had commanded a troop of demilances in the battle, was an obvious choice; and though Lipton lacked the well-born refinement the queen liked about her, he knew the specialized business of artillery as well as young nobles knew the chase.

"Ah, it is all display these days," Lipton said. "We bow, and salute, keep our doublets brushed, and polish the linstocks to a gleam. And they of Loretto sneer at us for our country ways." He sniffed. "You would have thought it was they who won the last war."

"It might be claimed they won the peace," said I. For Loretto's captured king had never paid his ransom, and his grand-nephew and heir had married our queen, and for his condescension had been made king regnant, sharing equally the powers of his wife.

"Ay, that's true enough."

"But why the long face, Coronel?" said I. "You cannot fairly complain, for you are master of Her Majesty's artillery!"

"True enough, youngster," Lipton said. "Yet the changes they come, and not all are good." He gestured over his shoulder at the scaffolding covering the palace walls and towers. "It is all show and extravagance here. Look you, they gild the gilding. And now they will call the Estates to pay for it."

"Their Majesties are calling the Estates? For new taxes, I assume?"

"You have not heard? Ay, for the crown needs money, not least to pay my wages, which are two months in arrears."

I privately thought that for a soldier's pay to be no more than two months late was excellent luck for the soldier. "We are at peace," I said. "The great storm has ruined this year's yield in Fornland, but for the last few years we've had good harvests, and trade has expanded. Why does the crown need more money?"

Lipton waved a hand. "They gild the gilding, youngster. These Loretto nobility have their own ideas of grandeur, and it seems we must pay for it." He raised a hand and pointed across the lake, where cranes and scaffolds marked the building of some great project. "And there the monarchs raise the Monastery of the Holy Prophecy, to be the greatest in the kingdom, which will be made rich with donations of land from the crown. And it has also come to the royal attention that the crown possesses twenty-three palaces in different parts of the kingdom, and that some have been neglected and others allowed to fall into ruin, and that the dignity of the House of Emelin requires that all these palaces be restored and made as bright as day."

"Is it likely the Estates will agree to pay for this?"

"The chancellor will get his way. He always does." He looked down the row of bronze guns all facing out over the quay. "It is not enough for royalty to take a salute of twenty-three guns, but they must also be greeted by a chorus of nuns, all singing praise to the Pilgrim."

"Nuns? I met their concert-mistress the other day." I gestured at the bronze guns. "Why are you set to bombard the lake? Are Their Majesties looming?"

"Expected this afternoon." He cocked an eyebrow at me. "Are you still banned from court?"

I shrugged. "Doubtless I shall find out. It may be that Her Majesty will not remember me."

Lipton showed his crooked yellow teeth. "I think she remembers every little thing that has ever thwarted her in her life."

"I never thwarted her!"

"You made her look closely at things she wanted not to see. Did you expect thanks?"

I spread my hands. "That was three years ago. Surely Her Majesty has had more to attract her disapprobation in the years since?"

His white brows came together. "Disapprobation?"

"It's a new word. I made it up."

"It is unlovely. I don't know that I approbate it."

There was the clop of a horse on the quay, and a demilance trotted up along the line of guns. His helmet and breastplate had been plated with gleaming brass, with the royal badge on the breast and the cypher, the entwined *B* and *P* on the helmet, and in the afternoon sun the trooper dazzled though he had covered miles and was very dusty. I thought of gilt on gilding.

"Where is the coronel?" asked the trooper.

Lipton turned to him. "I am the coronel, sure," he said.

The cavalryman raised a hand to the beak of his helmet. "Captain Leyton's compliments, sir. Their Majesties have just come onto the north lane past the guard lions, and you may begin the salute."

"I shall commence directly."

The demilance saluted again, turned his horse, and trotted back the way he had come.

"They are very proper here, sure," Lipton said. He brushed his blue doublet with his hands. "I will be busy the next hour, youngster."

"Come see me at Rackheath House," I said. "It's just down the lake, and you'll see my flag flying."

Lipton bustled away, I returned to my galley, and we pulled onto the water as the guns began to boom. The wind streamed the clouds of gunsmoke onto the lake, and so the galley seemed to float in a world of mist, with the towers of the palace shining gold above, as if they were a vision of another world. The effect was enhanced when the guns fell silent, and Mistress Concini's choir began to sing, the unearthly music shimmering over the waves, as if it were dropping from the spheres.

I tasted the gunsmoke on my tongue and contemplated this singing, floating fantasia, the palace as fata morgana, and I thought of Orlanda, equally nebulous as this vision, and deadly as any artillery. I knew that she would be present in the court, invisibly perhaps, perhaps whispering in the inward ear of the queen and the courtiers. She had poisoned the queen against me once, and I had no doubt she would do it again.

I wondered how foolish were my intentions at Howel in the face of Orlanda's enmity, and whether I was no more than an insect prepared to be crushed beneath the boot of my own ambition. Yet Orlanda would oppose me no matter what I did, and even if I donned a smock and hood and turned cotter, I thought she would blight my turnips. So if I were to play her game, it seemed to me that the stakes should be worthy of my effort.

As Mistress Concini's choir sang in the white mist, I wondered if I were still unwelcome at court. The scandal that I had uncovered seemed a very long time ago, and I a different person.

The question, I decided, was not whether I had changed, but whether the queen had—and, for that matter, whether Orlanda would allow her to change. And that we would see soon enough.

CHAPTER SEVEN

I f your ladyship will take my advice," said I, "you will consider these deep yellow diamonds, for if you wear them by your face"—I held one of the stones near her ear, and affected first to study the picture I had created, and then to approve—"you will see they compliment the gold lights in your eyes. If your ladyship will permit?" I touched her chin with my other hand and tilted her head into the light. "Yes," I breathed. "That is your ladyship's color exactly."

Lady Westley blushed. I could feel the warmth of the rising blood on the back of my hand.

I withdrew my fingers and showed her the stones again. "Let me demonstrate," I said, "with a mirror and a candle."

I drew to her side a table with a mirror, took the candle in one hand, and knelt by her side. I brushed back the warm chestnut-colored hair to reveal her ear and held the stone against the warm curve of her neck, where an earring might dangle. She gave a little shiver. "Can you see?" I said into her ear. "Should I move the candle?"

She reached for my hand with the candle, her fingers closing on mine, and moved the light so it shone into her blue eyes. "Ay," she said. "I see."

"I think the effect would be dazzling," I said. "Your ladyship should wear the stones on earrings, or perhaps on a headdress that would place them near your eyes."

Lady Westley let her hand linger on mine. Her bergamot scent teased my senses. "I have never seen diamonds so yellow."

"The color of these stones is unusually intense," said I. "People often buy pale yellow diamonds and put them in gold settings, because then they can pass for white stones to the untrained eye. But the color in *these* diamonds is too extraordinary for such tricks. Your ladyship should put them in settings of white gold, the better to let them shine in their true glory—and of course you should enhance them with lesser stones, of which I have none, but which your jeweler would be pleased to provide."

I drew back from her ladyship, and set the candle on the table. I could see that her face was still a little flushed.

"Would your ladyship like some more wine?" I asked.

The court had returned to Howel eight days before, and the palace and the city at once came alive with dinners, receptions, concerts, masques, hunts, and the rattle of carriages as courtiers, diplomats, and suppliants passed my house on their way to Ings Magna.

I had gone to the palace several times, bowling along in Lord Rackheath's carriage with my shield now painted on its door. No one had turned me away. I had bowed to Her Majesty at receptions, and she had looked at me without interest.

Perhaps she did not recognize me. In the past I had dressed in the robe and cap of an apprentice lawyer, for I could not afford to compete in the glitter and display of the court, and as an incomplete lawyer I was at least respectable. But now, though I still could not outshine the jeweled and painted raiment of the high nobility, I could at least glitter in my own distinctive way.

I took my cue from the chancellor of the exchequer, Sir Denys Hulme, who dressed simply in black, perhaps to avoid the resentment of the nobility unhappy with his common birth, a resentment sharpened by his elevation to the peerage as Baron Hulme. Had he paraded like a glittering peacock and built a shining palace in the vicinity of Ings Magna, he would have been suspected of making away with revenue belonging to the crown.

Instead he lived in a large house in town and dressed like a sober man of business, which he was, though he set off his severe clothing with brilliant gems, which he wore on his gloved fingers. It was to let the world know he was a man of substance—and indeed he was, for his substantial fortune he had made himself before being appointed to office. And though I'm sure his fortune had increased since his becoming chancellor, I'm also sure he had no need to steal—the man in charge of the treasury will always know where to put his money to make himself a fine profit.

Having no office, I had no need to pretend to such sobriety as the lord chancellor, so I indulged myself with suits of satin, velvet, and silk—but without the pearls, purfles, paint, and slashings that were so popular among the courtiers—and which I set off by immaculate white linen. But I had reserved the best and largest of my gems for myself, and wore rings on every finger, a blue-white diamond on a gold chain about my neck, and a great sapphire dangling from a gold belt about my waist, a belt composed of tiny links knit one to the other, the most precious chain mail in the world. In the brightly lit Chamber of Audience, amid the fantastic carvings and the bright silk tapestries, and even among the courtiers in their furbelows and fancies, I stood out like a species of fantastic animal.

Thus did I proclaim myself worthy of the court. And though Her Grace of Roundsilver very kindly wore the blue pear-shaped stone I had given her, and told others where she had got the diamond, I hardly needed her assistance, for my diamonds, rubies, and sapphires in their precious settings told a tale of their own.

Nor was I entirely a stranger, for I had made the acquaintance of some of the courtiers three years before, and I was gratified, and somewhat surprised, by their remembering me at all. They introduced me to their friends, and related anecdotes—some vastly exaggerated—of my time in the court at Selford. Time had drawn a rosy veil over the escapades that had once caused outrage or suspicion and lent them a charming anecdotal quality, like the subject of a ballad or a stirring episode in a play. From its origin as a bare sequence of events, which seemed to me a collection of episodes all unrelated one to the next, it appeared that in my absence my life had become a tale. And of course, once I saw the shape that time had made of my life, I was able to form new tales in that mode, and so I spoke of my voyages and the shipwreck, along with my modest narrative—for those of nautical inclination—of the invention of Quillifer's Haul.

Thus, as I offered a modest relation of my adventures to some of my new friends, was I introduced to Lady Westley, the wife of a knight from Lake Gurlidan who held a post in the Royal Mews as master of the henchmen. Her interest in gems was plain, for with her gown of bright forest-green silk she wore emeralds, turquoise, chrysoberyls, and cabochons of jet and of tourmaline, and carried on her girdle a golden pomander set with pearls. A beautiful, if rather miscellaneous, array, which did not complement to the fullest possible extent the broad forehead and generous lower lip, the mass of chestnut hair, and the level brows over the blue eyes, with their flecks of gold.

And so Lady Westley became my first visitor at my house, and I knelt beside her with the yellow diamonds in my hand, admiring the flush that blossomed and faded in her cheeks.

"I will take some more wine, thank you," said she.

I rose and poured sauternes from a decanter into her goblet. While she sipped, I shifted some scales onto the table by her side and put the diamonds in one of the pans. I knelt by her again, unstopped a bottle, and began, with silver tweezers, to draw out carob seeds and place them in the other pan.

"These *karatioi* are used in Sarafsham to measure gemstones," said I, "for their weight does not vary from one to the other. And as you can see, the stones together weigh somewhere between ten and eleven carob seeds—let us say ten. Because you are the first to come admire my collection, and because your beauty so compliments these stones they might well blush red when you wear them, let us say that I will part with them for thirty royals."

Thirty royals would keep one of my tenants and his family roistering and dancing the sarabande for three years or more, yet it was a very good price for such rare stones. Others might have paid fifty or sixty without protest. Lady Westley looked at the diamonds with her lips parted, and I could see the gold flecks glitter in her eyes.

"I think that is fair," said she.

"Your ladyship's judgment is exquisite," I said. "Shall we drink to our agreement, or would you like to see some other gems?"

She gave me an appraising look. "Why not both?"

I laughed. "Why not?" I reached for my own cup and poured sauternes, and then turned to Lady Westley, raised my glass, and touched it lightly to her own. "To beauty," I said, "and to the loveliness which my stones can only enhance, but never supplant."

She blushed again, most becomingly, and drank. For the next quarter hour I showed her some of my prizes and spoke of the Street of the Shining Stones in far Sarafsham, and the deep mines that had been worked for centuries, protected from collapse by the great cedar beams hewn on Mount Safavi and dragged thirty leagues to the diggings. The close-knit families of merchant princes who controlled the gem trade, each rich as King Timaeus and proud as a Lorettan lordling. The keen-eyed cutters who studied the raw stones, propping them between mirrors so the sun would come at them from all angles and reveal their structure. The caravan guards, grim and fierce, who escorted the gems from Sarafsham to the port of Tabarzam, and whose dour temperament was belied by the warm hospitality they offered me around their campfires, and by their sad and sentimental music. And while I offered these memories, I illustrated my words with gems, which I set on a length of black velvet that I had placed on her ladyship's knees.

Lady Westley listened with interest, but paid more attention to gemstones than to my tales. I refilled her cup again. At length she sighed.

"I should like to possess them all," she said. "But that is hardly possible."

"I understand," I said. "These stones each have their story, and I feel as if I could relate all of them." I carefully took the black velvet away and placed it atop my strongbox.

I rose from my kneeling posture and helped Lady Westley rise to her feet, and then found myself looking into her gold-flecked eyes at a range of inches. Her lips parted. I could scent the sweet sauternes on her breath, and scent as well the bergamot fragrance she had dabbed on her throat.

"When you have the diamonds mounted," said I, "I hope you will come and model them for me. For well will they grace this neck." I kissed her below the ear, and she shivered as I took her in my arms. I let my lips travel from her throat to her mouth, and she kissed me with bright eagerness. The taste of her lips set my blood afire.

Two constraints fell upon our afternoon of love. The first was that she was not alone, having very properly brought a serving woman with her. This woman was being entertained in the serving hall, but could not be expected to wait there forever.

The second was that I had never before dealt with the complicated garments of a lady of the court. There was a corset to be considered, and the whalebone busk she wore to flatten her chest in accordance with the fashion; there was a farthingale, and a bumroll, numerous petticoats, a kirtle, and the gown over all. I had no doubt that with a degree of patience I could perform the necessary unlacings, but I had little confidence that I could stitch her up again and send her from the house in anything but scandalous disarray.

Yet she was avid, and I had scarcely more patience than she. I placed her upon a settee, and there was nothing but to push up the petticoats and gown, and reveal her legs and the stockings gartered with ribbons of peach-colored satin. I kissed along the soft, warm, fragrant flesh from her ankles to her velvet, where I lingered for a moment or two to enjoy the soft cries that came from her throat, and then I straightened and began to undo my own laces.

The rest you may imagine for yourself. Some span of minutes later, she lay at rest on the sofa in a froth of petticoats, her half-dreaming eyes gazing up at the ceiling; and I reclined with my head in her lap, watching the rose fade slowly from her cheeks while she stroked my hair. "My lady?" I asked.

"Yes?"

"In consideration of our degree of amity, I hope I may not be considered overly familiar if I petition to address you by your forename." The first of which, I happened to know, was Osgyth.

She gave a low chuckle. "Which one? I have six or eight forenames," she said, "all of elderly relations from whom my father desired money. And I care neither for the names nor the relations."

I considered. "May I call you Girasol, then? For your beauty has an opalescent sheen, yet you are passionate, and in my arms you blaze up like a fire-opal in the sun."

She teased a lock of my hair. "Are you the sun, then?"

"I am more like a moon, as my radiance is but a reflection of yours."

She flushed prettily. "Oh, with such flattery you will go far at court." Her eyes lost their dreamy quality, and she looked at me with speculation. "Yet you have only one name."

"A single name is not uncommon in the west of Fornland."

"Yet how would you know if I address you formally or informally? The name is the same."

"Choose a name, my Girasol, as I did for you."

"Heliodor," she said. "For you have sold me those sun-colored stones."

"It is a name out of romance," said I. "Heliodor, the beryl knight."

"Should I be ever confined in a dungeon," she said, "I will expect a rescue."

I kissed her thigh, and then went across the floor to my strongbox. I chose a stone, put it in a velvet bag, and returned to her side.

"We have done business together," I said, "and I would not tamper with those arrangements, for I would not have it thought that you coupled with me for precious stones. But yet a lover may offer a gift, may he not?"

She kissed me before opening the bag, which I thought was the proper order. The white diamond I had given her was small, only a fraction more than two *karatioi*, but it was flawless, and cut in a new fashion, adding eight new facets to the seven of the table cut, and showing a brilliance that had once only been possible in larger stones. Girasol gave a cry of delight and kissed me again.

"You must tell your friends that you paid dearly for your diamonds," said I.

She laughed. "Perhaps I have."

"If you think this payment dear," I said, "then what will you think of the exactions I hope to inflict on you in the future?"

By the time she called her maid, I had helped her adjust her costume so as to avoid scandal, and she carried all three of her diamonds in velvet pouches. I had some misgivings at allowing some of my best stones to leave without being paid for, but I found myself unable to deny Lady Westley her pleasures.

And my trust was not misplaced, for the next day came a draught on the Oberlin Fraters Bank for thirty royals, along with a pendant in the form of a cameo of a rayed sun carved in agate, and on the reverse side, a glass compartment that held a lock of chestnut hair.

In truth I must recommend to all young men that they find a wife. Not that they marry, though they may do that as well, but that they find a merry, pleasing wife, with whom they may delight the hours. For a wife, being married already, will leave a man his freedom and will not harry a man to join her in wedded union. Nor will they play such games as coy virgins play, saying "nay" one day and "maybe" the next; and because wives have knowledge of the world, they will know how to please, and how in his turn the youth should please them. A wife may therefore be a part of a man's education, and certainly the most pleasurable part thereof.

I have treasured all my wives, and warm memories of them take up a special place next to my heart.

So to young men I say: *Find you a wife! A wife! A wife!*

There is laughter in your black eyes, my love. Yet I remind you that for peril there is nothing like a single lady, and that you yourself are the proof. For you I will risk the gallows, where with wives I risked but the wrath of the husbands.

CHAPTER EIGHT

Y ou were amused, I saw, by my haplessness when faced
with Lady Westley's court dress. But as you know first-
hand, I have surmounted my handicap in the time
since, and I can tie up a lady's points as smartly as I can
a bowline. At need I could earn my living as a lady's maid, if any lady
were deranged enough to employ me, and for that I must thank the
practice I had with Lady Westley.

I have, after all, repaired your own costume on more than a few
occasions. Occasions which, I hope, we both found unforgettable.

"I have just viewed the lord great chamberlain's head," I said, "on
a spike in front of the Hall of Justice. He did not contribute to the
beauty of the scene."

"Yet it is more wholesome," said Lipton, "than to see a forest of
heads in the square, as we did after the rebellion."

Which was true enough. The bastard Clayborne and many of
his supporters had once graced a thicket of pikes in the square, but
most of the heads had been removed, and now only the usurper
and his close kin were visible, removed from the square to the top

of a crow-stepped gable over the hall's entrance. The Marquess of Scutterfield was the only recent head to be found on the square, and I hoped he was not a harbinger of more to come.

Lipton and I were dining in Rackheath House's great hall. Surrounding us was a riot of embroidered herbs, flowers, stags, and knights, all embroidered on brilliant silk tapestries, with the gold threads kindled by the noontide sun. We were served by two footmen, the master carver, and the two yeomen, respectively, of the ewer and of the buttery, who were to aid us in washing our hands between removes and to keep our glasses filled. Thus my intimate dinner with a friend was attended by five eavesdroppers.

The carver laid his knife to a carbonado of mutton, poured on a sauce of claret and camphire, and garnished it with lemons and capers, after which the footmen marched our plates to the table. "By your leave, my masters," they said, nearly in unison, and put the plates before us, before marching back to their place at the carving table.

The carver, I observed, was competent enough, but I could have done a better job.

"Did you know Scutterfield?" Lipton asked.

"Nay. By sight only."

Lipton looked to make sure the servants were not too close, then leaned across the table to me. "He ran afoul of Her Majesty's principal private secretary, Lord Edevane. He is said to be Berlauda's spymaster."

"And who does Edevane spy upon?"

Lipton spread his hands, as if to encompass the whole world. "He may have someone here, in your own household."

"Here?" I spread my own hands. "But I am harmless. I have no power. And I have demonstrated my loyalty to Her Majesty more than once."

Lipton applied himself to his mutton while he considered the matter, then he leaned again across the table. "There are many sorts of servants, youngster," he said. "There are the lazy servants, who will not work unless someone stands over them. There are servants who do their duty and nothing else, because that is what they are paid for; and there are also servants who will do their duty and seek to do more, in hopes of notice and advancement." His face turned sober. "And then there are servants who so understand their masters' minds that they know their masters' secret desires before even their masters know them, and they then act in advance to fulfill these unvoiced wishes. Their masters are oft surprised when such a thing happens, but ultimately they are gratified, and the servant prospers. And such a servant is Lord Edevane."

I ate my mutton while I considered the matter of Berlauda's secret desires. She had taken the throne in the midst of a civil war, when one city after another was deserting to Clayborne, and great men of the realm were flying to his banner. In the midst of this—and I must here admit my own part in bringing these facts to light—she had discovered murderous treachery on the part of her own mother, and also her most intimate friend.

After the victory at Exton Scales, she had not forgiven those who had betrayed her. While another monarch might have executed the leaders, then fined or forgiven the rest, Berlauda had hunted down everyone who had supported Clayborne's cause, executed or enslaved them, and confiscated their property to pay for the war. Even those who survived their ten years of hard labor would have to live with a *T* for treason branded on their face.

Berlauda's desires, I thought, were not complicated. She wished a realm that was her own, where her enemies were destroyed and she was free to live with her husband in security and pleasure. A gentleman who could provide that realm, or a plausible illusion of it, might prosper in her reign.

Lipton leaned across the table again. "Bear in mind also that a man whose job it is to root out conspiracy must *find* that conspiracy, or lose his employment. Scutterfield accused Edevane of sharking up cases against innocent men, and soon lost his head." He looked at me with unease plain upon his face. "Edevane is the only man at court who frightens me. If he has an ally who wants my place, I can be indicted for some peculation or other, be convicted on the testimony of paid inform-ers, and Edevane's friend slipped into my place as easy as winking."

"Sooner or later such people go too far," said I. "And that is the end of them."

"Ay, but how many heads will roll in the meantime?"

I leaned away from the conversation, sipped my wine, and sig-naled for the footman. "By your leave, my master," he said, and car-ried away my plate. Another dish was brought up from the kitchens. The yeoman of the buttery came out to refresh our wine, and the yeoman of the ewer brought his bowl and pitcher to wash our hands.

Again we put our heads together. "Are you sure you want to come live at court, youngster?" asked Lipton. "Walk open-eyed into this tan-gle of conspiracies, falsehoods, and right murder?"

"No man has reason to hate me," I said.

"Ha! You overvalue reason."

I threw out my hands. "What other game is there? I will play my best, alongside the best."

"You but make a target of yourself. Better to sail again to Tabarzam and defy the pirates."

The footmen were coming with the next dish, meatballs made with a paste of regia, the paste itself made of the meat of quails, par-tridges, a capon, and a few cock sparrows, all mashed together with pistachios and sugar-paste. (I do not know why hen sparrows are to be avoided.)

"By your leave, my masters." The footmen put down the plates and withdrew.

The meatballs were an interesting combination of sweet and sa-vory. I considered Lipton's warnings, then looked up at one of the room's tapestries, a scene of astrological figures dancing through the sky. "Perhaps the stars decide all such matters," I said. "Do you believe in such things?"

"I was born under the sign of the Boar, sure," said Lipton. "I therefore possess wisdom, and great appetite."

"My father had my horoscope cast when I was young," I said. "It said that I was studious, abstemious, steady in my habits, and that I would make a good monk, or a chandler. Every so often my father would take this document out of his strongbox, read it aloud at dinner, and laugh."

"A chandler can make a good living," Lipton said, "and not have to risk his neck at sea. Allow me to recommend this employment to you."

"I am invited to an astronomical evening tonight," I said. "At the palace of His Grace of Roundsilver. We are to hear a lecture about the Comet Periodical, and if the sky is clear, we will view the planets with telescopes."

"Comets fly like a flaming shell," Lipton observed, "and the planets are round like gunshot. Maybe the gods have artillery, and fire their bombards across the heavens."

"And the stars are the glow of their linstocks. You should recruit the gods into your Loyall and Worshipfull Companie of Cannoneers."

"Ay." He laughed. "You should sell this conceit to the playwright Blackwell. He would get a soliloquy out of it."

"Only if he has a cannoneer for the subject of his play."

Lipton laughed again. "And why should he not? Let the cannon rattle the theater, and strike the clowns dumb! They would not be any worse for having to perform in silence."

I picked up a meatball on a fork and contemplated it. "I will suggest to Blackwell that he employ artillery," I said, "but I think he would not agree unless he were allowed to direct his fire at certain members of the court."

"Well," said Lipton, "if the gods oblige us not in this matter, perhaps a poet will have to serve, if he have good aim."

The air tasted of smoke as I came to the Roundsilver palace after dark and found linkboys lining the road outside, their torches shining on the glittering dress of the guests as they stepped from their carriages. I stepped from the coach and let one of the linkboys conduct me to the door. I gave the boy his vail and a footman my wool boat cloak, and entered to the pleasing sound of women's laughter.

I turned into a parlor and saw the duchess in a wrapper of white samite trimmed with frogging and fringes, speaking with a group of ladies that included the princess Floria, Her Majesty's half-sister. For a moment I considered turning away and leaving the house, but I had been seen, and so I approached to bow to the princess and to greet my hostess.

"I see you have made something of yourself, Quillifer," Floria said. "Judging by those shiny boulders you wear on your fingers."

"I have achieved some little success, Your Highness," said I.

Queen Berlauda was tall and blond and stately, like her royal father; but Floria was short and dark and quick, like her mother, with hazel eyes that snapped from one point of interest to the next and missed nothing. She wore a gown of the royal gold and scarlet ornamented with embroidery of white flowers, a gold belt studded with rubies, and hung from her wrist a marabou-feather fan. A golden circlet and a net of gold mesh made an attempt to confine her tight, rebellious, dark curls, and she wore a galbanum scent that conjured shady pine woods, soft moss, and freshets of sweet water. Floria had played a vital part in the benign conspiracy that had given me a knighthood and a manor, but I had always suspected that she viewed me as a tool for her amusement, and I had been wary of her interest. I had once refused to be the plaything of a goddess—and having refused a goddess, would I then allow myself to become the court fool of a fifteen-year-old girl?

She might be eighteen or nineteen now, I realized, but those hazel eyes still viewed me as she might view a clown in Blackwell's theater company. I suspected that at any moment she might command me to perform a somersault.

"Sir Quillifer has brought a great treasury of gems from a voyage to Tabarzam," said Her Grace. "Perhaps Your Highness would care to view them?"

Floria gave me one of her sharp glances. "Are you a jeweler now? I thought you were a lawyer, or a soldier, or a sailor."

"Alas, Your Highness," said I, "I am myself."

"Next week," Floria decided, "you might be a haberdasher."

"Have you met Her Highness's ladies?" said the duchess. "Sir Quillifer, this is Countess Marcella, Mistress Chenée Tavistock, and Mistress Elisa d'Altrey."

Mistress Tavistock had light brown hair and an engaging overbite, and Elisa d'Altrey was tall, black-haired, and black-eyed. With pride she wore her classical features, the pale tall brow, the straight nose, and the full lips, and she viewed me with obvious disdain. Countess Marcella was the most striking, for she was an Aekoi, with golden skin and a lithe frame that did not sort entirely with the stiff corsets and gowns worn by ladies of Duisland. I knew of no Aekoi peers in our country, but supposed she might have come from Loretto. She was somewhat older than the others, who were twenty or younger, but I have no great skill at judging the age of Aekoi and guessed she might be around thirty.

I supposed there was a story behind Countess Marcella, but I would not learn it that night.

I bowed to the ladies, and then we made pleasant conversation as more guests arrived. I noticed that Floria's ladies all wore a badge of the same white flower with which the princess had embroidered her gown.

"It is appropriate that a great lady bearing a floral name should adopt a flower as a badge," said I. "But why a busy lizzie?"

Floria looked sat me in surprise. "It is a double impatiens."

"In Ethlebight we call them busy lizzies."

"Well," said Floria, "so you would."

Her ladies laughed, though I did not quite understand the joke, which made little sense unless the inhabitants of my native city were known for giving quaint names to vegetation, which they are not.

"Well then," I said. "Why an impatiens?"

"That is explained by the motto."

I saw now that a motto was stitched in silver thread on the badge, but in letters too tiny for me to read.

"To read the letters," I said, "would require me to peer in a rude fashion at your gown, which—"

Before I could finish, Her Highness snapped open the marabou-feather fan. The feathers were each affixed to a scarlet ribbon to keep them in order, and on the ribbon were embroidered, in New Aekoi, the words *SUB UMBRA CONVALO.*

" 'I thrive in shade,' " I translated. "Very appropriate, Your Highness."

"The more so," said she, "as I am always surrounded by big fellows like you, to stand between me and the sun."

But I thought there was more to the motto than that, for Floria would always stand in the shade of her elder half-sister, the queen. And though there was no overt hostility between the sisters, neither was there any visible affection. *Berlauda won't mourn if I break my neck,* I had once heard Floria say after a riding accident.

It occurred to me also that, as *convalo* had more than one meaning, there was another possible interpretation, which was "In shadow I gather power," which seemed more the motto of a villainous duke in a play—though if Floria had not intended the double meaning, she could have chosen a different verb, for example *vigeo.* I wondered what message this innocent white flower was intended to send.

My musings on Floria's choice of verbs were cut short as

QUILLIFER THE KNIGHT † 95

another group of guests strolled into the room. I recognized Master Ransome, the engineer whose alchemical skill had won him the post of queen's gunfounder, and who now cast giant artillery for the defense of the realm and for his own glory. He was a plump man with glossy mustaches and a self-satisfied air, as if the secrets of the universe had been opened to him alone, and he found them just as he had expected them. On his arm was a somewhat older woman, as gaunt as he was stout, with a narrow, rather beaked nose. The playwright Blackwell arrived shortly afterward and was clearly drunk. Prince Alicio de Ribamar-la-Rose shimmered in his white silk doublet.

Then I saw Roundsilver come out of his cabinet with Lord Hulme, the chancellor of the exchequer, and I assumed they had been discussing the forthcoming meeting of the Estates. Their Majesties wanted money, and it was Lord Hulme's task to rake it out of the peers and the Burgesses.

I excused myself and went to salute Hulme and His Grace. Roundsilver was dressed in a scarlet velvet doublet slashed to reveal his gold satin shirt, for as cousin to Her Majesty he was permitted to wear the royal colors. Hulme wore a black gown and skullcap, with rubies and smaragds shining on his gloved fingers. He was tall and carried himself with dignity, and his hair and beard had more gray than I remembered. The two made a strange pair, the small man shining in his finery, the tall man in darkling dignity.

The chancellor looked at my glittering rings with dry amusement and spoke in his deep voice. "Your privateering enterprises seem to have done well for you, Sir Quillifer."

"I have been lucky, your lordship." I gestured at his own ring-bedecked hands. "And in matters of fashion, I follow the wisest man in the realm."

The chancellor laughed. "There is no point in so flattering me, sir. I can bring you no advancement."

"Fie, my lord!" said I. "Have I asked you for work? I would bring no credit to the exchequer, I assure you."

The chancellor chose to change the subject. "And Ethlebight? Your city does well? The revenues from the port have risen this last year."

I was not surprised that Hulme had the figures firmly lodged in his mind, for he was a very good businessman in addition to being a superior royal servant.

"Very good progress has been made, my lord," I said, "especially since many of the captives have now been redeemed. But I'm sure the revenues are far below what they were before the reivers came."

"True, they have not recovered entirely. But the port is still silting up, is it not? Any recovery will be temporary."

"The port may be threatened, my lord, but the Ostra country is still rich, and produces a plenitude of wool and grain in most years, though this year the storm has ruined the crops, and there may be famine, even if aid is sent promptly."

"Her Majesty hopes that the Estates will vote money for the relief of the people," Hulme said.

"It is my home country," said the duke, "and the storm was a great blow, but the silt is killing it."

I had some idea for Ethlebight's revival, but to disclose it was premature. I thought therefore to encourage premature disclosure of a different matter, and so I looked at the two of them and put on my attentive-courtier face. "What are the prospects for the Estates, my lords?"

They were both practiced politicians, and I sensed nothing from them but amusement. "I hear there will be a fete tomorrow," said the duke, "at the Guild of Goldsmiths."

"Ay," said the chancellor. "I hope the weather stays fair."

"Perhaps we should go fishing on the lake beforehand."

"That will give you the privacy you desire," I said. I bowed in compliment. "You are too practiced, my lords. I give over."

The duke craned his neck and looked at his guests. "We have a goodly crowd, gentlemen," he said. "Perhaps it is time we call on Doctor Heskith to enlighten us."

In each of his palaces the duke had a room called the Odeon, intended for concerts, lectures, exhibitions, and readings. Straight wooden chairs were set out before a small stage, that night with a lectern and a candle. The straight chairs creaked, and when a speaker heard the creaking growing in frequency and volume, he would know he had lost his audience.

Theodore Heskith had the ill luck to provoke a deal of creaking. He was a young physician who displayed a thin, pale face above the fur-trimmed robe of his profession, and who had taken up philosophy and the problem of the Comet Periodical. This apparition had been shown to reappear in the heavens every seventy-seven years, and caused a great vexation for those who concerned themselves with matters transterrene.

For it had been held for millennia that our world was at the center of a universe, and that the moon, planets, and stars were fixed to a concentric series of crystal spheres perpetually revolving about our world in celestial harmony, and turned in some accounts by gods or spirits. This description of the universe had recently received two blows. The first was the invention of the telescope, which revealed that the moon was not a flat object fixed to a crystal sphere but was itself a sphere, and furthermore a sphere with mountains and plains and other features similar to those of the earth. Furthermore, the planets, heretofore visible as mere bright dots wandering about the firmament, were now visible as disks, sometimes full and bright, and at other times a crescent, and this transformation implied that they were spheres as well. And moreover, some planets seemed to have companions of their own, bright spots that drifted about them, as if they were satellites.

All this, the transterrene geometers maintained, could be explained by multiplying the number of crystal spheres, and so tradition was maintained until Magnus Prest of Steggerda, searching through old records, discovered the regularity of the Comet Periodical. For the Comet, in order to traverse its path every seventy-seven years, necessarily had to pierce all those spheres, which by now were numbering in the dozens, like a roundshot flying through a row of wattle cottages. It seemed that the spheres, being perfect and eternal, should have repelled the Comet, or failing that, should have been shattered, and the entire Cosmos broken into pieces.

Heskith attempted to retrieve the situation with a new theory, which stated that the Comet Periodical, and comets in general, were made of a new element called "non-corpuscular matter," which had the special property of being able to pass without hindrance through the material of the spheres. He maintained that the existence of non-corpuscular matter was proven by the existence of the comets' tails, for since no other object in the heavens was observed to have a tail, the tail was clearly a phenomenon peculiar to this special non-corpuscular element.

The questioning that followed the lecture was opened by Mistress Tavistock asking how the comets would affect the casting of horoscopes, and whether non-corpuscular matter, floating through the atmosphere, could harm people on earth. Heskith responded that there could be no interaction between his new element and any other, and that therefore no harm or benefit was possible. His answer to the question of the horoscopes was complex and recondite—which was not unexpected, for a physician would of course cast a patient's horoscope before prescribing any treatment, and would be familiar with astrology's intricacies—but insofar as I could understand it, Heskith did not seem to come to any conclusion.

"For the art of astrology is based on thousands of years of observation," he concluded, "of the stars and planets, of the tides, and of human character. No study seems to have been made of cometary influence."

I was more than a little surprised at this answer, for I had never known a physician to admit to any lack of knowledge, but instead to promptly contrive a diagnosis, whether or not it flew in the face of reality, then prescribe a remedy and pocket his fee. This seemed even more remarkable in a physician who could invent such a concept as non-corpuscular matter.

Ransome the engineer was quick to respond. "What evidence have you that this new element exists?" he said. "It cannot be found on earth. So it seems you observe a phenomenon, and then you claim it is something entirely new in the universe." He preened his mustaches with a plump finger, like a smug cat cleaning his face on the hearth. "Why" he said, "anyone could make such a claim, and about any phenomenon at all. You could observe a waterfall, and claim that the water that falls is a special form of water unlike water that flows through flat country."

Heskith did his best to ignore Ransome's insinuant tone. "Philosophy strives for logic and completeness of theory," he said. "My theory of non-corpuscular matter is in accord with all observations, and preserves the scientific traditions that have been passed to us by the great minds of the past."

Ransome's gaunt companion was eager to lodge her own objections. She spoke very quickly and in a voice that rang in the room like a clarion. "What evidence have you that even the crystal spheres exist?" she demanded.

"Why, Mistress Ransome," said the physician, "surely the planets and the stars must be suspended from *something*. And that something must be transparent, else it would be visible."

"What then suspends your comets?" she demanded. "It cannot be crystal spheres, if your non-corpuscular matter cannot be influenced by ordinary matter."

Heskith seemed not to have considered this, and his desperation became plain. "Perhaps there are spheres of non-corpuscular matter," he said, "which would account for their ability to pass through the spheres of crystal."

"If there are non-corpuscular spheres," demanded Ransome, "then *why do they not have tails?*"

That completed Dr. Heskith's rout, and the duke, in his mercy, rose to announce an end to the lecture. He added that there was a banquet awaiting us on the sideboard in the next room, and reminded us that telescopes were set out on the broad lawn that ran from his palace to the river.

The banquet was a new idea in Duisland and consisted of a meal without meat, at which the guests served themselves. The duke's banquet featured nuts, fruits, bread, cheeses, pastries, and sweets, all served cold, alongside hot wassail with cloves, nutmeg, allspice, ginger, cherries, oranges, sherry, and brandy to keep us warm as we viewed the skies. I thawed myself with the punch while nibbling a bit of cheese, and then I felt a degree of alarm as the princess Floria came marching up to me along with her three ladies.

"Sir Quillifer," said she, "why were you so silent during the lecture? I fully expected you to put forward your own thesis of the universe, and vaunt your superiority over everybody."

"To submit my theory at this time might be premature, Highness," I responded. "I should acquaint myself further with the subject, perhaps read a book or two."

Her darting eyes settled upon me. "That is uncharacteristically modest of you."

"I am very humble, Your Highness." I bowed and "cast my eyes down," as the saying is. "I am a mere naufrageous knight. My humility," I expanded, "is without doubt the greatest in the land."

She nodded. "I observe that it is."

I straightened and glanced over the crowd. "Is Mistress Ransome married to Ransome the gunfounder?" I asked. "I had not heard that he had wed." And indeed they seemed an unlikely couple, for I thought Ransome was too self-regarding to marry anyone who did not more closely resemble a bauble or an ornament.

"That is Edith Ransome," Floria said, "Master Ransome's sister."

"Ah. There is little family resemblance."

"Other than that they both enjoy an argument. I will introduce you." The princess suddenly cocked her head, like a bird, and fixed me with one eye. "Naufrageous?" she said.

"It's a new word. I made it up. It comes from—"

"Naufrage, in maritime law. I know. But you have been ship-wrecked? Or is your new word but a metaphor for a life gone tragically on the rocks?"

"I lost *Royal Stilwell* in the great storm in July," I said. "Though we saved all the crew, and most of the cargo." I showed her my hand, with its rings and crooked finger. "Including my box of shiny boulders."

"I am heartily sorry that the great ship named for my father has been lost," said the princess. "But was not *Royal Stilwell* a ship owned by the crown before it somehow came into your hands?"

"It was acquired legally," I pointed out.

"All great thefts are legal," the princess observed. "I should enjoy your tale of the shipwreck, as well as hear you boast of how you came by the ship in the first place, but at another time. For here is Mistress Ransome."

The gaunt woman joined us, wrapping herself expertly in shawls and pinning them in place. "Horagalles is well above the horizon," she said. "We should have a good view." Her voice was more pleasant when she was not shouting at hapless prey. I observed that she wore the badge of the double impatiens, and therefore was one of Floria's ladies.

Mistress Ransome came in company with her brother, who looked very sleek with his finely groomed head above the immaculate lace of his collar. "Quillifer!" he said. "I haven't seen you in ages!"

"You look well fed," said I. "I believe you've just devoured a theory of the empyrean."

Ransome was amused, but I was answered by his sister. "People say the most absurd things about the heavens," she said, "and as in truth we know so little, they feel they cannot be contradicted." She gave a thin-lipped smile. "But I *will* contradict them. If I cannot yet prove my own theory, I can at least reveal their ignorance."

"That is fine practice," I said. "In theory."

Floria gave me another of her looks. "Sir Quillifer says he may read a book or two, and thus arrive at a thesis of his own."

Mistress Ransome snorted. "The world hardly needs another thesis!" she said. "What we need is knowledge!"

"May the Pilgrim illumine you," said I politely.

Mistress Ransome snorted again, which I understood to be a comment on the likelihood of the Pilgrim to illuminate anyone at all. "And *your* thesis?" she asked.

"I have none," said I, "as Her Highness surely knows. But I spoke to Coronel Lipton this morning, of the Royal Regiment of Artillery, and he offered the observation that the planets travel through the skies like roundshot fired from great bombards, and that comets trail fire in an arc like bursting shot."

Mistress Ransome suddenly fixed me with her dark, intent eyes. "Your coronel," she said, "is not such a fool."

"My dear," said her brother. "Horagalles waiteth not."

Ransome and his sister bowed to the princess, and then made their way to where the telescopes waited. I fetched my good wool boat cloak and joined them.

There were half a dozen telescopes on the lawn, the largest five yards long with its barrel supported by a wooden framework, with footmen to help manhandle it about. Though the air seemed heavy with woodsmoke, the sky was clear above us, with the lake a dark, still plain, and on the far shore the palace twinkled like a constellation. Agoraeus, the sun's messenger, had set long since, but Horagalles and Ourania were bright in the sky, and Mavors was far in the west, near to setting. Accordingly, we viewed Mavors first, a dusky red disk shimmering on the edge of the horizon. I marveled at how different it looked from one instrument to the next, sometimes dark, sometimes wrapped in mystery, sometimes glowing like embers on the hearth. The telescopes, like witnesses at a trial, each told a different tale.

Then the telescopes were shifted to Horagalles and Ourania. Horagalles the King was nearly full and in some of the telescopes was a pale blaze, but in others seemed swirling shades of cream. The bright stars that were his companions were plain to see, bustling about their chief like courtiers around a monarch.

Ourania was a bright, full disk, almost too brilliant to view properly. She had no satellites visible, but swam alone in the heavens like a dazzling swan upon the water. Her outline was somehow less distinct than that of Horagalles, as if she were made of swirling white smoke.

Afterward the instruments were pointed at the stars, and so we viewed the Boar, the Ephebe, the Brilliant Triangle, the Horologist, the She-Goat, and other autumn stars and constellations. Never had I seen the stars so brilliant, or in their colors so distinct from one another: white, red, dusky, brilliant blue white. While I watched the sky, many of the guests drifted homeward, or went indoors where it was warm, but other than a journey or two to refill my cup with hot punch, I remained out of doors, perfectly happy with the revelations that I found in the heavens.

The taste of citrus and ginger was pleasant on my tongue, and the warmth was welcome in my belly. I found myself with a group of guests around one of the telescopes, and in the dim starlight I recognized Prince Alicio by his white leather jerkin and his Lorettan accent. "It is all interesting in its way," he was saying, "but I wonder that we spend so much time gazing at the unknowable sky and so little in perfecting ourselves."

"I think Mistress Ransome would disagree with you about the sky being unknowable." The voice came from near my right elbow, and in my surprise I realized the speaker was Princess Floria.

"It is the Pilgrim's doctrine," said the prince, "that the only thing we can know for certain is that we exist—or, to be more precise, that our *minds* exist, for our knowledge of ourselves *in extensio*—in our bodies, and our bodies in the world—we know only because our minds perceive them. Existence, for the Compassionate Pilgrim, was a mental phenomenon. And so, as we know only our own minds, it is to our minds that we must direct improvement."

"Yet how many people can be said to know their own minds?" Floria asked.

"Very few," the prince conceded. "Yet the Pilgrim's path is the most conducive to understanding."

Even in the darkness, I felt Floria's keen gaze settling on me. "And you, Sir Quillifer? Do you know your own mind?"

"Some corners better than others," I said. "At the very least I endeavor not to tell myself lies."

She was amused. "Ha! You reserve the right to lie to others!"

"When people so ardently desire a thing," I said, "why should I not give it to them?"

"*Mundus vult decipi,*" said Alicio. "It was Eidrich the Pilgrim who said that the world desires deception rather than truth. But he said also that the consequences of deception strike both the deceived and the deceiver, and that it was better to be neither."

"It seems to me that we are removing deception tonight," said I. "For we have long deceived ourselves about the heavens, and now we see them better revealed, and so many of those stories are now uncloaked, and shown to be phantoms."

"I am right glad to hear you say so," said Mistress Ransome, who had come up through the darkness. "If everyone could see in the sky what we see tonight, there would be much less nonsense in the world."

"We see stars and planets," said Prince Alicio. "But what *are* stars and planets? Of this we know nothing."

"Yet we know more than we did," said Mistress Ransome. "We know they are not objects, flat but somehow perfect, pasted for some inexplicable reason on crystal spheres. We know they are globes, like our earth, and we know also they are not perfect, for some, particularly the moon, show features, and so we know they are not uniform."

"You disparage the crystal spheres," said Prince Alicio. "But how do you imagine the stars and planets are suspended?"

"I do not think they are suspended at all," said Mistress Ransome. In the starlight I saw her pale, gaunt face turn to me. "I think your cannoneer friend was correct that heavenly bodies are impelled to move in arcs by some force. But I know not what that force might be."

"No celestial bombards?" I asked.

I sensed a smile. "Would it were that simple."

"From the perspective of a sailor," said I, "I wish to know more about the stars and planets, so that I can more accurately determine my longitude. Sometimes in bad weather we cannot take the noon sight on the sun, but must hope the clouds open up at night, to enable us to take a sight on a star. But the instruments we use to read the heavens—astrolabes, alidades, and the cross-staff—are inadequate, and such star tables as we find are filled with errors. Hundreds of mariners die every year because they cannot find their way."

"That is one of my projects," said Mistress Ransome. "With Her Highness's help, I will construct a quadrant that will measure the height of the stars with great precision, and produce correct star tables that will succor those mariners of yours."

I turned to Floria in surprise. "Your Highness concerns yourself with the height of stars?"

"Why should I not?" She waved a hand. "It is a thing I can do. I am building Mistress Ransome's quadrant at my home of Kellhurst."

"And there I shall reside, and make my tables." Mistress Ransome seemed very pleased by the prospect.

It would be a mural quadrant, I was told, mounted on a wall that was aligned with the meridian, and which could sight on each star as it journeyed about the earth. It would be the largest quadrant in the kingdom, and would be housed in a building that Princess Floria was constructing on her palace grounds.

"Most of my ladies-in-waiting wait, but only for husbands," Floria said. "I am pleased to help one of them to achieve a more original ambition."

"I will be thankful for the tables when they come," I said, "and I will see that each of my ships has a copy."

You were amused at my discourse on lies. Ay, I deceive as other folk deceive, to please myself or to please others, or to evade too long an explanation when such an explanation would be tedious.

You, too, employ deception. You are not so well placed that you can afford to speak the truth to those about you.

But our lies share one other quality, which is that we both know a lie when we speak it. Other people babble falsehoods without thinking, because these are the sort of lies that people believe without thinking about them, where a moment's reflection would reveal their falsity.

When you and I choose to tell a lie, we do so knowingly, and we know also that a lie can be a weapon, sharper than a razor. And thus, with our falsehoods, we are armed against those who oppose us.

We watched the stars till the middle of the night, and then went indoors to browse the duke's banquet and to warm ourselves before going to our beds. Mistress Ransome, her brother, and the footmen busied themselves by shifting the telescopes and other apparatus to a room where they could be safely stored till they could be removed, perhaps to Kellhurst. I watched as Floria thanked the duke and duchess for their hospitality, and as her ladies, the gold-skinned Countess Marcella and the disdainful Elisa d'Altrey, prepared for their departure. And then I remembered the name d'Altrey, and began to wonder.

For the Marquess of Melcaster had been surnamed d'Altrey. He was one of Clayborne's supporters, and had served in his Privy Council and fought on the field of Exton, where he was captured. He was among those proscribed, and after the war I had probably viewed his head set on a pike before the Hall of Justice.

I certainly remember looting his house and carrying off a silver-gilt nef big enough to hold in my two arms, which I had loaded with precious objects of silver, gold, and ivory.

I wondered if the black-haired Mistress d'Altrey was the daughter or granddaughter of the proscribed peer. She had not been introduced as a member of the nobility, as Lady Elisa, but then I supposed Melcaster had suffered attainder and lost his titles and land. If she had once been a Lady Elisa, she was now a commoner, no better than me.

No wonder she was disdainful. Disdain was probably all that supported the ramshackle remains of her pride.

But one of Floria's ladies had gone astray. Marcella and Mistress d'Altrey were sent in search of Chenée Tavistock, who had not been seen in some time, and I found myself in the hall with the princess.

"It is very good of you, Highness," I said, "to support Mistress Ransome in her project."

The hazel eyes looked into mine. "There are so few educated women," said she, "and of these so few wish to do anything with their education." Her face bore a self-amused smile. "Perhaps because I am permitted no ambition, I therefore admire the ambition of Mistress Ransome—and if I can be of service to her, perhaps other women will seek to emulate her, and I will have more learnèd companions at dinner."

"I wish you the very best of learnèd companions, Your Highness."

"And you, Sir Quillifer?" she asked. "Why have you returned to court? You did not receive such a warm welcome last time."

I made a gracious wave of my hand. "Those were misunderstandings, Highness. I hope I have grown in wisdom, and will be able to avoid such misunderstandings in the future."

She offered a little laugh and pointed at me her marabou-feather fan. "Do you hope to save my sister from another plot?"

"It is my understanding," said I, "she now has another gentleman for that duty."

A cloud passed across her face, and she gave a curt nod. "She does indeed."

I am permitted no ambition, she had said. For she was the queen's heir, at least until Berlauda and Priscus succeeded in producing a child, and that meant that Floria's only task was to wait, either for the child or for a crown. And if the queen's child made her redundant, then a mind attuned to danger and conspiracy might see her ambition as a threat to the child and to the safety of the realm.

Coronel Lipton maintained that Lord Edevane placed spies in the households of prominent men. Surely Floria was of greater interest to the throne than any number of the nobility, and I began to wonder who in Floria's household had turned spy. Possibly one, or indeed all, of the three ladies who now came bustling back from the parlor. Mistress Tavistock, spy or not, had been found asleep on a sofa.

"And that actor Blackwell is unconscious in front of the hearth," said Elisa d'Altrey, and for the first time I heard her cold disdain distilled into words. "He is ataunt, and reeks of brandy."

"I suppose I shall have to take him home," I said, and hoped I had not just volunteered to share my carriage with the poet's puke.

I bade good night to the princess and her ladies, and then sought out the duke and duchess to offer them my thanks. Her Grace had gone to bed, but her indulgent husband was in his study, conversing with Prince Alicio. I thanked His Grace for the pleasures of the evening, and then said I would take Blackwell home. "Apparently whatever he was drinking has submerged him," I said.

"His play failed," said the duke.

"Well," said I, "that is reason enough to be submerged."

I went to the parlor and prodded the poet awake, then supported his arm as we went outside. The linkboys had all gone home, and the carriage came up slowly in the dark, hooves ringing hollow on the deserted road. The footman and I boosted Blackwell's lean form into his seat, and I climbed in opposite him. The playwright was the picture of misery, his head hanging partway out of the window, half-closed eyes gazing in bleak torpor at the fine homes as we drove on.

"The next play will be better," I said, and Blackwell gave a half-laugh.

"Not if the new master of the revels has his way," he said. He cleared his throat with a great bearlike rumble and spat out the window. "For Queen Berlauda has appointed a prim little miss in the form of a half-monk named Shingle, who wishes there to be nothing in a play that may offend the royal sensibility." He pointed a wavering hand at nothing in particular. "I had, you know, a little success with *The Red Horse* a few years ago, about the queen's ancestor Emelin. You might think the queen would enjoy more plays praising her antecedents, but most of our celebrated kings won their laurels fighting Loretto, and now the queen has married Loretto, and it is impolite to hear of any such strife between the kingdoms in the past. Then there were the kings who fought in civil wars, but Master Shingle finds these civil wars uncivil, for no suggestion may be made that ever there was discord in the realm. Of the foolish or feeble kings who started the wars in the first place—well, we pass them in silence. And even the ancient world—even if I paint up the actors as Aekoi and have them enact a scene out of classical poetry, there may be no uncivil strife." He snarled. "Gods, I am in too sober a state to discuss Master Shingle. Have you a flask with you?"

"Nay."

"Let us go to Gropecoun Street and drink until we fall asleep in some harlot's arms."

"Now that you mention it," I said, "there is, I suppose, comedy."

Blackwell gave a bitter laugh. "Ay, there is, but Master Shingle permits no intemperate behavior. Lovers may not defy their parents and run away together, for it sets an unwholesome example for the young folk. Old husbands may not lust after young ladies, duchesses may not long for commoners, rogues and inebriates may not sully the scene with their indecorous braying."

"What is left?" I asked, in perfect puzzlement.

He waved a listless hand. "I write a masque now and again, in which a character called Rectitude evades the schemes of a fellow called Vice, and the verse is pretty, but very dull. But I fear the only story that Shingle would find really congenial would be one in which a pair of young people follow their parents' advice and marry each other, and they then produce nine children and raise them to follow the Pilgrim's footsteps." He spat again. "See if an audience will sit still for *that*."

"That would depend," said I, "on how much of the interval you show, in regard to how the nine children were kindled."

He barked a laugh. "Ay, I would like to write such a thing, if only to watch Shingle change color when he reads it." He looked at me again from out of a cloud of brandy fumes. "Have you a flask? I feel the dread hand of sobriety clutching at my vitals."

"I have no flask, but I have a bed, and I'm going to it." The carriage wheels crunched over gravel as we pulled into the drive before Rackheath House, and I swung myself out without waiting for the footman to open the door. "Take Master Blackwell where he wants," I told the coachman.

"Take me to *hell*!" cried the playwright.

"Take him *home*," I said firmly. "He lodges at the Cat and Custard Pot." And I sent the carriage on its way.

I looked up at the stars as the carriage drew away and felt a touch of my earlier wonder. They glittered above me in their inverted black bowl, and I wondered if they would be less wonderful once Mistress Ransome had numbered and catalogued them.

They would be no less beautiful, I thought, for that which is useful has its own beauty, and Mistress Ransome would make the stars useful to mariners.

CHAPTER NINE

I wore Lady Westley's sunburst pendant a few days later, at the season's first regatta on the lake, held at midmorning before the afternoon winds rose, and so that the court could celebrate afterward with a dinner. The day was sunny, and the morning chill faded quickly as we rowed to the starting line. Even on the lake we could smell our dinner cooking in the palace kitchens. The galleys would travel under oars alone, on a roughly triangular track across the lake. We would cross behind two low islands on the far side, then return to the starting line. Bright red buoys had been laid out around the islands to mark the intended course, and another pair of buoys had been laid out to mark the start and finish.

There were nearly a score of racing galleys in the water, all sponsored by the nobility or the great guilds of the town. To keep out the meiny, there was a bond of fifty crowns for each vessel, in return for which we were given a printed copy of the rules for the race. I paid very close attention to the rules, studied carefully, and thought I had found something to my advantage, but most of the rules were immaterial today, for they dealt with the management of sails, and today we would be under oars alone.

Most of the galleys were commanded by the owners of the boats, but some had professional captains. There was a good deal of wagering going on, and I had made my own bets with some of my rivals.

Their Majesties were also on the water, on their barge, which was ornamented with gilded reliefs of the tritons of Fornland, while its hull was painted in the royal colors of scarlet and gold. Their thrones were set beneath a silken canopy, and the barge's gilding was blinding in the sun.

I looked at Their Majesties through my glass, and I found Queen Berlauda much as I remembered her: blond and handsome, tall and adorned in satin, velvet, and jewels. From behind an ostrich-feather fan she wore a bland air of satisfaction that suggested the world matched her expectations exactly. Some of her ladies of honor stood about her, glittering rather less than the queen, but still a formidable array in their composed and dignified silence.

One man stood near them, and this I somehow understood to be Lord Edevane, Her Majesty's principal private secretary and supposed spymaster. The man who had encompassed the ruin of the Marquess of Scutterfield was about thirty, of ordinary height, and wore his hair and dark beard long. He dressed in purple velvet that set off his gold chain of office, and wore thick gold-rimmed spectacles that gave his eyes a blank, dead quality, like a pike that had been caught and lain too long in the sun.

His dead eyes were directed toward the courtiers around our king, and he wore an expression of polite attention. I do not imagine he failed to hear anything he cared to.

Her Majesty's husband, Priscus, to whom she had awarded the style, honors, and power of king regnant, was tall and swarthy, with a large beaky nose like a blade, and a beard so short that it might have been taken for a week's failure to shave. He wore a tall conical hat with badges in the red and gold of Duisland, and a white satin doublet absolutely covered in pearls, so closely sewn onto the garment that the doublet seemed solid, glowing softly like an opalescent breast-plate, and like a breastplate seemed to be propping him up on his throne.

Priscus was more lively than his bride and spoke to his circle of gentlemen, a group that seemed equally from Duisland and from Loretto. Standing a little apart, frowning and white-haired, was Lord Thistlegorm, the attorney general, who was also the judge of the race. Dressed in the white silk doublet, hose, and trunks that marked him as a Retriever, he watched as the galleys jostled for their place at the start. At the sight of the attorney general, I raised a hand to my breast, for I had tucked a copy of the printed rules into my doublet, and I wanted to be certain I could quote from them at need. I had trained as a lawyer, though the sad death of my master prevented my ever being certified to practice at the Bar, and against the attorney general I knew that I would need all my lawyer's skill.

I saw Thistlegorm glance toward the quay, and I followed his glance to find my friend Coronel Lipton and a group of his cannon-eers, all shining in their uniforms and clustered about the small field gun that would signal the start and completion of the race.

I was obliged to put down my glass and maneuver *Dunnock* to avoid collision, and I looked at a nearby galley and locked eyes with the Count of Wenlock. He looked at me with a fierce expression on his pale face as a gust of wind tore at his grizzled hair.

He hated me for reasons that were obscure, at least to me. I had been a friend to his son Lord Utterback, who had commanded at Exton Scales and had fallen in the battle, and Wenlock blamed me for the fact that Her Majesty had not advanced the count in rank after the battle, or given him grants of land. I had won a knighthood and a manor, and in Wenlock's way of thinking, I had stolen these rewards from him and sullied his dead son's glory. Yet it had not been Wenlock who had been the hero of the battle, but his son Utterback, and I did not understand why Wenlock expected to be rewarded for his son's success.

Because Utterback had been Wenlock's heir, and his wife was past the age of childbearing, he had been forced to divorce his wife and find a younger bride in order to insure his title's succession. There was now a two-year-old Lord Utterback toddling about his house, and Wenlock had added to his collection of gray hairs. I suppose he had reasons for his choler, but I still don't know why his ire settled on me.

Wenlock snarled when he saw me, and though I felt a thrill of apprehension, I grinned at him. I had faced battle, storms, and shipwreck, and I had no reason to fear a disgruntled nobleman.

Or so I told myself.

I turned back to Thistlegorm, and I saw him raise a hand with a white flag, and I told my lads to cock their oars and be ready to pull. I tucked the tiller securely under my arm. The flag fell, the gun went off with a bang, and the oars came down to turn the water white. The galley surged forward, and I felt a breeze on my face and a fine, cool spray.

Off we sprinted, and I kept *Dunnock* in the middle of the pack until we approached the first island, when I steered off to larboard— for I was aiming for the tail of the island, and the others were heading for the first buoy that was meant to mark the course. I was thus able to cut inside them, and save my crew a deal of rowing.

Because I stayed inside the buoys instead of outside, my course was at least a quarter league shorter, and though my men were rowing easily, I was ahead by a great margin as I swung around the second island and headed for the finish. The others were clustered behind, rowing furiously as they battled one another for the lead—for they paid no attention to me, being confident that I had fouled out of the competition for not staying on the marked course.

As my lead was considerable, I kept my oarsmen at a moderate pace and only ordered them to sprint when the leaders of the pack threatened to overtake me. I crossed the finish line five or six boat-lengths ahead and immediately swung *Dunnock* round to the royal barge in order to deliver the protest that I already knew I would have to make.

Coronel Lipton's gun signaled the end of the contest when the first of the pack crossed the line—*Ostra*, owned by His Grace the Duke of Roundsilver and captained by the duke in person. Second place went to the Count of Wenlock, which meant that captains from Ethlebight had taken the topmost three places, a great compliment to my native city.

I let *Dunnock* hover off the royal barge's quarter as I waited for the song of trumpets and a herald to announce that His Grace had won the race. After the applause died down, I had my crew give a single stroke to their oars and drifted to where Thistlegorm stood on the prow of the barge, his white suit shining like silver. I donned my respectful-apprentice face. "My lord!" I said. "Surely you err! I won the race plain as the sun in the sky!"

He frowned down at me as the scent of gunpowder drifted on the breeze. "Sir, you fouled out of the race," said he.

"I protest!" I said. "For I committed no foul!"

He spoke as if to a simpleminded child. "You strayed from the course," he said. "You failed to stay outside the buoys."

"The buoys are nugatory," said I. I reached into my doublet and withdrew my copy of the printed rules. "The rule book does not mention buoys at all, my lord. It says only that we must pass behind the island."

"Not mention buoys?" The attorney general's face reddened. "Why in the blessed Pilgrim's name did you think the buoys were there at all?"

I lofted the rules again. "My lord, the rules do not oblige me to think about the buoys in any way at all."

His brows came together. "What is your name, sir?"

"I am Sir Quillifer the Younger of Ethlebight," I said. I donned my innocent-choirboy face and offered the rule book. "If your lordship would consult your copy of the rules . . . ? Or you may borrow mine, if you like."

I saw Her Majesty's fine blue eyes glance at me sharply when she heard my name, and I wondered if this adventure would see me banned from court again. Lord Thistlegorm, on the other hand, clearly knew my name, probably from that business of the would-be assassin Burgoyne. He had one of his secretaries bring him a copy of the rules.

"My lord," said I, "if you would view part the third, 'Concerning the Course,' which I believe you may find on page seven?"

I adopted a patient air while I waited and concerned myself with keeping *Dunnock* from drifting too far from the royal barge. I saw His Majesty conferring with his gentlemen, and the flash of white teeth in his dark face as he laughed, a kind of *caw-caw-caw* like a crow. While I had probably not pleased the queen, at least I had provided the king with amusement.

From the dead-fish eyes of the man I assumed to be Lord Edevane I received an interested look, and I felt a cold finger touch my neck. I did not rejoice in having the man's full attention, not least because he seemed to be mentally dissecting me on the spot.

Lord Thistlegorm read Part the Third, and then read it again. With great impatience he flipped through the rest of the rule book, found nothing that pleased him, and rolled the rules into a tube, which he clamped in his fist. He signaled the trumpeter to play another sennet and reached for a silver-chased speaking trumpet.

"The results of the previous race are ruled invalid!" he said. "The race will be repeated as soon as the competitors can be brought to the start." He lowered the trumpet, then raised it again. "No wagers may be settled! Wagers may be settled only after the race is run again!" There were cheers at this, for apparently few people had wagered on my success. Then, his mouth twisted in frustration, Lord Thistlegorm called out again. "All boats must stay outside the buoys! *All* boats!" he added, with an eye on me.

I bowed to him. "Your lordship's ruling displays surpassing wisdom," I said, "and fully justifies the trust Their Majesties have placed in their attorney general."

Then I took off my cap, bowed to Their Majesties on their thrones, and maneuvered my galley to the starting line, nearing again the Count of Wenlock, who sneered at me. "Stealing another victory, Quillifer?" he asked.

I ventured a laugh. "Victories are the result of good planning, my lord!"

In the jostling at the start, I managed to claim for myself the place farthest to the larboard, giving myself the best chance to remain inside the others as we rounded the course.

In the end this was not necessary, for I had kept my crew at an easy pace for most of the preceding race, while the others had had their oarsmen flailing the water in a perfect frenzy for the entire length of the course. My own men were much fresher than the exhausted crews of the other galleys, and *Dunnock* pulled ahead easily from the start and kept the lead for the entire race. We won by a greater margin than we had the first time and were saluted by Coronel Lipton's gun as we crossed the finish. We all disembarked at the quay, and His Majesty presented me the victor's pennant as I knelt before him.

"I offer this to Sir Keely-Fay, the only captain who has read the rule book." He smiled, his words hidden amid a thick Lorettan accent, and then cawed thrice at his own wit, sounding more like a crow than a king.

The flag, which bore the triton of Fornland and the hippogriff of Bonille, I brought to *Dunnock* and placed on the staff where I normally flew my own flag. I would possess the flag only until the next race, when it would be awarded to the winner, but in the meantime I could flaunt it on the water.

Though many would find my day's victory, and the means of it, comical, I supposed an equal number would find it insufferable.

My own ambitions were to be neither comical nor insufferable, but *known*.

I could loiter about the court like every other provincial knight, hoping to be noticed and employed in some office or other; or I could trot at the heels of some grand noble in hopes of becoming a part of his affinity; or I could take some action that would put me before the eyes of the court, and this had I done.

I would be dismissed as a jumped-up coxcombical rudesby, but those inclined to that opinion would be certain to dismiss me anyway. To those of a more open cast of mind, I hoped to be seen as someone possessing gifts that might be useful.

And even those who disliked me, I thought might soon be wearing my gemstones.

I sent my boat's crew to my house for their dinner and told them to come back late in the afternoon. I collected my winnings from the other captains and saluted His Grace the duke.

"I am sorry to have deprived you of a victory," I said.

He cocked an eye at me. "I think you are not so sorry as all that."

"In faith, you think correctly."

He smiled. "The next race, I think, will not be so easy for you."

I bowed. "I know you will make certain of that, Your Grace."

I strolled down the quay to Coronel Lipton, standing with his gun crew, and offered him a salute. "I hope you put money on my galley," I said.

He grinned at me with his yellow teeth. "I have won a little white money, sure."

"I hope you will use it to drink my health."

"Ay, as soon as the Carters and Haulers can be bothered to carry the leather gun away."

I looked in surprise at the small field piece. The barrel, wrapped in brown suede, was about four feet long, and the carriage light. "Do you mean to say the gun barrel is actually leather?"

"Come, youngster, I will show thee, so." He took me before the barrel. "A thin barrel of brass, with leather wrapped around it, and secured with iron hoops. It will fire a six-pound shot, like a saker."

"And will it do so without bursting?"

Lipton made an equivocal gesture with one hand. "They have all burst, so far. I have yet to find the right prescription for the metal. Yet they will fire half a dozen or more shots before they fail."

"And you brought a bursting gun to Their Majesty's regatta?"

He laughed. "There was no danger, sure, for there was no ball in the gun, just a ropen wad."

"And the purpose of this leather bursting gun, Coronel?"

"It weighs but little, youngster. If the ground is too uncertain to pull the gun in the ordinary way, one man may carry the barrel in his arms, and another the carriage upon his back. And if the ground be firm and not too uneven, the crew may run along with it, and pull it on a rope. You can hardly do that with a demiculverin that weighs thirty-four hundredweight."

I remembered Lipton's guns in the fight at Exton Scales, stranded where the Carters and Haulers left them, to be overrun if the fight went against us. "This could be a formidable weapon," I said, "if perfected. For you could push these guns ahead of the foot, smash up the formations of pikes, and then send in our own pikemen to finish the enemy."

"That is my hope. But I have little support from my superiors. We are at peace, and they care only for pomp and show." He plucked at his splendid blue doublet and the sash that marked his officer's rank. "For *this*. And there is no knight marshal, and no constable, to make of the army anything but ornaments to the throne."

"The Marquess of Exton is no longer knight marshal?"

"He is dead, Pilgrim rest him."

I was surprised by the sadness I felt, for Sir Erskine had never liked me, and for my own part I had not been impressed by the shambling, superstitious old man, or his equally shambling campaign. "I am sorry, but not surprised," I said, "for he was old and ill."

"He was lucky," said Lipton. "That is all that matters, in a commander."

I looked down at the gun. "Does Ransome support your endeavors?"

"The queen's gunfounder has greater projects in mind. He cannot demonstrate his art on little weapons, and so casts guns greater and greater. Cannon that must be emplaced for an enemy to come to them, for they are too heavy ever to move to a battlefield."

"Who pays for your experiments, then?"

"I have some support from the Guild of Cannoneers, sure. But for the most part I pay myself—you will recall," said he, looking at me, "that we made some little fortune, in the late war."

I remembered him staggering beneath the weight of a great sack of loot, and smiled.

"Who casts the gun? Does he know metals? For I need a deviser for a project of my own."

"My engineer is a young fellow from Dun Foss called Mountmirail," he said. "He will make his mark, I'm sure—for he knoweth his metals and his alchemical prescriptions, and he knoweth his reduit and his glacis and his bastion and his contravallation, along with the names of the Thousand Gods of the Aekoi, and how many leagues a salmon may swim in a day. He maketh little toys that roll and tumble about his study, and perhaps one day he will put Howel on stilts and walk it about the countryside."

"I should meet this prodigy," I said, "though I care not for any report on salmon."

"He was called away to Deubec, to rescue a tower that was leaning over the lord lieutenant's quarters and threatening to destroy it. But he is now the savior of that tower, and the lord lieutenant also, and will be back within the week."

"Bring him to my house when he arrives," said I, "and in the meantime I would like to see this leather gun fire."

"You will see it explode, an you are unlucky."

At that point the trumpets blew again, along with a thunder of kettledrums. Lipton looked westward, toward the water gardens. "We are summoned to the feast," he said. "I to drink my fill, and you to have your fill of glory."

It being a fine autumn day, we dined out of doors, on an island in the water gardens, our tables surrounded by hibiscus, dahlias, camellias, and other flowers of autumn. Water-lilies stood like sentinels in the aqueous ways between the islets, and smiling statues of goddesses and nymphs viewed our revels with serene faces. Their Majesties sat on thrones at the high table, beneath a canopy in the royal gold and red. Behind them was the scaffolding of the great hall they were adding to the palace, and the cranes that were lifting the great golden blocks into place.

We were set out in strict order of precedence, so I was very far from Their Majesties, and found myself with a set of knights and the younger sons of the nobility, many from Loretto. I thought it would be some time before I had my "fill of glory," as Lipton had put it, and I would have told him so, but he was seated below me, in fact on the other side of a bridge. As a cannoneer, he ranked below the miscellaneous gentlemen who served the court as secretaries, and well below the officers of the Queen's Own Horse, who dined near Their Majesties.

There were ten or twelve removes, beginning with a thick frumenty pottage with almonds, sugar, saffron, and currants. This was followed by pike, caught in the lake, that had been cooked in a broth of white wine and horseradish, after which we had roast lobster swimming in sweet butter. There was roast pig stuffed with fig pudding and studded with cloves, venison backstrap wrapped in bacon, collared beef cooked in claret, ginger, mace, cloves, and nutmegs.

As the beef was brought forward, I caught a sweet whiff of rot behind the odor of spice, and I thought the condiments were perhaps intended to conceal a flank of beef that was far past its prime. I declined my share, but my companions were not so overparticular, and they ate with a will. Whether they became sick after, I know not.

There followed veal stuffed with mince, again flavored with many spices, and I wondered if I had brought any of the spices to Duisland in my *Royal Stilwell*.

Next came the fowl, for there had been a hunt a few days earlier and several thousand birds sacrificed for our pleasure. Bustards served with sugared mustard, pigeons in butter and rose water, and blackbirds baked in a pie, gravy bubbling out of slits in the crust. The last and greatest of the fowl were the swans, who were served roasted and clad in their feathers. The bird carried to the royal table wore a gold collar studded with emeralds.

I had seen swans served this way at Berlauda's coronation and wondered how it was done. Now I discovered that each roast bird wore the tanned skin of a swan with the feathers preserved. The skin was laid like a cape over the roast bird, with some internal stiffening so that the head was curved gracefully on its long neck.

The most impressive skins were reserved for the royal table, and the best of what remained for the nobility, with the rest spread out down the lines of tables, again in strict order of precedence. The cape that covered my table's swan was old, much used, and decrepit, with more than half of its snowy coat gone.

The bird, however, tasted perfectly fine.

Afterward came the sweet finale to the meal, a sugary blood pudding, a quaking pudding served on a plate of sugar, a stepony drizzled with rose water, and almond cakes cooked with musk and ambergris. These did not entirely please me, for so many of the previous removes had been sweetened that the pudding seemed superfluous.

Throughout the meal there was music, beginning with the trumpets, sackbut, and drums of Her Majesty's demilances. Their martial music was not suited to digestion, and so they were replaced by Mistress Concini's choir of nuns singing their devotions, then by a boys' choir that sang morally improving songs of the type approved by Berlauda, and lastly by strolling musicians wandering up and down the lines of tables. One of these, a black-eyed young man with a scant beard, a turned-up nose, and hose stitched in gaudy yellow and black checks, came to my table, bowed, and began.

> *Quillifer, Quillifer, active as miniver*
> *Waited on water for sound of the gun*
> *Quillifer, Quillifer, aqua-philosopher*
> *Heard the big blast, and the boat it did run*
>
> *The oars struck the water and turned it to white*
> *In the midst of the mellay sailed the tall knight*
> *The pace of the race was a heartening sight*
>
> *All of the galleys rowed for the first turn*
> *But one boat alone that custom did spurn*
> *For jewels and rules were his tools of concern*
>
> Refrain:
> *Quillifer, Quillifer, never did malinger*
> *As the boat sped on for the far isle*
> *Quillifer, Quillifer, trader of mace and myrrh*
> *Had conned the rule book and learned to beguile*
>
> *First came the knight across the line*
> *His galley bold had held the bowline*
> *His ploy of the buoy was all his design*

"Hold!" cried the judge. "For you have fouled out!"
But the knight's reply brought the ruling in doubt
He footnoted and quoted his foes to a rout

Rather than sing the refrain, the minstrel then played it on his guitar, with fancies and flourishes that excited my admiration, and with clever triplets that stood in for the syllables of my name. When he was done, he returned to his song.

Tempers were foul as all bets were suspended
At the start of the race the boats were re-blended
"On!" was the call, and the brawl was contended

The knight took the lead, and the buoys were passed
Sure-eyed was the hero, and his crew was handfast
The pack was outrun, and the gun it did blast

Refrain:
Quillifer, Quillifer, unwilling to defer
The pennant of victory placed into his hands
Quillifer, Quillifer, the racecourse geographer
The best in the test, and the best in the land

I laughed and reached in my purse for a pair of crowns, which I pushed across the table. "I believe I would like to hear that song again."

Again he sang it, and I and some of my companions sang along with the refrain. I pushed another pair of crowns his way.

" 'Best in the land,' " I said. "And some call *me* a flatterer."

He placed a hand over his heart. "Yet you have given me a generous vail," he said. "How is that not the best?"

"Very well," said I. "I must therefore be the best. And you must be congratulated for finding so many rhymes for Quillifer."

"Some I did not employ," he said. " 'Scrofular,' for example."

I laughed. "That was wise—though while we are on the subject, I am not entirely satisfied with 'miniver.' I am not certain I enjoy the comparison with a weasel."

"With an *ermine*, sir. A royal animal, for none but the Emelins and the peers may wear ermine on their cloaks."

"True." I considered him. "What rhymes with your name, good-man?"

"There are too many. Begot, besought, bowknot."

"Your name, then, is Naught?"

"Knott, sir. With a *K*. Rufino Knott, sir, at your service."

"Well, Goodman Knott, I hope you will sing that song before Their Majesties."

Knott raised an eyebrow. "I think I have not been paid enough to croon such an impertinence before the high table."

"Then sing it for everyone else." I pushed another coin across the table, and Knott snatched it up, bowed, and continued up the line of tables.

"Ay, this Duisland is a different sort of country," said Dom Nemorino d'Ormyl, one of the Lorettan knights. "For Dom Keely-Fay, if you had flouted the rules of the race in Loretto, you would even now be off to prison on a warrant royal. And that little rogue"—nodding at the minstrel—"would lose his head."

"I did not flout the rules," said I. "I followed them strictly. And His Majesty was amused."

"That would not matter," said the knight. "King Henrico would never stand for such an affront to his dignity."

I reached for my wine. "Should I ever stand before King Henrico," I said, "I will restrain my impudence."

"You would be wise to do so, Dom Keely-Fay."

Trumpets and drums sounded as Their Majesties rose from the high table and retired to the palace. We stood as they did, and then

I finished my wine—of indifferent quality, slightly better than that given to servants—and excused myself. The gardens were filled with people, the ladies floating over the grass like lilies gracing the surface of the water. A great many ladies, I saw, were from Loretto, and were in search of husbands. I have spoken, I believe, of how our Duisland nobility are more rare than that arrogant rabble that infect Loretto, and the ladies of Loretto had taken note of this and were hunting down our bachelor peers.

Strolling, I saw Lady Westley in a gown of blue watered silk that trailed on the green grass, with a partlet and kirtle of brilliant white samite patterned with gold threads and puffs of blue and black. For a day at court, she had whitened her face and then brightened her lips and cheeks with alkanet. The blue gown, reflected in her eyes, made her eyes seem even more intense, and the gold flecks more brilliant. I came to her and bowed, the sunburst pendant dangling. She remarked it, but made no comment.

"I have heard that songster's ballad," she said, "and admired its ingenuity. For I'm blessed if I could have come up with a single rhyme for Quillifer."

"I never had occasion to find one," I said, "for I have never made songs on myself." I considered the question and added, "Though I see no reason I should not."

She smiled. "I'm sure you would praise yourself with a fine eloquence." She turned and looked at the palace, partly concealed by the bulk of the new great hall. "Do you know I have an apartment in the palace?"

"I was not aware," I said.

"My husband's position comes with lodging," she said, "though the rooms are very small, and we use them rarely as we keep a house in town."

"Yet it must be convenient," I said, "if, for example, you find yourself fatigued after a great feast."

She gave me a look from beneath her fine level brows. "I believe I am fatigued in just that way," she said. "I think I shall retire for a while. But I remember that I promised to show you something, and if you could come to my rooms in, say, half an hour, I would be in a position to receive you."

"I would be honored to oblige you. Though will your husband not be present?"

She smiled. "He is at Entham Lodge, making arrangements for the stag hunt in two days."

"Then I will be very pleased to keep the appointment, my lady."

She strolled away, toward the palace, the blue gown trailing on the grass. I wandered about for a while, enjoying the water gardens and idle conversation, and then I encountered Rufino Knott again, where he sat on a marble bench, contemplating the statue of an oread, and eating a blackbird pie that had managed to escape the guests. He jumped up with an apology, and I told him to sit and eat his dinner. I examined his guitar, which had six courses and a convex back, like a viol.

"You play it well, Master Knott," said I. "I admired those dextrous figures you played when you were resting your voice."

Knott swallowed a bite of pie, then spoke. "Thank you, Sir Quillifer."

"Where did you get a guitar with that rounded back? I've never seen one."

"The work is signed 'Blanco.' I understand he was, or perhaps still is, an Aekoi luthier from the Empire, but who lives, or lived, in the south of Loretto, in Pantano Morto, I believe. But he did not make the instrument for *me*, for I won it in a game of cards."

"I have a seven-course guitar from Varcellos, which I found there on a voyage. But while I can strum it well enough, I learned from sailors who learned from other sailors, and I lack your proficiency. I wonder if you would consent to give me lessons?"

He lowered the pie that he had lifted again to his lips. He seemed surprised. "I would be honored, sir."

"Can you come to my house—Rackheath House, that is—the day after tomorrow? In the afternoon, following dinner?"

"Yes, of course."

I rose, and he rose with me until I waved him back to his seat. I walked toward the palace through the dispersing throng, passed around the incomplete structure of the great hall, and then entered through the grand rear portico past the Yeoman Archers in their black leather doublets and red caps. I found a stair, went up several flights, and made my way to a part of the palace divided into small apartments, either for officials or pensioners. I had never been in this part of the palace before. The smell of the place was unwholesome, and the apartments I saw through open doors were small, and some were wretched. The contrast with the glittering public parts of the building was unmistakable.

I found the door to Lady Westley's rooms, battered oaken planks painted black, with the name *Sir Edelmir Westley* picked out in graceful painted script. I knocked lightly, and then I heard Lady Westley's voice. "Who is it?"

"Heliodor."

"Please come in."

The room was small and dark, with only a small window high in the far wall, but it was lit by a dozen candles that filled the air with the mysterious scent of hyacinths. Mirrors and radiant wall hangings served to make the room seem larger and brighter than it was.

But I paid scant attention to that, because of what I found in the center of the room, pale and lovely in the candlelight. Lady Westley was naked, rising like a goddess from the milky pool of the robe that she had just let fall from her shoulders. The yellow diamonds in their new settings of white gold glittered below her ears, and the single white diamond hung on a silver chain between her breasts. Candlelight glittered knowingly in her gold-flecked eyes.

For some seconds I was struck dumb, and I felt little but my own scalding blood as it sluiced like molten bronze through my veins. She raised her head and arched her brow.

"Why are you surprised?" said she. "I promised I would model the stones, did I not?"

I finally managed words. "You did not promise to outshine them so, my Girasol."

I had just enough presence of mind to bolt the door, and then I took her in my arms. We spent the afternoon in an exchange of delights, each discovering new ways to please the other, and then, as the candles burned down and the sun neared the horizon and sent its rays in a long bright beam through the window, I began my practice as lady's maid, in aiding her toilette, and making her presentable for a return to the court. Yet I found dressing her too stimulating, removed her clothes again, and disported a while before I could, in a less frenzied frame of mind, resume my task. I tried to banish all distractions from my mind, and so I tied her garters, tightened her corset, inserted her busk, tied on the farthingale and the bumroll, added the kirtle, forepart, and partlet, and then helped draw the blue gown over her head. I laced the points, and then helped her feet into her scarlet latchet shoes.

Her chestnut hair had become disordered, and I did my best to put it in order, but my mistress was much more proficient at such things than I. In the end the mirrors showed a properly dressed court lady, and I helped her pin on her cap and then put my arms around her. I kissed her ears with their dangling jewels, and then her mouth. She melted against me for a moment, then drew back and considered the room.

"The servant may make the bed," said she.

"I will do it. I will also remove any material evidence." For I had employed scabbards, so as to prevent a cuckoo appearing in the Westley nest.

She lifted an eyebrow. "You are thorough in performing your maid's duties," she said.

I bowed. "I am entirely at your service, Girasol."

"You should leave first, I think."

This required another toilette, my own this time, before I could put the sunburst medallion around my neck, kiss my lady good-bye, and slip away into the corridor.

Outside the palace, an autumn wind had come up to chill the twilight. I walked to the quay and found my boat's crew, who by now had been waiting for hours. At a modest pace we returned to Rackheath House, the winner's pennon snapping over my head. I sent my crew a bottle of brandy to warm them after their long wait on the quay, and then went into the house and ordered up my supper.

Even after such a banquet as I'd had that morning and over the long afternoon, I still found myself hungry for more.

Do you know, my sweet, I am so very thankful that I may speak so frankly in your presence. So many others, uncertain perhaps of my love, would find my candid talk of other women vexing, or hateful. But you know I am completely devoted to you, and understand that I view my other amours as but imperfect versions of yourself. If I praise Lady Westley or some other, it is as if I praise a mere shadow, for your light is such as to cast all others into darkness.

It is you, of course, with whom I choose to commit treason, and it is your courage that inspires me to the daunting tasks that lie before me. So kiss me, my dear, and I will return to my modest narration.

CHAPTER TEN

F rom Lady Westley, in her candlelit chamber in the palace, I learned more of the world of the court. She knew it well, for after being orphaned as a child, she had been raised in Howel by an uncle who served as a judge. She knew most of the figures who graced the palace, and had played hide-and-seek through the corridors with their children.

She lay in my arms, her warm dark hair cloaking my shoulder, her bergamot scent tingling in my senses. I felt a pleasant lightness in my loins. At this moment, after this sharing, the rituals and residents of the court seemed far away, and therefore a suitable topic for amused conversation. Even the queen's spymaster seemed a distant figure, as if I were looking at him through the wrong end of a spyglass. "Lord Edevane's father was a country baron," said Lady Westley. "But the son's poor eyesight made him unsuitable for country sports, like riding and shooting, and he applied himself to his books, and went to the university to learn law."

He had served as a lawyer in the chancellery before Berlauda called the Estates at her accession, and he had himself elected to the House of Burgesses in his family borough. He had made himself useful to

Berlauda in her wrangles with the houses over her war taxes, and had been working his way upward in her service ever since.

"He has but recently inherited his father's title," said Lady Westley. "And he will take his seat in the House of Peers when it meets."

"Has he a family?" I asked. "A wife?"

"He has a wife and children at home, and an Aekoi mistress here in Howel."

That was not unusual. Aekoi courtesans were prized, not only for their supple, gold-skinned beauty but because no human could get them with child.

"Do people fear Edevane, Girasol?" I asked.

"They do since Scutterfield fell," she said.

"I did not care for the way he looked at me in the regatta."

She was amused. "You shouldn't have made such a spectacle of yourself, then." Her tongue teasingly touched her teeth as she sang. *"Quillifer, Quillifer, lord of the gem-coffer."* She laughed. "People are bound to wonder how to get that gem-coffer for themselves."

"Fortunately, I have a reputation as a doughty soldier. Fear of my arms will keep those gems safe."

She raised her level brows. "You have a reputation as a soldier? I thought you were a sea-captain of some kind."

"I am, above all things, a lover," said I, and held her close while I kissed the smooth skin at the juncture of neck and shoulder.

"Ay," she said with a pleased sigh. "That you are, Heliodor." She touched my neck while I caressed her, and then sighed again. "I am expected for a game of cards at Hallmeet House," she said. "Will you help me dress?"

"Of course, Girasol. Helping you into your gown is almost as pleasing as helping you out of it." And we began the complicated business of making Lady Westley suitable for an appearance in public, which began with donning her smock.

"What of Countess Marcella, lady-in-waiting to Princess Floria?"

I asked as I knelt before her and carefully drew her stockings up her legs. "I don't imagine it's common to take Aekoi into a royal household."

She raised an eyebrow. "Do you fancy her? She is handsome, I think."

I kissed her thigh. "In the light of a blazing Girasol, all others seem mere shadow."

She laughed. "That courtier's language again!"

Her stockings having been sufficiently gartered, I offered her the corset. It was lashed to a steel busk in front, and the ingenious busk itself was split, but could be hooked together, which both enclosed her waist and saved the trouble of re-lacing. "Countess Marcella?" I reminded.

"She is a widow," said Lady Westley. She tugged and smoothed the smock beneath the corset. "Her husband was conducting some kind of mission to Pisciotta, and he died there. Before she could return to the Empire, there was a political change at home, and her husband's faction was exiled. She has plenty of money, so she travels until it's safe to return."

"And how did she come to be in Floria's household?"

I held the farthingale low to the floor so she could step into it. "I know not. But Floria enjoys the company of interesting people, provided their interests are not in politics."

"Floria mislikes politics?"

"Floria knows politics are dangerous for her." She drew the farthingale to her waist and tied it in place. "Berlauda, you know, has miscarried twice, and once given birth to a stillborn girl."

With satin ribbons I lashed the bumroll in place. "I was unaware."

"You were at sea." Lady Westley regarded herself in the looking-glass, and adjusted the farthingale, "But there was great anxiety here, more for Her Majesty's life than the life of any children. For if the queen died, Priscus would remain a foreign king here on the throne of Duisland—unless perhaps the people's choice fell on Floria, and then there would be war."

"I see where Floria might have a goodly share in that anxiety."

I helped Lady Westley lace on her kirtle, with its forepart of dusky-orange embroidered satin that would set off the deep blue of the gown. "Until Berlauda gives birth to a living child," she said, "and if you leave Priscus out of the business, then Floria is the heir, and if powerful men flock to her, she could be accused of conspiring to gain the throne." She straightened. "So Floria occupies herself with harmless pastimes, like dancing, and masques, and music, and natural philosophy."

"Astronomy," I said. I helped settle her ruffled partlet about her neck and shoulders.

"Ay, with Mistress Ransome. Who is another of Floria's collection of curiosities."

Reflectively, she gave her reflection a reflective look. "I will say this for Edith Ransome," she added. "She has twice the brains of her brother. Though if she ever publishes her catalogue of stars, it will have her brother's name on it, and not her own."

"Why is that?"

"The brother desires to enhance his reputation. Edith cares for the work, not for acclaim. And—" She looked over her shoulder at me. "Do you think the world would credit an arcane astronomical work by a woman?"

I kissed the shoulder. "I know not what astronomers might think, but I know I would not care to contradict Edith Ransome in any way," I said. "Yet if prejudice against her sex is a problem, she can publish the work under a pseudonym, Asteria or something."

I brought out the silk gown and held it open so that Lady Westley could back into it. This was the same dark blue gown of watered silk she had worn for the regatta, but embroidered sleeves of dusky orange satin had been laced onto the gown in place of the sleeves of white samite, and with the kirtle's orange forepart made the ensemble seem very different. I helped lace up the front and then adjusted its folds. Then Lady Westley attended to her hair, while I dressed myself.

"Floria's other two ladies?" I asked. "What of them?"

Again she gave me a look over her shoulder. "Are you looking to replace me, Heliodor?"

"You are irreplaceable, my Girasol. And I think Floria's ladies look for husbands, not lovers."

She was amused. "You can't be both?"

"I fear it would overstrain my gifts."

She returned her attention to the mirror, and to her hair. "Very well, then," she said. "Chenée Tavistock is a poor relation. Elisa d'Altrey is a niece of the Marquess of Melcaster, who supported Clayborne and was attainted. The family has lost everything and is now quite poor."

"Yet she remains very much above me."

"Ay, she is very concerned with her fallen dignity. I think also she may have something of the character of a hostage, for her family's good behavior."

I considered this. "That must weigh on her mind. If the family considers some crime or other, do they even care whether Niece Elisa will suffer as a consequence? I don't suppose they would."

I finished dressing and put my sun medallion about my neck. Lady Westley turned to face me, her white diamond about her neck, and the yellow diamond earrings glittering like little suns. The effect was dazzling, and my breath was quite taken away. She saw my breath so taken, and gave herself a catlike smile of satisfaction.

"Help me with my shoes," she said, "and kiss me good-bye."

I tied her shoes, then rose and touched my lips to hers. "I will see you again?" I said.

"Perhaps," she said, "if you promise not to talk so much of other women."

"You choose the topic, then."

She bobbed a little curtsy. "I shall think of some pithy matter that will heighten the brilliance of our intercourse."

"I hope you will."

And so we both left the palace, each going our own way. The strange enchantment, the sense of distance that the afternoon had given to the court, was slow to fade. The bustling servants, the bright tapestries, the brilliant courtiers, and even Their Majesties seemed of less consequence than characters in one of Blackwell's plays. They seemed nothing more than puppets capering before an audience of children.

But if they were puppets, I thought, I wondered who controlled them, and who wrote their lines. And who, for that matter, controlled me?

I thought perhaps I would not care for the answer to that question, and so I left the palace, summoned my carriage, and rode in splendor to my home.

"Please excuse me," said I, "but I am not a tradesman. I do not visit others, nor wait in hallways for admittance. If you wish to view my stones, you must come to my house."

The man's name was Scarnside, and he was something called the premier baron of Bonille, which I supposed meant he was just like any other baron, but with an invented ancestry that went back further than the fabricated genealogies of his peers.

"But you sell diamonds," he said.

"As well as rubies and sapphires. But I do not keep a shop." I made a gesture with one hand, and my rings glittered. "Precious stones are my amusement. If it amuses me, I am willing to part with them."

Baron Scarnside gave me an icy glance. "I do not set myself to amusing tradesmen."

"I am not a tradesman."

"Better a tradesman than a rampallion knight," he snarled, and stalked off.

I suppressed laughter behind my innocent-choirboy face and consoled myself with the thought that he had at least recognized me as a knight, however much rampallion, and not called me a butcher's son.

So, I concluded, we must thank the nobility for their courtesies.

I did not care if I lost Scarnside's custom, for I had many visitors now, and my supply of precious stones had waned as my acquaintance had increased. In addition to my new connections, many from the nobility of both Duisland and Loretto, my lord of Roundsilver had bought gems for himself and his lady, and so had Prince de Ribamar-la-Rose.

Lady Westley also had I seen, both in my house and in her apartment at Ings Magna, and she gave me more practice at my new, delightful profession of lady's maid.

I had joined Coronel Lipton in test-firing one of his little leather guns—or rather, I joined him in a trench while a cannoneer's journeyman named Peel put a portfire in its touchhole, lit the fuse, and ran for cover. The gun fired nine times before it burst, which Lipton said made it the best of these engines he had yet constructed. And when it burst, the leather jacket restrained somewhat the flying metal, which made it that much safer for any crew.

The second regatta had been run, *Dunnock* had placed third, and the pennant of victory had gone to the Worshipfull Companie of Ale-Conners, or at least their hired captain. His Grace of Roundsilver took second place. I would have done better had not I been run aboard by a galley belonging to the Conte Ricardo, a noble of Loretto, so that his oars tangled with my own. So willful did this collision seem that I wondered if it were a deliberate attempt to take me out of the race, but then I decided that it was unlikely that Ricardo had been bribed by the Ale-Conners, and that he was more likely another captain who had not read the rule book.

I had begun guitar lessons with Master Knott, though by now my calendar had become rather full, what with tennis lessons, practice on the lake, visits to court, stolen hours with Lady Westley, and the necessity of inventing stories to go with all my gems.

I had encountered Baron Scarnside at Howel's old Aekoi stadium, where we had gone to view that new wonder from Loretto, the horse-ballet. This new species of spectacle had premiered in Loretto only two years before, and had been a sensation. King Priscus had summoned the troupe from his homeland, and all the court would view its debut on this fine October afternoon.

The ancient stadium stood north of Howel and was used for jousting and athletic contests. The stone seats on the south side of the arena were reserved for the royalty and nobility, and were shaded by a canopy, while the rest of us stood in the open, like groundlings at the theater. I fetched myself a cup of wine from a vendor, then discovered Coronel Lipton standing in the line behind me.

"Well, youngster," said he, "you have cost me some silver, for I put money on you in that last race."

"I think you have not lost as much money as I," I said. "For I planned to win that race, and if Conte Ricardo had not fouled me, I would have."

He shrugged. "Well, you will race again, sure." He turned to a young man standing behind him. "I promised I would introduce you to Master Alaron Mountmirail the engineer, did I not?"

Mountmirail was a tall, lank young man who looked no older than sixteen. He had pale red hair all crimped into tight curls, a round moon face with the wispy beginnings of a mustache, and large hands covered with scars and burn marks.

"How may I serve you, lord?" he asked.

I sipped at my wine. "That pleasing appellation is at best premature, for I am a mere knight," said I. "Though I will take it, if I may, as an omen for the future."

He nodded, showing scant signs of embarrassment. I continued.

"As I understand, you are an engineer and artificer of mechanisms. I wonder if you can make me a grinding machine."

He affected to consider this. "I suppose I could, sir. What must it grind?"

"Hard vegetable matter—nuts, for example. You might practice on oak galls, they are cheap enough. The mechanism must grind them in quantity, and to a fine powder."

We discussed my requirements for a while, and Mountmirail said he would consider the matter, and then call on me at my house. With our wine, we walked to the arena, and Lipton's uniform and coronel's sash gained us a spot at the rail, where we encountered the playwright Blackwell, who had drunk more wine than was good for him. He sagged against the arena's rail, and his ultramarine eyes narrowed in disgust as he looked at the neatly combed sand and straw that filled the ring.

"Is something amiss?" I asked him.

He snarled. "I know that if these horse dramas become fashionable, people will desert my plays."

"I hardly think they are a threat. I saw your *Waldemar* the other day, in the old Aekoi theater, and there was no lack of audience."

"*Waldemar* is an old play, a favorite of the mob. It replaces another play that did badly."

"Old play or new, the spectators parted with their pennies, and you had profit without the trouble of writing something new."

He gave me a narrow look. "I *did* write something new. *Rinaldo*, the play that failed."

"*Rinaldo?* You wrote a play about the poet?"

"Ay." Blackwell reached for a wineskin he carried on a cord, opened it, and filled his cup. A brandy reek stung the air.

"Is there anything dramatical about the poet's life?" asked I. "I thought he had a quiet existence, with a cottage and a garden, a plump mistress, and a rich patron."

"He lived a life devoted to contemplation and to beauty." Blackwell took a swallow of brandy. "He wrote the most sublime verse in his generation, if not all generations. I wished to inspire the audience as Rinaldo inspired me, but my own verse failed." He gave a twist of his lip. "Well, the duke liked it, or said he did."

Certainly a play about a poet reciting verse and worshipping beauty seemed to lack a degree of dramatic vigor. I decided to be helpful.

"You should publish it," I offered. "Perhaps it reads better than it plays."

Blackwell made an equivocal wave of his hand, and then—as if the actor had just given a cue—trumpets played a sennet, and Their Majesties's party mounted the stands. Beside them Princess Floria, though grown to as full a height as she could manage, seemed a half-grown child next to her tall, blond, sturdy sister. It would require some effort to thrive in that shade.

With them was a monk from Loretto, which I knew because instead of the plain unbleached wool favored by monks in Duisland, he wore a jeweled belt over robes of purple satin edged with gold and scarlet. Behind the tonsure that shaved the forepart of his head, his black hair was caught in long, oiled ringlets, and gems glittered on his fingers. His posture was erect, his glance imperious, and clearly he obeyed the Fiat of Abbot Reynardo. He shared King Priscus's dark complexion, and his nose was only slightly less impressive than the king's hooked beak. It occurred to me that he might be some kind of royal relative. I turned to Coronel Lipton.

"Who is that ultra-luxurious cenobite?" I asked.

Lipton looked upon the monk with distaste. "His name is Fosco, a kinsman to the king. He headed one of the princely houses, until he chose to serve the Pilgrim, passed the title to his younger brother, and become abbot to a score of monasteries."

"The Pilgrim seems to have done well for him."

"The Pilgrim gives gold and silver with both hands, sure, and keeps none for himself."

The royal party took their places beneath the canopy, and we of the audience bowed to the presence. They took their seats, the king waved a hand, and the entertainment began.

I am not a natural rider, and my relations with the equine species have had moments both of low comedy and of high drama. I had survived the battle at Exton Scales in part because my ill-tempered charger Phrenzy behaved as savagely toward the enemy as he did to me.

Yet for the next hour I fell in love with horses. An orchestra began to play, and the chargers of Loretto floated onto the field in defiance of all the custom of gravity, hanging in the air in time to the long slow throb of the tambour. Their great loose manes and tails drifted in the breeze like clouds. They came forward and knelt to the king and queen, one foreleg stretched out before them like a line of courtiers making their reverence. Then they began a complicated weaving dance, passing about and through one another, turning in small, tight spirals, all in time to the music.

They danced left and right, forward and back. They leaped over their kneeling trainers. They reared on their hind legs, forelegs flashing as they bounded across the field; and they stood on their forelegs only, lifting their rear legs off the ground, then kicking out. They bounded high into the air, or strode with forelegs reaching out as if to paw the air, or walked in place with dainty marching steps.

Horses came forward, one at a time or two by two, to display their specialties. There was no one grand narrative, as might be seen in a more conventional ballet; but there were little stories woven into the display, simple stories of love, war, and conquest enacted by horses who seemed able to communicate passion even in their silence.

At the end the line of horses came forward again to bow to Their Majesties, and the audience burst into cheers and applause. I turned to Blackwell and saw his indigo eyes gazing bleak from his ashen face.

"This is obscene," he said. "A sham entertainment, with animals taught like whores to please the ill-tuned mob. I will see no more."

And then he stalked away, the one doleful wretch in all the happy crowd. I thought I should follow him, but I knew not what comfort I could bring. My pleasure in the horse-ballet was all too obvious, and I did not credit his claim that the horses would replace his acting company—for one thing, when the spectacle grew stale, the horses would take too long to learn any tricks.

So I let him go, like a black squall storming over a calm ocean, and then I chatted with Lipton and Mountmirail as we left the tiltyard. We parted as I went to my boat at the quayside, and they headed south into town. Along the way I encountered the duke's guest, Prince Alicio de Ribamar-la-Rose, who was dressed in a suit of brilliant green silk, slashed to reveal his saffron satin shirt. His silken doublet was painted all over with fantastic animals, and he wore the short Loretto cloak. I greeted him, and he bowed in that Lorettan way, with one leg thrust toward me, the bow that the ballet-horses had imitated at the beginning and end of the spectacle.

"Your clothes are no longer white, Highness," said I. "Is it a sign that you have reconsidered your philosophy?"

He seemed a little abashed. "I have changed my colors, true," he said, "but unwillingly. Prince Fosco is here, and he is King Henrico's champion of orthodoxy. I did not wish to parade my beliefs before him, Sir Keely-Fay, lest he report to the king and I be ordered home, or even to prison."

I considered the fierce mien of the abbot Fosco, more like a warrior than a monk, and thought that Ribamar-la-Rose might well be forgiven. "Surely a little discretion is in order," said I. "The Compassionate Pilgrim did not insist that his followers turn martyr."

"I shall leave the city ere long," said the prince. "And lodge in a monastery till Fosco leaves. But my own station and standing, as head of another cadet branch of our royal house, require that I meet with him, and I would prefer this to be on cordial terms."

"I understand completely," said I. We walked over the ancient flagstones that led to the quay, and I saw the golden towers of the palace rising above the blue waters of the lake. We approached my boat, and the crew stepped to the quay to help me aboard.

"May I offer you a ride, Highness?" I said. "I can put you ashore at the Roundsilver palace on my way home."

"I am returning with His Grace," said the prince. "But he was delayed by business with the chancellor—" He gave me a sly look. "*One* of the chancellors. He was *monopolized*."

I laughed. "His Grace is an exquisite monopole, to be sure."

The music of female laughter floated on the afternoon air. I turned to see the princess Floria walking over the flags in the company of her ladies, and for a moment considered skipping for my boat and rowing away. But my flight would have been too visible to Her Highness, and so I waited with the prince and bowed as Floria approached. Bowed like a man of Duisland, with my two feet under me, while Prince Alicio bowed gracefully over his advanced leg.

Floria was dressed in the royal gold and scarlet, with a gold circlet on her cloud of crinkly dark hair and a carcanet of rubies close about her throat. She acknowledged the prince's salutation, then turned her sharp eyes on me.

"I've seen you ride, Quillifer," she said. "I hope the horse-ballet will inspire you to improve your horsemanship."

"I fear that horses and I are ever at odds, Your Highness," said I, and then hoped to turn the subject away from myself. "I trust your royal mother does well?"

"She thrives, as always. Though she fears the fire-drake reported in the Cordillerie near her house at Bonherbes."

I was surprised. "A dragon? In Bonille?" For those unnatural creatures that flew, or swam, from the Land of Chimerae to Duisland usually landed in the far west of Fornland and plagued the stubborn, resilient people of that stormy coast. "A monster in the heart of Bonille," said I, "is a wonder indeed."

"I should love to see this marvel," said Prince Alicio. "It has been many generations since Loretto saw such a prodigy."

"I expect it's been up in the mountains for years," said Floria. "Eating its fill and growing fat. And now that the sheep have come down from the summer pastures, the worm has followed its dinner to the plains."

"How large is it?" I asked.

"I know not," said Floria, "save that it dines on sheep and calves, and must be killed before it begins to devour my mother's tenants."

I remembered the great ocean serpent that I had seen from *Royal Stilwell*'s quarterdeck, the scaled writhing body shimmering with uncanny light, the great bared fangs, the glint of intelligence in its eye. "At sea I have seen a watery version of this monster," I said, "and even though it did not spout fire, I know not how to kill one."

"Did not my lord duke's ancestor Baldwine hunt such prey?" asked the prince.

Amusement tugged at Floria's lips. "I would not sacrifice Roundsilver on this quest," said she. "He is too lovely a lily to scorch in the drake's fire."

"Does not the queen have her own regiment of horse?" asked I. "A monster hunt would prove a diversion for them, I'm sure."

"They are not trained to fight serpents."

"Nor is anyone, I suppose. Yet here they are, with weapons, horses, and armor, and with nothing to do."

"They guard Her Majesty's person. It is their sole duty."

I considered the facetious remark that, for a small recompense, I could undertake that task while the troopers went to fight the dragon, but decided against it.

Floria's eyes narrowed, and she looked at Lady Westley's sunburst medallion. "Have you run out of precious stones?" she asked. "Or do you compare yourself to a sun god?"

She had seen the one element of my raiment that did not tally with the rest. I concealed my annoyance behind my respectful-apprentice face and strove to shift the topic. "It is an amulet," I said. "Bought of a mountebank in Tabarzam, to guarantee fair weather. As a sailor, you see, I worship the sun, as an antidote to storms." And then I added, "And I have gems aplenty, an you care to view them."

"Bring me something fantastical tomorrow," said she, "and tell me the tale of it, a tale at least as good as that of this Tabarzam mountebank."

I had just told Baron Scarnside that I never visited another's house to sell gems, but I considered that an exception might be made for the heir to the throne.

"I will be pleased to call upon you. At what time?"

"Come after dinner." A smile tugged at her lips. "I don't want to have to feed you."

I bowed. "I shall dine, then, on the rich and pleasing airs of court."

As I rose from my bow, I glanced over Floria's shoulder, and saw another royal party coming down the walk, Berlauda and Priscus surrounded by a bright cloud of courtiers. As soon as I saw them, I realized that while I had been engaged in colloquy with Her Highness, the idea of the fire-drake had not entirely left my mind, and I found that I had built an elegant little formula in my thoughts without ever having devoted any actual thought to the matter whatever.

So when Their Majesties' party joined ours, I bowed to the royal presence, and then went down on one knee.

"Your Majesty," I said to Berlauda. "I beg of thee a quest!"

Everyone looked at me in some surprise, and Floria was the most surprised of all, for but a moment ago I had been engaged with her in a perfectly ordinary conversation with no mention of a quest or favors, and now here I was on one knee addressing the monarch.

Berlauda looked down at me with mild blue eyes. Her placid face remained expressionless. "You may send your petition to the Chancery," she said, and turned to sweep along the path toward her barge.

"Your Majesty," said I, "I have no petition but to be allowed to fight the fire-drake that endangers Your Majesty's subjects and their property." The queen paused, and the shadow of surprise passed across her face. She looked at me again. I offered her my dutiful-apprentice face and an apologetic smile. "I believe fighting dragons is what knights are *for*, Majesty."

While Berlauda absorbed this, another man came out of the crowd and knelt on the path to my left. "I beg Your Majesty's permission to accompany this knight," he said in the accent of Loretto. He was a tall man, about my height, but with much greater breadth of shoulder and depth of chest. I recognized him as Dom Lorenso d'Abrez, a *couceiro* who had won the prize at the joust, three years before, that celebrated Their Majesties' impending nuptials. I was annoyed at this great conceited lump of brawn trying to force his way into my expedition, and even more annoyed as another man knelt on my right.

"And I, Your Majesty." And this man I recognized as the master of the henchmen, Sir Edelmir Westley. My lover's husband had become inconvenient in a completely unexpected way.

Vexed at this ridiculous circumstance, I said that I intended to take the quest alone, but no one heard me, as courtiers were swooping in from left and right to join us. Apparently questing was the new fashion, like brimless hats or shoes with scarlet heels. Among the newcomers I saw Dom Nemorino d'Ormyl, the Lorettan knight who had sat beside me at the regatta dinner and urged me not to tempt his king with impudence.

Berlauda looked at the growing pack with what seemed to be amusement. After a baronet tried to join us, the queen said the quest would be for knights alone.

At the end there were twelve of us. The queen wished all luck and went on with her ladies to her barge. King Priscus lingered a moment, surveying us, and then looked at me and smiled. "I hope at least one of you has read the rule book," he said, and then laughed at his own joke, *caw-caw-caw!*

After the king left, I rose and invited the others to my house to plan the expedition, but none cared to hear me, and they wandered away in twos or threes, engaged in animated conversation. At the end I stood more or less as I had begun, with Floria and her ladies. Floria's face was split in a merry smile.

"I thought you said you didn't know how to kill one of these beasts!" she said.

"Nor do I. But I shall find out."

She laughed. "Gorge it with those idiots," she said, "and kill it while it's sleeping off the feast."

I snarled. "I will if I can."

"If you succeed," she said, "you will have the thanks of a royal queen of Duisland." And then she paused and smiled. "Not my sister, of course," she added, "but my mother."

And then she and her ladies laughed, and trailed their merriment all the way to the royal barge.

CHAPTER ELEVEN

I will take the star sapphire," said the princess Floria. "Though I don't know quite what I'd do with it. Use it for a doorknob, perhaps."

The sapphire, a remarkable dark blue color, had not been faceted, but cut as a cabochon, which made its shape something like a flattened egg. The six silver rays of the star blazed across the gem's dome like an exploding firework, and there were times when I thought it was the finest thing in my collection.

I had not brought my strongbox to the palace, but only a selection of the largest and finest stones, each wrapped in velvet, and the whole array carried in a leather bag. For each piece I had a prepared a story, and I felt justified in doing so, as Her Highness had practically commanded me. The star sapphire, for example, I said had been set on the crown of an idol in Mirandazar, until it had been looted at the fall of the Kangavid Dynasty. I continued the gem's history with a series of lurid murders until I sensed Her Highness growing weary of the tale, at which point I brought the sapphire to Tabarzam and put the stone into her hands, and with a candle showed her the magic of the star, the rays that moved with the light over the gem's dome.

"It's large enough for a doorknob," I said, "but I think it would make a fine pendant or ring."

"Oh, ay." Floria turned the stone in her fingers and watched the star shift across the cabochon. "I will think of something."

"Your Highness wishes no other gems? This may be your last chance, for I may be eaten up by a dragon."

Her darting hazel eyes steadied as she gazed at me. "Whatever possessed you to volunteer for that quest?"

I had come to think this was an interesting question. In truth, the idea had come in a rush of inspiration, and before that moment I had had no intention of going on any adventure more perilous than a regatta. Which made me wonder if the idea had been mine at all.

According to the ancient epics of Bello and his imitators, divine beings float invisibly among us, whispering their ideas into the ears of mortals, and moving us like pieces on a chessboard, to war or love or doom—all of which I had thought a poet's conceit, until I had met such a being. Orlanda, I knew, was working to blight my life. She had poisoned the queen's mind against me, and caused the wreck of *Royal Stilwell*, and wrought I knew not what other mischief.

I had wondered if Orlanda had put the idea in my head, and was even now in the Cordillerie, teaching the fire-drake how best to encompass my ruin.

"Why did I volunteer?" I asked. "Purely out of compassion for your distressed mother."

Floria barked a laugh, and I saw amusement on the faces of her four ladies. For we were not alone in her parlor—no royal lady would ever let herself be found alone with a man, for her chastity was an instrument of the state, and subject to the state's necessities.

"You know," said the princess, "you didn't need Her Majesty's permission to fight this dragon. You needed only to go and do it, if that's what you wanted. The queen would hardly have stopped you."

"I felt I should tell someone," said I, "so that if I am lost on this adventure, someone might search for me."

Floria was amused. "My sister has no reputation for scouring the wilderness after lost gentlemen."

I prepared an invoice for 190 royals, offered it to Floria, and then hesitated.

"Perhaps I should give it to the lord chancellor?" I said. "Or the lord treasurer?"

"The money will come from my household accounts." Floria took the invoice, and I felt a pang of trepidation. If a member of the royal family chose not to pay money owed, what was the remedy? I could hardly take her to court.

But I decided to trust Floria, as if I actually had a choice in the matter. And I consoled myself with the thought that, if she had intended to rob me, she would have taken my every stone.

From Floria's parlor I went to the Chamber of Audience, the tapestry-brightened, sunlit room where Their Majesties' thrones sat golden beneath the canopy of state. It was what I thought of as an adulation day, for there was no activity or entertainment planned, and instead the courtiers strove to outdo one another in praising the appearance, wisdom, and every single utterance of the monarchs. This was not a game that I could play, not because I was more honest than the others, but because I was beneath Berlauda's notice, and the monarchs would rate my flattery as of less consequence than the buzzing of a fly.

I entered the room in hopes of finding His Grace of Roundsilver, who I found standing by his golden duchess. I approached them and bowed. Her Grace turned to me with concern shining from her blue eyes.

"You purpose to fight dragons now?" she said. "What prompted you?"

"I have asked myself that question," said I, "and I have no answer. But at least I shall have a bodyguard of eleven gallant knights." I turned to the duke. "Perhaps your ancestor Lord Baldwine employed a stratagem that would be useful?"

"That was a long time ago, in the period of the Sea-Kings," said the duke. "He left no prescription for monster-fighting, and there are few written records of him. But the legend states that he covered himself with muck and slime, dug some sort of tunnel beneath the place where the serpent came to drink, and stabbed the drake with a sword as it passed."

"I have seen Baldwine portrayed in a pageant," said I, "and no muck or slime was presented."

"Place not your trust in pageants," said the duke, and made a slight gesture of his hand that seemed somehow to encompass the entire pageant of the great palace, the strivings and rivalries of the courtiers, and perhaps the world itself. I shook my head.

"I cannot imagine Dom Lorenso d'Abrez and the others covering themselves in muck." I smiled. "Though I should like to see it."

"Here comes another of your band," said the duchess.

Approaching came the master of the henchmen, Sir Edelmir Westley. He was a self-assured man of five-and-twenty, with long, well-dressed black hair, black eyes, and a pointed beard. He clearly shared his lady's passion for gems, for stones glittered on his fingers and belt, and he wore a pendant set with baroque pearls. He bowed to Their Graces, and then turned to me.

"Sir Quillifer," said he, "those of us on the expedition had a meeting this morning—"

"Was I not invited?" I asked.

The black eyes did not blink. "I suppose we could not find you," he said.

I gestured in the direction of the lake. "I was on the water this morning," said I, "in plain sight of all."

Sir Edelmir paused to absorb this, a picture of amiability. "I am heartily sorry that no word came to you. I was not among those who organized the meeting, and truth to tell, it was barely organized at all."

I bowed by way of accepting the apology. "What was the substance of the meeting?"

"It was decided that we should all leave the day after the Burning Bull Festival, after meeting at Oliver's Cross in the morning."

"When is this festival?"

"The first of November, Sir Quillifer."

I knew nothing of burning bulls. In Fornland this would be the Final Flowers Festival, to mark the end of autumn.

"Did the meeting decide anything else, sir?" asked I.

"That we should draw lots to determine the order in which we fight the dragon."

I looked at Sir Edelmir in surprise. "Why don't we fight it all together?"

He gave me an easy smile. "That would hardly be sport."

"Sport? I thought we were to kill a dragon, not challenge it to a game of tennis."

Sir Edelmir laughed. "I think it is better this way. If we were to fight all together, twelve knights could never agree on what to do, and we'd get in one another's way."

I thought all eleven of them were in my way before we even started, and was tempted to say so. But Sir Edelmir had apologized very gracefully to me, and I supposed I might in theory owe him an apology as well, for sporting with his wife. So by way of changing the subject, I complimented him on his pendant.

"I shall hardly afford another," said he, "not after you sold those diamonds to my lady. The white stone is very pretty, but who ever heard of diamonds in that bright shade of yellow?"

"Such diamonds are rare," said I. "That makes them valuable."

His look was skeptical. "Possibly so, but it was a lot to pay for a pair of ear-pickes."

Her Grace was quick to speak up. "If you like not those stones, Sir Edelmir, I might take them. I think they would suit me."

He gave an easy laugh. "Nay, Your Grace," he said. "My lady likes them too well, and does not rank my opinion."

"Perhaps in this case," said the duchess, "she is right to do so."

"That may be," said Sir Edelmir, and, smiling, he gave us his adieu.

I thanked the duchess for her spirited defense of the diamonds.

"I should like to own them," said she. "I am sorry that Sir Edelmir does not know their worth."

My mind had turned to the message Sir Edelmir had brought. "The Burning Bull Festival," I mused. "That is nearly two weeks from now. These knights are in no hurry to find the worm."

"Perhaps that is wisdom," said the duchess.

"It will give me more time to prepare," said I, "and to reacquaint myself with the arts of weapons."

"I should buy myself a large shield, were I you," said the duke.

"I know not how to fight with a shield," said I.

"You need no training to hide behind it," said His Grace. "If you are to avoid the fiery breath, you need a wall to shelter behind."

This reasoning made uncommon sense, and I said so. "You might also consider draping yourself in wet cloths," the duke added. "And your horse as well."

"You are an uncommon great resource for a knight-errant," I said.

"My father knew the last great dragon-slayer of the realm, Lawton Triphorne," said the duke. "And I was told he always drenched himself thoroughly before a fight. He also soused the padding beneath his armor."

"With your guidance," said I, "I believe I may survive this adventure."

The duke's advice, I thought, would be of great service.

But I would never have volunteered for this mission if I had not already had a scheme or two of my own.

I made the most of the time before the festival of the Burning Bull: I put aside tennis lessons and reacquainted myself with riding, and with the wearing of armor. I bought a shield and padding and thick draperies that would hold a great deal of water. I also acquired a small wagon with a canvas top to carry supplies and stores of food for the journey. My experience in the cavalry, as secretary of the Utterback Troop, stood me in good stead, for I knew how to provision a journey.

I consulted with Coronel Lipton, and with Alaron Mountmirail the engineer, who had produced the first version of my grinder. It looked like a wooden box with an iron handle, and it crushed oak galls with ease, but the result was too coarse.

"To add a fine grinder would result in too complex a mechanism," said Mountmirail. "It might be simpler to have two grinders, one for coarse, one for fine."

"Perhaps something like the grindstones of a mill?" I said.

He grew intrigued. "We would need small millstones only. Do we know anyone who makes millstones?"

"Unless you can find someone with that skill," said I, "build the fine grinder, and then we may consider a mill later."

The court did a deal of hunting in the autumn, and I decided to join them when I could, by way of exercising my riding skills. I rode my charger Phrenzy that had brought me through the fighting at Exton Scales, and he tore through the woods and over the jumps with a vicious, sullen, persistent fury that more than justified his name. I don't know if my riding improved, but after the terrors of one such hunt I feared the dragon less.

I did not attempt to teach Phrenzy any of the feats of the horse-ballet. He might leap or rear or kick or dance, but only when he willed it: My own commands were received with the contempt they probably deserved.

Because I knew that horses were mortal, and horses on campaign doubly so, I bought another charger called Spitfire that was scarcely less belligerent than Phrenzy, along with a palfrey for its peaceful glide over the roadway. All, along with the wagon's draught horses and the sumpter mules, were under the care of my groom Oscar, who had looked after my beasts since I served in the Utterback Troop.

I received a letter from Kevin Spellman, and he informed me that the insurors had finally paid out on the loss of *Royal Stilwell*, and that our partnership's exchequer was enriched by 19,436 royals, eight crowns, and a halfpenny. Most of this would be spent on a new, large galleon to replace *Stilwell*, intended for the long trade to Tabarzam and the Candara Coast.

Our other large ship, originally named after the arch-rebel Lady Tern but renamed *Sovereign* out of discretion, was now provisioning for that same journey, under Captain Gaunt. To him I sent some private monies, so that he might replace the gems in my strongbox. He had been privy to the business I had conducted in Tabarzam, and I trusted he would prove a canny enough agent in those foreign lands.

From the profits I sent money to Ethlebight, to relieve the suffering of those who would go hungry on account of the great storm. The price of grain had almost doubled in the kingdom, and everywhere the poor complained for lack of bread.

Lady Westley came to visit when she could, and wore her diamonds for a select audience of one.

There was one more regatta before the festival of the Burning Bull, this with the galleys under sail for the entirety of the course. This meant that one leg of the triangular route would be into the wind, which would necessitate a good deal of tacking back and forth. My crew of professional sailors, drilled by me and by Boatswain Lepalik, performed with faultless skill, and I stood to take the pennant until a bobolyne marquess from Loretto swerved in my way and would not surrender the right of way to me, even though he was on the larboard tack and I on the starboard. Because of milord's ignorance, I was forced to come about to avoid collision, and finished second, after His Grace of Roundsilver.

You find it amusing, I see, that I hold so firmly to the rule book, when I have made so much of my reputation by defying custom. Yet when I choose to flout convention, I at least understand the convention I am flouting.

I feel that one should have perfect command of the rule book before throwing it away. That should itself be a rule.

Due to my encounter with the blundering captain I was not in the best of spirits the next day, which was the Burning Bull Festival, which opened with a parade in Howel sponsored by the guilds. Their floats came down the street, each with its orchestra or choir or a troupe of acrobats, or with actors performing a playlet of some fantastical legend. The equestrians of the horse-ballet took part, and they performed some of their tricks, to the crowd's great enthusiasm. After their command performance before the court they had continued to perform in the stadium, and had become wildly popular. I could not imagine this pleased at all the playwright Blackwell.

After the parade the crowd went to the stadium for the main entertainment. There were more acrobats and songsters, along with ribald comedians performing gigues and knocking each other on the pate. Then the bull was brought in, a magnificent animal with a vast spread of horns all wrapped in straw and tallow, and led into a pen.

A chant began to spread over the crowd. *"Red day bring the new day! Red day bring the new day!"* The chant rose up and up, sounding through the cool autumn air. Men left their seats and jumped down into the stadium. They leaped and danced and chanted, and for a moment I thought there would be a riot.

The chant rose to a peak. Then a torch was touched to the bull's horns, and the little pen opened as the horns were wreathed in flame.

The bull went mad, of course, and dashed into the stadium, through the crowd of jack-a-dandies, swashbucklers, and runagates who had flocked onto the field in order to defy fate and demonstrate their courage. The men roared and scattered. I saw one man tossed from the horns high into the air, to land lifeless on the sand like a straw poppet. Others were trampled or knocked down before the fires burned down and the bull, trembling and sweating but having suffered little in the way of permanent injury, was led off to honorable retirement.

I have since inquired as to the origin of this ritual, for we have nothing like it in Fornland, but no one could enlighten me. It is of such an ancient foundation that its purpose and intention is obscure, and no one has seen the rite performed anywhere but Howel. Yet it is enacted on the first of November, which by our old calendar was the first day of winter, and I suspect it was intended somehow to preserve the sun over the dark wintertide. And of course it is a blood sacrifice, though if the crowd is lucky, it need not be a fatal one.

Because of the heathen origins of the ritual, our pious king and queen did not attend, and the lord mayor presided over the event. I did see a number of monks in the throng, so the prohibition was not universal.

I learned afterward the identity of the man who was gored: Sir Albert Winstead, who was to quest for the dragon the next day. He died a few hours after the festival ended. Our company was reduced to eleven before we had even set out.

Perhaps this meant we would have no luck with fire-beasts. The omen oppressed our spirits as we assembled the next morning at Oliver's Cross south of town, and our spirits were further depressed by the weather, which was chill, and the rain, which fell in a continuous mizzle all the day long. My crooked finger ached. I was not the only knight who had brought his own wagon, for some of the others seemed to have brought a small village with them; but I was the only man who had brought his own minstrel. For I had asked Goodman Knott to accompany the journey, and to provide entertainment as we crossed the countryside.

It had occurred to me, after Lady Westley brought up the matter, that I could make songs on myself, or at least that Knott could. And if I killed the fire-drake, I would quite properly deserve a laudatory ballad.

Not that anyone felt like singing as we left the crossroads and turned southeast along the right bank of the Dordelle. The rain pattered on my broad hat and on the oilskins I wore over my old cheviot overcoat. The river was gray and turbid and speckled with raindrops.

We came to an inn mid-afternoon, and as everyone was tired of riding in the rain, the decision was to halt. I viewed my bed with a careful eye, on the alert for fleas or lice, but this close to the capital the inns were very clean. That evening in the common room, the others were polite but for the most part ignored me. Some were the sons of lords, and most were knights of the great orders of chivalry; whereas I was a mere knight-bachelor and the son of a butcher. No king or queen had knocked me on the shoulder with a sword, and I wore no ribbon across my chest. I wore a duke's ransom on my fingers, but no one was interested in buying gems, and I had not brought my strongbox, in any case.

Yet I had been knighted for military service, and of the Duisland knights I was alone in this. The rest had received the honor on account of their birth, and the great majority had been knighted on the occasion of Berlauda's ascent to the throne, when she had handed such rich compliments to the sons of her followers. The two knights of Loretto had fought in one or another of King Henrico's wars, though I understood that they had been knighted first and fought after.

Lorenso d'Abrez suggested that we fight the dragon in order of precedence, which would place him first, as a knight of the Seven Words, a cousin of King Henrico, and a descendant of Queen Margaretha of Steggerda. Once this became apparent, the other knights opposed his idea, and we drew lots as originally planned. Sir Brynley Wilmot, the third son of His Grace of Waitstill, drew first place. D'Abrez drew second, and I sixth. D'Abrez seemed content enough with the result.

As no one wished to talk to me, I called on Rufino Knott to bring out the guitars, and he sang and played his dextrous little figures, while I strummed an accompaniment. While we made our music, the heavens opened, and rain beat on the roof and the shutters. The others played cards and drank. I thought there would be a late start the next day, and I was proved correct.

It was midday before the company deemed the roads dry enough for our carts and wagons, and we set out into a biting cold breeze. It seemed that we had embarked on a winter campaign. We spent only four or five hours on the road before finding an inn. The next day squalls roamed over the countryside, and we spent half the day getting across the Dordelle on the ferry. The fifth day was bright and cold, but one of the wagons broke down, and we advanced only a few leagues.

Each night, there was more drinking, and more cards and dice. I began to think I had joined a traveling carouse, and not a quest at all. The only excitement came when Sir Edelmir's horse stumbled while fording one of the Dordelle's western tributaries, and he was pitched into the river. He flailed madly in the water, unable to swim. Aware that irony lurked in the very act of my having to rescue my lover's husband, I turned my palfrey and was prepared to launch myself into the river to fetch him out, when two of his own henchmen swam their steeds after him and brought him gasping to the shore, his fine black hair straggling in his face like seaweed. Shivering, he was bundled into one of the wagons and changed into dry clothes, and by evening,

having warmed himself with hippocras, was laughing about his mis-
adventure. More laughter came later, when he lost a small fortune at
dice.

The sixth day, in the forenoon, we arrived at Bonherbes, the house
of Queen Natalie, Floria's mother and the third wife of King Stilwell's
four wives. She insisted on providing us dinner, which dragged on
into supper. Her Majesty was not at all disturbed by the existence
of the dragon, and spoke merrily for hours, pausing only to ask for
news of court, which news she interrupted with scandalous reminis-
cences of those being mentioned. She had a group of ladies to wait on
her, and one lean gentleman dressed in a robe of black velvet, with a
skullcap on his gray head. He was introduced as Doctor Smolt, and
he spoke in a deep, measured voice, as if weighing his every word.

"Oh none of us believed little Botilda was really Count Conmouth's
daughter," said Queen Natalie, "for everyone knew Lady Conmouth
loved Sir Jasper Cherrier, and both he and Botilda had that blazing
red hair. Yet Conmouth never seemed to know what was going on
under his nose, possibly because his affections were directed at Lady
Gildrum, and always had been. . . ."

Truly she was an indiscreet woman, though she never seemed
to speak out of malice, but rather because she seemed unable to
stem the great flood of scandalous reminiscence once it had started.
Anecdote followed anecdote. I looked at her ladies and saw that some
restrained yawns, while others had that glassy-eyed look that comes
with trying to seem interested. I supposed they had heard all this
many times before.

"It has always been an open question whether Lord Fonteynis was
poisoned," Natalie said. "But I suppose when my daughter the lady
Floria is finally queen, she will have access to the archives, and we
can find out."

This statement so startled all Her Majesty's guests that none of us
knew how to respond. Her Majesty saw our expressions and laughed.

"Oh, ay," she said, "Floria will be queen. Doctor Smolt has cast her horoscope, and assured me this is true."

"Is it not against the law," I asked, "to cast horoscopes of the royal family, or to give out the hour of their birth?"

"Oh please," said Natalie, "I certainly know the hour when my own daughter was born. And I am assured that it was an auspicious hour indeed."

"Her Majesty speaks truly," said Smolt in his deep, ponderous way. He stared intently from one to another of Natalie's guests, as if judging our credulity.

From one of her ladies, I later learned the history of Doctor Smolt. He was a sorcerer and, being a necromancer, spoke to spirits. When Clayborne had rebelled, Smolt had become Berlauda's philosopher transterrene. The previous holder of that office, a venerable but tedious abbot named Ambrosius, had been willing to cast spells for the safety of Berlauda and the realm, but his holy office forbade him to cause harm through his magical arts, and Berlauda wanted magic that would blast her half-brother to ashes. Smolt was less scrupulous than his predecessor, and was employed for the express purpose of laying curses on Clayborne and his supporters. After Clayborne's defeat, for which Smolt was more than willing to take credit, he was dismissed and replaced with a monk, but the crown awarded Smolt a pension, and Natalie employed him and gave him a tower in which to conduct his experiments.

This seemed unwise to me, and I thought Smolt, with his black robe and staring eyes, was likely a mountebank.

The next day was sunny and fine, ideal for the journey, but the sense of our fellowship was that we should continue to enjoy Queen Natalie's hospitality. Natalie was enjoying our company and did not object. And so the day was spent in idleness, or rather in more games of dice or cards. The games played were simple, if not childish, and the sums wagered would have shocked the richest mercer in the land.

I could afford to lose, but I misliked losing to a mere cast of the dice and preferred a game with an element of skill. I joined a game of nine-men's-morris and won twelve royals, but then lost it again in a game of fox and geese, with seventeen of us playing—the eleven knights, Queen Natalie, and several of her ladies.

Afterward I settled into a game of imperial, in which—as the game involved skill and I had but a single opponent—I better fancied my chances. Yet Sir Brynley Wilmot, a knight of the Red Horse and the third son of His Grace of Waitstill, was a skilled card player, and after several hours' play, each of us having won a number of games, I managed to win but two royals, and only because he drank a deal more wine than I, and allowed me to trump his knave.

He gave me his note with ill grace. I think he viewed me as a capon ripe for plucking, and was willing to put up with my undistinguished ancestry if it promised amusement and money. Alas for him, I thwarted him of his pleasure.

Sir Edelmir Westley seemed to suffer the greatest losses in the gaming, but he lost with such easy grace that the others were probably encouraged to win more off him.

Stilwell's former queen gave us a very fine dinner, and then, after nightfall, a supper made largely of game caught in Her Majesty's own park. I heard talk going around the table of spending another day at Bonherbes, perhaps including a stag hunt in the park, but I'd had enough of this meandering, drunken adventure with a band of interlopers who would not treat me with civility, and so after the last remove I stood and called for attention.

I raised my glass and offered a pledge to Queen Natalie, whose noble generosity and hospitality, I said, was matched only by the grace, excellence, and charm of her person. The others thumped the table and cheered. After we drank, I addressed the others of the party.

"Gentlemen," said I, "it has been an honor and a pleasure to travel in your company. But I have set out to kill a fire-drake, and as I have pending business in the capital, I purpose no further delay. I will set out on this quest tomorrow after breakfast, and I hope the rest of you will join me."

Sir Brynley Wilmot spoke up, his pale mustaches bristling. "Who are you, Sir Quillifer, to decide on behalf of this company?"

"I do not decide for you, or for any of these gentlemen. I decide only for myself." I bowed toward Queen Natalie. "I hope that Her Majesty will provide me with one of her huntsmen to serve as a guide."

Her Majesty acceded, though clearly both she and her ladies had hoped to enjoy our company for a few more days. I was early to bed, after telling Rufino Knott and the others of my following to have the horses and wagon ready by dawn.

I encountered the other knights at breakfast. Many showed the ill effects of the previous night's revelry, and none were in any humor to speak to me. I finished as quickly as I could, praised again the charms and hospitality of our hostess, kissed her royal ring, and made my way to the courtyard, where my minions waited with my horses and wagon. Sir Edelmir Westley had arrived ahead of me and was already in the saddle, supervising his sumpter horses as they were packed.

It must be admitted that Sir Edelmir was a capable royal officer and had prepared his own part of the expedition with efficiency. He had brought along a half-dozen of his own henchmen from the royal stables, and they were accustomed to one another and to taking his orders, and did their work well and almost without speaking—and of course they had acted to save their chief from drowning.

("Henchman," by the way, is an ancient title used by the grooms of the royal mews, though as these fellows are available and handy, they are used for other tasks as well. The term dates from the time of the Sea-Kings, and combines "man" with "hengest," their word for horse. In exchange for this tidbit, you may pass the wine and kiss me.)

Sir Edelmir gave me a jaunty wave as I jumped into the saddle. I looked about the courtyard, dark in the shadow of the great house even though the sky had grown light, and saw the other knights' followers moving vaguely about their errands. I turned to Sir Edelmir.

"Shall we move on, and let the others catch up?"

"Her Majesty has not yet sent us her huntsman."

Doctor Smolt arrived first, padding into the courtyard in his black velvet robe. "I will cast spells for your success," he said, "and it will take three days."

I thanked him civilly, and he retreated to his tower to begin his chanting. In time the huntsman appeared, a gray-bearded lean man astride a dun cob, but by then most of the knights were ready, and we waited for the laggards and then set out in a troupe. I put myself with the huntsman in the lead and set a steady pace until noontide, when I allotted an hour for a cold dinner and a watering parade for the horses. Then I was back in the saddle for a long afternoon's riding.

We were very much in the country, and there were no inns. Under the bright, cool sun of winter, the land seemed prosperous enough: Sheep spotted the pastures, orchards lay on all sides, and the farms were snug and tidy. The great storm of that summer seemed to have spared this country, tucked in the shadow of the Cordillerie. The roads were fenced with hedges, and sometimes were mere sunken tracks. We were obliged to ford the rivers, and by afternoon were in the foothills of the Cordillerie, the long folds of mountains and steep hills that formed the spine of Bonille. Here there were no great fields, but lynchets only, with terraces stepping up and down the hills.

By this point the huntsman was out of his reckoning and regularly spurred his cob ahead to get directions. It seemed that the Princess Floria had greatly exaggerated the danger to her mother, for the worm was nowhere near Her Majesty.

Before nightfall we pitched camp in a field, and the grooms took the horses off for water. Soon fires were kindled, wine was set near the blaze in pots and leather jacks to warm. Pottage was prepared, and sausages and smoked meats were grilled on skewers. My crew set up my tent beneath an awning of sailcloth, and in my old cheviot overcoat I was as warm as a cat by the hearth. Goodman Knott played his guitar and sang "The Queen of Albiz," his fine tenor soaring over the camp.

Brynley Wilmot's eyes glittered firelight from the far side of the camp. "Sir Quillifer," he said, "I wonder if you will carve this ham?"

A warning note sang in my blood, clear as a trumpet call. I replied cautiously. "Do you not know how to carve?" I asked. "I had thought it was an accomplishment for all gentlemen."

"I practice rather at carving the enemies of Her Majesty," said Sir Brynley.

"A futile practice," I observed. "For Her Majesty in her wisdom has married the heir of our greatest foe, and now she has not an enemy in the world."

He glowered. "Yet I think you are more suited to carve than I."

"Then I must teach." I fetched a fork and a carving knife and walked around the camp to where Wilmot had draped himself in a folding chair by his own fire. One of his men had the ham on a skewer, with the trotter pointed skyward.

"First we must find you a trencher, Sir Brynley," I said. I cast about for a platter, or at least a slab of cheat bread, but then I saw the knight's armor laid out on a blanket by his wagon, where one of his following was oiling and polishing it. I snatched up the backplate, and laid it on Sir Brynley's lap. He gave a start and made to rise, but I put a hand on his shoulder "Not yet, Sir Brynley, for the lesson now begins."

I took the skewered ham from Wilmot's minion and dropped it on the backplate. "Now rest you," said I, "and pay attention, for I will slice you some fine collops." I showed him my knife, passing it close enough to have thinned his yellow beard. "Now you must first of all have a knife of fine steel," I said, "and keep it well sharpened. It need not be one of your thick heavy bilbos, for you will soon see that while my blade is thin and light, it slices very well. And for control, you must hold the knife with the thumb and forefinger steadying the blade."

I thrust my fork into the meat. "Now it is said that the trotter should be facing upward," I said, and touched the trotter with my knife. "But I find that is not the universal rule." I cut several long slices from the part of the ham closest to Wilmot's nose. Fine sizzling portions fell into the backplate. The scent of saffron rose in the air, for the ham had been cured in that spice, and its rind was golden.

When I had cut enough long slices to make a flat surface, I turned the ham so that it rested on the flat side. "Now you see I have made a fine rest for the meat," I said. "It matters not how the trotter points. And we may now proceed without accident. For accidents"—and here I casually held the knife before his face, the point making lazy circles—"accidents are all too common." I placed the knife against the meat. "Had this been warming longer before the fire," I said, "I would cut along the shank end, thus—" I made some thin cuts down to the bone. "But the joint has not been on the fire long enough to be heated all the way to the shank-bone, but it is warm in the outer layer only. So I must make some thin cuts along the surface. Cuts this thin take a fine eye and a steady hand, as you will observe."

All conversation in the camp had ceased. My lesson had become the object of all eyes. Goodman Knott's song had fallen silent. Wilmot, I could see, was turning scarlet as the cooking fire, and he was gnawing his lip beneath his pale mustache. Words burst from him like bubbles at a slow boil. "What—!" he cried. "What is this—"

"Be careful, Sir Brynley," I said. "You may do yourself an injury."

Wilmot snarled. "You, sir, are *nothing*! You are a base—"

I pointed the blade straight at his face. "Before such words as 'cullion' or 'barber-monger' pass your lips," I said, "you should reflect that I have a sharp knife, and you do not. I advise you to sit still, and learn your lesson."

I cut a long series of collops. Steam and scent rose from the backplate. Wilmot trembled in every limb, like an angry boar trapped in a pen. I stepped back.

"There you have it, Sir Brynley," I said. "You have a fine supper, and I hope you will enjoy it."

I began the walk back to my own fire, and then there was a crash as Wilmot leaped to his feet and hurled the backplate and the ham into the dust. "I will end your sneering now, you butcher's son!" He walked to where his armor had been laid out and drew his sword.

"Sneering?" said I. I backed away, keeping Wilmot always in sight. I stooped by my fire and picked up a jack of hot mulled wine, from which I then took a sip. At need I would hurl it in his face as he charged.

"I have not sneered," I said. "You asked me to slice your ham, and all these gentlemen are witnesses to your request." I pointed around the circle with my knife. "I obliged, and gave you a lesson in carving in the most civil way. Yet I am repaid with insults and threats. To this, these men are also witnesses."

I noticed, out of the slant of my eye, that the two sailors in my company had equipped themselves with whinyards, and that Rufino Knott had circled around just beyond the light of my fire, and that he carried a heavy falchion in his hand. If Wilmot ran at me, Knott could come in from the flank with a weapon weighty enough to take off an arm.

I had never thought to find a staunch ally in a minstrel, but I was pleased to find in my retinue such a loyal supporter.

Wilmot brandished his weapon. "Pick up your sword! I'll fight you!"

I was half-inclined to indulge him, for I was fed up with this clodpoll and his clodpoll friends, but I managed to restrain my temper, and reflected that murdering him would scarcely do me good outside the relief of my feelings.

"You have a dragon to fight first, Sir Brynley," said I. "And I, after you. An we both survive, and you wish to pursue a quarrel, I may oblige you. But until then, it seems we must endure one another."

The other knights stepped forward to calm Wilmot, and eventually he jammed his sword point-first in the ground and stormed off to his tent. Rufino Knott quietly put away the falchion and began again to play his guitar. I recognized the refrain to the Quillifer song, but Knott knew better than to sing it aloud.

I drank the mulled wine, and ate my own supper, and went to my tent. I took my carving knife with me, in case I needed to defend myself.

I was up at dawn for a cold breakfast warmed by a cup of brandy, but a rain squall struck us and turned the road to muck, and the party was obliged to wait a few hours for the lane to dry. During that time Queen Natalie's huntsman struck out on his own, and found someone who agreed to guide us to the haunts of the great worm. So before we set out, the knights donned armor, in case the drake descended on us, and the others kept weapons near to hand.

I rode my charger Phrenzy and wore the breastplate and burgonet I had worn at Exton Scales, with the dimples and creases where the usurper's bullets had nearly struck me down. I had my broadsword in its scabbard, carried a pollaxe across my saddle-bow, and bore on my back the large shield recommended by the duke. I covered myself with a thick woolen cloak, which kept me warm, and which my supporters would drench with canisters of water were we menaced by the fire-drake. More draperies covered Phrenzy, and I hoped he would not grow too hot as we traveled.

I took off my rings, put them in my saddlebags, and drew on thick leather gloves armored with articulated steel plates.

Sir Brynley Wilmot spoke only to his servants and looked at the rest of us with cold hauteur.

The squalls had passed, and the water-droplets that hung in the grass were turned to gems by the sun. We came upon shattered holly-hedges, which our guide said had been broken down by the dragon. The holly-berries were still bright red. Torn sheep lay in the fields.

"It is a vicious worm, sirs," said our guide. "For it kills for sport, more than it can eat."

We turned into a shadowed lane with rows of hornbeam on each side, the limbs of which had grown into an arch above us and gave the impression of a tunnel. The leaves had turned, and we were bathed in golden light as we advanced, but Phrenzy seemed to mislike the lane and rolled his eyes and snorted. I began to think he was scenting an enemy. Then our guide pointed out a place where one of the hornbeams had been knocked askew, and through the hornbeam hedge we could see the fire-drake itself, lying in a field spotted with its victims.

CHAPTER TWELVE

The dragon lay in the sun on a tawny field spotted red and white with murdered sheep. It rested on the grass in shimmering, tumbled coils, and it seemed to gleam with shifting colors like a fire-opal. I had seen that scintillation before, in that great serpent that rode the storm earlier in the year, and I knew it was a sign of the supernatural power that animated the worm. The drake was difficult to look at, and I did not care to look at it directly, but only from the slant of my eye, and even then I felt uneasy, and there was an eddy in my thoughts at the touch of the extramundane.

The dragon's head, which I judged to be as long as my leg, dripped red from its overlapping fangs. Its unwinking eyes were gold, and it had a feathery mane of scarlet.

Wilmot, who had won the sortilege and was the day's first sacrifice, let his servants douse him and his charger with cold water. His horse was a heavy-framed chestnut, a destrier of the sort that carried knights of legend, and Wilmot was armed cap-a-pie, encased in shining steel from his crown to his toes, with a surcoat in his colors of green and white. He carried a lance with a green-and-white pennon.

Water streamed off him as he rode through the hedge and onto the field. There he paused to check his gear, then spurred his destrier toward the dragon. At the last moment he lowered his lance to pierce his target.

The worm's motion was so fast that I could not properly see it, but the beast lunged out fast as a whipcrack, and Wilmot was hurled from his seat to land in a crash of steel four or five yards away. The lance shattered into a hundred splinters, and the big horse was bowled right over, landing on its back with a scream, its legs flailing in the air. Then the drake was away, whipping through the grass fast as lightning. It swarmed between beech trees planted atop a march dike, and vanished in a blizzard of scarlet leaves.

The rest of us stood stunned, and then Wilmot's servants dashed out into the field to succor their master, and the rest of us followed at a more thoughtful pace, contemplating what we had seen. The worm was at least thirty feet long, and as big around as a wine barrel. It moved like a snake, in fast, smooth, sinuous curves, and we disagreed about whether we had seen legs. Nevertheless, the reality of the monster was far more formidable than it had presented itself in our fantasies, and as we crossed the field, we all dwelt in silence and cold introspection.

When Wilmot's servants drew up his visor, we could see his eyes staring sightlessly at the sky. Yet his pale mustaches fluttered with his breath, and it seemed that he lived, despite having been rattled in his steel suit like dice in a cup, and had only been knocked witless.

The destrier was dying with a broken back and unable to rise. One of Wilmot's men dispatched it with a pistol shot to the brain.

Now that it seemed the knight was likely to live, we all looked toward the march dike, where the worm had disappeared. The huntsman carefully approached the dike, twenty yards distant from where the dragon had broken down the beech-hedge, just in case the drake lay in ambush by his own track. The worm had long gone, and the huntsman rode through the gap and followed the track. He came back after a brief time and reported that the beast was two fields away and had taken up residence in a pear orchard.

We looked at Dom Lorenso d'Abrez. "Well," he said in his Lorettan accent, "I must fight it then, yes. But I wonder how it is best to do it."

"Perhaps you should not ride at it directly," I said. "And ride a horse more nimble than that great destrier."

Some other suggested that he not use a lance. D'Abrez brooded on the suggestion for a moment, then shook his head. "I may be able to strike it in the eye." As he was a champion jouster, I supposed this was possible.

"Take a heavy hand weapon," I said. "Have you a pollaxe or a halberd?"

He had not, but he had a variety of lances, a heavy broadsword, and a hand-axe. He wore his heavy tilting armor, without the "grand guard," the extra concave steel plate bolted on the left side of the chest to serve as a kind of shield, and, viewing Wilmot sprawled on the grass, he decided to have his servants mount that steel plate. This was done in a few minutes.

Wilmot did not recover his wits. His servants stripped him of his armor, wrapped him in a blanket, and carried him down to the lane, where they put him in his wagon and turned for the nearest town.

Now we were ten.

With caution, we followed the worm over the march dike, which was only three or four feet tall, and then we advanced to the next hedgerow. This too was an earthen dike topped with a row of beech trees, and our horses crunched over a carpet of fallen beech-nuts as we peered between the brilliant red leaves into the pear orchard with its trees still full of brown-skinned Winter Nelis. The drake, bright as a beech-leaf, was easy to find amid the trees, its shimmering coils thrown out wide. It was at rest again, though I could not imagine it was unaware of us, for surely it would detect the rumble of our horses' hooves on the ground, perceived through the six or seven fathoms of serpent body stretched on the earth.

D'Abrez dismounted, and his servants swathed him in a thick wool cape with a hood and poured water over him. They brought a charger to replace his tourney horse and put on it a long wool dress and hood, belted the surcingles, then shifted the saddle and tack over. I wished to suggest at this point that he not go face the worm alone, but he was a proud knight of Loretto, a champion, and I decided it was not my place to say such a thing.

His groom helped him into the saddle, and then he chose a lance from those on offer. He was not wearing a heavy tilting helm, but a lighter bascinet with a pierced visor to give him a good view, and through the visor I could see his dark, frowning, thoughtful face. He was a professional, expert in combat, and I supposed he was making calculations that I could only guess at.

His servants drenched his horse with water. Then he took the reins in hand, turned his mount toward the gap in the beech-hedge, and easily leaped the dike.

I think he was one of the bravest men I have ever seen. Wilmot's courage I did not rate so highly, because he knew not what he was challenging; but d'Abrez had seen Wilmot struck down, and still he advanced alone to fight the fire-drake.

I watched the fight through the leaves of the hedge. D'Abrez came on slowly, keeping the pear-trees between himself and his quarry, and then at the last second put the spurs to his charger, lowered the point of his lance, and made a perfect, beautiful turn around a pear-tree to bring him face-to-face with the worm. There was a crack, the brilliant rainbow serpent-coils recoiled as if in surprise, and I was sure that d'Abrez had struck the dragon even though the lance had broken. He threw the broken lance down, reached for his hand-axe, and spun the horse about neat as an evolution in the horse-ballet. And then the grove lit with flame.

The fire was so bright it seemed to burn a great white hole in the world. I was blinded, and the air filled with screams. The hair on my neck rose at the sound. I blinked until my sight returned, and the first thing I saw was the horse and man both on fire, galloping blindly through the grove. Knight and charger screamed alike, d'Abrez in a deep howl, the horse a high-pitched shriek. They rebounded off pear-trees but kept flying, leaves and Winter Nelis tumbling to the ground in their path. I tore my eyes away from the horror to find the fire-drake, which for all I knew was charging us—but the worm was flying again, thrashing away through the grove.

The burning gallop ended when the horse fell and pitched its rider to the ground. We rushed through the hedge as quickly as we could, but by the time we arrived, there was no longer fire, but only smoke and death. The great champion of Loretto had been cooked to death in his coat of steel, and, cooking, he had screamed his lungs to tatters. I felt a great cold void where my heart should be, for I knew not how to view the shattering of such a titan.

The knight's servants had to wait for the armor to cool, and then they stripped it off the body. I wished not to look at it, nor to smell it either. I desired myself back in Howel, sipping brandy before my tame domestic fire, with a volume of Rudland's comic verse in my lap. Yet here I and the others were forced to cope with the occult fire of a great worm, a blaze from beyond the world.

More than one of d'Abrez's servants burst into weeping at the sight of the corpse. Yet weeping, they wrapped it in a blanket and carried it away.

Now we were nine.

The huntsman and his guide crept after the dragon and reported that it had gone to ground in a cave. We all advanced to view the lair's entrance and saw only a baleful darkness beneath an overhanging ledge. Before the cave climbed a meadow made for grazing, dotted with faded wildflowers, and with the sweeping track of the worm plain on the grass.

A cloud obscured the sun, and rain began to patter down. Drops rang off my helmet.

According to the sortilege, there were three knights who would attack the dragon before me, and their names were a testament to the erratic and often pretentious nature of Duisland spelling: Majerle (pronounced "Marley"), Molyneux (pronounced "Mollinju"), and Woolfardisworthy (pronounced "Woolsery"). I took them aside.

"Gentlemen," I said, "I make no imputation against your courage, and neither do I make no extraordinary claims for my own bravery, but I think I might see a way to cope with this monster. If you would oblige by deferring to me, I will take your place, and fight the worm myself."

They looked at each other. Woolfardisworthy scowled. He was a big man, with a russet-colored beard that he'd tied in little ribboned tails that draped over his gorget. He blew a contemptuous breath through the thick mustache that overhung his lip. "I will not have it said that my courage is any less than that of Dom Lorenso d'Abrez."

That put the others in a dilemma, for even if I did not dispute their courage, it was clear that Woolfardisworthy did. Majerle cast an appraising eye at the cavern. "Yet I should not care to go into that cave," he said. "Let us wait out the night, for the worm may come out, and then we can track it in the open."

Relief descended on me. The matter of courage was postponed till the next morning, which I found myself pleased to do. Truly, though I hope I put on a brave enough face, I was no happier in facing the monster than Majerle.

We brought up the wagons and sumpter horses and pitched our camp on the far side of a shallow stream. It was a sober, cold, wet company that cooked its supper and went early to bed. We stood watches all night, in case the drake attacked, and so I stood in the dark for some hours with rain pouring off my oilskins and my pollaxe in my hand. I knew not what we would do if the worm attacked, other than die.

The rain faded before sunrise, and we cooked our pottage and porridge over damp, smoking wood while gray clouds streamed high in the firmament. Wrapped in blankets for warmth, shaking the water out of our possessions, and the breath of our horses steaming in the chill air, no one seemed very eager for battle. Yet, when there was no longer any reason for delay, we began to arm and mount our horses. Majerle resolutely avoided my eye as we crossed the stream and began to climb the hill that led to the meadow and the cavern.

The grass had rebounded and no longer showed the track of the fire-drake, and there were no new tracks, so Queen Natalie's huntsman pronounced his opinion that the worm was still in the cave. Majerle looked from beneath his visor at the entrance shadowed by the great overhanging ledge. "Dom Lorenso may have mortally wounded it," he said. "I think it may be dead."

No one replied. Majerle took a halberd and stepped onto the field.

He was not a jouster and was dressed as a demilance trooper, with a breastplate over a thick suede buff coat and a burgonet with a full visor. He already wore a cloak for warmth, and he drew the hood over his head and let his men drench him with water. This had not helped d'Abrez, but perhaps Majerle would be more lucky.

He could not ride his charger into the cave, so he left his horse in the lane and advanced on foot. His cloak swept a dark trail on the dew-brightened grass. He did not aim directly for the cave, but took a roundabout way so as to avoid alerting the dragon. When he neared the entrance, he crouched low and peered around the corner into the darkness. Whatever he saw must have encouraged him, for he crept forward and prepared to descend into the cavern.

The cave lit up bright as the sun, and when the bright blooms faded from my eyes, Majerle was gone, leaving behind only that dark trail in the grass. The worm had taken him.

Now we were eight.

We looked at each other in silence, and then I turned to Molyneux. "Sir, I repeat my offer of yesterday," I said. "If you will defer to me in the succession, I will do my best to bring the worm to heel."

Woolfardisworthy made a scornful sound. "For you to advance," he said to me, "two knights will have to give way, and Molyneux may, but I will not. I will not let it be said that you have more courage than I."

Sir Edelmir Westley tried to intervene. "It is not a question of courage, sir," he said. "It is a question of killing this dragon. We have not laid a finger on this beast, and two men have died. It is not cowardice to admit that our plan has failed, and that we should attempt something else."

Woolfardisworthy folded his arms across his big chest and blew a contemptuous gust through his overhanging mustache. "I will not yield my place," he said. There was a silence.

"Well then," said Molyneux. "Cavaliers, rest you merry. I must hope that my shield will serve."

Again we went through the business of draping and dousing one of our number, and Molyneux strapped on his shield and took a cut-down lance in his right hand, to use as a short stabbing spear. The shield was no small buckler, but a large wooden mantlet of the kind used in sieges, for handgunners to hide behind. Molyneux had covered it with rawhide to keep it from bursting into flame. I viewed the unwieldy portable wall and thought it might serve as good protection against anything but the unworldly fires of the worm.

We watched with sinking hearts as he lumbered over the grass carrying his wooden wall. He dropped it on the grass before the cave, I think to catch his breath, and then he picked up the great shield and advanced upon the cave. No fire jetted forth, and Molyneux stepped over the threshold and vanished into shadow.

We waited. There was no sound, no fire, no clash of weapons. For all we knew, Molyneux had vanished from the very earth.

We were seven.

I turned to Woolfardisworthy. "Well, sir," said I, "your turn has come at last. I wish you joy in it."

He looked up at the cave beneath its overhang. His face had gone pale, and his eyes seemed big as blue platters. "Molyneux may have yet to engage," he said. "We should give him more time."

"He may be in trouble," I said. "You will have the honor of rescuing him."

He blew breath out through his thick mustache. "Let us have dinner first. I fight better on a full belly."

"Nay," said I. "It is your turn. You insisted on taking your place, and you would not yield it to another. Now you must follow Majerle and Molyneux." I pointed at the cave. "And after you have gone into the dark tomb that awaits you, I may do what should have been done first thing this morning, before two brave men died."

"I say again," Woolfardisworthy insisted, "that I fight better on a full belly!"

"I have had a belly full of *you*," cried Dom Nemorino d'Ormyl. "By the Pilgrim's nose, must I throw you into the cave myself?"

The wide blue eyes turned to me. "Do you truly know how to kill that monster?"

"I have an idea that may serve," I said.

Woolfardisworthy threw his hands up into the air. "At Sir Quillifer's insistence," said he, "I will yield my place to him."

I snarled at him. "The time to yield your place was an hour ago!"

Woolfardisworthy folded his arms across his armored breast. "I have decided," he said. "You may have my place. It is at your own request."

"Coward!" said Dom Nemorino. "Turd!"

Woolfardisworthy scowled at him. "These aspersions are immaterial. Once I have chosen, I am immovable!"

"I'll move you!" The Lorettan knight punched him over the ear with an armored fist. Woolfardisworthy clapped a hand to his head and reeled. "Fight me or fight the worm," said Dom Nemorino. "But I tell you I am more terrible!"

Perhaps I inadvertently saved Woolfardisworthy from being massacred, because I seized him by his gorget and the skirt of his cuirass and hurled him through the hornbeam hedge and onto the field, where he fell in a crash of steel. I threw his burgonet after him. "Draw your sword," I said, "and get you to the cave!" Never have I been so inclined to commit murder.

Woolfardisworthy picked himself up. "These affronts are unbecoming, incivil, and refractory," he said. "I have done nothing to provoke them but accede to Sir Quillifer's request."

"Oh I have had enough," said Sir Edelmir, and reached to one of the holsters on his courser and drew out a horse pistol nearly as long as his arm. He cocked it and pointed it at Woolfardisworthy's head. "Go to the cavern, sir, or die here in the field."

"They were fools," you say, with that narrow look in your eyes, and you are perfectly correct. I had nothing to do with these high-born, tautstrung cavaliers, and I had never wished to be in their company. It was of no consequence to me if any of them died, or if they killed each other. But when all is considered, it were better Woolfardisworthy died fighting the dragon than being cut down by his friends.

Woolfardisworthy stared at the barrel pointed between his eyes, and then he shrugged and blew air through his overhanging mustache. "Ay, if you insist," he said. "I will retrieve the matter, and you may surrender all the glory to me." He put on his helmet and dropped his visor over his face. He did not bother to clad himself in wet wool, but drew his sword and marched out onto the grass. From the center of the meadow he paused to survey the cave before him, then crouched and went off on a slant, like Majerle, as if to take the cave by surprise.

Yet when he reached the hedge that bounded the meadow, he did not begin to move along it toward the cave, but climbed over the march dike and vanished, leaving behind only a few beech-boughs waving in the wind.

I stared after Woolfardisworthy for a few seconds, and then I could not help but burst into laughter.

"He has gone for his dinner!" I said.

Sir Edelmir laughed as well. "Well, the whey-guts fustian has fled! He may walk to Howel with my blessing!"

It seemed that we were now six. Woolfardisworthy's servants were abashed at their master's flight and seemed not to know what to do. "Bide here for a while," I told them. "You may yet be of service."

Sir Edelmir looked at me. "Well, Sir Quillifer, as Woolfardisworthy is *perfugio*, it seems the lottery has at last fallen on you."

At last I would be allowed to do what I'd intended to do from the first. All it had cost was the lives of two men.

I turned to my followers. "Come, my brave engineers! You know your business!"

They busied themselves in my wagon. Two men brought out the carriage on their backs, and the strongest carried the leather-wrapped barrel. The cart's driver and Rufino Knott followed, bowling the spoked wheels before them.

The wheels were fixed on the axles, and then the gun was dropped into the carriage, and the capsquares bolted over the trunnions. In swift order, the ammunition was laid out before the gun, and the sponge, worm, and rammer laid on the grass nearby. The cartridges were brought out in a wooden bucket to keep the damp from the powder. Two of my sailors stripped the canvas top from my wagon, and a pair of swivel guns were fixed on the corners, and the slow-matches lit.

For I had long ago decided that Coronel Lipton's leather gun deserved a field trial against the dragon, fire against fire, and to that end had acquired a crew from the Loyall and Worshipfull Companie of Cannoneers, three apprentices under the command of the lank-haired journeyman called Peel.

While the cannon was being readied, I pulled my cloak about myself and consented to a drenching, and Phrenzy's dress soaked also. He misliked this and snorted in anger. I stayed away from his rolling eyes and threatening hooves, planted my pollaxe in the ground, and returned to the gun.

Peel handed me the linstock, with two burning matches set in its tip. "Load first with a carcass, Goodman Peel," I said.

A cartridge, a flannel bag filled with costly corned powder, was rammed down the short barrel, and then a wad. The carcass, sticky with tar, was rammed down next, and there was no need for a second wad, for the barrel was tilted upward and the munition would not roll out. Peel pushed the vent prick into the touchhole to pierce the cartridge, then lifted his powder horn and poured fine, corned powder into the hole.

I peered along the barrel. "A little to the left, Goodman Peel." One of the crew used a handspike to crow the trail around.

Peel looked along the barrel himself and adjusted the elevation with the quoin. I do not blush to admit that it was he who actually laid and commanded the gun, being a professional who had worked with Mountmirail and Lipton in the weapon's development. I held the linstock and pretended, for the sake of my dignity, to be in charge.

The knights looked at me with great surprise. Yet there had been cannon for two hundred years or more, for all that no one had entered legend through the use of such a weapon against a great monster.

"Gentlemen," I told them. "It may be that the gun may provoke the worm to attack us. In that case, we should retire behind the wagons, and let my shipmates here fly at the beast with their murderers. And if the drake continues to vex us, I think we should then attack it all together. The worm is so long each of us will have a fathom of serpent to ourselves, to hew as we may."

I looked along the short barrel again. The range was about seventy-five yards, which was point-blank, even for a small fieldpiece, and we could scarcely miss. I reached out with the linstock. "Stand back, friends," I said, and the gunners stepped away and clapped their hands over their ears.

Standing well to the side, I touched the priming powder with one of the burning matches on the linstock, and the gun went off with a clap and bounded back four or five feet. I was trying to spot the fall of shot, and I saw the carcass strike the underside of the overhanging ledge and rebound into the cave.

Gunpowder scent stung the air. Peel's crew leaped to their work. The gun was rolled back to its position, the sponge was dunked in water and run down the barrel to douse any burning flannel or tar, and another cartridge rammed down, and then a wad. Peel looked at me, a silent question on his attentive face.

"Bide a moment, goodman," said I. "But ready a roundshot."

Tendrils of smoke began to rise from the cave. The carcass was a type of ball shot covered with tar and filled with a mixture of sulfur, tallow, saltpeter, antimony, and other tools of the alchemist. In sieges they would be used to set fire to buildings, but I was interested more in the possibility of suffocation.

I looked at the knights and grinned. "We'll see if the worm needs to breathe!" I said.

Billows of white smoke rose from the cave. Perhaps fire was the drake's natural element, and it was basking in the flames like a dolphin dozing on the sun-kissed waves; but I thought the worm seemed more like an animal than an alchemist's salamander, and should not care to breathe sulfur for long.

I waited until the smoke began to grow thin, and then I fired a second carcass into the worm's lair. The art of making these munitions is inexact, but this particular carcass seemed more successful than the last, for the smoke fairly gushed from the cave with a great hissing noise. The leather gun was loaded with cartridge and wad, and I had it trained on the cavern entrance. Two gunners stood by, one carrying another carcass, the other a roundshot. I stuck the butt end of the linstock in the ground, took my telescope out of its case, and viewed the mouth of the beast's lair.

I hoped that I did not have to fire more than once or twice more, for Lipton had told me that his guns always burst sooner or later. Yet he had assured me that this particular gun was an improvement on the others, and I tried to take some comfort in that.

It was difficult to see anything properly amid the gushing, swirling, gray smoke, but a surge of blood prickled my arms as I thought I saw a dark shadow bob up in the cavern entrance and then duck down again. I said nothing, and waited for the worm to more plainly show itself. Then the drake heaved its great coils out of the cave and appeared in plain sight, its rainbow colors shimmering against the smoke, its head bobbing as it tried to make out its surroundings. Perhaps it was blinded by the sun, or the smoke had brought tears to its eyes.

It was about seventy-five yards away, point-blank range even for a small gun.

"Roundshot!" I cried. The six-pound ball was rammed down the leather gun's short barrel. I looked at Peel and gave a silent command with my eyes, and he jumped behind the gun to train it. His crew made a few fine adjustments, and Peel pushed the quoin in to lower the barrel.

"Now, sir!" he said, and I brought the linstock down.

The gun bounded back with a crash, and I saw the ball strike the worm just below its neck. For a brief moment there was frantic writhing, like a nest of snakes that had been stirred with a stick, and then the drake fell still. I ran for my Phrenzy and found Rufino Knott ready, bent over with his hands cupped. I put my boot in his hands, and he threw me up into the saddle. I reached for my pollaxe.

"Grape atop roundshot!" I called, in case my next stroke failed, and struck spurs to my horse. Phrenzy gave a ferocious snort and bounded up the meadow. The gunshots and the taste of powder had perhaps reminded my steed of his warhorse days, for he seemed more angry and more animated than he had been in years.

The gallop was over in an instant, and the fire-drake was stretched before us. A sulfur scent tainted the air. The body, with its shimmering rainbow scales, lay slack in its coils, and the beast's scarlet mane stretched on the damp grass. The fanged mouth snapped at the air, and the golden eyes rolled toward me, filled with malevolence. The drake was not dead, but stunned.

I realized as I dropped out of the saddle that I had forgotten my large shield and could not stand the beast's fire, and therefore I should not give it the chance to breathe on me. I jumped behind the head somewhat, raised the pollaxe in both hands, and brought the axe-blade down on the fire-drake's neck with the intention of severing the spine. The blade bit deep, and the serpent's great coils heaved up from the ground and snapped like whips. I jumped back to keep from being bowled over, and Phrenzy reared and struck the coils with his hooves. I did my best to locate the head in the coiling chaos and struck again with the axe-blade.

The fire-drake fell still, one golden eye staring at the sun. I stood with the pollaxe cocked, ready to strike again, but the scales' rainbow colors were already fading as the magic passed away. Phrenzy struck the worm with a disdainful hoof, then snorted and backed away.

The last of the carcass-smoke drifted away. I viewed the dead animal at my feet and saw that it had four small, rather delicate clawed feet. They seemed too weak to support the worm's great weight, and there were recesses in the body where the legs might be tucked when the beast writhed on its way like a snake. I supposed the claws were of use in climbing, or in dismembering prey.

There were also the remains of two leathery wings. They had been enough, I suppose, to support the young drake on its flight to Bonille, but would hardly sustain it once it had reached its full growth.

"Hurrah for Sir Quillifer!" The two sailors in the wagon led the cheers and fired their swivel guns into the air. "A salute to Sir Quillifer!"

I began the business of cutting off the dragon's head. Its ichor was dark and glittered like black diamonds. By the time I had severed the head, the other knights had arrived, having walked up from the lane with many of their servants. They marveled at the beast and pulled on its tail to stretch it to full length. I had been nearly right that each knight would have a fathom of worm to kill, for it was ten or twelve paces long. One of the servants came forward with a knife to dig the teeth from the dragon's jaw, and I told him to step away.

"The head is a gift for Her Majesty," I said. "I shall deliver it entire." I looked up and saw Sir Edelmir frowning at me.

"This is what you had planned all along," he said.

"Ay."

"We just got in your way."

I had no answer for that. *Gorge it with those idiots*, Floria had said, *and kill it while it's sleeping off the feast*. That was near enough to what had happened.

The cannon boomed, and I jumped at the sound, which was followed by the whine of brass shards singing. In salute Peel had fired the gun harmlessly toward the next field, but the weapon had burst under its double charge of roundshot and grape, and sent pieces of its barrel sawing through the air. None of us was hurt, but I sagged with relief that I had not had to fire the gun a fourth time.

And then I felt my heart lift. I had killed the deadly worm, and the world would have little choice but to take notice.

CHAPTER THIRTEEN

Though he return to Howel was accomplished with greater dispatch than the journey outward. I carried the worm's head in a sack in the wagon, and kept one of the claws as a memento. Another claw, one of the wings, and some scales I kept as a gift for the duke, to be placed in his cabinet alongside his carvings, coins, and other curiosities.

We bore as well a burden far more melancholy. We had found Majerle and Molyneux in the cave, partly devoured. As Woolfardisworthy had abandoned us, the remains were placed in Woolfardisworthy's wagon for transport to the capital. Woolfardisworthy's wagons and servants we kept for ourselves, in the middle of the convoy, so that he could not reclaim his belongings without confronting us. Along the way we commissioned a village carpenter to make some simple coffins, and the two fallen knights were given a better home.

The recreant Woolfardisworthy did not appear.

One night we spent as guests of Queen Natalie, who was as voluble and hospitable as before. Sir Brynley Wilmot, we discovered, was already lodging there. He had not entirely recovered his wits, and though he would walk and speak and knew his name, he could remember little else, and had no memory of the quest or his encounter with the dragon. He stayed in his room, waited on by his own servants. The others called upon him, but I did not, for I did not want him to recall the occasion of our quarrel.

Doctor Smolt admonished us. "I told you my spell would take three days," he said. "Yet you attacked on the second day, and lost two men."

"We lost two more on the third," I pointed out.

"I had not completed my spell," said he. "Sir Quillifer, you were fortunate to attack just as I had finished."

Success has a thousand fathers, I thought, *but failure is an orphan.*

When I left the divorced queen the next morning, I carried letters to her daughter and to friends at court.

The November weather was mild, for the Cordillerie blocks or weakens most of the winter storms that sweep in from the sea, and we made good time on the dry roads. It was the eighteenth of November when at last I bade farewell to the company at Oliver's Cross and made my way to Rackheath House, where Master Stiver promptly ordered me a bath, and set a plate of wine and cakes in my study.

There I paid off the cannoneers and gave them some extra silver to drink my health; and I gave a generous vail also to those already in my employ, like the sailors and my groom Oscar. To Rufino Knott, I paid the agreed sum, and while I ate and drank, he revealed the new verses to the Quillifer song he had composed on the return journey.

> *Quillifer, Quillifer, dragon-lord singular*
> *Brought to the battle the weight of a gun*
> *Quillifer, Quillifer, knight-errant counselor,*
> *Touched fire to powder, and the worm he did stun*

There was more in this vein, in which I inflicted vengeance for the death of the knights. I gave Knott more silver to play the song at Ings Magna and in the town, and then I made him another offer.

"Would you like more steady employment?"

He viewed me with surprise. "As what, sir? Do you wish me to recruit an orchestra, or to form a band of minstrels?"

"I do not at present have a varlet," I said. "I will give you the job if you want it."

Knott was surprised. "I do not know what a varlet's duties might be."

"You would be my body servant. You would look after my clothes, whet my razor, fetch my shaving water, make my ink, run my errands, tune my guitar, deliver my letters, and otherwise exert yourself to make my life comfortable."

"I have little training in such things."

I picked up a lemon cake and waved it. "I am an easy master. I would hardly starve you at all, and would beat you only on alternate days. Of course, I would still expect lessons on the guitar."

"And my wages?"

I ate the cake while I considered. "We'll start at ten crowns per quarter, not counting vails and special commissions. Plus, of course, you will have a room in my house that is cold only in winter, your livery will be at my expense, and you will enjoy the privilege of dining with the other servants, and the joy of lording it over all downstairs but the cook, the steward, and the housekeeper, who share with me the duty of beating you when your inconstant nature requires correction."

Knott affected to consider. "Sir, your liberality is beyond description."

"There is one condition only, and it is your discretion. Servants are the masters of tale-telling, rumor, and scandal, and as you will have unequaled access to much that is personal to me, I desire that my business remain private until I choose to reveal it."

Knott nodded. "Yet may I have leave to praise your ingenuity in regard to the dragon? And perhaps to sing the song for your staff?"

"You may praise me as you like." I gave the matter thought. "Yet I pray you, keep the praise within the bounds of plausibility. I have not scaled the walls of the Castle Perilous, nor retrieved the Seven Pearls from the Floating Island of the Fay, nor ridden the Comet Periodical through the sky."

He smiled. "I'm sure it is only a matter of time."

"It is indeed a rare master who basks in the admiration of his servant." I took a sip of moscato bianco, sweet as a summer strawberry, and considered what I had heard about Lord Edevane, the queen's spymaster. "It may be that someone will ask you for information about me. He may offer to pay you. In that case, you may take the money, but report to me, and we shall decide between us what you shall tell him."

Knott nodded. "That is prudent, Sir Quillifer."

"Now, if we have reached agreement in the matter of your employ, please report to Master Stiver, have yourself enrolled in the books, and then have someone show you to my wardrobe. I go to court this afternoon, and I wish my costume brushed and laid out for me."

Knott put a hand to his breast and bowed. "I obey, my master."

Hiring Rufino Knott and paying off my gunners had given my bath-water enough time to heat, and so I went to my bath and emptied the copper reservoir into Lord Rackheath's marble tub. I thoroughly enjoyed scrubbing the scent of horse and saddle-leather off my person, and, with the aid of a steel mirror, I shaved, after which I went to my chamber, where Knott and one of the footmen had laid out a selection of clothing. I chose a brilliant blue doublet of watered silk and matching trunks, finely contrasted with white silk hose and linen, matching the blue and white of my banner. I told Knott to make himself presentable and bring his guitar to the boathouse, and while I waited for my boat's crew to assemble, I skewered the fire-drake's head on a half-pike I had found mounted in a display of weaponry in Rackheath's great hall.

My boat's crew turned out in livery, blue and white like my flag and my person, and they took me along the lakeside to Ings Magna.

The air was balmy with the scent of autumn flowers. The lawns that ran down to the river were filled with courtiers brilliant as butterflies, and I saw that the day being so fine, Their Majesties had decided on a day of lawn games. So I summoned my boat's crew, who in their livery looked very like an escort, and, with Knott, I carried the dragon's head past the games of bowls, of lawn billiards, of battledores and shuttlecocks, of shovel-board, of quoits and lawn darts, to where Queen Berlauda stood over her mallet on the palle-malle court. I had with my parade attracted a large crowd, and I led them to the royal presence, where I dropped to one knee and pulled off my cap.

"Your Majesty—" I began, but I saw that Berlauda was concentrating on a shot, and I fell silent while she gave the wooden ball a solid hit with her mallet. She failed to make her iron hoop, and the ball rolled out of bounds.

"It is my fault you were distracted, Majesty," said I. "You should take the shot again. But while someone fetches your ball, please allow me to present the head of the fire-drake that lately spread terror in the Cordillerie."

The royal blue eyes looked down at me in benign surprise. "We were told that you were killed," she said.

I had not expected that answer. "The report was, at best, premature," said I. "But three of our party were slain, and another injured. Dom Lorenso d'Abrez was the first to fall, and—"

Here I fell silent for a moment, for the death of the great champion caused a stir in the crowd. "We are saddened," said the queen. "He was a doughty man-at-arms."

I then reported the deaths of Molyneux and Majerle, and Wilmot's injury.

By the time I finished this narration, the crowd had grown, and now included King Priscus. "And you killed the beast yourself?" he said.

"I cut off its head, Your Majesty," I said, "but prior to that, I stunned it with a roundshot from a cannon."

There was a stir in the crowd. The king viewed me with some surprise. "You brought a cannon in your train?"

"It was a leather gun, designed by Coronel Lipton of your Royal Regiment of Artillery. It is small and light, and required only three men to bring it into the field."

"We have seen such a gun," the queen said. "Coronel Lipton has shown it to us. We found it winsome, as guns go." She approached the drake's head and examined the dagger teeth and the lifeless golden eyes. "How large was the animal?"

"It was more than twelve yards long, Your Majesty, and nearly a fathom across at its widest part."

"Most formidable!" she said. "We are gratified that you returned without further mishap."

"Thank you, Your Majesty."

Berlauda called for grooms to bear the head away, and then she picked up her mallet and returned to her game of palle-malle. "Fifty royals I make my hoop," she said, and as soon as one of her company took the wager, Her Majesty took her shot again, and again missed.

Fifty royals vanished, I suppose, from the treasury.

"Well, Sir Keely-Fay," said Priscus. "It is very good that you read the rule book, yes? *Caw-caw-caw!*"

Pleased with his witticism, and also with hearing that witticism praised by his retinue, he strolled away.

I rose from my kneeling position and brushed soil from my white hose. Though the royal couple seemed to have lost interest in my adventure, there were still a great many in the crowd who wished a more thorough account, and this I was pleased to offer. Rufino Knott, strolling over the lawn, found an audience for his ballad.

After relating my tale several times, I found myself dry, and went in search of refreshment. I got a glass of cider from one of the refreshment tables, and, turning away, I saw Lady Westley, who stood on a path from the palace, framed by a pair of topiary shaped to resemble rearing hounds. I paused for a moment to appreciate the sight. Her gown was a deep red, almost purple, and in the shadow cast by the great bulk of the palace seemed almost black. Her lustrous face and hands seemed to rise from the shadows about her like pearls coming up from the sea. I saw that she wasn't wearing her yellow diamonds, or any other jewelry beyond a few rings, and that she seemed to have paused on the path, uncertain of her next step. I approached and saw that her eyes were rimmed with red.

"My Girasol," I said, "are you distressed? May I be of service?"

She looked at me. Her eyes glittered with frustration. "I'm *furious*," she said. "There was a report that you and my husband were killed. So I went to our house to change into mourning, and while I was there, my husband arrived on the doorstep."

"The queen mentioned something about such a report. Who gave it?"

I thought I knew the answer before she gave it. "A knight called— was it Woolsey? He arrived this morning and said he was the only survivor of your party, because in the fight with the dragon he'd been knocked into a river, and was thus saved from the drake's fiery breath, while the rest of you were consumed." Her gaze turned fierce. "And he said it was all *your* fault, for your cowardice disordered the company and caused them to miss their strokes."

I laughed at Woolfardisworthy's audacity. "And your husband told you about Woolfardisworthy when you met him, did he not?"

"Ay, he did."

Woolfardisworthy must have heard the leather gun firing, I thought, and assumed it was the sound of the dragon annihilating us. He had felt free to return to Howel and spin his tale of heroism and survival.

Lady Westley's blue eyes darkened. "I came back to the palace to slap his face, but I couldn't find him."

"Leave the slapping to me," I said. "I'll howster him out."

"My husband also seeks him." She looked at me, her red-rimmed eyes searching. "Do you think Edelmir knows that we are lovers, Heliodor?"

"I said nothing that might give him any misgivings. Nor was his behavior in any way suspicious."

"He told me I may not buy more gems from you. He said that we could not afford it, but that is nonsense, for though we have borrowed, it is against my inheritance, which will clear our debts once it is paid."

I thought about how those cavaliers so casually wagered great sums in absurd games of chance, and how gracefully Sir Edelmir had lost, so gracefully that one might think he'd had a deal of practice at losing. I also thought that I would like to know the details of Lady Westley's inheritance, and how and when and under what circumstance it would be paid.

"He lost at cards on the journey," I said. "I do not know how much, but the sums wagered were not small."

She was troubled. "He must have lost a great amount."

"Perhaps it is nothing, and he was so angry at Woolfardisworthy's malicho that he diverted some of that anger on you. But you should ask him for an accounting of how much the two of you owe. It was he who brought up the matter, after all."

Her fine, level brows drew together. "I see that I must," she said.

I took her hand. "I hope to see you soon, Girasol. But I should find this Woolfardisworthy before he can work more mischief, and before your husband murders him in front of witnesses."

As I departed, I cast my eyes over the revelers on the lawn. The sun was far in the west, and the warmth of the day was fading. Many of the courtiers had gone indoors or gone home. I hadn't seen Woolfardisworthy on the lawn that day, so if he were still here, I reasoned he was indoors, and I thought I might know where I could find him.

I entered the palace and went up the grand marble stair with its gilded mirrors, and found myself in the midst of a series of parlors, all filled with gamesters. I passed through a door and found myself at a table where courtiers were playing at dice. At the far end, the Count of Wenlock laughed behind a pile of crowns, a leather die-cup in his hands. He looked up at me and scowled.

"There are only gentlemen here, Quillifer," he said. "You are not wanted."

I gave him a cold bow. "If my gold is so tainted by my person that you would not have it in your purse, I shall withdraw."

I went in the other direction and passed through two parlors before I found Woolfardisworthy in a scene of merriment, playing at fox and geese with a stack of silver crowns in front of him. I watched him for a while as he basked in his glory, and then his eyes turned to me and grew wide. I smiled and donned my hearty-lad face, and walked around the table to give him a hearty thwack on the shoulder.

"I find you thriving, sir! After such a submersion, I would have thought to find you suffering a quinsy, wrapped in blankets and with your feet in a bath of hot water."

He gave me a calculating glance. "I am tolerably well."

"We had feared you strayed in the foothills and lost, but now I find you here, amid a host of admirers, all enthralled by your tales of martial glory. Your friends will be delighted to know you thrive so—in fact I know of six brave knights even now searching the palace, who desire nothing so much as to *meet* you." And on the word "meet" I punched him with my big fist between the shoulder blades—not such a blow as to be considered battery, but hard enough to rattle his ribs.

He took my meaning, for "meeting" was a term for a private encounter, an affair of honor with bright, sharp steel. He rose from his seat. "Perhaps I shall go find them, then." He made a gesture toward the crowns on the table. I put a hand around his wrist.

"Nay, sir. The game is not over. I will finish it for you." I guided him toward the door. "Perhaps the back stair," I suggested, "would best suit your purpose."

I took him through the crowd to the stairway door. His expression was wondering, and he puffed air through his overhanging russet mustache, but things were moving too quickly for him, and he never regained his bravado while I rushed him through a series of drawing rooms. "This will take you to the water gardens," I said, "and from there you may find a boat to take you home." I pushed him through the door onto the landing. He looked at me, poised on the verge of thanking me—but something stopped him, for I had no reason to help Woolfardisworthy, and he knew it.

I looked about and listened, and no one was on the stair, or near us; so I took hold of his collar and his belt and hurled him head-first down the stair. He landed with such a great crack that I thought his skull had shattered a sandstone block. I left him a motionless, huddled figure on the landing and returned to the game, where I took his place and won eighty crowns.

"His luck was in," I said, as I pocketed the money.

I understand he did not die, but broke his crown and some other bones, and was found the next morning by a footman. The staff of the palace is experienced at removing such embarrassments as drunken courtiers who fall and suffer injury, and a surgeon was called and accompanied him home in a litter. Anything after that is rumor, for I never saw him from that day to this.

You are amused. "Your ruthlessness is exemplary," you say, "but why did you soil your hands with him? The others would have ended him for you."

I contemplate your question. "I think my loathing got the better of my reason. I simply could not abide him. And after all, I had just killed a dragon—one runagate knight was small by comparison."

Your deep-voiced laughter rings like water pouring along a stream. "You drove him like a sheep to slaughter. I know you, Quillifer—you prefer to humiliate your enemies, not kill them. You leave them raging and impotent. It is by far the most superior form of revenge."

"I am but a low-born knight," I say. "Revenge is a luxury I cannot afford."

Again that low laugh. "And yet you rise, and leave in your path the broken fortunes of lesser men. If you had not so fittingly degraded those who despised you, I could not love you."

"Well," I say, "I must then accept your admiration, and take pride in hurling wretches down stairs and dropping hams in the laps of arrogant cavaliers. But that seems poor enough in comparison with what we are about to attempt."

"True." There is a smile in your black eyes. "Your fortune is in the wind. You must seize it, or go down."

"As always, my dearest." With a kiss. "I will comply with your desire."

I was going down the great mirror-walled stair in the palace when I encountered Sir Edelmir Westley coming up. He offered me his easy laugh.

"You might have waited, Sir Quillifer," he said, "for us all to assemble before you presented your trophy to the queen."

"I wanted to get rid of it," said I. "It was beginning to stink."

He waved a hand. "Perhaps it is best. The rest of us would have been mere auxiliaries." He peered up the stair.

"If you are looking for Woolfardisworthy," I said, "he is not in the rooms above."

He gave a twist of his lips. "I'll stick a knife in him, an I find him."

"He has probably fled by now."

He started up the stair. "Is there gaming? Perhaps—"

I restrained him with a hand on his arm. "I left your lady in some distress," I said. "You should take her home."

He considered this. "Ay, you are right. Woolfardisworthy's tales gave her a dreadful blow."

I took his arm as we descended and left him on the lawn to find his lady. I rounded up my sailors, who had made free of the beer and cider, found Rufino Knott where he played with an impromptu orchestra, and took my party and myself across the lake. I found my featherbed as welcoming as I remembered it.

In the morning I was readying myself for exercising my boat's crew on the lake when, to my vast surprise, the queen's private secretary was announced. I told Master Stiver to bring Lord Edevane to the parlor and met him there in my buff jerkin and baggy sailors' trousers.

"I apologize, my lord," I said. "I'm not in a proper state to receive visitors."

"That is quite all right," he said in a dry, soft voice. "After all, I came unannounced."

"May I offer refreshment?"

He offered a cold-eyed smile. "I bring an offer from Her Majesty. An you accept, we may raise a glass afterward."

In the most congenial way Edevane relayed Berlauda's offer. I accepted, and we pledged Her Majesty's health.

So it was that later that day, in front of all the court, I knelt before Queen Berlauda in the Chamber of Audience and placed my hands between hers. I swore to be a true and loyal liegeman to herself and to her heirs and successors, that I would be faithful and bear true allegiance, that I would honestly and sincerely defend Her Majesty, her heirs, and successors, against all enemies, and that I would sincerely and to the best of my ability fulfill the duties of my new office. A courtier placed a chain about my neck, and I rose no longer a free man, but a royal officer.

Tomorrow I will shatter that oath, and shake the monarchy, I hope to death.

And I will do it for you, my love.

CHAPTER FOURTEEN

L ord Warden in Ordinary Against Monsters," said Princess
Floria. "You would seem to be rat-catcher to the realm."

"The rats may be somewhat larger than any you may
have seen in the palace," I said.

"Possibly," Floria said, "but many of the rats in the palace are man-sized."

I was still in the bustling Chamber of Audience, crowded with
people come for the Estates General. The murmur of business echoed
from the vaulted ceiling. I stood before a brilliant tapestry of a heroic
Emelin II leading a storming party at the Siege of Avevic. My friends
had been offering their congratulations until they were shuffled aside
at the appearance of royalty.

Floria was accompanied by two of her ladies, Countess Marcella,
the regal Aekoi, and the disdainful Elisa d'Altrey, whose upper lip
curled in a way that suggested I might reek of offal. I looked at the
princess, who wore a gown of royal scarlet and sleeves of a particularly vivid shade of blue, and I noticed the star sapphire that graced
the helve of a lacy gold pomander that hung from her belt.

"I see you have found a use for that old doorknob I sold you."

"I did," said she, "but it put me to more inconvenience than I desired. Its color would not complement any of my clothing, so in order to wear it, I had to commission this gown, with its kirtle and virago sleeves of blue."

"I'm flattered that the stone was able to justify such an exercise in taste and beauty."

Floria fixed me with a narrow-eyed look. "It's meant to flatter *me*, not you."

"And it succeeds, Highness. Though," I offered, "to save you such trouble in the future, when next you search for gems, let me see your gowns first, and I will try to find something more suitable."

"I see," said Floria. "You wish to add dressmaker to your baffling series of occupations."

I waved a hand. "I cannot devote all my hours to monster hunting." Mistress d'Altrey gave a sniff, as if she expected to soon find me crawling through Her Highness's petticoats. I looked at her ladies. "Mistress Ransome is not among you. Is she in Kellhurst, building her observatory?"

"Ay," Floria said, "the work is beginning."

I looked at the two ladies. "Do either of you gentlewomen have such projects?" I asked.

Countess Marcella tilted her head at a graceful angle. "I will not be in Duisland long enough for any such project to conclude. Though if you wish to turn shipwright and build me a boat to take me home, you would have my thanks."

"You are stranded, Countess?"

Floria grinned. "Surely you mean, 'Are you *naufrageous*?'" she said.

The princess's interruption failed to ruffle Marcella's serenity. "I am not so much stranded," she said, "as waiting for the right ship."

I smiled. "But aren't we all of us waiting for such a ship?"

The countess nodded. "That is apt."

I turned to Elisa d'Altrey. "Do you wait for a ship as well, mistress?"

The disdainful lip curled. "If Her Highness is so minded as to build me a ship, I will sail in it."

A page appeared and bowed first to the princess, and then to me. "Lord Edevane's compliments, sir," he said, "and he would see you in his cabinet, at your convenient."

"Well." Floria's hazel eyes looked up at me. "I think you are about to be introduced to your first monster."

"Hardly my first, Highness."

"In any case, I hope you survive the encounter." She nodded and turned from me, then turned back. "Though it pains me to acknowledge that as you have maintained your existence in this world, I must pay the hundred and ninety royals I owe you."

I bowed. "I apologize for my continued existence, Highness."

She swept on, like a sprightly little ship, with her two ladies in convoy. Friends closed about me again, to congratulate me, while others hovered about, calculating how much they would profit from a friendship with a lord warden in ordinary. I could have told them, but decided they should discover the answer for themselves.

I let the page conduct me to Baron Edevane, and on my way to his cabinet I passed through his outer office, where a number of men in velvet gowns and skullcaps worked in silence at their desks, surrounded by shelves piled with papers neatly wrapped in red or blue ribbon. No other color ribbon was visible.

Her Majesty's pale principal secretary rose from his desk to greet me and told the page to pour me a goblet of moscato. "Lord Warden, I wish to give to you your first commission," he said. "Please take a chair and read it."

His voice was soft and measured, and I found myself leaning forward in order to hear him. He handed me a cardboard folder, with papers, tied in blue ribbon.

I sat, sipped the sweet wine, untied the ribbon, and read a letter from the lord lieutenant of Inchmaden, on the far coast of Fornland. His county had been afflicted with an infestation of iron birds, fierce raptors the size of eagles and made of metal—vicious, unnatural fowl that devoured crops, attacked sheep and calves, and perched in trees in such numbers that limbs were broken and the trees ruined. The birds were ravenous and repelled the missiles of expert hunters. Their beaks and talons were so sharp that they could cut their way out of nets in only a few minutes. The lord lieutenant had attacked the birds with his militia, but the birds had flown away. Occasionally a hackbut loaded with steel shot might injure one, but then came the trouble of hunting down and killing a wounded, vicious animal that came complete with its own armor. The lord lieutenant asked for aid from the crown.

I returned the document to the folder and turned to Edevane. His dead eyes looked at me through his thick spectacles.

"Your lordship, do you know if the iron birds have been seen before?" I asked.

"I'm afraid not, Lord Warden."

I frowned down at the cardboard folder and its dangling ribbon.

"You said yesterday that my office had been vacant since before King Stilwell's time," said I.

"The wars of the time took up all the crown's attention," said Edevane. "The lords lieutenant were left to handle the matter on their own. But—" He offered a thin, considered smile. "The request from Inchmaden came at the same time as news of your success with the fire-drake. It seemed a fortunate coincidence, and I persuaded Their Majesties to make your appointment."

"I thank you for your consideration, my lord," said I. "Perhaps you know if there is any archive of correspondence from any of the previous wardens?"

"I am unaware of any."

"Because it occurs to me that we are sadly ignorant of the proper tactics to be used against these chimerae. If there were an archive of what contrivances had been employed against monsters in the past, and what success had been achieved against what threat, then we would be better armed against future events."

Lord Edevane considered this idea, the finger-pads of his right hand tapping against those of his left. "It is my experience," he said, "that while documents are often misplaced, they rarely go missing forever. I will instigate a search."

"I thank your lordship. Should you find any, could you send them to Rackheath House?"

Again his lordship offered me his considered smile. "I cannot loan state papers on such terms," he said, "but I can arrange for you to view them here."

"May I bring a scrivener to copy them?"

"So long as the originals remain."

"Thank you, your lordship."

Edevane looked at his cup of moscato, then decided against drinking it. "May I write to the lord lieutenant that you will soon arrive?"

"I will take the business in hand immediately."

As the interview seemed to be over, I finished my moscato and rose. Ever polite, Edevane also rose to his feet.

"Please leave the lord lieutenant's letter with me," he said.

I returned it to his desk and tied up the blue ribbon. "I have seen documents in blue ribbon," I said, "and in your outer office I saw documents in red ribbon. May I ask if the color is significant?"

"Blue ribbon is used for matters that are still in progress," said Edevane. "Red ribbon for those matters which have reached a happy resolution."

"An admirable system, my lord."

As I made my way out, I wondered if the happy resolution involved the spilling of any liquid matched in color by the red ribbon.

My answer came a few hours later, when I heard of the fall of Lord High Admiral Mardall, who had lost his office and been carried off to the prison at Murkdale Hags.

When I'd had my interview with Lord Edevane, his men had been breaking down the admiral's door.

I know what you would say about the admiral's fall. *The more room at the top, the more room for us to advance.* And I suppose it matters little to me, for I had never met the lord admiral, and I suppose he was little better than other politicians.

Yet it seemed a shame for him to be so singled out, when so many others could be hanged with perfect justice.

"Ay," said Lipton, "my lord admiral objected to Their Majesties' plans to halve the funds for the navy."

"Why should they do that?" asked the engineer Mountmirail.

"The chief purpose of the navy is to protect us from Loretto," Lipton said. "The queen has married Loretto's heir, and our country no longer needs such protection. Or so they reason."

"The high admiral is one of the great offices of state," said I. "Her Majesty could have merely replaced him. Why drag him to Murkdale Hags?"

"He will be accused of peculation, sure. Those to whom he awarded contracts for supplying the navy and building its ships expressed their gratitude, sure, and in good silver."

"But that is the case with all the great officers, and most of the minor ones," I said. "There are perquisites and sweeteners customary to each office. For why would anyone serve the state, except to make himself rich?"

"Mardall was a great sea-captain," said Lipton, "and fought with the late king in all his wars. With a man as popular as he, it were better to kill him than to permit him the freedom to rally his friends and engage his enemies." His lips twisted as if he were tasting something foul. "This is Lord Edevane's work," he said.

"I hope you are not so outspoken elsewhere," said I. "You should be wary in mentioning that name, for your own safety."

Lipton cocked a bushy eyebrow. "It's *your* safety that concerns me, youngster. For now you are an office-holder, and under Edevane's eye. If you offend him, or Her Majesty, or anyone powerful—and of course you already have achieved a reputation for doing exactly that— you could be mewed up, or your poll clipped."

"That could be true whether I held an office or not," said I. "And as for peculation, I have no idea why anyone would offer me a bribe to fight monsters, or how I could extort one."

"For a courtier," said Lipton, "you have a very small imagination."

We were in Mountmirail's workshop, set in an old foundry north of the river. A turgid canal that ran beneath the window filled the air with its fetor, and the stench vied in my senses with the hot greasy reek from the forge that had been set up under an awning in the court behind the building. One of Mountmirail's assistants was hammering out a piece of iron on the anvil, and another sat at a scarred wooden table, working with feathers and glue.

"Your grinder is complete, sir," said the engineer. Mountmirail pulled a tarpaulin off the machine. "You wanted an engine that will grind your substance to a finer powder, and so you see I have created a chute that feeds the coarse grind from the old machine directly into a second grinder." He picked up a wooden scoop and thrust it into the hopper that contained the finer product, then let a thin stream fall through the air. "'Twould make a fine ink, if ink is what you are after. Though I cannot see what you would want with so much ink."

"I would like three more of these engines," I said.

"Erskine would be happy to make them for you," Mountmirail said, and nodded toward the assistant at the forge. "But he must finish this other project first, for we are repairing damage to the old temple of Horagalles. A wall has cracked apart, and we are making iron staples to stitch it back together."

"Does Horagalles still have worshippers here in Howel?" I asked "Or has the temple been converted to some other purpose?"

"People still worship the Old King," said Lipton. "But it's hard to find priests, because men with ambition want advancement, and advancement comes only from Their Majesties, who disparage the old gods and hold to the path of the Compassionate Pilgrim."

"It is a grand old building," said Mountmirail. "The largest temple ever built here. But it's in poor repair, for it's in a poor part of town, and the god's followers are mostly poor. The statue of the Old King is quite wondrous, though, made of gold and ivory, and sapphires for eyes. You should visit it, on a sunny day when you can see it properly."

"I shall." I looked at the assistant who was gluing feathers to a wooden frame. "What are you making here?"

"A flying bird." Mountmirail went to a rack and took down a bird-shaped machine, about the size of a thrush. He wound the mechanism with a twist of his fingers, and then tossed the bird into the air. At once it began to thrash the air with frantic beats of its wings, and to my immense surprise the bird began to bound through the air, darting high amid the blackened old roof beams. It seemed to have no sense of direction, for it ran into the beams and the walls, and then fell; but it eventually recovered and flapped off on a new course.

While the bird was still darting through the air, Mountmirail sent a second aloft, and then a third. I began to hear twitters and tweets, and for a moment I thought the birds were calling aloud, and then I realized that the engineer's assistant was making the sounds by whistling.

The first bird began to falter, and Mountmirail caught it as it fluttered gently down, and it beat out the last strokes of its wings in the engineer's arms. He likewise caught the other two, and then put them on a table for our inspection. Once we were able to look at the machines, the little gears and cogs and eccentrics were plain to see.

"They are powered by a spring," he said, "of the kind used in a wheel-lock pistol. Goodman Dowd, yonder, is working on an improved version that will sing as it flies, and without Dowd's whistling. But there is no real purpose to the thing; it is merely a toy—and an expensive one, for those gears must be made by workmen, and the spring alone is costly."

"You don't think you could make one large enough to carry a man?" Lipton asked.

"Ay, I could," said the engineer. "But what would make it go? A spring would not be powerful enough—nor would a man, I think."

"There is a place where such toys would be popular," said I. "And that would be at court. But no—do you know Master Blackwell, of Roundsilver's Company?"

Mountmirail blinked at me. "I don't think so. I've never been to the theater."

"Never?" I was astonished. "You have never seen a play?"

"Should I?"

"Well, my friend," I said, "you should know that many plays contain wonders, such as gods flying down from the sky, or ghosts rising from below the floor, or chimerae appearing onstage, or transformations from one sort of being to another. And he who can engineer the greatest wonders will have employment and fame. Now if we can persuade Blackwell or some other poet to write a play on the theme of birds, and if your birds are set in flight over the audience, while the actors appear in bird costumes designed wondrously by you, then I flatter myself that your fortune will be made, and your fame also."

Mountmirail pondered this. "I may have to view a play," he decided.

I picked up one of his little birds and viewed it. "I have heard of some other metal birds," I said, "and these are not pleasant toys."

I told Mountmirail of the iron birds now flocking to Fornland's coast, and asked if he could imagine a remedy. His broad face turned thoughtful. "Larger hackbuts," said he, "with larger bullets of fine steel to crack the armor."

"I should not care to pay the cost of equipping a company of militia with such weapons," said I. "Especially as they would be useful only for this one purpose."

Mountmirail swept aside the cloud of red hair that shaded his eyes. "Chain shot," he offered. "Cannon balls tied together with chain, to sweep these pests from the trees and wrap them in neat bows."

"Cannon and special shot," said I. "You go from one expense to another. I thought perhaps small mortars, to loft a metal net over the intruders."

Mountmirail was skeptical. "That metal net will cost both money and time. For consider that a smith must forge every link by hand."

"But the birds can cut through a rope net."

"Nets are easily repaired." He smiled. "And the birds cannot cut them instantly, and in the meantime they are helpless and you may kill them."

"With what?"

"To smash iron?" He waved a hand. "No need for elegance. A big enough hammer will serve."

Lipton and I recruited Peel, the lank-haired journeyman cannoneer, and we made some experiments with nets and small mortars. After some failures we succeeded in capturing in the net's coils a herd of sheep, and I reckoned this was the best we could do until we had the iron birds in our sights. With a battery of mortars, a half-dozen apprentices, shot and powder, and a letter to the lord lieutenant of Inchmaden, I sent Peel on a barge down the Dordelle to find transport to West Fornland. I presumed he could find enough war hammers, pollaxes, and halberds in the lord lieutenant's stores and need not bring any with him.

After which I continued with my other projects. With my skilled crew of sailors, I won a race on the lake that took place under sail alone. The Count of Wenlock had won two races while I was gone, with His Grace of Roundsilver placing second, and so Rufino Knott soon wrote a song extolling "The Three Great Lords of Ethlebight" for our nautical prowess. I was neither great nor a lord, but I did not object to being included.

Using Mountmirail's grinding machine, I began to experiment with ways of making and bottling ink, and I visited the headquarters of the Worshipfull Companie of Dyers, to see if I could find a man to head my ink works. The art of the dyer was the closest I could think to that of ink-maker, an occupation that did not yet exist. I interviewed several journeymen, but they seemed dubious. "Don't people make their own ink?" they said.

I found Blackwell in a bagnio in Gropecoun Street, dragged him to Mountmirail's workshop, and showed him the flying birds. "Consider a meeting between the kingdoms of Earth and Air," I said. "Duisland may serve as a model for the former, and the rare exquisites of Loretto will serve for the latter. You may have a comedy of wonder and mis-understanding, with a marriage at the end, and thus a happy union of the kingdoms is achieved."

"Do you think the master of revels would permit even misunder-standings?"

"If you made them innocent enough."

I sensed a glimmer of interest in Blackwell's indigo eyes. "I will give the matter some thought."

The streets were crowded with members of the Estates, their friends, and their servants. On my way home I stopped in the Flesh Shambles to compare prices in a pair of butcher shops. My father had been a master of the Worshipfull Societie of Butchers, and I was

myself a member in good standing of the guild, with the rank of journeyman. I passed the time with my guild brothers, then returned to
Rackheath House and fired my cook.

When I'd examined my first set of accounts, I'd been shocked by
the amount it cost me to feed my household. It required but a few
calculations to show that my cook had been marking up his cost of
meat and poultry, and pocketing the difference between what he
paid and what expenses he passed on to the household. Presumably
he'd practiced this also upon Lord Rackheath, possibly for years, but
Rackheath had no practical experience in buying and selling meat,
and hadn't realized he was being fleeced. After having the footmen
heave the cook out into the road, I wrote to his lordship telling him I'd
sacked the man, and why.

For the moment the undercook was promoted into his place, but I
began a search for a more seasoned replacement. Visiting the butchers' shops had given me an idea, and I wished to have a cook in place
before I put my own recipe to the test.

Lord Edevane managed to find some of my predecessors' reports, and
these I came to his offices to read. I brought a scrivener to copy anything that I might have found useful. In reading the old despatches, I
was disappointed when it came to discovering ways how these beasts
were vanquished, for while the old lord wardens wrote that they had
done their duty and killed the chimerae, they rarely reported how
they had done it. Yet the descriptions of the beasts themselves were
of great interest, and from these I understood that kings of old were
more interested in tales of fantastic monsters than in practical methods of fighting them.

It seemed that whatever powers directed the Land of Chimerae
took the notion of change as a watchword, and had no sooner created one beast than they replaced it with another. There were dragons
that breathed fire, dragons that spat poison, and dragons that fought

only with teeth and talons. There were dragons that walked on four legs, dragons that crawled, dragons that had many legs like centipedes. There were dragons with only two legs, commonly known as wyverns, and there seemed as many sorts of sea-dragons or serpents as those that dwelt on land.

Nor did the chimerae consist entirely of worms. There were giant crabs that spat fire, leopards with poisoned spines and adamantine talons, sables that slipped into human dwellings at night, wound themselves around any they found lying abed, and overcame them with intoxicating breath before drinking their blood. Bulls with the heads of men, apes with the heads of goats. Mantichores with the body of a lion and a scorpion's tail, harpies with the body of an eagle and the head of a hag. Black, stinging flies with the figure of a horned skull on their abdomen.

There were no reports of savage iron birds. It seemed I would have to write those reports myself.

I did notice that many of the older despatches mentioned prayers and sacrifices conducted to the local gods, with thanks to the gods afterward. Perhaps the lord wardens were pious, or perhaps gods had actually helped.

But now we lived in a different age, and if I were inclined to pray, I would not know to whom to address my prayers. The only divine being I knew would laugh my pleas to scorn.

I would have to use such talents as nature had provided me, and fight chimerae with whatever tools came to hand.

My new office came with lodging at Ings Magna, and the privilege of taking dinner with the pensioners, who, having received no reward but poverty in exchange for a life of service to the crown, were given humble lodging at the palace, provided they stayed out of sight generally and did not lower the tone. The dinners were served in a depressing undercroft, and the food would hardly tempt the palate of an epicure, but the pensioners themselves were an interesting crew, full of tales of King Stilwell, his wives and companions, and of the high nobility. They retailed as well a long list of palace scandals, crimes, and improprieties long forgotten by the great world outside the undercroft.

My little room high in the palace was small, dark, dirty, and noisome, but a crew of sailors equipped with swabs and prayer-books soon cleared away decades' worth of grime. I put down three layers of rush bundles, which I sprinkled with basil, sweet cicely, and lavender, and then laid down carpets. I added a small table, chairs, a wardrobe, a mirror, and toiletries, along with goblets, bottles of wine, and a dozen silver candlesticks with perfumed candles. Most importantly, I added a bed with seven feather mattresses and perfumed sheets.

Thus I was able to welcome Lady Westley to a convenient bower, where we might meet to kiss, caress, and kindle, and thus forget the world for a little while. While she expressed delight in the sanctuary I had created, I sensed a distraction in her manner, and I sat her in one of my chairs, poured wine for her, and asked her what was the matter.

"I have got a better idea of how much money we owe," she said. "That is bad enough, but I fear that my uncle's forthcoming marriage might mean that we will never be able to meet our obligations."

The uncle who had raised Lady Westley had no children of his own, and he had made no secret of his intention to make her his heir. But his wife had died, and now he, at the age of sixty, had announced his intention of marrying a maid of seventeen, a granddaughter of one of his colleagues in the Treasury Moot.

I could understand Lady Westley's concern, for I could imagine only one reason a seventeen-year-old would marry a man of sixty, and that reason had to do with assets, reserves, income, and deeds to real property.

"If my uncle gets that girl with child," said my Girasol, "then his estate will go to his offspring, and Edelmir and I will be bankrupt. With my uncle's estate, we have a chance to pay much of what we owe, but without it we will be lost."

"I hope your husband is not trying to win himself a new fortune at dice," said I.

Lady Westley waved a distracted hand. "He says he doesn't bet so much that it will make a difference."

I feared that this might be true, for I supposed there was little practical difference between being bankrupt, and being bankrupt three times over.

"If only the gaming in Howel was not so high!" Lady Westley said. "But Their Majesties set the fashion, and they play for mad stakes!"

I remembered Berlauda betting fifty royals that she would make her hoop in palle-malle, and I wondered how many hoops she had missed that day, and what that game had cost the treasury.

"Your husband's gaming must stop," said I. "You must be very firm."

Candlelight shivered in her wide blue eyes. "But how can we recoup?" she asked. "We have borrowed so much against my expectations."

"Let me consider. There are many ventures that would bring in a greater profit than laying bets with tricksters and coney-catchers."

Tears sped from her eyes, and she reached for a handkerchief. My heart dissolved at this sign of distress, and I wished to kiss the tears away. Instead I took her hand and put on my superior-prefect face, all conviction and assurance.

"There is no immediate danger, yes?" I said. "Your creditors are content to wait for the present?"

"Ay."

"And this child of your uncle's is not born, nor is your uncle yet wed."

Her hand clutched my fingers. "Nay. But—"

"Is your credit still good? Can you still borrow money?"

She looked at me in some surprise. "I think so."

"You have time," I said. "Time to make an investment. I would offer you cargo space on my *Sovereign*, but I fear it has already left the Saelle on its way to the Candara Coast. Yet something of that sort is called for."

She seemed perplexed. "We know nothing of the shipping trade."

"But I do. I will find you a good ship and a good captain, and the profits on a single long voyage may come near to ending your troubles."

She looked at me helplessly. "I—Edelmir doesn't know that I've spoken to you. If you come to him with an offer of help, he will be angry with me for telling you of our misfortune—"

"I will manage it. I'll ask him to help *me*. I'll tell him of an opportunity that's risen, and that my own resources have fallen short."

Her blue eyes made little leaps right and left, as if she were reading an invisible text written on my forehead. Her lips trembled. She began to speak, then fell silent. Her diamonds glowed in the soft flickering light.

"You must also speak to your uncle," I said. "Tell him frankly of your situation."

The prospect seemed to frighten her a little. "We borrowed in anticipation of his death. Telling him will be hard, Heliodor."

"Bankruptcy is harder," said I.

Her eyes fell to the table. She squeezed my hand. "Ay," she said softly, "I see that I must tell him."

And then, as she gave a little sigh of resignation, I heard the thump of a cannon shot. The gun had been fired on the other side of the building, down by the quay, but I felt the palace shiver, and two silver goblets on the shelf rang against each other. A bell began to clang. As I straightened in surprise, another big gun thumped.

"Is that an alarm?" asked Lady Westley.

"The one o'clock gun has already fired," I said. "I hope the palace isn't ablaze." I rose, opened the door, and looked out into the hall. Only a few servants were visible, and they were as perplexed as I.

When I returned to Lady Westley, she had risen from her chair. She came to me and took my hand.

"I had hoped the afternoon would be full of enchantment," she said, "but instead there is only alarm and sorrow."

I knew from her tone that our brief rendezvous was at an end. The world with its guns, bells, and terror of failure had entered my little bower like a great wave, and our love was too fragile not to be swept away by the inundation.

"There will be other afternoons," said I, and I grazed her knuckles with my lips. She made her way to the door, looked out, and then went into the hall.

I looked ruefully at my room, all scented and glowing and filled with the promise of delight, and then I snuffed the candles and followed her.

There was a seething crowd along the quay, where a full eight-gun battery of Lipton's demiculverins was spending colossal amounts of powder sending great roaring salutes out over the lake. The gunsmoke towered in great sunlit clouds in the still air. The bell still clapped out from its belfry atop the palace. I looked for Lady Westley in the throng but couldn't find her. On the palace stair sat Their Majesties beneath a canopy of state, with state officials gathered about them, a line of demilances to keep the crowd at a distance, and little Princess Floria almost submerged beneath the crowd of dignitaries. A herald on a white horse stood just behind the line of cavalry, his tabard glittering with gold thread and his trumpet propped on his thigh. Apparently he'd just made an announcement, because the crowd was buzzing with what they'd heard, for the most part imperfectly, the words buried beneath the ringing bell and the thundering cannonade.

"War!" I heard. "We're at war!"

"Who are we fighting?" I asked. No one quite seemed to know.

"It must be the Aekoi, mustn't it?" said a courtier. "They attacked Ethlebight, after all."

While I would have cheered for a war of vengeance against the Aekoi reivers, I thought it unlikely. Ethlebight had been sacked over three years ago, and there had been no great demand for retaliation in the meantime.

"Three cheers for Their Majesties!" someone called, and cheers were duly given, though all seemed uncertain what the cheering might be about. I worked my way closer to the herald, and then he blew the trumpet and again shouted out his message. Between the bell, the crowd, and the gunshots, I heard none of it, but I read the word "war" clearly enough on his lips.

"Who are we fighting?" I asked again.

"Did he say Thurnmark?" said a lady.

"Of course not!" said another. "How could we fight Thurnmark? Our armies would have to march across the sea just to get there."

But Thurnmark, I thought, made sense, for Thurnmark shared a border with Loretto. If King Henrico had decided to attack his neighbor, and Priscus and Berlauda had decided to support him, then such a war was perfectly possible.

Though I didn't know how popular it would be. Duisland had no reason to fight Thurnmark, and could expect nothing from the war but increased taxes. We would gain no new provinces, and any treasure would be swept up by the armies of King Henrico.

The Estates would meet in a few days, and would now be expected to vote not only the new taxes Their Majesties were requesting, but additional taxes to support the war. I did not imagine this session of the Estates would be a happy one.

But yet Thurnmark had a coast and harbors and ships. In the last war I had acquired privateering commissions and much profit, including the captures *Royal Stilwell* and *Sovereign*. This new war would be profitable for privateers, if for no one else, and so I made up my mind to go the next day to the high court of the admiralty and seek commissions for those vessels in which I had an interest.

The bell-ringing and the cannonade went on. I pushed closer to the herald, who again blew his trumpet and cried out his message. Again I caught the word "war" and precious little else, but apparently war in the abstract was enough to set off another round of cheering.

I pushed closer, and then I saw Sir Edelmir Westley pushing his way through the crowd. "Sir Quillifer!" he said. "I must have words with you!"

The surging throng pushed us apart. I stumbled but regained my balance. "Did you hear?" I asked. "Who are we fighting?"

Sir Edelmir said something I could not make out, and then a few phrases slipped through. "This is an insult! It is outrageous!"

"The war?" I said. The crowd pushed us closer together. "Do you mean the war?"

"That song!" he cried. "That impudent ballad! It is an insult to chivalry itself!"

I was bewildered. A demiculverin roared out, and the echo came rushing back across the lake. "Who are we fighting?" I asked.

As if in answer to that question, Sir Edelmir Westley struck me on the face with his fist.

CHAPTER FIFTEEN

A y, you must fight him," said Coronel Lipton. "If you don't, you can't show your face at the court."

"Isn't dueling illegal?" asked I.

"Ay, but what of that?" Lipton spread his hands. "What does the law have to do with what men count as honor?"

I rubbed my jaw where Sir Edelmir had struck me. "I could be charged with murder."

Lipton pointed a thick finger at me. "Only if you win, youngster."

"Yet losing," said I, "does not seem the best option."

"To save honor," said he reasonably, "you might contrive an honorable wound. Let Sir Edelmir run you through the shoulder, or pink you in the hip."

I considered this. "Would that not require his cooperation?" I asked.

We walked along the quay in the light of morning, the day following Sir Edelmir's challenge. Silver flashed on the dancing waves, and sun-dapples frolicked on the sails of the pleasure-craft that tacked back and forth offshore. The winter day was so mild and perfect that it was difficult to believe that Lipton and I were talking of the deadly single combat to which the customs of knighthood now bound me.

"How bloodthirsty is he?" Lipton asked. "Does he truly want you dead? What is the source of this conflict?"

"Up till now our association has been perfectly cordial," said I. "Thanks to the shooting and shouting yesterday, I could not entirely understand his challenge, but apparently he objects to the ballad that Goodman Knott wrote about the fire-drake."

"Was Sir Edelmir ridiculed?"

"Not in any verse that I have heard," I said. "Knott denies writing mockery of anyone other than Woolfardisworthy. And in any case, I don't see why Sir Edelmir doesn't take the matter up with Knott."

"Knott is not a gentleman," said Lipton. "Sir Edelmir couldn't fight him."

"Surely that is all for the best."

Though I feared that Sir Edelmir had more cause to murder me than any words that might have passed Rufino Knott's lips. His challenge had not mentioned his wife's affections for me, though that might be to avoid naming her in a scandal—or to avoid Sir Edelmir publicly putting the cuckold's horns on his own head. Perhaps that afternoon he'd had a report that Lady Westley had visited me in my room at the palace.

Yet there was something peculiar about his challenge. I had seen him angry, when he had drawn a pistol on Woolfardisworthy, but he had not seemed angry even when he struck me. He had shouted out his challenge into the surging crowd, and not to me directly, as if the words didn't matter. It was as if he wanted to shout his challenge only because he could then move on to the sequel.

"Sir Edelmir named his second," I said. "Someone named Sir Hector Whyte."

"I know him." Lipton huffed. "A threadbare baronet, a laddered stocking, an eater of broken meats. One of Wenlock's mesnie."

I gave him a sharp look. "He serves the Count of Wenlock?"

"Oh, ay."

"It has escaped your memory that Wenlock hates me?"

Lipton stopped in his tracks, and he looked up with surprise. "Why did I not remember?" he said. "For did he not curse you on the day you gained your knighthood?"

"He has cursed me on other occasions as well."

"Well, well." Lipton turned thoughtful. "Yet what does Edelmir Westley have to do with Wenlock?"

"I don't know."

"It seems a plot to murder you."

"And I must survive it. Will you act for me?"

Lipton took longer to consider this question than I would have liked. "Ay," he said finally, "but only if the seconds are present to insure the fairness of the fight, and not to join in. My days of brawling with sharp steel are far behind me."

"I desire nothing more than fairness," said I, "or at least a pretense of it."

"What weapon do you choose?"

I waved a hand. "It hardly matters, for I am inexpert with all of them," said I. "I received some instruction in broadsword play when I served with the Utterback Troop, but Westley also served in the cavalry at Peckside, and has been training all his life."

A sailboat approached the quay in perfect silence, and then its sails rattled as it changed course and swept out onto the lake, its smiling captain hauling in the sheet and trimming the sail with expert ease.

"Rapier?" Lipton asked.

"I have never handled one. It is a prodigious long weapon, to be sure, and I should think very awkward."

"And Westley carries one, and I suppose knows what to do with it."

"Well then. No rapier."

"I saw you with a pollaxe at Exton Scales," said Lipton, "and you did execution with it."

I watched the boat as it receded, its wake a series of black *V*s on the blue water, and I wished myself aboard, and bound for Tabarzam. "That execution is precisely the objection," I said. "For if I were to hit Sir Edelmir with a pollaxe, he would be dead, and then I would be taken and hanged for murder."

Lipton seemed amused. "So we desire a weapon with which both combatants are unfamiliar, and which will not be too deadly."

"Billiard balls?" I suggested. "Do you think we might hurl billiard balls at one another?"

The cannoneer's eyes turned dark. "He seems to want you dead, youngster. He will not want to play with toys."

"Ay." I considered this sobering likelihood as I watched the boats turning like dancers on the lake. "Very well," I said. "We may fight with whatever weapons you and Sir Hector Whyte can agree upon. But I will choose where the duel will take place—and if he likes it not, he may withdraw his challenge."

"You have a place in your mind, then?" asked Lipton. "Let it be at dawn, with the rising sun in Westley's eyes."

"Ay," I said. "We may as well have that, as well."

Between us we set out plans in order, and Coronel Lipton went to seek Sir Hector Whyte while I returned to Rackheath House, where I found a hired carriage waiting in the road. Master Stiver, the steward, met me at the door, and bowed. "Sir Quillifer," said he, "a lady has come to see you."

"Who is she?"

His face was grave. "She is masked, sir."

I looked at him. "Surely you must have some idea."

I was forced to admire his practiced manner, for his expression failed to alter in any way. "I did not venture to guess, sir. I put the lady in the parlor."

"Very well," I said. I was only a little perplexed, for there were not so many ladies who would visit me in disguise. I went to the parlor, and there found Lady Westley in her mask, traveling cloak, and a whisper of her bergamot scent. She rose from a settee and rushed to me in a rustle of gabardine, and gripped my hand in both of hers. She spoke with frantic desperation.

"Heliodor," she said, "you must spare my husband's life."

I was perhaps a little displeased that she had not offered so much concern for my own well-being. "I will spare him if I can," said I. "But he is making it difficult for me to rescue his financial affairs."

"But now there is war!" she said. Her tone was strangely hopeful. "Edelmir says he will go to the fighting in Thurnmark and make his fortune."

I suppressed bitter laughter. "Are there no cards or dice in camp? He will lose that fortune ere he can win it."

She looked at me for an anguished moment, then turned her head away. "Please do not say these things."

"Do you know what prompted his challenge?"

"He said only that he had been insulted, but he would not say anything more than that." She turned to me again, and looked at me from behind her striking mask of shot silk, pale gray with a shimmering undercast of blue that mirrored the color of her eyes. Her voice rose to a desolate pitch. "What has happened? Did you say something to him?"

"No, I didn't. Come and sit with me." I drew her back to the settee. "Does he know we've been meeting?"

"No," she said, and then added, "I don't think so."

"And if he knew, would it drive him to this kind of violence?"

She blinked, then shook her head. "I do not think so. He is not a possessive man. We have both had our adventures and there was no great jealousy on either part."

"He parts with his money gracefully enough," I said. "But possession is a curious thing, and perhaps he did not know how well he valued you until I threatened his control of you."

I drew back a little and looked at her, her face wan behind the mask. "Girasol, I am afraid I must query you about your marriage," I said. "We haven't spoken of it—we have instead tried to create a sanctuary of our own, a harbor free of the cares of the temporal world—but there is now much I need to learn."

"What do you want to know?"

"How long have you known Sir Edelmir?"

"All my life," she said simply. "We were both raised at court."

"And his family?"

"Edelmir is the fifth son. His father was unlucky—he guaranteed some loans for a friend who fled with the money—so there was little for Edelmir but a few properties by Lake Gurlidan."

"And yet your guardian permitted the marriage to a man without money?"

She shrugged. "It was not Edelmir's fault that he was not rich. He had friends at court and was master of the henchmen with the chance to rise to greater office."

"But if his office is like mine, it costs him more money to maintain his place than it brings him in earnings."

She looked away. Light from the window blazed up in the gold flecks of her eyes. "That is probably true."

"Do you know if your husband is friendly with Sir Hector Whyte?"

She looked at me in surprise. "We know everyone at court, but Edelmir and Whyte are not friends."

"Or my lord of Wenlock?"

"Again, we know him, but are not familiar." She cocked her head at a memory. "But I recall now that I saw them together, outside the mews. Wenlock had just come in from riding, and they spoke for a while."

"Do you know their business?"

"No. But I hardly think it was friendly, for Edelmir did not seem pleased."

I considered this news for a while in silence. Lady Westley had not ceased to clasp my hand with both hers, and now I folded my second hand atop the others, in what I hoped was a comfort. "Girasol," I said, "I think for your own safety you must divorce."

She looked up at me sharply. "Divorce?" said she. "That would not reflect well on me, with Edelmir going to war!" She shook her head. "Do you understand what scandal will result? The whole court will look for a reason behind the divorce, and they will find one—they will find *you*. Especially if you and Edelmir fight, for no matter what reason lies behind the encounter, people will assume you fight over me."

"Scandals are brief," said I, "but bankruptcy is long. Listen to my reasons, and remember that I studied law."

She seemed puzzled. "Did you? I thought you were a sea-captain."

I refused to allow myself to be distracted. "You must separate your money from your husband's. If you are divorced, your husband's creditors cannot pursue your inheritance. Not unless you have also signed for the loans."

"I haven't." But she was impatient. "I won't *have* an inheritance!" she cried. "Not once my guardian fathers a child!"

"You don't know that he will, even if he marries."

With some effort, she pulled her hands from mine. "None of that matters now!" she said. "Not with you and Edelmir about to kill each other!"

"I have said I will try to spare him," I said. "If you can convince him to return the favor, I would be greatly obliged."

She jumped to her feet and began to pace the room. I rose and watched as she stormed back and forth, the dark gabardine cloak rustling.

"You must see a lawyer," I said. "You may not wish to take my word, for I am hardly impartial, but you should see a lawyer and lay out the whole matter before him."

She stood still and glared at me. "Divorce requires a vote in the House of Burgesses!" she said.

"Dozens of divorces are passed at every sitting. You know everyone in Howel, you must know some member who would introduce a bill of divorcement for you—ay, and he should be a lawyer, too. You can explain it's to keep your fortune safe; he will understand that."

Her fists doubled, and her lips pressed to a thin line. "You know what they will say about me. That I am a stewed harlot, that I spread my legs for diamonds."

"The best way to outface slander is to be armored in gold," said I. "Look to yourself and to your fortune."

"No respectable woman will speak to me!" she said. "No man will want me but a rake or a punkateero!" She came up to me, her eyes blazing. "Once scandal attaches to me, will even *you* want me? Not just in your bed, I mean, but in wedlock?"

"That scandal would attach to us both, and to our bed as well," said I. "But I may be dead tomorrow, if your husband has his way, and I would see you safe from ruin before that. For once blades are out, the matter becomes simple: Who shall survive, and who shall not." I made an effort to soften my voice, and to put on my earnest-lover face. "I desire your survival, Girasol. You once said that you hoped that Heliodor the beryl knight would save you, and I *want* to save you." And seeing this made no impression, I gave her a hard look. "Poverty will not become you, madam. To avoid hanging, your husband will have to go abroad as a soldier, and you will have to follow him. I have seen the women who follow their men to battlefields, and though they are not all wicked, in my view it is far better to be a scandalous lady of the court than the most virtuous of camp followers."

"You think everything is about money!" she cried. "Money and diamonds!"

"I can assume a measure of control over money," I said. "Over your husband's sword, I can do nothing. Perhaps you may have some influence there."

She stormed a while longer and wept. I did my best to offer comfort, but she accepted little of it, and eventually said she had to go. I had not told her what I suspected had caused Sir Edelmir to issue the challenge, for I did not wish her to have to view her husband in that way, but perhaps I should have urged a clearer sight upon her.

I walked with her to the door and saw her into her hired carriage. As the carriage turned and began its journey back to town, I saw her profile through the window. She sat very straight and looked forward, as if she were staring into a destiny empty of hope.

I hoped I did not have the same look as I returned to my house.

I went to the boathouse, where my galley was moored, and looked at the boats that Lord Rackheath kept there, then returned to the house and called Rufino Knott. I told him that I would soon be involved in an encounter with a knight, and that he would have a part to play. "Hold yourself ready for tonight," I told him, "for we shall conduct some experiments."

Coronel Lipton came to the house just before supper, with a long package carried in a cloak under his arm. "It is arranged for dawn the day after tomorrow," he said. "I insisted on an extra day so that Westley may have time to cool his temper, sure, but in truth so that you may practice with the weapons. For though you have your way with the setting, Whyte had his way with the blades, and you will fight with rapier and dagger." He unrolled his cloak and produced the weapons, matched pairs of blades. "I have brought you these to practice."

I viewed the blades as they lay on the table. "I am of two minds whether I should practice at all," I said. "If I know only a little, and try to use what I know, I will be overmastered by an opponent who knows more. Whereas if I know nothing, I may yet surprise both Westley and myself with something unexpected."

"Whether you know the art of defense or not," said Lipton, "yet I can still teach you a few things that may be useful."

"Well," I said, "stay to supper, and we'll discuss the matter."

We had as pleasant a supper as was possible beneath the darkling clouds of doom that hung over me, and then went to the tennis court to practice with the rapiers. They were indeed awkward weapons, being about four feet long, heavy, and useful mainly in the attack. The daggers, more nimble, were also used for the defense, to ward off the longer weapons, though they had other employment as well.

"If you can," said Lipton, "pass inside the compass of Westley's rapier, and with your dagger yerk him under the ribs."

"If I can," I repeated.

"And if all else fails," Lipton affirmed, "there is the strike of the peasant."

This strike, the name implied, was so simple that even an untutored dalcop such as myself could master it. With the left hand I would grasp the blade of my rapier below the hilt, and then, using the rapier as a spear, I would knock Westley's sword aside and skewer him through his vitals.

"So," I said, after practicing. "That is a brutal stroke indeed."

"It is despised as a barbaric stroke, sure, yet it may save your life."

"I must drop my dagger in order to use it."

"It is a last resort, youngster. It is drop the dagger or die."

I shared a last glass of wine with Lipton, then thanked him. The sun was near setting, and I made sure water was heating in my bath, and in the servants' bath-house. I met with Rufino Knott, and we went to the boathouse and conducted some experiments there, under cover of darkness. Afterward I warmed myself in my bath, and then made my way to bed.

It was some time before I managed to sleep. I was deeply concerned for Lady Westley, and I was frustrated by my inability to help her. I did not want her to share what would almost certainly be her husband's ruin, but yet I had no power to affect events. I could not file for divorce on her behalf, nor could I make her speak with her old guardian about her situation.

I could, I suppose, relieve Sir Edelmir by buying some of his debt, but that would not prevent him from incurring more debt. I had no power to keep him away from cards and dice.

I supposed that Sir Edelmir's challenge was prompted in some way by the Count of Wenlock, but I had little doubt that Orlanda was the ultimate source of the plot. I had not seen her since her appearance on Gannet Island during the last of that wild storm, but I was confident she had been working against me all this time, and I wondered how many traps she had laid besides the one she had just sprung.

I knew, for example, that Wenlock hated me, but it seemed past credit that he hated me so much that he would turn to plotting murder, not when I was no threat to him or to his position. Unless, of course, an ethereal voice whispered in his ear and suggested that now was a ripe time for me to die, and how my death might be accomplished.

I myself heard no voices whispering in the night, and after midnight managed to sleep.

I woke early, and then was faced with how to occupy myself during what might be the last day of my life. So I took my crew out on the lake for their exercise, and had my tennis lesson, and then went into the town to visit my notary and make some minor revision to my will. I left some money for my body to be carried to Ethlebight and laid with appropriate ceremony in my family's mausoleum. All my gems and jewels would be left to Their Graces of Roundsilver, in return for their friendship and kindness, and everything else to my friend and partner Kevin Spellman. I also made certain arrangements that, in the event of my not returning from the encounter, handbills would be printed giving the circumstances of my death, so that Westley would have to flee, and Wenlock might suffer some embarrassment. He was of the nobility, and so it was unlikely he would face a judge for the crime of killing a commoner, but at least I could proclaim him as a coward and a sneak.

That left me with most of the afternoon, and I did not fancy rambling about Rackheath House by myself with nothing to think about but the possibility that Westley's rapier might soon be lodged in my guts, so I dressed in my court clothes and went to Ings Magna, where I found myself a game of cards and won six royals.

I went home, supped alone, and went to bed early with a book of Erpingham's *Tales*. To my surprise, I slept well.

Clouds of fragrant woodsmoke drifted over the lake as the palace cooks lit their fires. My galley rowed to Ings Magna just as the eastern sky began to lighten, and there we met Coronel Lipton on the quay and took him on board. Then *Dunnock* sailed across the lake and behind one of the islands, where I was appointed to meet Sir Edelmir Westley in combat. Behind us we trailed a rowboat, about five yards in length, that I'd found in the boathouse, and which the servants used for fishing and running errands to town. Once we were concealed by the island, I cast the lead to find a deep spot, then anchored the rowboat in twenty feet of water.

A party waited upon the shore, all cloaked against the cold winter dawn. In the dim light I recognized Westley by his long black hair, and Sir Hector Whyte by his self-importance. That worthy stood on the edge of the shore, his legs spread as if riding a horse, the water lapping at his boots. He was older than I had anticipated, with gray in his hair and beard. His gross body stood square to us in an attitude of defiance, and his bearded chin was thrust out as if asking for someone to strike him on the jaw. His manner was so insolent I was tempted to oblige him.

Two other gentlemen lurked in the darkness behind, by the carriages that had brought them to the spot. I suspected they might be ruffians whose task, if Westley's stroke failed, was to see me to the next world, and was therefore glad I had armed my boat's crew against treachery with swords and pistols, concealed in a compartment in the stern.

The galley came gently to the shore, and Coronel Lipton stepped off, carrying his pairs of matched weapons under his arm. *Dunnock* backed away, then took me to the rowboat. I turned the tiller over to Boatswain Lepalik, let my boat cloak fall, put on my gauntlets, and stepped onto the rowboat. It rocked under me and sent waves lapping toward the shore.

As I stood on the boat and watched the gentlemen on the shore, I do not believe I felt fear, but instead I seemed preternaturally alert. I felt my senses prickling out in all directions, and I was conscious of the squelching of the mud beneath Coronel Lipton's boots, the sneer on Whyte's lips, the touch of the dawn breeze on the back of my neck, the scent of muck and reed and smoke, the last stars fading in the west. It was all of intense interest.

It occurred to me that perhaps I might be all the better for a touch of fear. I did not want to be a dispassionate observer at my own death.

Lipton spoke to Sir Hector for a few moments, and then Sir Hector tossed a coin. It fell into the dew-soaked grass at Lipton's feet, and he pronounced it heads.

Lipton waved *Dunnock* toward the shore again, and Sir Hector stepped aboard. He was taken out to the rowboat for an inspection, to make sure I had laid no traps and hidden no weapons. As he stepped aboard, the boat rocked beneath the ponderous weight of his guts. There was very little for him to see on the small craft, and as he passed me standing on a thwart, he glared up at me and gave a sniff.

"It is a damned poor shallop you bring to this encounter," he said.

"It will serve well enough for a coffin," said I.

He sniffed again, then returned to the galley and was taken to the shore.

I had insisted that the fight take place on the water, for I was a sailor and wished to fight for the honor of sailors. Westley, who had made the challenge, had no grounds to refuse so long as the boat gave him no disadvantage; and if he refused, I could proclaim him coward. So he had accepted my condition, but insisted on choice of weapons.

Next Lipton came out, to bring my rapier and dagger. "Whyte won the coin toss," he said, "so we use their blades. The weapons are matched, but I chose the ones I liked the best."

I took the rapier and dagger and made with them some inexpert motions in the air to judge their weight and utility. They were much as the weapons I had practiced with, the rapier with a web of steel protecting my hand, and the dagger with an enlarged cross-guard for defense.

"They will do," said I. "Thank you."

"Luck to you, youngster," he said in a hearty, artificial voice, and thumped me on the arm.

"I thank you," I said. "Be on your guard, now, when I come ashore."

His bushy brows contracted as he considered my words, and then *Dunnock* returned him to the land, then brought Sir Edelmir Westley aboard. I went to the bow of the rowboat and waited for him to arrive.

Westley was, like me, in his shirt, and carried his weapons in his hands. I had tied my hair back, but he wore his loose, and his face bore a black look that twisted his mouth. He scowled down at the water as he stepped onto the rowboat near the stern, and he stood still, a little pale, as the boat rocked under his weight and the water made bright splashing sounds against the chine.

"So," I asked him, "how much of your debt did Wenlock buy?"

His head jerked upright, and he gave me such a startled, hunted look that I knew at once that I had guessed aright.

"If you kill me," I said, "I have arranged that you will be published as an assassin. I do not expect the queen's justice will be merciful, so you had best fly the country while you may." I paused for a moment while I juggled the sword in my right hand, as if in thought. "You had best tell that young wife of yours to divorce you, before your crimes bring her down with you."

He gave me a dull, resentful look, and his lip curled. "Pray let us get on with this business," he said.

"Ay," said I. "*Business* indeed. For my life is worth crowns to you."

"Gentlemen!" called Whyte from the shore. "Are you ready!"

Westley nodded, and then realized that in the half-light no one had seen it. "Ay," he said briefly.

I laughed. "As my friend Sir Edelmir requires," I said.

"I will count to three," said Whyte, "and then I will wave my handkerchief, and so you may begin."

Westley carefully took his stance, his left leg advanced over a thwart, his body bent forward with his right hand above his head, the point of his sword directed at my breast, a stance recommended by the masters of defense. The left hand held his dagger lower down. I adopted the same stance except that I advanced the right leg, which I propped on a thwart.

In spite of the cool air my flesh prickled with sudden blazing heat. I felt my breath catch in my throat, and as the dawn ran along the bright steel, my heart gave a loud thump against my breastbone. Perhaps I was feeling fear after all.

"One," cried Whyte. "Two. Three!"

As soon as I saw the white handkerchief out of the slant of my eye, I launched myself from the thwart and landed on the starboard gunwale with all my weight on the left foot. There was a great surge of water as the boat tipped, and Westley staggered with a wide step to larboard, his dagger-arm thrashing the air for balance. His shifting weight brought the boat toward a more even keel, and so I leaped again and landed on the larboard gunwale with my right foot.

This brought the boat right over, the lake pouring over the gunwale in a great wave, just as it had when Knott and I had practiced two nights before. Westley was pitched backward into the water, hair flying, arms flailing. As the boat dipped beneath me, I stepped out into the lake with a long stride. The water was desperately cold, and I felt my heart lurch in shock. When the water closed over my head, I scissored my legs, and I popped above the surface to see Westley thrashing the water just as he had when his horse had pitched him into the river during our dragon quest. I let go my rapier, and once I saw that both his hands were empty, I used my dagger to give myself a cut on the right arm just above my gauntlet. The cold water numbed the pain. Then I let the knife fall, seized Sir Edelmir Westley by his long hair, and dragged him to shore.

He lay puffing and sputtering in the shallows, a picture of cold, sodden misery, while I rose with the water sluicing off me and joined Lipton on the shore. Whyte glared at me, his beard jutting out.

"That was foul villain's work!" he said. "You shall fight again, and this time on dry land!"

"Nay," said I. I showed him the wound on my arm, which by now was coursing blood. "Sir Edelmir gave me a wound. Honor is satisfied."

"*Satisfied!*" he snarled. "*Honor!*"

I felt Lipton reaching under his cloak for the hilt of his whinyard, and knew he remembered my warning to be on guard once I had come ashore.

I was aware of my galley coming aground just behind me, and I knew that—if Rufino Knott had followed his instructions—my crew was now armed.

"Ay," I said. "Honor is satisfied, even if the Count of Wenlock is not."

At that Whyte stared, his eyes wide, his mouth chewing unspoken words, and I took Lipton's arm and drew him back to the galley. We pushed off from the shore and went aboard to stand on the foredeck. I was half expecting a dagger or a bullet in the back, but Whyte and his friends made no move, and *Dunnock* backed out of the shallows.

We righted the rowboat, which swam keel upward on the surface, put the boat on the end of a line, then set out onto the lake.

"Well, Coronel," I said, "I am for a hot bath, and then breakfast. Will you join me?"

Coronel Lipton looked at the swords and the pistols that lay beneath the thwarts of the galley, and he looked up at me with a little smile. "All has gone as you expected?" he said.

"Better," I said. "I feared we would have a fight on shore." I held out my arm, where blood now stained my white shirt. "Will you help me bind my wound? We can use the sleeve, it is ruined already." As Coronel Lipton made of my sleeve a neat bandage, I turned to Rufino Knott.

"If you make a song of this, goodman," I said, "I trust you will be discreet in the matter of names."

"As you wish, sir," he said, and, with the tiller tucked under his arm, turned us for home.

CHAPTER SIXTEEN

I remained at home for the rest of the day in hope I might hear from Lady Westley, but instead I received an unexpected visitor just before suppertime. I was sitting at one of the great bay windows in the library, reading the bittersweet poetry of Tarantua.

Oh, be not careless then and play
Until the star of peace
Hide all his beams in dark recess.
Poor pilgrims needs must lose their way
When all the shadows do increase.

And indeed the shadows increased as the sun neared the horizon, and I felt the darkness lay fingers upon my heart. Master Stiver entered to announce my guest, but she arrived on his heels, and he had barely begun to speak when she ducked under his arm and came into the room.

"Quillifer!" she said. "They said you were wounded!"

I rose in some surprise. "A scratch, Your Grace," I said. "I have already forgot it."

Stiver withdrew as the Duchess of Roundsilver approached, tall heels rapping on the parquet. She was dressed for court, in a wrap of amethyst-colored satin with frogs and swags of gold. A hooded traveling cloak was draped about her shoulders, and rubies clustered about her throat and wrists.

"I thought to find you dying alone in your bed," she said.

"And instead you find me at ease in my library," said I. "I prove a poor object for your noble and admirable compassion. Yet, in some small recompense, I can offer you wine, or a tisane, if Your Grace will tarry."

She looked at me carefully before she answered, perhaps to make certain I wasn't hiding a serious injury, and then consented to a tisane. "May I take your cloak?" I asked, and when she gave permission, I rang for Stiver. When the steward arrived, I gave him the cloak, ordered the tisane and some cakes, and then helped Her Grace to sit at one of the library tables.

I sat by her. "What have you heard that had me mortally wounded?" I asked.

A charming blush touched her cheeks. "I'll admit that was my imagination," said she. "I'd heard that you'd received a wound from Sir Edelmir Westley, after you'd thrown him into the water during a fight and then had to rescue him from drowning. It was I who feared the wound was mortal."

"Sir Edelmir did not attack me in that blackguardly way," I said. "He was half-drowned and could barely move."

She viewed me with grave blue eyes. "Perhaps you'd better tell me what happened."

This I did, having no reason to alter the story in any way. I even admitted that I had cut myself, with my own knife.

"And thus it has fallen out to my satisfaction," said I in conclusion. "For I wished not to be killed, and still I live. And I wished to kill no other man, and this I have avoided."

"And you have suffered no dishonor," she said, "which, considering your pacific intent, was the most difficult object of all."

"I am gratified that Your Grace thinks so."

Stiver arrived with the tisane in a copper pot, and two footmen who carried a tray with cups, plates, cakes, napkins, forks, and a sauceboat of jam. All these were distributed—"By your leave, Your Grace"—and then the servants withdrew. The soft scent of anise rose in the room from the steaming cups. Her Grace turned to me.

"The court buzzes with speculation about the cause of the fight. Can you tell me—" She hesitated. "Tell me, that is, without compromising the honor of any third party?"

I admired her for wishing to save Lady Westley's reputation, so I hastened to tell her the true story. "Westley said I had insulted him," I said. "I don't believe I did any such thing. I believe he was urged to the fight by another party, a man who wishes me ill."

Her gaze turned acute. "Who is that?"

"Wenlock."

She seemed puzzled. "How have you offended his lordship?"

This required a lengthy explanation, and perhaps one that seemed not entirely convincing. Alas, the only way I could make the tale plausible was to bring Orlanda into it, and that would make me seem like a madman.

"I believe Westley was deeply in debt," I said in conclusion, "and that Wenlock bought up so many of his notes that Westley was unable to resist him."

Her Grace's face was troubled. "If true, this speaks to a deep dishonor in both," she said.

"It would be easy enough to discover the truth," said I, "for I need only ask those who held Westley's debt who bought it from them."

Which was easier than it might sound, for there were brokers in Howel who would buy at a discount the signed notes given by gamesters and other debtors, and then try to collect the full amount for themselves. There were only a few such men, for they needed to be so highly placed as to be able to pursue courtiers into the palace itself, and most were courtiers themselves, or office-holders.

"I do not know if I wish to pursue such an investigation," I said. "For having thwarted Wenlock, and defeated his instrument, he would be foolish indeed to pursue his enmity. Perhaps it is best to let the matter lie."

"Quillifer, I think you must investigate, not least for your own protection," said she. "If this was an attempt at murder, then it must be brought to the light." She gave me a serious look. "There was another time," she said, "when a great nobleman tried to murder you."

I winced in remembered pain. "I recall it all too well."

"Her Majesty exiled him to his estate, and there he has remained."

"That lord flirted also with the rebel cause, though it could not be proved, and Her Majesty wished to punish him for his friendship with Clayborne." I considered my situation. "Would Her Majesty take action against yet another great noble, on behalf of a mere rampallion knight?"

"You are not a rampallion but a royal official, and one well known in the court," said Her Grace. "An attack on you is an attack on the royal dignity. The throne would have to respond in some way, though perhaps you would not wish to make a formal, legal complaint, but allow the chancellor to handle it beneath, as they say, the rose."

I found this good advice, for I did not want to instigate any form of legal proceeding. I did not think Wenlock would wish to be brought into court, and I rather thought he would set a great many murderers to lurking behind the arras before he would allow that to happen.

"I will follow your counsel," I said, "and I thank you for it." I looked at her, the slim, small form with its fruitful curve about the middle. "And you, Your Grace?" I asked. "Are you faring well?"

"I am much better now than those first few months," said she, and raised her fork. "For see, I am able to enjoy your cakes. For some while even the very sight of food made me ill."

"My mother would have made you a pottage that would have restored your appetite," I said. "But perhaps your cook knows the recipe, for I see you now at the summit of health. And my kitchen will rejoice that you have had a second cake."

"It seems I am not the only fertile mare in the stable," said the duchess. "At court they say that Her Majesty is again with child."

"It distresses me that you refer to yourself as a mare," said I. "For surely you are a sprightly young jennet made to dance lightly over the fields, and toss your bright palomino hair in the wind."

"I will not be dancing lightly for some months yet," she said. "But I thank you for the compliment."

"Has Her Majesty confirmed that she is *praegnas*?"

"Nay, but some preparations have been made. For after her miscarriages she no longer trusts the physicians here in Duisland, and has said more than once that if the fates are ever again kind to her womb, she will travel to Loretto and give birth there, under the supervision of the royal physicians of her husband's house. And now she is making plans to travel to Loretto."

I sipped my tisane as I considered this news. "In this season? If one of our winter gales rises, that will not be such a sweet voyage for a woman but newly with child."

"Priscus must go in any case, as his father will give him an army against Thurnmark. So Berlauda has put it about that she wishes to accompany her husband as far as Longres Regius, where she will accept the hospitality of King Henrico. But we suspect she may have other reasons for going."

"Are these Lorettan physicians so superior to our own? And would Berlauda not better profit to banish all physicians from the court? For my father told me I should never see a physician, nor go to a hospital, unless I was already dying; and then the doctors' cures might save my life, but at least they would not shorten it if they proved deadly."

Her Grace smiled. "Perhaps your father's wisdom has reached Her Majesty, for she is avoiding her doctors' draughts and purges."

"My father would be pleased to hear it." I ventured a bite of cake. "But when she goes to Loretto, she must travel with the whole court, must she not?"

"With the Privy Council, at least. And she can't leave Howel until the Estates have finished their wrangling, and my husband says the wrangling will be prolonged."

"In the last war, with Clayborne's rebellion sweeping all of Bonille, the Estates fought each other over war taxes. And now they are to vote for war taxes when there is no threat to our country?"

The duchess contemplated her second cake. "The queen wishes to oblige her husband, who wishes to bring to the war an army suitable for the maintenance of his kingly greatness and majesty."

"And His Grace? How is your husband disposed?"

"He is the queen's kinsman, and a member of the Great Council. He must support the queen." Her expression failed to conceal that her husband's support was reluctant.

The duchess took another bite of cake and a sip of her tisane, and rose. "I must return home. But I am so happy to see that you've taken no hurt."

"I am likewise happy on that score," said I, "and I will be at pains to remain thus happy in the future."

Her blue eyes looked up into mine, and she touched my arm. "Should you fall afoul of any more of these plots," she said, "I want you to remember that I and my husband are your friends, and that we will help you."

"Your Grace, I did not wish to involve you in anything so sordid as an encounter with rapiers."

She gave a smile. "Oh ay, you were clever, and you survived. But it were best that the encounter never happened at all, and my husband could have arranged that."

I was intrigued. "How, Your Grace?"

"A few of the sheriff's men, sent to the place of rendezvous. You and Westley might have spent a few hours in jail, and you might have been fined, but there would have been no danger to either of you."

I bowed. "It is the superior plan by far. I will be sure to consult you on all such matters in the future."

I showed the duchess to her carriage and watched as it rolled away into the growing evening. It was all too easy, in a place like the court, surrounded by ambitious, arrogant, and unfeeling men, to feel that I had no friends, and that the entire burden of my life rested on my shoulders alone. Her Grace had just provided a lesson that this was not the case, and as I went to my supper, I felt a growing sense of gratitude.

The next day I put on my armor and rode to the palace. Not to fight, but to accompany King Priscus to the opening of the Estates. He was to be accompanied by no less than a thousand men in glittering armor, a glorious pageant of steel and power, perhaps aimed at cowing the Estates before the session began.

Priscus himself was dressed in magnificent cloth of gold, with an ostrich feather in his hat and gems on every finger, and his ermine-trimmed scarlet robe of state over all. He was surrounded by lords and kinsmen in full armor, and by heralds carrying the royal standard and his own personal banner. Each lord or official had his own standard-bearer, so the front of the great procession resembled a great advancing wall of brilliant standards, ensigns, banderoles, and pennants, all bravely flying in the wind.

As a new-made royal official, I had been assigned my own part farther back in the column. I did not own a complete set of full armor, but rode as a demilance, with breast- and backplate, gorget, helmet,

and thigh pieces, and my lower legs encased in great shining boots ornamented with the silver spurs of my knighthood. Behind me, carrying my blue banner, rode Rufino Knott, dressed less grandly in some
of the surplus armor I'd won, three years before, from the bandit
knight Sir Basil of the Heugh. My charger Phrenzy trotted along with
neck arched and his head high, his ears pricked forward, and a kind
of snarl fixed to his upper lip, as if he were bidding defiance to the
other horses, and ready to challenge them if they did not keep clear.

We rode along the lake's edge, past all the grand palaces of the
lords, and into Howel itself. Thousands of the townsfolk had come
out to cheer the king, and he waved with gracious ease at those who
waved their handkerchiefs, threw posies or garlands, or called on the
Pilgrim to bless His Majesty. The road shivered beneath the hoof-
beats of a thousand horses, and the city echoed to the call of trumpets. I felt my heart lift at the sheer magnificence of it all.

And then we rode past the Hall of Justice, and I saw there the head
of the Lord High Admiral Mardall, newly severed, next to that of the
unlucky Marquess of Scutterfield. Dogs lapped at the blood until they
fled the thunder of the horses. My heart fell again, and it was with pur-
poseful resignation rather than high spirits that I continued my ride.

I looked for Sir Edelmir Westley, but I saw neither him nor his
banner.

Our journey came to an end before the House of Peers, an old
shambles of a building with its foundations dating from the old
empire, and its gables, towers, and belfries raised rather miscella-
neously over the last several centuries. Here we waited for the queen,
for Berlauda had spent the night in the Monastery of the Hallowed
Pledge, where the leaders of the Burgesses had joined her that morning for prayers and chants to assure the success of the day's under-
taking.

Berlauda arrived in an open-topped carriage, magnificent in her
scarlet robes decked with ermine and gold thread, with a jeweled

crown atop her blond head. Her sister and the abbot Fosco also rode in the carriage, both magnificent in silks and satins, purfles and swags. They were escorted by a company of the Queen's Own Horse, who rattled up in their armor, and whose coronel, my old companion Lord Barkin, helped the queen alight from her carriage.

Those of us in the king's party doffed our helmets in salute and cheered Her Majesty while our banners waved overhead; but I thought of the lord admiral's pale head atop its pike, with blood-drops falling from its long hair, and my cheers were not so lusty as they might have been.

Berlauda took her husband's arm, and the two of them entered the House of Peers, followed by heralds and the members of the Great Council. Those lords who had ridden in the procession followed in haste, for they had to doff their armor and put on their scarlet robes before the business of the house commenced.

There was then a pause, and then bells tolled to announce that the formal business of the day had commenced, and that Their Majesties sat beneath the canopy of state, with the peers arranged about them. In accordance with tradition, the herald of brass was sent to the House of Burgesses to summon the members to wait upon Their Majesties and to hear the address from the throne, but was refused. The herald of silver was sent likewise, and likewise sent back. But lastly, after the Burgesses had asserted their independence, the herald of gold was admitted, and returned with the Burgesses following in formal procession. After the doors were shut behind them, the bells rang again, and the business of the Estates commenced.

At this point the king's escort was dismissed; the Queen's Own would be sufficient to escort Their Majesties back to Ings Magna. I considered greeting Lord Barkin and offering to stand him a jack of wine or beer, but he disappeared into the house, I suppose to await further orders. The taverns I knew would be crowded, and so I turned Phrenzy about and rode back to Rackheath House, where Master

Stiver brought me a small package from which wafted the faint odor of Lady Westley's bergamot scent. It was with great foreboding that I opened it and read words written in haste, and blotched with careless splashes of ink.

> *Heliodor—*
>
> *I must thank you for my husband's life, though I could wish you had not saved him at such an expense to his pride. So humiliating has he found the outcome of his encounter that he has resigned his position as master of the henchmen, and will travel at once to Loretto to take part in King Henrico's war. There he may recover both his dignity and his fortune.*
>
> *I must go with him, for he has no one else, and he believes that even his friends will despise him for the manner of his defeat.*
>
> *I must therefore disregard all your advice, though I know it was well intentioned. There is little time, and there is scandal enough without my adding to it.*
>
> *You and I must never meet again, for I would not have my husband humiliated once more. I will remember you always, and remember also that you tried to save me from what the world will call my folly.*
>
> *Some of my jewelry I may have to pawn, but I wish to return the enclosed. I would rather you keep it than I fail the test, and find myself selling this precious memory in order to meet some debt.*
>
> *Yours in sorrow,*
Girasol

In the small package was the white diamond I had given her as a love-gift, with its silver chain and simple setting. I held it in my clenched fist while I contemplated my own helplessness in all these dealings, and I wondered if I should have told her what I suspected of Westley's dealings with Wenlock, and if that would have altered her decision.

For a wild moment I considered riding to her house and pleading with her to fly with me. But no, I thought, I could not swerve her now from the course she had so decided upon, be it ever so unwise.

And so concluding, I went to my strongbox and laid the diamond to rest in a pouch of velvet black as mourning, and beside it I laid the sun medallion, and as I closed the box, I felt that sun in eclipse, and the world seemed a little darker.

That evening I tried to cheer myself by playing guitar with Master Knott, and as we tuned our instruments, he turned to me. "What you predicted, Sir Quillifer, has come about."

"I'm pleased to know of my prescience," said I. "But what is it that I prophesied?"

"That someone would come to me and offer money to inform on you."

"Ah." I considered this. "Who was it?"

"He said his name was Darnley, but I know no more than that."

I plucked the D string, found it flat, and gave a twist to the tuning peg. "How much does he offer?"

"Three crowns per month. More if I report something of great moment."

"In that case," said I. "We shall invent a tale worth the telling. And I will match whatever he pays you."

"Thank you, sir. That is very generous."

I gave the matter more thought, and then said, "Try to find out if Darnley is paying anyone else in the household."

Knott nodded. "Very good, sir."

"And now," said I, "let us play."

CHAPTER SEVENTEEN

The next day, Lady Westley's plight filling my mind with a storm of anger and despair, I went to the House of Burgesses and watched the proceedings from the narrow gallery. The peers met in a ramshackle old palace, but the Burgesses met in the former great hall of Howel College, built before the college became a part of the great King's University built on the watery meads east of the city. The gallery had been added in recent decades, and it creaked and groaned beneath the weight of the spectators. High windows brought in the dull winter light, and old tapestries, blackened and worn, draped the walls.

The chain of my office and a vail to one of the porters gained me a good seat, and I found myself near Sir Denys Hulme, the chancellor of the exchequer. Before he gained his peerage he had sat among the Burgesses and overseen the king's business there, but now as Baron Hulme he could not speak in the Burgesses, and had to manage them through a deputy. But because the passage of Berlauda's new taxes was crucial, more here than in the other house, he sat in the gallery of the Burgesses, and communicated with his deputy through notes carried by a messenger.

Because Their Majesties also viewed the Burgesses as of primary importance, they tended the day's business themselves, from beneath the canopy of state they had set up at the head of the chamber. They wore their ermine-trimmed robes of state, and Priscus wore a gold circlet about his dark head, while Berlauda had a small crown perched atop her blond hair.

For myself, I hoped that the Burgesses would raise money for the relief of Ethlebight and the other districts ravaged by the summer storm. For the war and the raising of palaces I cared little.

The session began, however, with a wrangle over the delicate matter of free speech. For the members begged leave of Their Majesties to speak freely before the throne, a liberty which the co-sovereigns were reluctant to grant. "We do not grant liberty to cause us offense," said the queen.

"We pray the truth cannot offend Your Majesties," said the spokesman for the Burgesses. He was a dark-visaged, scowling man from Selford, a rich silk merchant named Umbrey.

"We will be the judge of truth!" said Priscus. His face had turned scarlet with anger, and his hands clenched into fists. He was no longer the pleasant king with his *caw-caw-caw*, but an autocrat, raised to rule a nation where no one contradicted the monarch and lived. "The Blessed Pilgrim has given unto us the mastery of the state, the courts, and the Estates," he said, "and there is no greater judge in the land than we ourselves."

"The Pilgrim then give you the wisdom to judge wisely," said Umbrey.

Priscus understood this as defiance. "You desire liberty?" he said. "We give you the liberty to say 'ay,' or to say 'nay.'"

Umbrey looked over the assembly and saw crackling resentment rise in the Burgesses at this curt treatment, and he folded his arms. "In that case, Majesty," said he, "we may call for the vote now, and see whether the result pleaseth you."

Next to me in the gallery Hulme wrote frantically on a wax tablet and, without bothering to summon his messenger, tossed it below to Sir Edmund Tryon, his deputy in the Burgesses. Who then rose and, begging Their Majesties' permission to speak, began an attempt to redirect the storm that had built in the chamber.

"Why should Their Majesties consent aforetime to slander and derogation?" he said. "We of the Burgesses are honored by the royal presence, and the demands by mannerless rudesbys to offend the dignity of the house by baying their coarse opinions in this sacred chamber are an insult to all members."

"As we speak of slander and derogation," Umbrey said, "perhaps the honorable member would care to name these mannerless rudesbys?"

Tryon ignored the interruption. "Their Majesties desire naught but decency and order," he said. "There is no intention to forbid speech, but rather to keep the speech on point. We are summoned to this house on urgent business that is confronting all Duisland. So I beg Their Majesties to grant liberty of speech on the matter of the bill placed before the house, but to forbid distraction, disorder, and insult."

Berlauda, too, had sensed the danger that might result from a revolt of the commons, and was relieved to be offered an alternative.

"This we grant right willingly," she said. Her husband glowered, but said nothing.

Another member rose. I recognized him as the silver-haired Sir Cecil Greene, from my own city of Ethlebight, who had served as lord mayor and long been an alderman alongside my father. He was an apothecary, but a rich one, for he owned property and loaned money on merchant ventures.

"Your Majesties," he said, "and honorable members of the house, I wish to say that I have studied the bill that is brought before us, and I desire to say before Their Majesties that insufficient monies are allocated for the relief of the victims of the summer's great storm. Their Majesties desire that we raise and victual an army of twenty thousand men, but more than twenty thousand of our own people— men, women, and babes—will starve this winter if they have not succor. I remind the honorable members that the storm was nearly four months ago, and precious little aid has been given in the time since, even as the price of a loaf of cheat bread has risen to two pence."

Tryon responded that the crown would entertain a greater sum for the relief of the districts afflicted by the storm, but that this should be voted after the bill now placed before the house. Greene respectfully disagreed, and Umbrey rose to support him. "For it should not be said," he observed, "that the care of Their Majesties' own subjects should take second place to a war against a people far away, who have done us no harm, and with whom our trade is worth four hundred thousand royals every year."

King Priscus still burned with anger. "And how much for the honor of the nation?" he demanded. "How much is that!"

The spokesmen for the Burgesses wisely did not offer an answer, and the debate continued. It became apparent that Umbrey, Greene, and others in the leadership were determined to debate the bill clause by clause, and that the Burgesses would revisit the debate on carucage, ship money, and the salt tax that had been so thoroughly disputed during the last war.

Other Burgesses spoke loudly in favor of the war and the bill. They expressed no strong conviction against Thurnmark, but seemed in favor of war generally, and it mattered not against who. It was as if the army was like their favorite jouster, and they wished to see that jouster trample his rivals no matter what colors they wore. War was a great jubilant sport to them, an entertainment that they wished to enjoy, particularly if they could enjoy it from the safety of the House of Burgesses.

After listening to a few of this faction's speeches, I decided that if someone made a motion in North Howel to invade South Howel and kill all the inhabitants there, at least a fifth of the population would cheer for the idea.

After some hours the Burgesses rose for dinner, and a messenger in the cap and gown of an apprentice lawyer approached me. "Sir Quillifer," he said, "Lord Edevane hopes to speak with you."

"I am happy to wait upon his lordship," said I, and followed the messenger across the square to the House of Peers. Berlauda's private secretary I found in a small, crowded office lit by beeswax candles, with his peer's scarlet robes hanging behind him on a stand clearly made for the purpose. Edevane himself was gazing pensively at papers, his spectacles drawn down his nose, and he made a note on one of the papers before rising to greet me.

"How went the Burgesses?" he asked.

I looked into the dead-fish eyes while I considered an answer. "I think it may be a long winter," I said finally.

"There is ever a want of goodwill in the Burgesses," Edevane said. "Yet it will be managed, one way or another."

The image of those two heads before the Hall of Justice came to my mind, and I wondered what sort of managing Edevane intended.

Edevane sat again behind his desk, and he gestured me toward a stool standing by a cabinet. "I apologize for the scant comfort," he said in his soft voice. "Yet I can offer you a cushion."

"I thank your lordship." Placing the cushion on the stool elevated me somewhat, so that my knees were not quite level with my ears, and Edevane looked down at me with an expression of mild satisfaction, as if he desired me to know that I was below him, in life as in his office.

"I wished to say that I think you handled wisely the encounter with Sir Edelmir Westley," he said. "It is well that no injury resulted."

Even though Lord Edevane had seen fit to compliment me, I found it an unpleasant surprise that he raised the matter at all.

"My intention was to prevent bloodshed, your lordship," I said.

"No bloodshed, yet Westley has thrown up his office, and seems intent on fleeing," he said. "Yet who pursues? I trust you intend no vengeance upon him."

"None whatever," said I. "We were comrades, or so I thought. His challenge came as a surprise."

He gave me an incurious look. "It has not escaped my attention that not everyone at court is your friend," he said. "Do you think Westley might have been acting on the part of another?"

For a moment my breath stopped in my throat. Here, I thought, was a chance to serve Wenlock as he deserved. Yet I hesitated—for I had no wish to become one of the secretary's loathsome little creatures, going to their master with tales.

Yet Edevane might know more than I, and to dissimulate was dangerous for me.

"Westley is a gamester, and may have been in debt," I said. "I had thought to inquire among the brokers who handle such matters, and discover if anyone had purchased Sir Edelmir's notes."

"You need make no such inquiries," said Edevane quickly. "I will look into the matter myself."

For Edevane, I thought, would gather what evidence he could find, and use it for his own purposes. Wenlock in prison, or exiled in disgrace, was of no use to him, but a great nobleman under his thumb would bring its own rewards.

Well, I supposed, at least my hands would be clean in the matter. And my life would be that much simpler if no more mercenaries tried to kill me.

Edevane gazed at me, and for the first time I saw his face change expression, to something like curiosity. "Is it not past time, Lord Warden," he asked, "for you to travel to Inchmaden, to undertake your commission against the iron birds?"

"I sent a deputy, my lord. If he is not in Inchmaden by now, it is because he has not yet found a ship bound for the west coast."

For the second time Edevane's expression changed, this time to something approaching surprise.

"You are not authorized a deputy, Lord Warden," he said.

"Surely I can employ men at my own expense," said I. "I've sent a crew west equipped with mortars and other gear that may serve to trap the monsters. I thought I myself might serve better in the capital, corresponding with all the lords lieutenants about chimerae and researching the archives."

Edevane asked me what and who I had sent to Inchmaden, and I told him. "That seems very well reasoned," he said.

"Thank you, my lord."

By this time I had begun to understand the purpose of his soft, studied measure of speaking. All within his hearing would have to lean in toward him in order to hear him properly, and to anyone standing by he would seem the most fascinating presence in the room. And even if there were no observer, those in his company would have to pay close attention to his words.

He leaned back in his chair and regarded me with his blank eyes. "As you will be in Howel for the present," he said, "I wonder if I can ask for your impression of—of certain individuals."

It required no great intelligence to understand that he intended to employ me as an informer. I had no wish to serve him in this manner, yet, again, refusal might mark me as the enemy of the deadliest man in the realm.

I ventured a response. "I doubt that I know very many people who would interest you."

His dead eyes regarded me from across his desk. "You know, for example, Their Graces of Roundsilver," he said.

"Ay," said I. "But we are hardly intimates. I can't conceive how my ideas regarding Their Graces would be of any significance, not when they are better known by practically everyone at court."

"It is not the Roundsilvers who interest me," said Edevane. "But some others who have been seen in their circle. The Countess Marcella, for instance."

I was relieved to have nothing to say about the Aekoi lady-in-waiting. "I have spoken to her on a single occasion, nearly two months ago," I said. "She said she would return to the Empire as soon as she could manage it."

"Is she even from the Empire?" asked Edevane. "Is she truly a countess?"

"Surely the lady must have some credentials," I said, "else Her Highness would scarcely employ her."

Edevane waved a hand. "In truth, I know nothing against her. But she touches the royal family, and so she is of interest and perhaps concern."

"If I were to employ someone as a spy," said I, "surely I would choose someone less conspicuous, and preferably a human instead of a gold-skinned Aekoi."

"She might not be a spy, but a fraudster." Edevane gazed at the flame rising from one of his wax candles. "In truth, I fear for Her Highness."

"You fear that Countess Marcella might defraud her? Of what? Money?"

The candle sent leaping flames reflecting in Edevane's spectacles. "I fear Her Highness might be used by unscrupulous men," he said. "Because she is near to the throne, she might become the unwitting center of a faction aimed at opposing Their Majesties. She is young and, having grown up away from the court, is inexperienced in the ways and wiles of the palace. She might be manipulated and compromised by those who wish the kingdom ill."

He spoke these words in his grave, thoughtful tone, and as he spoke, I felt as if insects were creeping up my spine. I suspected these phrases were not speculation on the secretary's part, but a kind of *rehearsal,* a preparation for the case he would make against Floria when the time came.

When, I thought, Berlauda gave birth to a healthy heir, and Floria was no longer needed.

"The Pilgrim forbid such a thing," I said with absolute sincerity.

Edevane turned to me. "You know the princess, do you not?"

"I have met her half a dozen times in the last three years," I said.

The gold-rimmed spectacles glimmered. "Yet she exerted herself to save you when you were accused of brawling in the streets of Selford."

"I should like to think this was due to Her Highness's innate sense of justice. I had been set on by a pack of murderers."

His measured speech went on, pacing along with his relentless thought. "Yet it was due to Her Highness's influence that those murderers went to the scaffold, and not you."

"They had put her in danger as well."

"Yet," he insisted in his mild way, "I think she must favor you in some way."

I put on my exasperated-bailiff face. "I fear I amuse her," said I. "She looks on me as a jester, or a performing dog."

"Perhaps you should exert yourself to amuse her further," said Edevane.

He was giving me little choice. I could comply, or I could become his enemy, and he would be a far more formidable enemy than Wenlock or Westley.

"Well," said I, "if I am to guard Her Highness from those who would oppose the crown, I shall do my best. But I cannot simply appoint myself buffoon to a princess, she must choose to accept my company."

"You are an ingenious man," said the secretary. "I think you can play whatever part will serve." He paused for a moment, and then said, "I could offer you a stipend, if you feel that would aid you."

I felt heat burn in my blood, and I hoped I was not showing the rage this suggestion had ignited in me. "My lord," I said, "I hardly need to be paid to uphold the crown. I have done so, you may remember, to my cost."

"I beg your pardon, Lord Warden," Edevane said. "I am so used to the crooked ways of the court that I sometimes forget there are honorable men in the world."

A bell rang out from somewhere above the roof leads, and Edevane rose from his chair. I rose from the low stool, my knees creaking. Two varlets entered and, without a word, took his red robe from the stand and helped him into it.

"The house is about to convene, and I must attend," said Edevane. "I thank you for your visit, and I hope you will let me know how the matter of Inchmaden falls out."

I bade the principal private secretary farewell and walked to the House of Burgesses to listen to the afternoon's debate. It was much the same debate as had been heard that morning, and I saw that Priscus could barely restrain his impatience, twisting and shifting on his throne, his baleful eyes turning from one member to the next, as if marking them for some bloody private vengeance. Perhaps that was in fact what he was doing.

I found myself thinking of the princess Floria and the menacing shadows that seemed to surround her, shadows that seemed to have taken on a more tangible form in the last half hour.

My crooked finger ached, as if to tell me of a coming storm.

CHAPTER EIGHTEEN

---

he storm broke the next day, and cold rain sluiced off the roof in sheer, shimmering sheets while a freezing wind whipped up white wave crests on the gray lake. My crooked finger throbbed, and I thought of Lady Westley fleeing through the cold, and I felt thoroughly miserable. I decided not to brave the weather in order to witness another day of argument in the Burgesses, so it was not until the afternoon that I heard that Umbrey and Greene had been arrested and carried off to Murkdale Hags. The Burgesses, thus rendered compliant, voted the funds for the war and then began the complicated business of working out a means of raising the money.

This news I heard at the Admiralty Office, where—once the storm had abated somewhat—I had gone in search of privateering commissions for my ships. I owned two ships outright, the *Sea-Holly* galleon, which I'd acquired in the war, and the *Ostra* pinnace of eighty tons, which I'd built in Ethlebight out of my profits. *Sea-Holly* was a slow merchant, but *Ostra* was a fast, agile little ship, ideal for a privateer. Ideally I would want privateering commissions for both, for though *Sea-Holly* was not suitable to cruise for enemy merchants near Thurnmark, yet she might meet Thurnmark ships by chance on the seas, ships that had not yet heard they were at war, and with a letter of marque might legally seize them.

Against this I had to balance the fact that for each commission I had to bond myself to the tune of two hundred royals, and I debated with myself whether *Sea-Holly*'s commission was worth the expense. Yet the money would come back to me after the war, and so in the end I purchased the commission.

I also purchased commissions for some ships I owned along with Kevin Spellman and his father, including the pinnace *Able* that had aided in the salvage of *Royal Stilwell*, and the great galleon *Sovereign*, which would not act as a privateer, but which was so large and well armed that it could easily overcome any Thurnmark vessels encountered on its long trip to Tabarzam.

Some other ships I decided not to commission, but instead left the matter to the judgment of my partners.

I sent the commissions by messenger either to Kevin's father in Selford, or to the ship captains themselves, if I knew where to find them.

The Admiralty Office was a small building and served but as an auxiliary to the Admiralty itself, which was in Selford, in an old basilica. The place was busy, and while I waited my turn in the chill lobby, I heard of the arrest of the unfortunate Burgesses. It was the common opinion that they would soon be hanged on some pretext or another.

Later that afternoon I went to the Flesh Shambles, where most of Howel's butchers had their shops, and I made some inquiries about cooks. I wanted to know which of the city's cooks had showed a fine and discriminating knowledge of animal flesh and the ways of preparing it, and of these, which might be amenable to work for a new master. Most of those recommended to me came almost daily to provide for their masters' kitchens, and so I left messages for them asking if they would call upon me at my house.

This led to my hiring Harry Noach, who had been the undercook to Count Older, a cousin-german to Count Wenlock who normally resided in Amberstone but had come to Howel for the meeting of the Estates. Noach brought to my house samples of his work, which included some drawings of the great marchpane centerpieces used at formal banquets, where sugar-castles or fabulous beasts or landscapes with rivers of fine wine were placed for the delectation of the guests. I bought him away from Count Older and put him in charge of my kitchen with instructions to develop dishes according to my plan.

After a few days Greene and Umbrey were released from prison and resumed their places in the House of Burgesses. Neither Hulme nor Tryon could manage the Burgesses without them, and Their Majesties had ceased to attend once the Burgesses had voted the bill that most concerned them. Priscus had got his twenty thousand soldiers, and the details of how he was to pay for them did not concern him.

The issues of taxation were not resolved when the old holiday of the Silly Shepherds blossomed in mid-December, and work ceased for a day while everyone in Howel, from the palace to the meanest apprentice in the tallow-chandlers' guild, dressed as rustics and tried to play the syrinx. At midday there was a regatta, to take place entirely under sail, and *Dunnock* and the other galleys came to the start on a fine sunny day, with a light breeze blowing from the northwest. I had confidence, for Boatswain Lepalik and I had drilled the crew to perfection under sail.

Boatswain Lepalik deserves perhaps a mention. He comes from an island far to the south and east of the Candara Coast, past the celestial equator and beyond the border of any map I have ever seen. His people have black skins, and the men shave their heads and work hard to sculpt their bodies like ancient athletes, in order to attract the women, who they prefer corpulent. Lepalik often complained to me that the women of Duisland were far too thin, and the slender Aekoi women ridiculous. Lepalik's people are great sailors in their outrigger canoes, and Lepalik hunted whales, hurling the great harpoon tipped with obsidian.

One day a harpooned whale dragged the canoe for many miles before dying, after which a storm carried the boat far away from its prey. The mariners were quite lost and wandered the sun-soaked sea until a foreign ship rescued them. That began Lepalik's travels through eastern realms whose names come to us as legends, for there is always work for a good sailor. Through good service he was awarded the silver whistle of a boatswain, and he worked his way to Tabarzam, where he came aboard *Royal Stilwell* as a replacement for a man who had died.

He is well liked by his crew, but he has begun to long for home, for he has had no word of his family since the storm carried him away. There are a few other black men in Duisland, but none hail from as far away as his subequatorial island. Now that he is over fifty and there is gray in his bushy beard, Lepalik wishes to return to see how his family and friends have fared. I have vowed to aid him in this, and will send him as far as Tabarzam, and give him some money to buy passage to his island, if he can find it.

On the day of the regatta we circled and circled before the start line, the sail booming and slatting overhead, and then Lord Thistlegorm had the signal gun fired, and we set out on a reach, with the wind coming over my left shoulder. No sooner had we begun than fine wisps of mist began to rise from the water. The wisps grew thicker, and as I made the first turn, I saw white towers of fog on the northern horizon, towers that came down slowly before the wind, like dancers in the stately pavane.

As we passed behind the islands, the mist engulfed us completely, and I felt a fine, fresh drizzle on my face. Now my galley seemed alone on the lake, the water chuckling beneath the transom as the mainsail shivered close-hauled. I could hear boats all around me, but they were all invisible, and I was worried that one might accidentally come aboard us. I called out *"Dunnock! Dunnock!"* to let the other captains know where I sailed, and soon I heard others take up their own calls, but the cries echoed eerily in that fine mist, and it was hard to know where any vessel was by the sound alone.

I knew that soon I must clear the tail of the second island, and then come about onto my new course for the finish line, but I could not tell where the island was, or the finish line, or for that matter where my own galley might be. For all that I knew, I might be sailing entirely in the wrong direction, or about to run aground on the western bank. So I made my best guess, called the crew to tend the staysail set forward of the mast, and put the helm down.

"Helm's alee!" I called, and then immediately began to call *"Dunnock! Dunnock!"* for I knew I was about to cross the path of the other vessels, and that I risked a collision. Water sloshed against the rudder, and the sails flogged as we came into the eye of the wind. A ghostly form appeared just ahead, a dark sail looming directly before the bow. My blood froze, but the other galley crossed just inches ahead of *Dunnock*'s bow, and I caught a glimpse of the terrified, staring eyes of the towheaded helmsman as we crossed his stern. He wore a shepherd's smock, and I saw a flute tucked into his belt.

Then we seemed alone on the water again, moving much faster now, with the water laughing as it ran down the strakes and the mist cool on my cheeks. I called out *"Dunnock"* every few seconds and braced myself to run aground on one or another of the islands. Yet the minutes passed, no islands appeared, and I began to feel myself more at ease.

Which ease came too soon, for a galley appeared before us, crossing our bows. I threw down the helm, but the rudder bit too late at the water, and we swung slightly to starboard and rammed the other vessel on its port quarter. Planks shrieked and snapped. *Dunnock* came to a smashing halt, its sails and gear crashing. I was thrown forward onto my knees. The other vessel rolled, sending up a vast white wave, but it then came back upright. I heard the chuckle of water as the lake began to pour into the stricken vessel.

I told the crew to douse the sails, so that we would not sail away and leave the other galley stranded and sinking, and the canvas came down with a rattle. I rose from my scraped knees and ran forward, only to encounter the formidable glare of the Count of Wenlock. We stared at each other for a few seconds, and then I recovered from my surprise and found my tongue.

"Well, my lord," said I, "it seems you have once again chosen a flawed instrument."

Wenlock's pale face darkened with anger. "Curse you to hell, Quillifer!"

"I believe the correct form of address is 'Lord Warden,'" said I.

Wenlock brandished a fist. "Damned if I'll ever call you 'lord'!"

"Then you may sink with your boat," I said, "though I will do your crew the courtesy of saving their lives."

One of Wenlock's crew reached for *Dunnock*'s gunwale and pulled it close to come aboard. Wenlock fixed him with a furious eye. "Don't you dare!" he snarled.

The crewman shrugged. "I can't swim," he said in the most sensible way, and came aboard my vessel.

At that moment a gun boomed out from the shore. I thought it perhaps signaled the end of the race, but after we had finished taking Wenlock's crew aboard, the gun fired again, and I realized that it was meant to guide us home. I looked at Wenlock, whose boat was far down by the stern.

"Last chance, my lord."

"Go and drown yourself!"

"I am not the man in danger of drowning," I said. If his own foolishness filled his lungs with water, it was none of my affair. I would be rid of an enemy, and Edevane of an instrument, both of which developments I thought could only improve the world.

I told the crew to stand by the halliards and be ready to raise the sail. And then, in less time than it takes to relate, another boat raced up from behind us and stove in our stern. None of us saw it coming until it struck. I was thrown back onto the stern counter, and by the time I regained my feet, my shoes were splashing in lake water.

I lunged out over the stern counter and seized the other ship's forestay, to keep it from sailing off, for now two crews needed rescuing. The three vessels spun in circles, powered by the third boat's sails. The captain of the other boat was a gentleman from Loretto, and he babbled apologies as our boats spun around one another.

"Get your sails down!" I told him. Holding the two galleys together by main strength, I felt as if I were being stretched on the rack.

Lake water gurgled beneath me. My feet grew cold and wet. Crewmen hopped up onto the stern counter and jumped to the Lorettan captain's boat, and sometimes uncivilly used me as a bridge. Last of all came Wenlock, who used my boat to cross without asking my permission. Like a proper captain, I was last to abandon *Dunnock*.

Neither *Dunnock* nor Wenlock's boat would sink. They were built of wood, and it is a property of wood to float. But as they filled with water, the weight of the masts and sails would roll them over, and the crew would probably have drowned or frozen before anyone could come out from the shore to rescue them, even if the wrecks could have been located in the fog. As soon as the fog cleared, I would take a boat out and tow *Dunnock* to shore, where I could hope to have it repaired in time for the next race.

The Lorettan captain raised his sails, and we forged off into the mist, the galley riding low with all the extra weight of the two rescued crews. The gun boomed out from shore every minute or so. It seemed to me that the sound grew louder with each fire, so we were on something like the right track.

I looked at Wenlock. "It is a shame that we shall neither of us know who would have beaten the other, my lord," I said. "Unless we manage to settle it now."

"You rammed my boat," Wenlock said, "and you did it deliberately, like the cullion you are. It is only justice that you lost your own galley."

"Yet we can finish the race between us." I began to undo my jerkin. "We can still race to shore. But we will have to do it without boat or crew."

He looked at me in scorn. "You mean to swim?"

"If you will swim with me."

He sneered. "I hardly think so."

I tore my leather jerkin off and began to unfasten my doublet. "It may be that you are afraid of the water," I suggested. "That can't be helped, but perhaps I can spur you with a wager. Twenty-five royals?"

His face was stony. He had not liked the suggestion that he was afraid. "I'll want odds. Two to one."

I laughed. "I am not so foolish as that, but I will wager thirty-five against your twenty-five."

Hatred warred with doubt in his eyes, and hatred won. He began to pull off his jerkin.

We stripped to our shirts and stood clinging to shrouds on either side of the galley. The captain looked at us as if we had been struck mad. The crewmen began to make wagers among themselves. I turned to Wenlock.

"At the next gunshot," I said. "Swim well, my lord, and you may recover some of the money you spent buying Westley."

Wenlock tried to snarl at me, but there was a hollow quality to his anger and a haunted look in his eye. His plan to kill me had gone astray, and now I had brought the matter out in public. And possibly Lord Edevane had already raised the subject with him, and he knew himself now for a base, crawling creature who would spend his days as the secretary's cringing lackey.

The cannon echoed through the mist, and Wenlock and I leaped into the lake. As I landed in the frigid water, my heart in its shock seemed to boom out louder than the gun, and I felt the sting of lake water in my nose and throat. I bobbed up behind the boat and struck out in its wake. Beside me I saw Wenlock's white hair rising from the water, and his long arms began to thrash the water. I wondered for a moment if he would view this as an opportunity to murder me, but he did not look at me, but instead directed his gaze at the boat as he pursued it. Encouraged by the violent thunder of my heart, I put on a burst of speed, and soon we were separated. I knew not where Wenlock was, but that was not surprising, for once the galley vanished into the mist, I did not know where I was myself. I tried to choose my path based on the firing of the cannon, but the gunshots were too far apart for me to be sure of staying on a bearing, and the shots themselves seemed to come from no constant direction.

I was surprised at how quickly I had managed to get lost. I began to tire, my breath rasped in my throat, and my fingers and toes grew numb in the cold. I plodded on at a deliberate pace, uncertain whether I was moving in the right direction. I knew that the distance from the islands to the quay at Ings Magna was about a league and a half, and I was confident that the galleys had covered most of that distance before I leaped into the water. The distance to shore should be no more than half a league, and I had reckoned less than five hundred yards, but that reckoning assumed the galleys had been heading in the right direction. But still I assured myself that if I kept swimming, I must encounter land sooner or later.

The cannon roared out every minute, and I seemed to grow no closer to the sound. I thought that I might be turning circles in the middle of the lake and half expected to encounter the overturned hull of *Dunnock*. I was panting for breath, my heart was hammering in my breast, and I had lost feeling in my arms and legs. Even my nose seemed to burn with frost.

Then the gun went off, and through the mist I saw a distant blos-som of fire. Coarse energy filled me, and I swam with greater speed. I tasted gunsmoke on the air. The mist swirled before my eyes, and then I saw Lady Westley's face looking at me with her gold-flecked blue eyes, and then the face dissolved into the mist. Anger filled me, and I struck on until I saw the quay, with galleys bobbing in the water and Lipton's crew loading the leather gun.

Panting, I let Lipton's gunners draw me from the water, and then I sat in dripping fury on the quay while I caught my breath and curses chased each other in my head. It was a while before I could speak, and then I looked up at Lipton and said, "Has Wenlock come yet?"

"I have not seen him, youngster," said Lipton. "And I sense a tale forthcoming."

A shudder ran through me, and then a bout of shivering. Lipton signaled the gun, and it went off, the sound a storm breaking on my ears. I began cautiously to stand on my bare feet.

At that moment I saw a white head on the water, and Lord Wenlock came swimming up with the same deliberate, methodical stroke he had used when he first set out on the water.

"You swim well, my lord," I said, "but you still owe me twenty-five royals." My teeth were chattering so badly that I could barely speak.

Wenlock was too exhausted to reply, but only floated in the water, blowing like a whale. Lipton's gunners bent to help him rise, and I remembered that I had a warm room in the palace, with a bottle of brandy and a change of clothes, and I walked away on my bare, frozen feet. Along the way I found my boat's crew, just ashore, who had my shoes and clothing. I stripped off my shirt and donned my doublet, jerkin, and trousers, which were far warmer, and then I told my crew to wait and went to the palace, where the corridors were filled with people dressed as shepherds and shepherdesses.

As I grew warm, the anger that had been simmering in my blood burst into flame, and when I went into my room—the room with the fresh, scented rushes, perfumed candles, and soft bed that I had prepared for Lady Westley—I saw the room flare with a coruscating light, and radiant in the center of the light, imperious in a jeweled gown of forest-green satin, Orlanda stood with her hair tumbled down about her shoulders in massy red waves. A coronet that looked as if it were made of delicate crystalline leaves circled her brow.

"Did you think I had forgotten you?" she asked.

I closed the door behind me and reached into the wardrobe for a shirt. "I need never blame myself for my misfortunes," I said. "You are present always."

"I hardly thought you would jump into the wintry lake," said she. "That was your idea alone."

"I was giving Wenlock a chance to drown," said I. "But he is stronger than I expected. Here."

I handed the shirt to Orlanda, who took it without thinking, and then looked at it in surprise. I walked past her to the mantel, where I poured myself a glass of brandy and drained half of it in a single draught. Orlanda looked at me sidelong.

"Do you offer none to me?"

"I'm not your servant, madam." I took another sip. "An you want some, a glass lies ready."

She tossed my shirt at me, lightly, as if she were discarding a piece of trash, and I snatched it from the air.

"You have done well with the obstacles I have put before you," she said. "Though at least I have sent running away that greedy gem-loving vixen for whom you prepared this chamber."

I managed not to grind my teeth. "So you inspired Wenlock to employ Westley against me."

Orlanda gave a lazy, catlike smile. "It is so easy to move these mortal lords, these tiny insects who believe the world spins about them. And Westley had a perfectly good reason to challenge you, though he knew it not. You may thank me for choosing not to tell him you dallied with his wife."

"That courtesy made little difference in the end."

"It saved the lady from scandal, and scandal is what she most feared. She knew that you would not marry her if she divorced."

"That is far from proven," I said. "Though it is true I consider myself a poor candidate for marriage, not least because an other-worldly being has cursed me." I reflected on the matter. "Should I pity Wenlock, then? That his ill deeds are due to your prompting, and that you are his puppet-mistress?"

Scorn twisted Orlanda's lips. "Wenlock was nothing," said she, "and now he is less than nothing. A worm that will writhe along Lord Edevane's trail, leaving a trail of slime."

"You conjure a lovely picture, to be sure." I looked at her. "Lady Westley's eyes, for example, were perfection itself. You must have studied her for hours."

Her scorn deepened. "None of your women are worth studying, Quillifer."

"That seems not to keep you from studying them." Warmth was enfolding my limbs. I sipped more brandy to encourage it. "The mist, then, was entirely yours, along with Lady Westley's image?"

"I wished to bring you and Wenlock together, to see what might result. And, I must admit, your swimming game was unexpected, though the finish was uninspired, with both of you wet but well."

"If you wanted blood, you should have conjured up a couple swords. Perhaps you should study drama with Blackwell." I appraised her. "Was your hand in any of my other recent adventures? The business of the dragon, maybe?"

She smiled. "I do not give orders to dragons. That was entirely your own affair, though it may be that I encouraged your companions to despise you, just a little."

I shrugged. "I had no great opinion of them, either."

"They were brave, and died. You were less brave, and triumphed." Her eyes turned hard as jade. "Yet what did you do with your triumph? You are the servant and slave of Lord Edevane, no better than Wenlock. You are an informer, a mere creature who will indict anyone at the behest of your master."

"That, also, is not proven," said I.

"Ah?" She feigned incredulity. "And when Edevane tells you to provide evidence against one of his victims, you will refuse? When to refuse means your own present death?"

"I refused him once already," I said.

"You refused his money, and it only served to make him suspicious. He will not let you refuse again." Again that catlike smile crept across her face. "Edevane, I think, may be my masterpiece. It served for a while to make people hate you, but I think I may serve my purposes better by making the wrong people love you."

And with that she vanished, and her radiance also, leaving me alone and blinking in a small, dark room that smelled of brandy and stale lake water.

CHAPTER NINETEEN

Warm both with brandy and the fury running through my veins, I dressed in dry clothes and left the palace for the gardens. The mist had evaporated along with Orlanda, and a cold winter sun shone down on brown grass and the bare earth that awaited spring flowers. Shepherds' flutes were twittering, and shepherdesses walked with crooks dressed with garlands or ribbons. I turned the corner of the palace to return to the quay when bells began to toll. I remembered the last time the bells at Ings Magna had rung, followed shortly by Edelmir Westley's fist striking my jaw, and so a foul mood deepened as I stalked through the withered gardens, kicking pebbles out of my way as if they were an army of my enemies.

I stepped out onto the quay and saw, walking toward me, Princess Floria and her ladies. They were dressed as shepherdesses, wearing broad hats and carrying ribbon-decked crooks.

The anger in my mind seemed to reach a peak, and then receded as I began to consider my situation more carefully. Orlanda had predicted with her smug little smile that I would turn into a vile informer and send the little princess to the scaffold. In that moment I decided that I would defy this fate that Orlanda had arranged for me, and that I did not care if it made an enemy out of Edevane. I would cope with that when the moment came.

I stepped off the path and bowed as Floria approached. "Highness," said I, "it seems you thrive in the shade, and in the sun, too."

"Ah," she said, "it's the naufrageous sailor."

"More naufrageous now than ever, Highness," said I. "My galley was rammed and sunk in the regatta."

"You seem to have no luck on the water," Floria said. She flourished her crook. "Perhaps you should consider the bucolic life of a shepherd. I believe it is one of the few occupations you have not yet adopted as your own."

"Alas," said I, "I have no dog to bark the wolves away."

"Dogs are easy to come by," said Floria. "Here at court, every great officer of state walks at the head of his pack, each hound snuffling at his master's heels for a whiff of power and treasure." She gave me an appraising look. "Even the lord rat-catcher should be able to find such a pack."

"Such dogs are useless in the face of wolves, Highness," said I. I glanced over my shoulder at the palace, with its ringing bells. "Have we declared another war?" I asked.

"Possibly on the Estates General," said Floria. "But no—my royal sister has announced that she is with child."

I donned my pious-anchorite face. "May the heir thrive," I said.

I detected a flicker of awareness below Floria's eyelids. By this I knew that she understood my meaning, that the heir I hoped to thrive was Floria herself. Yet surrounded by ladies whose loyalty could not be guaranteed, she could not respond directly.

"Amen," she said simply.

"I heard that Her Majesty was planning to migrate to Loretto," I said.

"The court will travel with her," said Floria. "I shall go myself, after I have finished some business at my house of Kellhurst."

"Mistress Ransome's observatory?"

"That and a garden I am building." She looked at the palace, and then at me. "Should you not be offering your congratulations to Her Majesty, like all the other courtiers?"

"In my leather jerkin and trousers I am dressed for sailing, not the court."

"Another reason to take up the shepherd's craft," said Floria. "You would fit among the other shepherds . . . and their dogs."

"Perhaps I merely anticipate the festival of the 'Silly Sailors.'"

"That's *every* regatta, Quillifer," Floria said. "You have no idea how dull it all looks, seen from the shore."

"Perhaps Your Highness should build a boat and enter the races yourself," said I. "I would help you find crew."

She laughed. "The courtiers would defer to my rank by losing deliberately. You would see the worst sailing in the world."

"Do it in disguise."

Again she laughed. "As Tom Bowlin the Miniature Sailor?" She looked at her ladies, amused. "I think I shall stay on shore, and guide my flock."

"That is probably wise, Highness. But now I must rescue my half-sunken boat."

"Best do it now, sir, before it becomes a full-sunk boat."

"Your Highness." I bowed, and she went on, along with her flock.

By his galley I found the Lorettan captain who had rammed *Dunnock*, and whose extravagant apologies I found useful, for he took me and my crew out in his boat, and together we towed *Dunnock* back to Rackheath House. With some effort we righted the boat, and then beached it. While lake water gurgled from the stove planks, my crew stripped away the gear, unshipped the tiller, and lowered the mast. I would contact a boatyard tomorrow for repairs.

The bells continued to ring across the water, and were joined by a salute from a battery of Lipton's guns. From the shore I could see the gunsmoke blurring the horizon, obscuring the palace that had become Orlanda's playground. The intrigues and factions of the court were complicated enough without Orlanda subtly organizing them around me. I perhaps enjoy being the center of attention, but not in this way.

Anything or anyone could be a trap, or could be turned into a trap. Yet I needed to avoid all traps.

I thought this might oblige me to acquire more foresight than I currently possessed.

"Welcome to the first Savory Supper," I said, and raised a glass. "I thank you for joining me, and I hope we may enjoy many feasts in the years to come. And now let us drink to Their Majesties, and the peace they have brought to our two realms."

The ladies remained seated while the gentlemen rose, and then we drank. I had instituted a loyal toast before every meal, and Master Stiver enforced it also in the servants' hall. If Lord Edevane had informers in my house, let them report that we saluted the throne three times each day.

I had by now been to enough fine feasts in the capital to perceive a gap in the bill of fare. The fashion was for foods that had been spiced or sweetened, as with carp served with a paste of blanched almonds, currants, and cinnamon; or leg of mutton with sugar, cloves, and nutmeg; or quails with apricots and pistachios; or the meatballs made with a paste of regia that I had served to Coronel Lipton. These sugar-gravies and fruit-sauces could be exquisite, but over a feast of ten or twelve removes, served with sweet wines, the very sweetness could grow heavy and monotonous. The spices could also disguise meat that was of poor quality.

So with my new cook Harry Noach, I had planned a Savory Supper, with choice cuts of meat, fish, and fowl, all served with sauces that would enhance, rather than submerge, the native flavor. We began with a pottage of pigeon stuffed with parsley, then went on to pick-led oysters, a pike-perch served with a fine cream of horseradish, a capon roasted simply and basted to crisp perfection, stewed pheasant, calf's tongue hashed, a dish of marrow, a venison pie, a chine of beef roasted on a spit so that the exterior had a hard crust but the interior was pink and filled with juice, all the meats served with vegetables such as celeriac, carrots, parsnip, turnips, and other fruits of the season.

Nor did I neglect those whose tastes were entirely biased toward the sweet sauces. A roast pig I served with a honeyed sauce of apricots, a chicken in a paste of almonds and pears, and a duck cooked in rosebuds and cloves.

We ended, of course, with nuts and sweets: cakes with almond cream served on plates made of sugar, the colorful sweet bread called ginetoes, tarts with clotted cream, and a sweet frumenty made with rice. This I served to my principal guest, for frumenty was something of a joke between us.

I had been somewhat surprised that Princess Floria had accepted my invitation, and yet here she was, seated by precedence at the top of the table, and her ladies somewhat below. She had Prince Alicio to talk to, and Their Graces of Roundsilver, while I occupied the middle reaches along with Dom Nemorino d'Ormyl, Countess Marcella, and Sir Cecil Greene, Ethlebight's member in the House of Burgesses, he who had been clapped in prison by Their Majesties. Below were the commoners and mechanicals among whom I had till recently counted myself: Ransome the queen's gunfounder, Floria's other ladies, Coronel Lipton, Blackwell the playwright, and Alaron Mountmirail the engineer.

The table's great centerpiece was made of marchpane and consisted of a pair of falcons each a yard long, with feathers of sugar-paste and fierce eyes of carnelian. This was in honor of Blackwell, whose play *The Kingdom of the Birds* had been a great success, with Mountmirail's mechanical birds flying over the heads of the audience, and another of his creations, a great kingly eagle twice the height of a man, which had been made to walk about the stage, turn its head, talk, and raise its great wings.

An equal sensation had been made by a beautiful young actor, Webb, known in the company as Bonny Joe. He had played a princess, and so outperformed many of the adults in the company that he was thought to have a great future on the stage, if his fellow actors did not kill him out of jealousy.

Music floated down from the gallery to aid our digestion, where Rufino Knott had recruited an orchestra.

For the dishes that required it, I served as my own carver, for I felt I could carve more nicely than my servant, who for the feast now assisted the yeoman of the buttery in serving the wines. I sliced fine and fancy collops and joints, and ladled out gravies and sauces with a careful eye.

"I do not know this word 'savory,' Sir Keely-Fay," said Dom Nemorino during one of the interludes, as the previous remove was swept away. "But it seems to me this is very plain food, which might be served in an inn."

"An inn could never afford meat this fine," I said. This was not precisely true, but it appeased him somewhat, for his objection was not to the flavor but to the lack of expensive ingredients. If a dish had not cost a cotter's yearly income, it was not worthy of his aristocratic palate.

I had been lucky in my choice of date, for my feast was taking place the day after the Estates had adjourned. Because Greene and the duke were not required in the Estates, all my guests could arrive early in the afternoon and take part in an afternoon's pleasures, including bowling on the green, games of darts and billiards indoors, and tennis in my court. This was the first time I had played tennis against anyone but my tutor, and I fancied I did well enough. I lost a match to Prince Alicio when he drove a ball right past my guard into the dedans, and then won a match off Dom Nemorino with an angled shot off the penthouse roof.

I turned to Sir Cecil Greene. "Do you leave now for Ethlebight?" I asked.

"After the solstice," he said. "I hate a winter crossing, but I must inform our city that the crown will do precious little to keep our people from starvation."

"May I send money with you?" I asked. "You will know best how to bring relief to the city."

"I will do what I may, and thank you," said he.

"I shall contribute also," said Floria, calling down the table.

"You are very good, Your Highness." And then to me, Sir Cecil said, "Well, the crown has its loan. But we shall see if they can collect it."

For the Burgesses had not agreed to a new tax, but instead made what they called a loan to the crown, which in theory would be obliged to pay it back. The crown would never pay a penny, of course, but forgiveness for the loan would be a club the Burgesses would hold over Their Majesties at some future negotiation. In the meantime, I could enjoy the fact that Their Majesties would be in my debt.

The loan idea had arisen at the revelation from Umbrey that Their Majesties had paid nearly six thousand royals in gambling debts in the last year. Umbrey had examined the royal household accounts and deciphered the rather obscure wording in which such payments were cloaked. This report had increased the Burgesses' truculence, and indeed won the crown very few friends even among the peers.

The loan had not yet been collected, but the crown was already spending it, raising troops and hiring mercenaries for the war against Thurnmark. Pikemen were already drilling on the Field of Mavors, and Ransome was planning to cast whole batteries of cannon.

"Sir Quillifer," said Floria. "What is your recommendation for a crossing to Loretto? Should I take the northern route, or the southern?"

"In midwinter you stand an equal chance of a stormy crossing," said I. "But the northern route is shorter if you embark at Ferrick, and when you land, you are closer to Longres Regius."

"My royal sister goes by the southern route."

"There is a great royal galleon at Bretlynton Head, flagship of the southern fleet, which can carry most of the royal household. But when you travel, may you not take a naval ship, like Her Majesty?"

"I believe I may," she said, "but I wish to send some of my ladies ahead to make certain that my accommodation is suitable."

"If they leave around the new year," said I, "I will be pleased to escort them."

She offered a skeptical look, as if she doubted any of her ladies would be entirely safe with me, but instead said, "That is a kind offer. But you plan to join the court in Loretto? Your office of lord warden scarcely requires it."

"I'm a hardened traveler," said I. "I desire to see Longres and the palace."

"Well," said Floria, "you will find plenty of custom for your gems in Longres Regius."

I refrained from remarking that Floria had not yet paid me for the star sapphire I had sold her, though at least she was doing me the compliment of wearing it.

The waiters brought all the nuts and sweets that made up the last remove, and I stood. "I should like to offer each of you a memento of the evening. I hope you will find it useful, and that it will spur your inventiveness and inspiration."

The waiters came forward again and placed before each guest a small, squat, black bottle, with a wax-sealed cork stopper. Floria picked up her bottle and looked at the label, which bore a large letter Q, and in smaller letters the words "Sable Ink."

"You named it after yourself, I see," Floria said.

"There wasn't room for my whole name," I said.

"What is sable ink?" Blackwell asked. "I don't suppose it's anything made from actual sables."

"It's black ink made up and put in bottles," said I.

"Why would we need such ink?" Blackwell asked. "Everyone makes their own."

"How many hundred hours of your life have been wasted in making ink?" I asked. "Now you will have those hours back, for writing poetry, for the pleasures that leisure brings, or for simply pondering the vasty parade of life."

Blackwell seemed skeptical. "Do you plan to sell this?" he asked. "I doubt very much that very many folk will buy it."

I could have answered that people would have little choice, since I had taken the trouble to purchase every oak gall available in the city, and also tracked down those who shipped oak galls into the city and signed them to two-year exclusive contracts. I had *monopolized* oak galls. Many had already been rendered into powder by Mountmirail's grinding machines.

While it is true that oak galls are not uncommon, and could be found in any of the oak groves around the city, it was also true that those who made their living by the pen were not the sort inclined to search through oak groves in order to climb trees and hack away the galls.

In the morning, my footmen and other servants would travel to the palace and to all the various departments of state, and offer complimentary boxes of Q Sable Ink. If they wanted more, they would have to pay.

And, I rather thought, they *would* want more. The state consumed ink as a drunkard consumed ale.

After the footmen carried away the last remove, His Grace of Roundsilver offered me a toast of thanks, and the ladies made their way to a withdrawing room to loosen their stays, or whatever other activity might assure their comfort. For the gentlemen, there was a pot in a sideboard drawer in the next room, but for myself, I walked outside to the pier and relieved myself into the lake. Then I stood for a moment contemplating the dark, still night and listening to the waves lapping against the shore. Wine drowsed in my veins. I heard a tread upon the pier and saw Prince Alicio de Ribamar-la-Rose.

"You will be traveling soon to Loretto?" he asked.

"I hope to leave before the new year," I said.

"If you find the suggestion congenial, Sir Keely-Fay, we may travel together."

"I would be honored, Your Highness."

Prince Alicio gazed out at the night. "When we come to Longres, you are welcome to stay in my house, though I shall not be there long." He gave a sigh. "I am obliged to join the fighting, now we are at war."

I was somewhat surprised. "Does that sort with your philosophy?" I asked.

I had not seen him in the white costume of a Retriever since Prince Fosco's arrival, though he usually mixed white with some other colors, as if to proclaim his divided conscience. Tonight his doublet and hose were white, though he wore them with sky-blue trunks, and sleeves tied with scarlet points.

"I came to Duisland to find peace," he said, "but I can be no common pilgrim, for I head a princely house, and my proper task is war. I must fight or disgrace my ancestors."

"The Compassionate Pilgrim had little good to say of war," I said. "What does he recommend, when your duty wars with your convictions?"

Prince Alicio sounded unhappy. "He would have little sympathy with me, I fear. I have chosen prudence, first when Fosco appeared, and now when my king chooses war."

"I can hardly call it prudent to ride into battle," said I, and then

I remembered that I had joined the queen's army in order to avoid a threat I deemed more deadly than Clayborne's rebellion.

"Joining the war is more prudent than defying my king," he said. "My father raised up an army against King Edouardo, and aided your King Stilwell against him. He and Edouardo's son eventually made peace, but my family remains under suspicion, and I don't want my mother and sisters to be punished for something I failed to do."

"Such as ride at enemy cannon?"

"I will be given a large command," Alicio said. "I will not have to charge the enemy myself, but will instead send others to die."

In Duisland we hear of King Stilwell's great wars a generation ago, and how he captured Edouardo and held him to ransom, along with several of Loretto's cities. But there was civil strife in Loretto at the time, with both peasants and princely families in rebellion against Edouardo's pretensions, and in Duisland this tends to be discounted in favor of tales of Stilwell's heroics. I think our armies would have had a more difficult time if Edouardo had fought Duisland alone.

So Prince Alicio was paying the penalty for his ancestors' misdemeanors, just as Elisa d'Altrey was paying for her uncle's treason. I wondered for a moment if my own children would find themselves paying for my errors in judgment, and then decided that my true challenge would be to survive long enough to sire any children at all.

"Speaking as a former soldier, I hope you will husband the lives of your men," I said.

"I hope I shall not be obliged to spend their lives at all, Sir Keely-Fay." He looked at me. "You will not fight, yourself?"

"One battlefield is enough for me," said I. "I will not be so foolish as to seek another."

"You are blessed with more freedom than I."

"Yet did not the Pilgrim say that existence is mental phenomenon? If so, freedom is to be found in the mind, if anywhere. You may cultivate your philosophy in the privacy of your own thoughts."

He seemed downhearted. "I shall endeavor to accomplish at least that, Sir Keely-Fay."

We returned to the house, where we found most of the party in the game room, gathered around tables for games of cards and dice. Countess Marcella approached and handed me an envelope. "Her Highness asked me to give you this," said she.

An idea of billets-doux half formed in my mind, but then laughter at the idea drove the notion from my thoughts.

"I shall accept with pleasure anything Her Highness chooses to offer." I took the envelope. "Does Her Highness wish me to read it now?"

A slight smile touched the Aekoi's lips. "I think Her Highness cares not whether you read it now or never," she said.

"Well," I said, "if she cares not, why should I?" I began to put the envelope on a table, and then I took it up again and looked into Marcella's dark eyes shimmering in candlelight. "Yet I should never disdain a letter from a high-born lady," I told her, and opened it.

It was a note for my 190 royals, drawn upon the Bank of Howel. "I hope you will thank Her Highness," I said.

"You may thank her yourself."

"She wished an intermediary for this business," I pointed out. "I but follow her example."

Amusement touched the corners of her lips. "Princesses do not handle money. It somehow taints their majesty. But the gratitude of subjects is always received with pleasure." With that she turned and made her way to one of the dice tables.

I went to a card table and joined Floria and Their Graces of Roundsilver, where I made a fourth for rentoy. The Roundsilvers were partnered with one another, which made Floria my partner. While the duke dealt the cards, I turned to Floria.

"I thank you for your timely message," I said. "I shall put it to good use."

"By making ink, apparently," said she as she sorted her cards. "Have you exhausted all possible occupations, that you have to invent one?"

The duke turned up the final card to choose trump. It was coins.

"Perhaps I grew tired of making my own ink," I said.

"You could have given the work to your varlet." Floria showed me the tip of her tongue, which startled me as a strangely mischievous and intimate form of communication until I remembered that this was the signal that she held the deuce of trumps, which was the highest-ranked card in the deck.

Rentoy would be a very straightforward game were it not for the signals, which are permitted by the rules. The signals are systemized and known to all players: to raise the shoulders for the low trump card; to twitch the mouth for the knight of clubs; to wink an eye for the varlet of coins; and so forth. What would be considered cheating in another game is thereby turned into a species of art, for there are signals that you attempt to give privately to your partner, and other, false signals, that are meant to mislead your rivals.

Sometimes the results are quite comical, as all four players simultaneously engage in winking, shrugging, twitching, raising eyebrows, sticking out their tongues, and biting their lips. It is like a congress of lunatics.

There can also be private signals outside those that were known to all players, but Floria and I had not the time to arrange these, and we were matched against experienced players who had all the time in the world to create their own private system. I resigned myself to losing some money.

And indeed we lost the first few hands, until I noticed the duchess make a small movement with her little finger, brushing the surface of the table as she raised her eyebrows, which was itself the signal that she held the king of trumps. As I had the king myself, and had already covertly signaled that fact to Floria, I knew Her Grace was lying, and that the movement of the little finger was meant to convey that fact to her partner. In sudden elation I looked up at Floria; I saw a glimmer of triumph in her hazel eyes, and I knew she had seen the same signal and understood it.

After that we began to win, for if we did not always know what cards our opponents had, at least we knew when they were not telling the truth, and this in itself gave us an advantage.

But the cards themselves had their own favorites, and on that night they favored the Roundsilvers; and so by the time the duchess decided to retire, I had lost some money, though, because I had deciphered their signal, the amount was small.

I walked with the Roundsilvers to their coach. "Do you travel to Loretto with the court?" I asked.

"Nay," said the duke. "After the birth, we will take a leisurely journey to Selford, and spend the summer there, until the Estates are called again in the winter."

"You think the Estates will be summoned again? So soon?"

"Their Majesties raised enough money for a year of war. Unless there is a miraculous peace . . ." The duke gestured hopelessly with one hand.

"Ay," said I. "Or we must hope the king raises the money by plundering Thurnmark."

"Thurnmark well knows its danger, and its river lines are well fortified," said the duke. "It will be a war of sieges, of famines and plague. Those twenty thousand men will fall sick in the ditches, or freeze, or starve, and the Burgesses will be asked to replace them."

Following this happy thought, His Grace helped his lady into the carriage and joined her. I bade them good night, the carriage creaked away, and I returned to the party.

Floria and her ladies were the next to leave. "If fate had granted me but a single trump," she said, "we would have won that last game."

"Yet we lost only a trifle," I said. "I thought we would do better, once I saw that you had understood Her Grace's signal."

Glee sparkled in her eyes. "I assumed from that signal you had the king, and so we won that hand."

"And the next, where your deuce trumped the king."

She looked at me. "It is pleasing to trump the king."

"And to do it with a deuce," I said. "Which in any other game is a low card."

I bowed to her and said farewell to her ladies. Countess Marcella looked at me with what seemed to be speculation, and Elisa d'Altrey sniffed and ignored me. I was surprised she was not in better humor, for I believe she had won some money from Dom Nemorino at dice.

The dice game had come to an end, and Dom Nemorino and Prince Alicio were playing darts, tossing cut-down crossbow bolts at the target and wagering sums that would have beggared a country baron.

Sir Cecil Greene, Ransome the gunfounder, and Coronel Lipton were involved in a discussion of gunpowder, and of amending the law that required the army to purchase powder from the Royal Powder Mill outside Selford, which on account of its monopoly produced an inferior product. I had little to add to this discussion, so I joined Blackwell and Mountmirail, who sat by the fire planning a new spectacle. It seemed that the master of the revels had found little to object to in *The Kingdom of the Birds*.

"Because," said Blackwell, "it is set in a realm of fantasy, and could therefore have nothing to do with the Kingdom of Duisland or its people. It seems that all I have to do to get a license for my plays is to set them in fairyland, where I can write about war, forbidden love, conspiracy, treachery, and the death of kings, and no one here will suspect it has anything to do with them."

"I thought your play was clearly set in Duisland and Loretto," said I. "But with feathers."

"For heaven's sake don't tell the master of the revels!" Blackwell said. "I have enough trouble with Bonny Joe Webb!"

"Your pretty young leading lady?" asked I. "Has his success turned him into the petulant backstage tyrant of the tiring-house?"

"Nay," said Blackwell. "We are besieged by an army of his admirers. He has become the eidolon of other children, and we're always having to pluck these youngsters from under the stage or from behind the scenery, from which they hope to view him. And he has mature admirers, also, grown men and women who wish to corrupt him." He gave an exasperated sigh. "Quillifer, I have been offered fortunes! I will have to hire guards to keep him safe, but how honest will the guards be?"

"You worry about Bonny Joe's virtue? When I was his age, I thought of little else but being corrupted."

Blackwell almost snarled. "His mother and father are friends of mine, and I made them some promises when I took their son onto the stage. And truly," he added, "his years are tender. But in another year or two, when he has grown a little, I will let him follow his pleasures wherever they lead, so long as they lead him back to the stage."

"I'm sure he longs for the day. Do you work on another play?"

"I'm planning another excursion into the world of make-believe." He looked at me and raised his brows. "I think I will make a play about a dragon-slayer."

"How is that make-believe?" I asked. "Dragons exist. And how are you going to get the cannon onstage?"

"I rather thought the dragon would be killed in a more conventional manner," Blackwell said. "I think the play will be about Baldwine, the duke's ancestor. I have already writ a little playlet on the theme, performed at the Mummers' Festival a few years ago."

"I would like to suggest a more contemporary setting," said I. "And Goodman Knott has already writ a ballad, which the players may sing during the gigue."

Blackwell laughed. "Remember that we are Roundsilver's Company, not Sir Quillifer's Players. If you wish me to flatter you before the court, you may give us silver for our trouble."

"How much?" I asked, but at that point Mountmirail jumped into the conversation and began to excitedly describe the mechanical fire-drake he planned to construct. He had not yet worked out a mechanism that would allow the beast to breathe flame, and Blackwell doubted that he should.

"I should not like to set the scenery on fire, or the players."

"You can spare some of the clowns," said I.

"I can make smoke," said Mountmirail, "and blow it out with a kind of bellows."

"Yet you must build a fire to make this smoke," said Blackwell, "and I think Their Majesties would object if I set fire to the palace during the course of the performance."

"They would just call the Estates to pay for a new palace," I said. "But Master Mountmirail, may I speak with you for a moment in my cabinet?"

I took Mountmirail away to my private study. "I wonder, good-man," I asked him. "What do you know of rocks?"

"Rocks?" he said.

The next day came the news that the chancellor, Baron Hulme, had been dismissed from the Council, and that his deputy, Sir Edmund Tryon, had also lost his place. They had not managed the Burgesses as Their Majesties wished, and now were cast aside.

I thought there might be two heads on pikes ere long. I went to Hulme's house to offer condolences, but the steward said he was not receiving company. I asked that I be remembered to his lordship, and the steward said he would deliver the message.

There was to be a regatta on the holiday of the solstice, but a great winter storm came, with freezing rain sheeting down out of the sky as if in mourning for Baron Hulme's fall, and the race was canceled. The celebration at Ings Magna was as dull and cold as the weather, and I went home, sat before the fire, and read more of Tarantua's melancholy verse. I thought of Lady Westley and hoped she was safe and warm in her exile.

The day after the solstice, warrants were issued for Tryon and Hulme, but Tryon alone was arrested. The chancellor had known what was to come and fled. I wished him every success.

In those days Q Sable Ink sold mainly as a curiosity, but this did not perturb me, for I knew that when Howel ran out of oak galls, the ink would no longer be a curiosity, but a necessity.

I made arrangements for my trip to Loretto, and wrote to Floria that Prince Alicio and I would be traveling together, and that we would provide escort for her ladies if she wished it. Floria was more receptive to her ladies being escorted by a pious prince than a rat-catcher knight, and so plans were made for the journey. Dom Nemorino, also going to war, volunteered to join us.

I heard from Peel the cannoneer that he had arrived in Inchmaden. The mortars had been employed against iron birds lured to a field by grain poured out on the ground, and there had been some success in destroying the birds with halberds and war hammers. Peel expected that his tactics would only improve, and he hoped to eradicate the birds within weeks.

I dutifully relayed the news to Lord Edevane, and he replied that he wished to see me. I packed up a box of a dozen bottles of ink and called for my carriage.

It was another day of rain, and I huddled beneath an otter-fur cloak as my carriage rattled toward Ings Magna. The Estates having been dismissed, Edevane had left his little closet in the House of Peers and returned to the palace, and so I climbed the stairs to his office and walked through the room of clerks, all wrapped in wool or fur. Their breath steamed in the cold, and their blue-white fingers seemed frozen to their pens. The room smelled of mildew. Condensation marred the stone walls and trickled to the floor.

I was shown into Edevane's cabinet, where I was privileged to sit upon a chair and not a little stool. The room was warmed by a fire, and a page helped me out of my fur cloak.

"I hope that the matter of the iron birds shall soon be tied with red ribbon," I said, and presented the box of ink with my compliments.

"Her Majesty will be pleased to hear it," said Edevane in his soft voice. He reached into the box and took up a bottle of ink. "I don't believe I have ever received such a practical gift," he said. "Though of course one of my secretaries makes my ink for me."

"That secretary may now be better employed," said I.

"Perhaps." He replaced the bottle and fixed me in his spectacles. "You intend to travel with the court to Loretto?" he asked.

"Ay, my lord."

"But you will not serve in the army?"

"I guard the realm from monsters, my lord," I said. "And I also commission privateers, though not against monsters."

"You have a martial reputation," said Edevane. "I thought you might seek battle."

I spread my hands. "I have an office now, and owe a different duty to Their Majesties."

"Just so." He touched the pads of his fingers together, left meeting right. "I understand you will be in the company of Ribamar-la-Rose and two of Her Highness's ladies."

I wasted no energy on surprise, for years ago Floria had confided to me that her correspondence was read by servants of the crown. Now I had the honor of knowing which royal servant had scanned my letters.

"Prince Alicio returns to serve his king," said I, "and we offered to escort the ladies on their journey."

"Her Highness revealed to you her plans for her voyage?"

A log on the fire cracked like a pistol. I felt smoke clutching at my windpipe and cleared my throat. "She said only that she wished her ladies to go in advance, and make sure accommodation in Longres was suitable."

"You are in her confidence to that extent?"

"So it would seem. But we are hardly intimates."

"Yet Her Highness came to your feast." His index fingers, still pressed together, dropped to point at me.

"You asked me to amuse her. I set myself to do it."

"Sir Cecil Greene was also present," said Edevane, and from this I knew that Edevane probably had a spy in my household who kept track of my guests.

"Greene is the honorable member for Ethlebight, my representative in the capital. I wished to consult him regarding merchant ventures, but I never had the chance."

"Did Greene speak to Her Highness?"

"I don't believe they exchanged a single word." I cleared my throat again. "If you are still concerned that some man may prove a bad influence upon Her Highness, I can't imagine Greene would be that man. Indeed, Her Highness has such a strong, pronounced character that it would be a great man indeed who could influence her, particularly for ill."

"I fear not greatness," said Edevane, "but cunning."

I waved a hand. "I flatter myself that I was the most cunning man at that feast, and no one there was my equal."

His dead eyes flickered. "You will accompany Countess Marcella and Mistress d'Altrey to Loretto. I hope you may find out more about them."

"What does your lordship want to know?" I affected to consider the matter. "Again, I am hardly on terms of intimacy with either. The countess has been polite enough, but Elisa d'Altrey has shown me only disdain."

"I should like to know if Countess Marcella is what she claims to be."

I shifted in my chair. "I doubt that her ladyship will confess any imposture to me, but I will find out what I can."

Edevane dropped his hands to his desk and toyed with a blue ribbon that had fallen from some document. "Their Majesties have prorogued the Estates."

It took me a brief moment to follow Edevane's swerve from one topic to another. "I should think Their Majesties would be happy to see the last of them," said I.

Edevane did not comment on this observation. "Their Majesties may recall the last Estates, or hold new elections," he said. "You are well known in Ethlebight, I believe. Have you ever considered standing for election yourself?"

It took me a moment to master my surprise. "My lord," I said, "I am too young. Not yet two-and-twenty."

"Ethlebight deserves a representative of proven loyalty," Edevane said. "As for elections, they may be managed, if the candidate is plausible. You are young, ay, but you possess wealth and reputation."

"I cannot imagine the Burgesses await my wisdom with any degree of anticipation."

He regarded me. "I hope you will consider this. It would be a great advancement for you."

"Perhaps too great," said I. "But ay, my lord, I will think further on it."

"I would consider it a favor. But now I must be about other business." He stood, and I rose with him. I bowed, and as I began to leave, he said, "But stay."

I turned. "Yes, my lord?"

The dead, lifeless eyes gazed at me with mild curiosity, as if I were a small, undistinguished, mummified animal in someone's cabinet of curiosities. "You do not know whence Lord Hulme has fled?" he asked.

Surprise surged through me, followed instantly by a blaze of fear. I would not be surprised if my hairs stood on end.

"I know not, my lord," I said. "I have not spoken to him since before the Estates met."

"You know him."

"I do," said I. "He dealt generously with me, and with ravaged Ethlebight, when I first came to Selford."

He raised his chin a little, perhaps so he could look down at me. "I hope he tries not to fly on one of your ships."

"I hope so too," said I.

Somehow, as my nerves jangled and jumped, I remembered to take my cloak when I left. I wondered if Edevane had raised the matter of Hulme as a threat, to point out that he could bring down any office-holder, even so mighty a figure as the chancellor, or if he actually suspected me of hiding Hulme in my closet, or in a passenger's cabin.

And then I began to worry if he knew something I did not. Perhaps Hulme *would* take passage on one of my ships. So I began a mental inventory of where my ships might be, both my own and those I owned with Kevin and his family; and I thought none of them were in Bonille now, except perhaps the pinnace *Ostra*, which might have arrived early in Ferrick or Stanport to take on the large fighting crew necessary in a privateer. But Hulme could hardly expect to take passage in a privateer, and so I was safe.

And then I was able to consider Edevane's notion that I would try for election to the House of Burgesses, running, I suppose, against Sir Cecil Greene. Greene had vexed Their Majesties, of course, and spent a few nights in prison on that account, but I thought he had represented my city well, and I had no desire to challenge him for his seat. Nor did I want to appear in the Burgesses in the character of one of Edevane's creatures, parroting the arguments written by the crown, and with no more freedom than a slave.

I would flee the city, I thought, and go to Longres in Loretto. Though of course the court would follow, and Edevane with it. His spymaster's trade would best be conducted in Duisland, where his informers lurked in every shadow, but his power came from his nearness to the queen, and he would not dare leave her to her own thoughts.

I wondered if Orlanda had been in the room with us, whispering suggestions into Edevane's inward ear, and tying me ever more firmly into my role as informer and pawn.

There were fireworks at Ings Magna on the night of the new year, and a great banquet. I drank too much brandy punch, and rather than go home, I slept for the first time in my little apartment in the palace, the room I had furnished for Lady Westley. I slept not alone, though I don't remember the woman's name—I believe she was the granddaughter of one of the Burgesses. She was hardly sober either, and laughed when I mistakenly called her Girasol.

All I remember of her is that her hair was chestnut, and she had blue eyes with flecks of gold.

New Year's Day was celebrated at the palace with a feast, which started late because I was not the only person who had drunk too much the night before. My leman was profoundly unconscious, her hair and one bare arm hanging over the edge of the bed, and so, against the cold, I built up the fire and left her. When I returned a few hours later, she was gone, and never again have I seen her.

It seemed the court had spent all their vitality the previous evening, for most walked about dull-eyed and dull of speech. Their Majesties appeared amid a blare of trumpets that prompted wincing among the courtiers, and then Her Majesty announced that, when they left for Loretto in a few weeks, they would appoint a viceroy with demi-royal powers to rule the kingdom, and that this viceroy would be the monk Fosco, the king's kinsman, who was also given the Monastery of the

Holy Prophecy that Berlauda was building across the lake from the palace.

These honors opened more than a few dull eyes. It appeared to all that Their Majesties could not find a single trustworthy Duislander, and so committed the realm to the mercies of a princely foreign ecclesiastic. Yet, as Fosco knelt before the thrones, swore his oath, and was given a signet, all in the court applauded the choice, as was expected.

Now the courtiers would have someone new to pursue with their flattery.

I looked for Princess Floria, to see if she might show a more honest face, but she seemed at least as pleased as the rest of us.

On the second day of the year I visited Master Mountmirail, and we discussed the matter of rocks. I was sending him to Ethlebight in the company of a young surveyor named Radford, to chart the course of a canal from the Ostra just above Ethlebight to Gannet Cove, which I intended to make the finest port city on the south coast. Silt-starved Ethlebight, cut off from the sea, would be reborn in all its glories, and provided with a harbor that could hold a fleet of deep-draught ships. I had not the money for this project, and so I would have to form a company and sell shares, and that would mean that the idea would be made public and perhaps others might attempt the work—but I had protected myself by buying the sole right to purchase the village of Gannet Cove, and without the village there would be no new city.

But I could not raise money unless the project were proven possible, and to that end I employed Mountmirail and Radford. To build a canal would mean carving a path through hills, building dams and locks, and perhaps constructing aqueducts to carry the canal over low-lying areas and allowing the barges to sail like swans over valleys and swamps. The terminus of the canal would be in Gannet Cove, and in order to reach the harbor, the canal would have to somehow go through the cliffs behind the village, either by cutting a trench or making a tunnel. For this I needed an expert in rocks to tell me how to go about it, and though Mountmirail disclaimed any particular lithic knowledge, I knew he could assemble all the information that was available, and with less time than it took him to build Master Blackwell's dragon.

Which, he informed me, would have a blunderbuss in its snout, to discharge smoke and flame at an appropriate point in the play. I cautioned him that a flaming wad might hit someone in the audience, or set the stage on fire, but he told me that the actors would be careful where they aimed it.

"I think you lack sufficient experience of actors," said I.

The dragon would be built by Mountmirail's assistant Dowd, while his engineer Erskine would construct more grinding machines to be shipped to Fornland. In the spring, when Viceroy Fosco and what was left of the court moved to the summer capital at Selford, I would open another branch of my ink-making business there.

I seemed to have instigated a surprising number of ventures. I was owner or part owner of merchant ships; I dealt in gems; I had privateers on the sea against the enemy and a galley racing on Lake Howel. I had killed a dragon, I planned a canal venture to save my native city, and I had invented the new industry of ink-making.

Yet what made me respectable was none of this, but rather the least of these, my manor at Dunnock. I was a landed gentleman with a grant of arms, and that had opened the great doors at the palace that had been so decisively closed three years before. And for that grant of arms, I had to thank the meddlesome Princess Floria, who had got me my knighthood because, I supposed, it amused her to do so.

And now Lord Edevane wished me to repay Her Highness by informing on her and her household, and to assist in dragging her to the scaffold. I could not think how I could avoid this, except by flight; yet while my flight might preserve my life, it would not protect Floria from the shadows that surrounded her.

Yet my many ventures kept me from thinking too much of these things, and so when I left Howel six days after the new year, in company with Prince Alicio, Dom Nemorino, Countess Marcella, and Elisa d'Altrey, I had almost put it from my mind.

Floria had sent riders ahead to alert staging posts and inns, and when we arrived at each destination, there were roasts and fowl turning on the spit, hippocras warming by the hearth, and snug rooms in which to take our rest. We traveled in five carriages, which included one for the baggage and two for the servants (I had brought only Rufino Knott, but the others traveled each with a suite of retainers). The ladies traveled in their own carriage with their maidservants, and I saw them only at mealtimes. We gentlemen traveled in near-martial splendor, in a carriage filled with pistols and swords, and with well-armed footmen riding on the top. We were accompanied always by the sulfur smell of the slow-matches burning on their blunderbusses. There were no bandits known to be on the road, but if there were, we would be robbed by nothing less than a small army.

The weather held fine for the days we were on the road, and then I scented the sea on the brisk air, though we were not yet within sight of the ocean. This came as we crossed the bridge at Ferrick, with the view of the estuary on our left, the silty river sending brown tendrils out into the ice-blue northern water.

I knew the harbor master and had sent a request for him to find us passage to Balfoy on Loretto's northern coast. He had obliged us by securing passage on the three-masted, two-hundred-ton galleon *Kiminge*, Captain Bodil, out of Steggerda. Bodil was a swaggering character out of the tales of Erpingham, with gold earrings, boots like buckets, a shaven head, and grizzled mustaches that fell like waterfalls to his chest. His ship, hailing from the Three Kingdoms, was safe from any warship out of Thurnmark.

We did not go on board right away, for *Kiminge* hadn't finished loading, and then another winter storm descended and kept us in port for another four days. While the ship pitched at anchor, we spent the days pleasantly in an inn, playing cards and drinking mulled wine while we watched the raindrops beating at the diamond panes of the windows.

At dawn on the fifth day one of Captain Bodil's officers thumped on our doors and told us that *Kiminge* would leave on the ebb, and that we had two hours to get ourselves, our baggage, and our cortege on board. We had time but for bread and cheese and a gulp of ale before we were bundled out of the inn and down to the harbor. The day was gray and squally, with a cold west wind whistling around the corners of the waterfront buildings, and brief spatters of rain showering down from the heavens. A pair of whaleboats waited at the quay, and the crew sped us to where the galleon lay at anchor. The anchor had already been hove short, and was ready to be drawn from the bottom on the captain's command.

We were bustled to our quarters while whistles blew and the crew rushed about the deck. "We have one other passenger just come on board," said our escort. "One of you will have to share a cabin with him."

We were in the aftercastle on the level of the main deck, with our cabins opening left and right off a central room with chairs and a large table. Large windows gazed aft, with small diamond panes interlaced together, and we had an outside balcony that wrapped completely around the stern.

The door of a cabin opened, and the other passenger came out to greet us. We stared at him in shock, and he gazed at us with an amiable expression.

"Sirs," said our guide. "This is Sir Brynley Wilmot, who will also be our guest on the voyage to Balfoy."

"I don't believe I have had the pleasure of meeting these ladies and gentlemen," said Wilmot.

I looked at the man who had challenged me to a duel before being knocked off his horse by the fire-drake and knew that if he had not recovered his memory yet, he would before the voyage was over. Orlanda would see to that.

"We've met," I said.

CHAPTER TWENTY

I am very sorry," said Wilmot, "but I suffered an injury when—" He paused, then laughed. "Well, of course two of you gentlemen were present when that happened." He shook his head. "I recognize your names, of course, and I know that we all journeyed together, and that Sir Quillifer killed the worm." He nodded at me. "But I'm afraid I don't recall anything of that journey."

Dom Nemorino spoke quickly, in hopes of turning the conversation to a safer topic. "Are you traveling to Loretto?" he asked. "Or are you going on to Steggerda?"

"My king has declared war," said Wilmot. "I go to join the army as a volunteer."

I remembered those volunteers from the last war. They attached themselves to the headquarters and plagued the queen's captain-general with their pretension and their quarreling, but they all came from important families, and were too well born to be sent home. Wilmot's character, from what I knew of it, was ideal for this demi-martial occupation.

Wilmot's varlet came into the room then, and I saw the shocked look on his face as he recognized me. He recovered swiftly and aided us in stowing our dunnage, but he kept casting looks at me over his shoulder. I wondered if he would find a moment to inform Wilmot that he was obliged to try to kill me, and clearly Prince Alicio and Dom Nemorino wondered the same thing.

Dom Nemorino bravely volunteered to share Wilmot's cabin, which saved me from wondering every night whether I would have my throat cut. Then I heard, from outside, the cries of the bosun and the stamp of feet on the capstan, and I excused myself, saying that I wished to go on deck and watch the crew make sail.

I put on my old cheviot overcoat and went up onto the poop deck just as the anchor broke free of the bottom, and *Kiminge* lurched as it fell off the wind, and the main topsail filled with a vast rolling boom. Even though only the spritsail, main topsail, and lateen were set, with the brisk wind and the ebb tide in our favor, we made our way out of the anchorage with good speed.

Rufino Knott joined me on the poop. The wind streamed his hair like a flag as he leaned toward me. "I spoke with Wilmot's varlet," he said, "and he's keeping the knight's weapons stowed away."

"I should like mine a little closer at hand," said I.

"I shall put a dagger and a pocket pistol under your pillow."

"Arm yourself as well."

He bowed. "I already have, sir."

Knott returned to his duties, and *Kiminge* left the anchorage in its wake. The fore and mizzen topsails were set, along with the fore-course, and *Kiminge* heeled far over as spray shot over the bow. I stood with my hand on a backstay and enjoyed the brave sight as the galleon swept over the estuary like a king riding in his majesty, with seabirds flocking about us like courtiers. Once the water shifted from brown to blue and we were on the open sea, the ship hove to in order to discharge the pilot, and then the yards were set, and *Kiminge* shaped a northeasterly course along the coast.

At this point Countess Marcella joined me, and anger blazed in her eyes.

"What is the matter, my lady?" asked I.

"That Wilmot!" said she. "He thinks I am a courtesan. He made me the most ill-bred offer, and I told him that if he were in my own country, I would have him gelded."

"Were you not introduced to him as a noblewoman?"

"Yes. Of course!" Her fury had not abated.

It is true that there is a class of Aekoi courtesans in our country, as human courtesans are found in the Empire. The two races cannot breed, and this fact is attractive to those who wish to indulge concupiscence without dangers of conception.

"His memory is badly injured, of course," said I. "But still it was ill-mannered and impudent."

"I should have slapped his face!" said Marcella.

"I apologize on behalf of my species. If you wish to return to our common room, you may take my arm, and I will offer you protection—"

Scarlet rage blazed up on her golden face, and she took a whirling step away from me. "You offer me your *protection*?" she cried. "You are no better than Wilmot!"

"I meant it not that way!" I said in haste. "I meant that I will shield you from Wilmot's insults."

She examined me with hard pebble eyes, and then she must have judged me sincere, for her anger eased. "If Wilmot insults me again," she said, "I will stab him to the heart. I am sick to death of the assumptions these humans make, thinking me naught but a whore."

"I am sorry you are so abused," I said.

At this point Elisa d'Altrey came onto the deck to say that she had made peace with Wilmot, and that he wished to offer her an apology if she would accept it.

"It's best, I think," she added. "For we are boxed up on this ship for a week or more."

"Well," said the countess, "if he is of a mind to apologize, I am of a mind to listen."

The two ladies departed and left me on the quarterdeck. Captain Bodil, who till now had been occupied with the pilot and with getting his ship under way, came down the slanting deck in his big boots to greet me, and I told him I was a shipowner and had recently returned from a trip to the Candara Coast. Bodil had never been so far from home, but he had a great many stories to tell of his years at sea, and we entertained each other with tall tales until it was time for dinner.

"I should perhaps warn you of one of the passengers," I said, with feigned reluctance. "Sir Brynley Wilmot suffered a recent injury to his head, and has lost part of his memory. I have heard tales of irregular conduct, but I have not seen it myself. I mention this only in case Wilmot should become irrational."

"No one is rational who sails along the north coast in winter!" laughed Bodil.

"So *Kiminge* is a ship of lunatics?"

"Oh ay! We reserve the dog watches for our raving, for we are all mad dogs on this ship!"

I ventured back to my quarters and found Countess Marcella, Elisa d'Altrey, one of the maids, and Wilmot playing cards while Alicio, Nemorino, and the second maid were moaning in their cabins, overcome by nausea at the pitching of the ship. The apparent cordiality of the scene eased my nerves, and I let the steward pour me a glass of ale and joined the others at the table.

The seasick voyagers declined dinner, which proved to be very good, as the ship was living on supplies purchased in Ferrick. The ale had not spoiled, and the turnips had not rotted in the hold.

Afterward we played cards. Wilmot, I remembered, was a keen player, and his head injury had not affected his skill in any way. After losing two games to him, I put on my overcoat again and went out onto the deck.

Supper was served at nightfall, and Prince Alicio was feeling well enough to eat a chop or two, and join us for cards afterward. Mistress d'Altrey had dropped out of the games, I supposed because she could not afford to lose.

Though my narrow bed was built for a smaller man, I slept well that night, and not merely because I found the knife and pistol that Goodman Knott had left for me. I sleep well on ships, in part because the sea rocks me to sleep in its watery cradle, and also because of a sense that the ship is somehow alive, and will be looking after me. A ship is never silent: The timbers creak; the masts groan; the wind cries among the shrouds and backstays; the canvas rumbles and shivers. The bell rings every half hour, and the watches change every four hours, the crew coming up and down the companionways and tramping along the deck in obedience to the calls of the officers. There is comfort in a life so ordered as that on a ship, and thus comforted, I slept.

The wind moderated overnight, and the log-line showed us making six knots on a quarter reach, our best point of sailing. I had convinced Captain Bodil that I was a competent practical sailor, and so I was allowed all over the ship, and went up the shrouds to view the world from the foremast, which obliged me to hang inverted from the futtock shrouds as I made my way first to the foretop, and then again to the crosstrees. I could have gone up by the safer route of the lubber's hole, but as a true sailor, I disdained it.

The view from the crosstrees, more than a hundred feet above the deck, revealed *Kiminge* alone on water the color of indigo. We seemed the only ship in the world, alone below the great deep dome of the sky. The hull had carved our wake a shade of darker blue, filled with turbulent shadows, and outlined by a spreading *V* of foam. Cloud-streamers scudded overhead, and the mast dipped and swooped with the motion of the ship. Below I could see the crew about their duties, and hear the calls of the mates as they gave their orders. So joyous did I find the scene that I remained there until I was called for dinner, and then I sprang for a backstay, and rode down that taut cable in a swift rush, but not so fast as to tear the skin from my palms. This rapid descent, and my earlier use of the futtock shrouds, showed the officers and hands my seaman's skills, for I hoped to be accepted in their company. The tales of the sailors would be a welcome contrast to the pieties of the prince.

I came into the common room, put my overcoat in my cabin, and washed my hands at the basin. The scent of cooking already filled the room. The other passengers were at table, their pewter plates neatly stacked before them, while cheese, pickled vegetables, and fresh loaves of cheat bread were laid for their pleasure. I sat in an empty place, across from Dom Nemorino. There were eight at the table, for the male servants dined with the crew, whereas the ladies' maids were housed with us, to keep them safe from the sailors, who—according to Captain Bodil and all custom—lacked an understanding of civility and chivalry where women were concerned.

First came stew, mutton cooked with raisins, prunes, and claret; and then the steward and his assistant came in with platters, and on the largest I saw a great ham, cooked in a honeyed sauce and spangled with dried cherries that had grown plump in a tub of brandy. We applauded this magnificence, and the steward bowed with pleasure. Countess Marcella spoke up.

"Sir Quillifer," she said. "I have had the pleasure of being your guest at your Savory Supper, and I know your carving skills are without compare. Will you play host and carve for us today?"

I could not help casting a glance at Wilmot to see if the chance occurrence of a ham and my carving of it would have brought back a memory of our quarrel. I saw no sign of danger, but I thought I should not tempt fate.

"I was the host on that occasion, ay," I said, "but I am not the host here, and I'm sure that our steward knows how to serve the feast that he has so obligingly cooked for us. So let us drink to him, and thank him for his good service." I raised my glass, and the steward bowed again, but then offered the carving-knife to me.

"If you please, my lord," he said.

The countess wore a sweet, imploring smile. "Please, Sir Quillifer?" she said. "Won't you oblige us?"

I felt unable to resist this polite but insistent pressure, and I rose from my chair to stand at the head of the table.

"Can you not tell us what you do?" asked the countess. "It would be useful instruction for those of us who lack the skill."

Curses chased one another through my head, but I smiled and took the knife. Wilmot sat on my right and would see the carving practically under his nose, as it had been in that camp in the meadow. His varlet might have stowed away his weapons, but he still had his eating-knife, and I did not fancy it plunged between my ribs. I racked my brain to remember what I had said to Wilmot around the camp-fire, and to invent paraphrases so as not to stimulate his memory too directly. I carved long slices out of the ham, then turned the meat so it sat on this base and began my fine cuts to the shank. The steward had honed his carving-knife to a razor's keenness, and my slices were thin as parchment. Steam and scent rose from the ham as I cut, and I observed Sir Brynley Wilmot from under my brows as he watched the carving, first with an affable aspect, and then a degree of puzzle-ment, and then rising anger. His face went red, a blazing contrast to his pale mustache, and I saw his knuckles grow white as he clutched his knife and fork. Then he looked up at me, his eyes blazing.

"You *cullion!*" he cried, and lunged at me with his knife. I was ready, and I leaped clear of the first stroke, but there was little oppor-tunity for jumping or dodging, for the table took up most of the room, and there were passengers and chairs occupying much of what was left. My carving knife was a superior weapon, but I wished not to use it even in self-defense, and I backed away as Wilmot made one rush after another while the steward and passengers tried to escape the slashing of Wilmot's steel.

Fortunately, I had not been alone in anticipating this turn of events. As Wilmot rushed at me, Prince Alicio rose and seized him by his arm. At this I stepped in close and brought the hilt of my knife up under Wilmot's jaw and knocked him senseless. One of the ladies' maids, thinking I had stabbed him, gave a shriek.

Prince Alicio drew the knife from Wilmot's nerveless fingers as he sagged to his knees, and Dom Nemorino and the steward both came up behind him to take him by the arms and shoulders. One of the cabin servants ran off to fetch help.

Wilmot was only stunned for a few seconds, and as soon as he realized his situation he began to bellow and thrash and threaten, and to make a lunge for the dinner-table in order to seize a weapon. Nemorino, Alicio, and the steward managed to wrestle him to the deck and pin him on his face until Captain Bodil and his mates came, bound Wilmot hand and foot, and threw him without ceremony into the cable tier, on a pile of sodden, weed-covered anchor cable. His unnerving howls and cries resounded through the ship and impeded the digestion of everyone on board.

Our common room was set to rights, apologies were made for the interruption, the captain returned to his own dinner, and I resumed my task of carving for a very subdued audience. Dom Nemorino explained the circumstances to the others, but the distant cries and threats from the cable tier echoed Wilmot's words, and his words fell into numb silence like pebbles into a deep, dark well.

"Perhaps some music would serve," I suggested, and sent for Goodman Knott and his guitar. I don't know that he managed to gladden the mood, but at least he helped to drown out Wilmot's bellowing.

Countess Marcella turned to me as the plates were carried away. "Please forgive me, Sir Quillifer," she said. "Had I known what happened between you and Sir Brynley, I wouldn't have asked you to carve."

"There is nothing to forgive, my lady," I said. "You couldn't have known." But Orlanda could have, I thought, and I was confident that malefic nymph had whispered the suggestion into Marcella's ear.

Some time later, Captain Bodil spoke with us. "I have just seen Wilmot," he said. "And if I had spent another minute with him, I would have fought him myself."

"He is resolute?" asked Nemorino.

"He insists he must fight Sir Quillifer," Bodil said. "He says that if he can't fight him here and now, he will pursue him in Loretto and challenge him in public, when honor will not permit him to refuse."

"While I hope to preserve my honor," said I, "I hardly think my honor would be served by a reputation for killing lunatics."

"If he *is* a lunatic," said Elisa d'Altrey, "can he not be confined to some convenient asylum?"

"He would not stay there long," said Dom Nemorino. "Remember he is the son of a *duque*. His family would have him out, and then he would be on Sir Keely-Fay's trail again."

"Dom Nemorino," said I. "You were a member of our expedition. Do you think that Sir Brynley has a just cause to challenge me?"

"He was insolent," said Nemorino. "You answered his insolence with your own. He set out to shame you, and you shamed him instead, and that drove him to a challenge. But I think the fault lies with him, not so much with you."

"Can you try to reason with Wilmot, then? Point out that he has no reason for a challenge?"

"I will make the attempt," said Nemorino.

"I shall try, also," said Prince Alicio. "There is no just cause for any such fight, and it is a stain on honor itself that our misplaced honor compels us to dishonor that honor. If there is to be fighting, let it be against the enemies of our king."

The two went to the cable tier and came back after half an hour.

"*Aï*, he is resolute," said Prince Alicio.

I toyed with my wine-cup for a moment. "I have no desire to kill him," I said, "but it seems there must be a fight." I turned to the captain. "Captain Bodil, may we turn your vessel into a dueling arena? For it seems to me that we are on the open sea, and no country's laws apply to what we do here."

"In that case," said Bodil, "why not knock Wilmot on the head tonight, and drop him over the side?"

"I don't wish to be a murderer," I said.

Captain Bodil shrugged. "These things happen more often than landsmen imagine," he said. "Thieves and *hexen*—witches—do not thrive on sea-craft, and no one asks what becomes of them."

There was a witch on board, I thought, but no mortal man could harm her. "A seaman might go overboard in the dead of night," I said, "but not a knight of the Red Horse and son of the Duke of Waitstill. It would raise too many questions."

"Even knights can stumble and fall in the dark," said Bodil. "But I will refrain from causing that stumble, if you wish it."

"Perhaps I can so contrive the fight so that no one is injured," I said. "I wonder if you gentlemen will give the plan your support?"

"Insofar as it is compatible with my honor," said Dom Nemorino. "But why, if he is not harmed, would Wilmot not challenge you again?"

Prince Alicio looked at me thoughtfully. "I think Dom Keely-Fay thinks of his fight with Sir Edelmir, that was so humiliating that Sir Edelmir dared not show his face in Howel ever again."

"There were other reasons Sir Edelmir fled," said I. "But yes, that is what is in my mind."

Captain Bodil asked what happened in the fight with Westley. Hearing it, he nodded. "I hope you will not up-end my boat!"

"I hope to manage without such a sacrifice," said I. I offered my notion to the others, and while some were dubious, none could think of a better.

"Very well," said Nemorino. "We shall do it! I will offer to stand as

Wilmot's second, and if he does not agree to your conditions, I will fight him myself!"

I turned to Prince Alicio. "Your Highness," I said, "will you do me the honor of standing as my second?"

Alicio viewed the idea without pleasure. "I disapprove of the whole foolish idea," he said, "but if this will help to resolve the trouble, I will consent."

Which is how, the next morning, I found myself standing on the end of the main yard, the sea rolling beneath me, while I held a top-maul in my hand and waited for the man who wanted to kill me.

Dom Nemorino had told Wilmot that, as the duel would be fought on a ship, I had insisted it be fought in a seamanlike way, high on the main yard, and with a sailor's weapons. Wilmot was so eager for the fight that he consented.

Prince Alicio had insisted the fight take place the next morning, to give Wilmot a chance to regain his sanity. I doubted that Orlanda would permit such a recovery, but I agreed that the attempt should be made. Once Wilmot assented to my terms, Captain Bodil removed his bonds and made his stay in the cable tier more comfortable, though he posted two strong seamen by the hatch to keep him from escaping and murdering us all in our beds.

Kiminge was hove to at first light, the spritsail and the foremast sails laid aback, and the mainmast still full, so that the forces on the ship were balanced, and she went neither forward nor back, but sawed gently back and forth. The wind had veered northwest during the night, and the blue-gray swells were regular, so the yard on which I stood pitched slowly to starboard and then to larboard. I steadied myself with one hand on the lift, the heavy rope used to raise or lower the end of the yard. I wore sailor's trousers and a leather jerkin, which I hoped might provide a bit of padding if things went badly for me. My feet were bare, to provide a sure grip on the yard.

The crew watched from the deck below, and I saw Countess Marcella and Elisa d'Altrey on the poop, their pale oval faces turned up to me. Smoke from the stove in the camboose reached me, and I knew that the crew would have their breakfast as soon as the fight was over.

Prince Alicio and Dom Nemorino stood with the captain in the maintop, and we all waited for Wilmot to make his way up the shrouds. Wilmot was stripped to his shirt, and I had a good view of his red bull neck as he climbed steadily, his eyes fixed upward, on his goal. When he encountered the futtock shrouds, he hesitated, then decided against the lubber's hole and made a slow inverted crawl to the top. I found this display of courage and surefootedness more discouraging than I would have liked.

Wilmot remained in the maintop for a while, recovering his breath and talking with the others. Then Captain Bodil handed him his top-maul, and for the first time Wilmot turned to face me. Fury seemed to twitch like lightning across his face. He swung himself around the topmast shrouds and took a careful step onto the main yard. The yard was a hundred feet long, and we were at least forty feet apart.

"Sir Quillifer!" called Captain Bodil. "Are you ready?"

I affected a casual tone, for all that my heart was beginning to knock at my ribs, and I was beginning to wonder how I found myself here, a hundred feet above the water, trapped on the end of a yardarm while a man glared at me with murderous intent.

"As Sir Brynley pleases," I said. "For this affair falls entirely on him."

"I am ready!" called Wilmot in a voice of triumphant rage.

"Then begin!" called Bodil.

I released the lift, waited till the ship's roll raised the yard under me, and then advanced toward Wilmot, walking slightly downhill on my bare feet. Wilmot cocked his maul over his shoulder and began a slow advance on his tight-laced latchet shoes. It was safe enough for an experienced sailor to walk here, for the center part of the spar was over a yard across in the middle, wider than the paved walkways on most streets, and it tapered but slightly toward the ends. The main topsail billowed out to my left, out of reach. If the wind veered very suddenly and the sail went aback, it might sweep both of us clean off the yard, but the odds were very much against this ever happening. Should either of us fall, we might make a snatch at the footrope, which lay in its stirrups below the yard. This was a rope the seamen would stand on when making or furling sail, their upper bodies folded over the yard as they fisted the heavy canvas.

If we failed to seize the footrope, we had a hundred feet to fall to the water. Captain Bodil had launched one of the ship's boats, and it waited to rescue us if we fell.

I held the top-maul in both hands as I advanced. It was a wooden hammer with a haft two feet long and a five-pound head that was pointed on one end and blunt on the other. The maul was used to bang home the wooden fid that supported the topmast or, when anchoring, to knock away the bight of the chain that kept the anchor on the cathead, or for any other task that needed a heavy weight, like knocking a half-mad knight off a main yard.

Wilmot had his maul cocked over his right shoulder, which meant he was restricted in his attack to a sidearm swing at my left side, or an overhand blow straight at my head. Given his homicidal intentions, I was inclined to believe the latter, but I hoped to be ready for the strike at my side as well. I stopped my advance and waited.

When he was just out of range, he hesitated, and I saw a flicker in his eyes that indicated he was appraising both his position and mine. I didn't want him thinking at all, so I donned my insolent-apprentice face. "Well, Sir Brynley," said I. "Here I find you in a common sailor's place, and with a workman's tool. Where is your brave knighthood now?"

Rage drew his lips back from his teeth, and he shuffled forward and let the maul fly at my head. I jumped back, confident that my bare feet would find purchase when they landed. I landed easily enough, but I felt the wind of the top-maul on my face as it whirred past. The maul spun on in its circle, and Wilmot was twisted around by the weight of his weapon, and so compromised was his balance that I had but to advance and prod his shoulder with the head of my maul to push Wilmot clean off the yard.

Wilmot gave a cry of pure spleen as he tumbled from the yard, but one hand reached out and snatched the footrope, and he bounced sharply in the air like a string-toy dangled before a cat. The crowd of watchers on the deck gave a shout, and I was surprised that his own tumbling weight hadn't torn his hand free. Wilmot dangled as his top-maul spun into the gulf below, and then he got his other hand on the rope and kicked his feet up to bring one heel over the footrope. With a cry of savage pleasure he rolled himself safely up onto the rope, where he paused for a moment, panting for breath.

"I will need another hammer!" he called.

"Sir Brynley," said Prince Alicio, "to continue the fight would be unseemly. Sir Quillifer spared you when he could have broken your head."

Wilmot turned toward the maintop and snarled. "I don't need a foot-licking giglet of a foreigner to tell me what I may do!" said he. "Someone bring another hammer to the what-d'ye-call-it—the platform."

Another top-maul was sent for. I stood over Wilmot as he went through the uncertain business of getting his hands on the yard and both feet on the footrope, and I considered how easily I could crack his skull, and wondered at this aspect of our fine civilization, that in these fights the lunatic is given an equal chance with a sane man.

Wilmot went back to the maintop on the footrope, then swung himself onto the platform. Prince Alicio turned his back on him, and was no doubt debating in his mind whether his princely honor demanded challenging Wilmot himself, and whether the

Compassionate Pilgrim himself would stand for being called a foot-licking giglet.

I retired to the end of the yardarm, held the lift for balance, and waited until one of the hands brought up a new top-maul. Wilmot took the maul without a word, then went back onto the yard.

"Are the gentlemen ready?" asked Captain Bodil. I heard scorn in his words.

Wilmot fixed me with a snarl. "I am ready," he proclaimed.

I merely let go of the lift and shrugged. Wilmot came forward, and I advanced toward him. He hadn't cocked the maul over one shoulder, as he had before, but held it before him like a quarterstaff. Whatever attack he planned would be more deliberate than the swing that had sent him into the abyss, and I suspected he'd been thinking again, a course I hoped to discourage.

"A fine ape you made, Sir Brynley," I told him, "dangling from the footrope with one hand and shrieking like a monkey." I affected to consider him. "What beast will you turn next, I wonder? Perhaps a salmon?"

"A better beast than you," he said, and dropped the head of his maul to swing up at me from below, a blow aimed straight for my courting tackle. I jumped back and let my own maul-head fall, and knocked his wide, preserving the next generation of Quillifers. I shifted forward to strike him in the face with the butt-end of the weapon, but he evaded the blow and swung his maul backhand. I blocked with my haft and felt lucky he had not managed to get all his weight into the blow, for it would have knocked me off the yard.

We both drew back to consider what might follow. "That was a foul blow, Sir Brynley," said I. "Hardly worthy of an honorable knight."

"I need not trouble my honor when fighting a butcher's son!" he snarled.

"Sir Brynley"—I smiled—"I am right glad to hear you say that. For here I have striven to fight in a way worthy of an honorable knight, and to cherish mercy and avoid spilling your brains into the sea." I ventured a snarl. "You claim gentle birth, but you have no more manners than a cockle-seller. And since you insist on viewing me only as a butcher's son, I will *be* that son, and I will treat you as my father would treat some old, useless, half-imbecile bull." And as I saw him turn pale, I added, "You are lucky I have not a shop here, for I would hang you from an iron hook, cut you into pieces, and make pies of you."

And though by this point of the encounter I meant every word I uttered, I was in fact delaying the decisive moment, for I knew a swell was about to lift the ship and cock my end of the main yard into the sky. And once the yard became a road leading down to Wilmot, I launched myself at him, thrusting the butt of the top-maul like a lance for his face. He ducked the strike but had no time to attack himself, for I was thrusting at him continually with the maul-butt and backing him down the yard. It was the strike of the peasant that Lipton had taught me, a vicious way of fighting inside an enemy's guard. He managed finally to swing the maul-head at me, feebly at first, and then with desperation, but I parried each blow and kept thrusting with my weapon. I thrust three times for his face, to get his guard up high, and then I dropped the maul-head low and crushed his knee. I saw the agony on Wilmot's face as his leg failed him, and I had just time enough before he fell to swing the maul round with both hands and smash him on the breastbone. That was enough force to throw him far from the footrope, and down he plummeted.

I had forgot that I had backed him up the length of the yard, and the ship was rolling, which put the hull below him rather than the sea. Wilmot fell, his limbs churning the air like those of a chick falling from the nest, until he struck the shrouds below, and from the shrouds he bounced into the water as if the ship itself was shrugging him off. He vanished beneath the waves, and though the ship's boat rowed straight to the place where he had disappeared, never did they find him.

Sir Brynley Wilmot, Knight of the Red Horse and third son of the Duke of Waitstill, now lodged in a watery grave.

I spent the day in disgust with myself. I had cudgeled my head with schemes to preserve Wilmot's life, and they had come to nothing, for at the moment I had swung the top-maul for his heart, I had intended nothing but murder, and I felt my own responsibility keenly.

I had probably killed men in battle at Exton Scales, but that was in a melee, with swords and pikes slashing at figures half seen in the gunsmoke. I did not know those men, and I had no quarrel with any of them. Whereas Wilmot I knew; the fight had been a personal matter. The quarrel, I thought, was not so much between me and Wilmot, but the result of a far more personal quarrel with Orlanda, who had made Wilmot her creature.

Everyone from Captain Bodil to Rufino Knott did their best to cheer me, but I was not minded to take consolation.

Yet one good thing came of it, for I think it finally made you take notice of me. I saw your black eyes on me in the common room, as we sat in silence around the breakfast table, and I felt as if you were regarding me for the first time.

"Sir Quillifer," you said, "you are a more interesting man than I suspected."

CHAPTER TWENTY-ONE

I remember your words a few months later. "He challenged you, and he died. You tried to save him, and you failed. Yet why blame yourself? It was his choice all along."

"At the last, I wanted him dead."

"So did I. So did everyone. The hearts of everyone on the ship were lightened when he fell." Your brows knit scornfully. "The world will not care if there is one halfwit knight the less." You took my hand and looked close into my eyes. "The world cares not about anyone, and that is why we must care one for another—and in order to do that profitably, we must first decide who is worth caring for." You leaned close, and I felt the touch of your warm breath as you whispered in my ear. "You and I, and no one else. Between us we *are* the world, and no one else matters."

I seem to recall that I played many hands of cards on that voyage. It was the most harmless activity I could think of, and kept my mind occupied with strategies that had nothing to do with death or war or conspiracy. Countess Marcella kindly partnered me in rentoy, against Alicio and Nemorino. She was most charming in sending me signals, winking and twitching her brows, sticking out her tongue and making signs with her fingers. At times the whole table was helpless with laughter, and my melancholy was forgotten.

Marcella also very kindly let you play in her place, and out of compassion for your lack of funds, let you play with her money. And so I came to know you as a subtle player, keen at sending false signals to our opponents and playing your own cards with skill. I had thought you haughty, and so you were, but now I realized that the haughtiness was a result of an honest estimation of your own worth. It is not for you to bandy words with lesser mortals.

We won enough money to buy a fine carriage, and four fine horses to draw it, though I believe we intended to invest it more wisely than in horseflesh.

Those of us from Duisland did our best to speak the language of Loretto on the voyage. My own knowledge of the language was crude, since it was acquired in various port cities, and my vocabulary was drawn from several local dialects. But yet I had studied in school the language of the Aekoi, who had conquered Loretto and Bonille fifteen hundred years ago, and it was from the tongue called "New Aekoi" that the language of Loretto had descended. After the Aekoi fell, the northern part of the country had been occupied by the Sea-Kings and then the Osby Lords, and they had left their imprint on the tongue, and provided most of the local nobility. In the north they said *aï* for "yes," but in the south *si*. In the north a cooking-pot was a *caudron*, in the south a *caldero*; and when a northern lord bordered his property with a hedge, it was a *fossé*, not a *haie*. When Prince Alicio marched to battle in the north, he went to *werre*; but if his battlefield were in the south, he fought in a *conflitto*.

As the royal family of Loretto had originated in the south, the southern dialect was considered "pure" and free of foreign influence, for all that it was a bastard child of the unrefined tongue spoken not by Aekoi philosophers and rhetoricians, but by the soldiers and merchants who occupied the country. But the vocabulary mattered less than the accent—the northern accent was considered coarse, and so I endeavored to polish the north from my tongue, and learn to make my words mince and strut and dance the pompous pavane. Dom Nemorino said I made good progress, though Prince Alicio withheld his opinion. Both, however, praised Countess Marcella's mastery of their language.

A voyage of six days brought us to Balfoy, on the river Lesse. We came as the herald of a storm that blackened the western horizon behind us as we raced for the shelter of the harbor; and by the time we achieved our anchorage, sleet was pattering like a rain of small stones on the canvas. Captain Bodil had been lucky and reached port before the wind began to roar. We left the *Kiminge* for an inn and invited Captain Bodil to join us for supper ashore. There we made a merry party while the storm battered the shutters, and when I went up the steep stair to my room, I swayed not because of drink, but because I had not yet grown used to footing that did not rise and fall to the scend of the sea.

The storm pummeled the town for two more days, leaving it cloaked in white; and then we departed on a barge for the south. We were eleven days on the barge as it went up the Lesse, the master trading at various ports of call, and I viewed Loretto in its winter colors, somber browns and grays, the fields half-flooded, the orchards stark and leafless. The land along the Lesse was fertile, and grand houses and castles overlooked the water, but the ordinary folk lived mean lives in little thatched houses that huddled together as if for warmth, with dogs and pigs walking in and out of the door.

"It is a fine rich country," I said to you as we drank mulled wine on a bright winter's day. We stood on the bow with the barge's lugsail rising behind us, and the tillerman the only crew on deck, the rest having their dinner in the roundhouse. You were wrapped in a coat of silver fox fur and a hat made of marten. I in my otter-fur cape looked plain as a shepherd.

"There should not be water standing in the pastures like that," you observed. "The farmers should have plowed for winter, to allow for drainage and keep the roots of the plants from drowning."

"I see you were raised in the country, Mistress d'Altrey," said I. "I know nothing of plowing, and it is not an occupation to which I aspire."

"The plowman toils all year long," you said. "He must plow to drain the fields, to kill the weeds, to plow dung into the soil, to prepare the ground for seed. If it is not being done"—and here you nodded at a field all a-shimmer with water—"that means the plowman is elsewhere. He has been swept up in the corvée, unpaid labor to maintain the roads and dikes, or to add a wing to the lord's palace. Or perhaps he carries a pike in the army."

"I defer to your knowledge of husbandry," I said. " But as ignorant as I am, to me this seems an unsound practice. The crops will suffer if the farmer is taken away."

"Ay, but the lords and the corvée care not for the problems of farmers." You pointed at a great fine house with a lawn running down to the water. "See that tall building on the left? The one shaped like a beehive?"

"I see it."

"That is a columbarium, a pigeon-house. There might be a thousand pigeons living there, to provide squab for the lord's table, eggs for his dinner, and a top-dressing for his fields. But as the pigeons belong to the lord, they have the lord's privileges, and are allowed to dine on the farmers' seeds, and to pluck the harvest from the stalk before the plowman. If the farmer retaliates by killing one of the lord's pigeons, he is himself hanged."

"You make me feel very sorry for those plowmen," said I.

"It is the way of the world," you said. "Those who can, take." I saw a flare of resentment in your black eyes, a flare that quickly died. "At the end of the rebellion," you said, "the crown took away the land that had been in my family for four hundred years."

"That must have been hard," I said.

"It was all the worse because I'd warned my father and brothers it might happen." The blaze kindled again in your eyes, and I saw your fists clench in your fine calfskin gloves. "Clayborne's uprising wasn't a rebellion—it was a sickness! And my grandfather, father, and brothers all caught the disease, were completely swept away by the dazzling prospect of riches and rewards granted by our brave new king." You laughed. "My brothers thought that gold and knighthoods would fall from the sky! I told them not to underestimate Berlauda, but they scoffed at the idea that a woman could hold the throne. So the queen ordered them all beheaded after Exton Scales, and my mother and I were turned out of our home. If I hadn't hidden away our jewelry and some money, we would have had to beg for our bread."

"Where is your mother now?"

"She is a guest of kin who avoided the rebellion and Berlauda's wrath. For myself, it is lucky that Her Highness took pity on me, and now employs me as one of her ladies."

"Did Her Highness know you?"

"Nay, but friends at court spoke for me."

I considered your story. "I am surprised that you went to court at all, with Berlauda having taken your lands."

You made a disdainful sound. "I went to court for the same reason you did. It is the place where advancement might be found. Which simpleton sits on the throne does not matter, so that simpleton does not simply take, but also dispenses favors."

I was amused. "You think Berlauda is a simpleton?"

"I think it is the act of a fool to share power with a foreign autocrat."

I smiled. "It is not the act of a woman in love?"

"If she loves Priscus, that makes her even more foolish. And to engage in a profitless war because that too-well-loved prince wants a pretty army to flaunt in front of his father, that is madness."

"It takes but a single monarch to make a war," I said. "Yet it takes two to make love."

You laughed. "You disregard self-love, Sir Quillifer. That is also a prerogative of kings."

"My mother always said that you must love yourself before you are worthy to love others."

Your eyes narrowed. "I think the topic has shifted somewhat from matters of state."

I waved a hand. "We move from matters in which we find ourselves powerless, to a matter in which we both have some influence."

Again you laughed. "Her Highness warned me about you. She suspects you of treating love too lightly."

I feigned offense. "Mistress d'Altrey, it seems to me that I accord love all proper respect."

You tilted your head to view me. "Yet you behave so recklessly in other things, I would be surprised to find you sober in matters of love."

"I do not believe love is a sobering thing." I spread my hands. "But, mistress, if you doubt me, you may lay down whatever rule you like, and see if I obey."

I could see calculation flickering behind your black eyes, and then you shook your head. "I am without power, Sir Quillifer. I have no one to protect me. I think it would be dangerous to love you."

"I?" I affected astonishment. "I am notoriously harmless."

You put a gloved hand on my arm. "One may ask Sir Brynley Wilmot how harmless you are, and he was a man you meant to save."

I was stricken to the heart, and my words bottled up in my throat. Yet at the last you took pity on me, and your eyes softened. "I am sorry to have mentioned that name, Sir Quillifer. But I wish only to remind you that what we do hath consequence for ourselves and the world, and that applies to our pleasures as well as our duties."

"I think you are wrong, mistress," I finally said. "You say you have no power, but I think you are wrong. You are powerful indeed."

You raised an eyebrow. "You are going to say that I have power over your heart?"

"Something less poetical, mistress," I said. "I was going to say that you are powerful, because you know what you want."

You gave a soft laugh and, as you went off, kissed me on the cheek. From that I took a little comfort.

It is strange to view that conversation now, when we are about to embark on our great emprise. You, who were so cautious, are now the epitome of daring. And I, so sickened over the death of Wilmot, am now ready to lay a nation in waste. If we succeed, tens of thousands will die, and only because we will it.

Neither of us would have dared this without the other. In this we complete ourselves, and will do so by shattering the world.

Prince Alicio joined me a few moments later at the prow of the barge. He wore against the cold wind a hat and coat made extravagantly of ermine, the pure-white fur recalling the white of the Retriever sect, where lay his philosophical sympathies. To hold the opinions of a Retriever in Loretto was of course a capital offense, but Alicio could merely claim that he wore ermine as a privilege of his princely house, for only those within a certain radius of the throne were allowed to wear the skin of that regal animal.

"I wonder, Highness," I said, "if you would enlighten me concerning a point of the Pilgrim's doctrine."

"If I can," said he. "I am not a divine."

"I'm confident the answer is within your competence."

He nodded. "Very well."

Over my shoulder I glanced at you, standing alone and magnificent by the roundhouse. "Why is it," I asked, "that the Compassionate Pilgrim is so opposed to the act of love?"

Alicio stroked his goatee. "Because the Pilgrim held that life is little but suffering," said he. "The act of love may produce momentary pleasure, but it also engenders children, and the children grow to suffer in their turn. Therefore the act of love produces suffering, and should be avoided."

"I feel that this doctrine may be true," said I, "yet I find it somehow incomplete. For does not a mother love her child, and take comfort in that child, just as the child derives comfort and sustenance from the mother? And should not people in a world of suffering seek relief in each other's arms?"

"The Pilgrim approved of the *sentiment*, as opposed to the *act*, of love," said Alicio. "For this sentiment comforts men and women in this realm of misery. But he felt that the carnal act itself led inevitably to suffering."

"Yet," said I, "if the Pilgrim's rule were followed strictly, the human race should become extinct. It is almost a way of declaring that the human race is a terrible mistake that should be corrected."

"I am not qualified to judge the human race," said Alicio, "but I rejoice in how much suffering would be ended."

"Consider how much other human activity results in suffering," I said. "Emptying cesspits. Working in Her Majesty's silver mines. Going aloft in a storm to shorten sail. Being clouted on the head by my schoolmaster."

Alicio smiled. "I perceive you have a grudge against that schoolmaster."

"I affirm that I do," said I, "and I heartily wish the Pilgrim had forbidden him to strike me."

"I believe that if you search the Pilgrim's writings," said Alicio, "you will find some remarks on the subject of violence."

"Well, that is a comfort." I lifted my mulled wine and inhaled the scent of clove and cardamom. "But my larger point," I continued, "is that the Pilgrim does not enjoin us from working in mines or emptying cesspits, but instead singles out an act of pleasure for his condemnation. It seems less a program than a prejudice on his part."

"*Aī*, but it is the only act that brings suffering to the next generation."

"Suffering, yes. But also love, family, amity, hope, curiosity, and discovery."

"If you are a lucky child, you may have that," said Alicio, "But you might also be born a cripple, or wander alone begging on the streets, or be set to climb into chimneys to clean them, or put to some foul purpose in a brothel."

"But the Pilgrim put forward no program to correct that sort of injustice," I said, "but instead wishes us not to make happy babies as well as miserable ones."

"The Pilgrim holds that happiness is transitory, but suffering eternal."

I ventured upon a laugh. "It seems that you are asking me to surrender much, and in exchange I receive extinction."

"Quillifer," said he, "you will become extinct in any case."

"And that extinction is another complaint I have, and one which, if the Pilgrim be divine—as so many of his followers allege—I wish he would address at once."

"Freedom can only be found in resignation," said the prince.

"Whereas I think that freedom is best found on boats," said I, "and on sailing on the free waters of the world."

When we arrived in Longres, I found it a discouraging sight, for behind its crumbling walls were shabby, ancient buildings crowded around narrow, dark lanes. I could all too easily imagine an ambush lurking around every corner. In Selford there were districts like this, like the Ramscallions down by the river, but from what I could see from the Lesse, the whole city was decrepit and stinking.

I have since learned that the city's appearance has much to do with the system of taxation. Windows are taxed, and so most are blocked up, and the interiors remain dark. Rooms are also taxed, so interior walls are knocked down, and no closets are built, for closets are considered rooms. Fresh paint and new thatch attract the attention of the tax collectors, and so are avoided. Even the wealthy strive to hide their success from the prying revenue agents, and hope to look poor as cotters.

The nobles, who are immune to taxation, live in quite a different world.

The captain had much business to conduct on the quay, and so we passengers disembarked into carriages summoned by the captain of the port and were carried five or six leagues to Longres Regius, where Henrico resided in his palace and the nobility crowded around on their own estates. But as we left the city, we first encountered the execution ground, where those judged guilty were broken on the wheel, and that wheel then mounted atop a pole, so that crows could feast on the victim and the citizens could pass that place of carnage and reflect on the vagaries of life, and of justice. There were dozens of these memorials, all black against the winter sky, some so old they held only bones clad in rags. I wondered how many had died for killing their lord's pigeons.

I remembered those heads in front of the Hall of Justice in Howel, and wondered whether these Lorettan notions of justice had come to my country along with King Priscus.

The broken bodies fell behind, and we viewed the highway to Longres Regius, flanked by the fine houses of nobles and courtiers, just like the road between Howel and Ings Magna. From the carriage I could see, rising above the bare black trees, the fantastic towers and chimneys of the royal palace, but I traveled on with Prince Alicio to his own house, where I was to be his guest. You, the countess, and Dom Nemorino would be lodged at the palace.

Prince Alicio lived at the Palace Ribamar, a gray stone house befitting his rank, with towers, gables, a thousand panes of glass, and a score of chimneys. Statues of royal ancestors occupied niches on the facade. There was a park, a lake where full-rigged ships lay ready for pleasure-parties on the water, and a garden laid out in an astrological design. A staff of two hundred maintained the buildings and grounds under the direction of the flint-eyed steward Braud, who kept the servants in order much as a sergeant-major disciplines his pikemen.

His Highness's columbarium lodged no less than two thousand pigeons.

Prince Alicio was an indulgent host, allowed me full use of his house, and introduced me at court. The courtiers were even more glittering than those in Howel, their gowns and jerkins of silk and satin and costly fur. I again made myself a contrast, my clothing comparatively plain but my fingers aglow with gems. I was presented to King Henrico and Queen Arletta, who were tall and lean, like Priscus, and looked so alike, both to each other and to their son, that it was plain they made up a marriage of cousins. As I was the first of the great wave of arrivals from the Duisland court, Her Majesty asked me about Queen Berlauda's condition, and I was able to report, quite honestly, that when last I had seen her at the new year celebrations, Berlauda had been at a pinnacle of health.

Their Majesties were gracious about my inexpert attempts to speak their language, and thanked me for coming to aid their country in war. Though they seemed to believe I intended to fight Thurnmark, I felt that small errors such as these were fully the province of majesty, and I did not correct them.

Later that day there was a ball in the great hall of the palace, with its gilded barrel vault a-drip with crystal chandeliers, and the walls splendid with mirrors and brilliant tapestries. Their Majesties opened the ball by leading a grave pavane. It is a simple dance, with couples slowly parading forward or back, and pauses every so often so the gentleman may circle his partner, the better to show off his fine costume. So many dancers followed the royal couple that they resembled the surface of the sea, rising and falling and doubling back as if moving at the will of a tide. Their Majesties paraded the length of the hall and back, and then, as is the universal custom, the pavane was followed by the galliard, a far livelier dance, wherein the lady shows off her dextrous footwork, and the gentlemen the fine shape of their legs in silken hose.

I observed the dances only, for I had no partner. Prince Alicio danced with some royal cousin or other, but I doubted that my touch would be allowed to sully the hands of my superiors, for the protocol in the palace was very strict, and I did not fully understand it, and rather than make an error, I chose to forego the pleasures of the dance.

Their Majesties returned to their thrones. What followed the galliard was a great surprise, for it was *la volta*, which in the language of the country means "the turn." The partners danced so closely that I was a little astonished, for that sort of intimacy would have caused a scandal in Duisland—and then I was dumbstruck by what followed, which appeared to be the gentlemen seizing the women by the bosom and groin, and hurling them in the air. The ladies took no offense at this, and many shrieked with delight.

Further observation gave me a better idea of this maneuver: The gentlemen seized not the woman, but either end of the busk that stiffened the front of their gowns and flattened their chests, and they also assisted the woman in her leap by some lift of the left thigh, the precise contrivance of which escaped me.

I realized I would have to hire a dancing master, and find a partner with whom to practice.

There were three galleries above the hall, one for the orchestra, and others for servants and observers. I procured a cup of wine and went up a marble stair to one of the side-galleries, for I thought that I might view the dancers below and find someone I knew. Perhaps Lady Westley was on my mind, or perhaps Elisa d'Altrey. Instead I found Countess Marcella in the gallery, speaking with two people I did not know. She saw me arrive and motioned at me with her fan to invite me to join her.

"I have found some people from your country," she said. "Sir Quillifer, this is his lordship the Count of Erquem, Berlauda's ambassador to Longres Regius, and his lady countess."

The count was a tall, spare man of sixty or so, with a pointed beard and white hair dressed in ringlets. His wife was about eighteen, with strawberry-blond hair and a warm, rosy complexion.

"I am very pleased to meet you," I said.

"As you can see," said Marcella, gesturing at my ring-bedecked hands, "Sir Quillifer is a connoisseur of gems. Perhaps you would care to view his collection."

The Countess of Erquem smiled at me, and a light kindled in her blue-gray eyes. "That would be lovely, Sir Quillifer, if you are willing."

Her husband frowned in thought. "What kind of name is Quillifer?" he asked.

Blaise Baldry, the Count of Erquem, was from one of the old noble families with lands on both sides of the Duisland-Loretto frontier, a status which complicated relations with the warlike monarchs on either side of the divide, but which probably explained his diplomatic avocation. His wife, Elvina, was from the gentry of southeast Fornland, and would never have been suitable as a first wife. Fortunately for the count, he had been widowed twice.

Her brother, anxious for a powerful friend at court, had seized an opportunity to throw his sister and the count together, then practically posted the banns himself. So Elvina found herself married to a worldly, elderly nobleman, and through his influence, her brother received an appointment as cofferer of the royal household.

"I don't blame my brother," she told me a few days later. "He is doing well, and my husband is kind, and I've met many more interesting people than I would have, staying at home."

"It is true that travel broadens the acquaintance," I said, and kissed her below the ear.

You have commented, I think, that in this period my private life became over-complex, and I own you are right. For I still had thoughts of Lady Westley, and I hoped that in the future you and I might develop a greater intimacy. But Elvina was present, lively, and willing, and I badly wanted distraction after the business with Wilmot.

Furthermore, she was one of a set of lively friends, and I soon found myself one of their company. I learned to dance *la volta*, with Elvina as a partner. We drank and feasted. We hunted, and I rode badly; I played tennis well; we made music, and while I enjoyed singing and playing my guitar, it must be admitted that my performance was somewhat short of a professional standard.

The Count of Erquem viewed his bride's friends with an indulgent eye. I suspect he had once been young, and understood that Elvina would find his friends dull and would resent being restricted to their company. Rather than preventing her from finding companions of her own, he allowed her to do what she wished, and openly, so that he could keep a benign eye on her. I found myself admiring him.

Prince Alicio stayed in his palace only ten days or so, for he traveled to his lands to raise forces for the war with Thurnmark. He allowed me to remain in his house, and committed me to the care of Braud the steward and his two hundred staff. They took splendid care of me, and when Elvina and her companions came to visit, I scattered silver among the household to pay for their extra labor.

You, I know, were less fortunate in your accommodation and your pastimes, as you told me when we met the day King Henrico and his court went hawking. I know nothing of hawks, their maintenance, or their uses, but Alicio had two hawkers in his household, and I took them and their birds along. The hawking was poor, as January offered little prey except His Majesty's own pigeons, some of which were sacrificed in the name of royal entertainment.

Yet it was good to be on a hunt that did not involve galloping full-pelt over ditches and fences, and the day was bright, the hawks were fierce and beautiful, and the still air had that fine crisp taste that you find only in winter. I saw you and Countess Marcella riding on the fringes of the hunt, and rode over to salute you.

"Well, Sir Quillifer," you said. "You seem to have made yourself at home in Longres."

"Thanks only to Prince Alicio," said I. "His Highness has been a very generous host."

"Would we could say the same about King Henrico," said Marcella. "The rooms allocated to Her Highness Floria are deficient—one miserable room, with one miserable bed! For the present, Mistress d'Altrey and I must share that bed, but when Floria comes, she will have the bed, and we will have to sleep on the floor. There will be no room for Floria's other ladies at all."

"Have you spoken to Their Majesties? Surely they cannot expect a royal princess to be so poorly lodged."

"They defer to the grand seneschal of the household, who says that no other arrangement can be made, for two royal courts must now share the same building, and there is no room."

"It seems only just that they pitch a few counts or barons out of their beds to make proper apartment for a royal princess," I said, and considered the situation. "I don't know if it would be quite proper to offer you rooms in Prince Alicio's palace, but I can certainly write him to ask if he would be willing to come to the relief of two gentlewomen."

"That would be pleasant indeed for the two of us," you said. "But when Floria comes, she must have a proper apartment at Longres Regius, and not a room given in charity by a royal cousin."

"I have written to Her Highness," Marcella said, "and advised her not to come until the matter is settled."

"But who can settle it?" asked I. "Beyond the grand seneschal, of course."

"Queen Berlauda," you said. "She can insist on a suitable apartment for her sister. We will petition her as soon as she arrives."

"I hope you succeed, mistress."

Hawks gyred overhead in search of prey. We walked our horses over sere grass, with Alicio's two hawkers following at a respectful distance.

"The story of your fight with Wilmot has reached the palace," you said. "And with it, the tale of the other fight with Westley."

"Need I worry about arrest, do you think?"

"You fought no one in Loretto, and you were supported by a prince, so there is no danger to you," you said. "But they are mad for dueling here, you know, and the court is full of bravos anxious to prove their mettle. And now you have gained a reputation as a fighter, so you should be aware that some may try to provoke a quarrel with you."

I snarled. "Cannot these bellicose gallants go to the war and relief their martial passions by killing a few of the enemy? Perhaps they will do us the favor of dying in a ditch." You laughed, but I sighed. "Yet I thank you for the warning, mistress."

"You seem a peaceable enough fellow. Yet there is always strife about you."

The strife is named Orlanda, I thought, but spoke not that name aloud. "I desire no harm to any man."

"Yet you will not stand aside for a fool or a madman," she said. "I find that laudable. And if you do not wish to soil your hands with blood, nevertheless you heap shame on your enemies, and put a fool's cap on their heads."

"That cap was always there," said I, "but invisible."

You laughed. In the bright winter sky, a hawk folded its wings and stooped to its prey.

"You will go far, Quillifer," you said, "so long as you fight only fools."

I waved a hand. "Why would a wise man fight me?" I said.

To this question neither of us had an answer.

CHAPTER TWENTY-TWO

Berlauda and Priscus arrived the first week of February, having made a stately progress from the west coast of Loretto. They paraded into Longres Regius preceded by Lord Barkin and two companies of the Queen's Own Horse in their brass-plated armor and red plumes, and followed by all the nobles in their finery and the court in procession. I was obliged to ride in the column of courtiers, though, fortunately, I was not required on this occasion to don armor, for I would have found all that steel cold indeed in the chill wind that rattled the trees and tore apart the low cloud over our heads.

The first part of the parade was witnessed only by cold, miserable stick-figures clothed in smocks and cloaks and blankets of thick, worn wool. Some were barefoot, the rest wore wooden shoes, and most leaned on their tools. These were the cotters subject to the corvée, torn from their homes to repair the highway and smooth the ride of Berlauda to the capital. I did not find that part of the parade very pleasant, for I felt there was judgment in the glances of these worn, cold men, and that they viewed me as they might view their lords' pigeons, untouchable until the hoped-for moment of vengeance. As we grew nearer the palace, however, the road became lined with the servants who worked in the fine estates of the nobility, and these cheered Priscus and Berlauda as the royal carriage rolled past. By the time the procession entered the gates of Longres Regius, the plaza before the palace was full of men and women cheering their hearts out, and the platform built before the front doors was filled with royalty and great officers, their forms wrapped in furs of mink and sable, while their plumes and cloaks flew in the wind. Elvina I could see there, her face rosy in the cold, with her arm in that of her husband.

A salute of great guns boomed out as Priscus and Berlauda left their carriage and came onto the platform, where king and queen gave the kiss of peace to king and queen. While gunpowder scented the air, the grand chancelier of Loretto met his counterpart, the lord high chancellor of Duisland; the grand master of Loretto met the lord high steward of Duisland; the keeper of the seals met the lord keeper of the great seal; the grand almoner met the philosopher transterrene; the grand chamberlain the great chamberlain; and so on down the line.

Alone among the worthies of Duisland was the new chancellor of the exchequer, a miserable being named Flinders who had replaced Hulme as the head of finance. It was he who would be expected to wrangle the Burgesses over taxes, and recent precedent suggested he would probably lose his head if he failed.

He stood alone not because he was doomed, but because there was no Lorettan equivalent to our exchequer, which possibly explained the chaotic state of Henrico's finances.

Likewise, on the Loretto side, their constable, their marshal, and their grand admiral did not meet their equivalents, for those offices had fallen vacant in Duisland.

Loretto had no equivalent to the lord warden in ordinary against monsters, which I considered sheer neglect on Henrico's part. I would have enjoyed exchanging pleasantries with such a man, along with suggestions for disposing of chimerae.

Riding amid the worthies of Duisland was the cofferer of the royal household, Elvina's brother. I had never met him, and so I looked for someone resembling Elvina, and saw no one.

Because of the freezing cold, the remaining ceremonies were moved indoors. There was drinking and feasting and speechmaking, but I was not ranked high enough even to view the table at which royalty sat; and so I was given a trestle table in a drawing room, and had a few bites of a wretched stew, made with greasy mutton and whatever half-spoiled bits of tuber were found in the royal larder, and so I called for my horse with the intention of returning to Prince Alicio's palace. There it was warm, the cook had learned my tastes in food, and I did not imagine the palace would miss me. But riding past the great train of vehicles waiting their turn to get into Longres Regius, all filled with royal servants frozen to the bone, I saw the face of Blackwell the playwright peering out of one of the carriages, and I hailed him.

"Your entire troupe is here?" I said.

"Ay," said he. "We are to show these folk of Loretto the greatness of Duisland's theater—or so we shall, if we don't freeze to death first."

"If you can find a horse, I will pluck you from the arms of death, and show you where it is warm."

Blackwell found not a horse, but a jackass, but nevertheless it carried him the few leagues to Prince Alicio's house, with his long legs nearly dragging the ground. As he arrived, he looked up at the house with fine appreciation.

"You have moved up in the world, Quillifer," he said.

"Indeed I have found excellent lodging, and a couple hundred servants to ease my days."

"The ink business must be good."

We drank and supped and warmed ourselves before a roaring fire, and he told me that his play of Lord Baldwine had been met with indifference, until Mountmirail's wondrous dragon was brought onstage, and that it had caused a sensation. Berlauda had decided to take Roundsilver's Players to Loretto, and of course His Grace of Roundsilver was happy to grant permission. The dragon had crossed the water to Loretto, along with the mechanical birds and marvels of *The Kingdom of the Birds.*

"Will you play using the Duisland tongue?" asked I.

"Indeed, we have no choice," said Blackwell. "But each scene will be preceded by a dumb show to explain the action, and, if necessary, a prologue will be delivered in the local language."

"That should serve," said I, "if you play before the court, for they are a sophisticated audience, and may respect poetry delivered even in a language they consider barbarous."

Blackwell turned to me, his deep-indigo eyes solemn. "Did you hear that they caught Hulme?"

A claw of sadness pierced my heart. "I am sorry to hear it. I thought he had got away."

"He had, and he ran to Bretlynton Head, but he could find no ships to carry him off, and the warrant caught up with him. His head has now joined that of the admiral and the lord great chamberlain."

Lord Hulme had treated me well, helped make me rich, and protected me from a powerful enemy. He had conserved Duisland's wealth, which of course made him the enemy of anyone who wished to spend it. Now he had been destroyed by an ungrateful monarch.

"Sir Edmund Tryon, his deputy, still lives," Blackwell said. "Hulme was an old man, and when he was shown the rack, he confessed at once to whatever charges were invented for him. But Tryon is younger, and defied them to do their worst. He held out, even against the rack." He shrugged. "They will kill him anyway, of course, but the trial will be less pat, and whoever prosecutes it will have to look to his wits, especially if Tryon is allowed to speak."

"If Tryon has been racked, he may be beyond speech," said I. "He may no better represent himself than a jerkin stuffed with straw."

Blackwell snarled. "The court was always a vile stew of ambition, but not since King Osmer have we had such tyranny. I am writing verses that will expose them all, that will reveal every crime, every unjust murder."

"You cannot expect the lord chamberlain to license such verse," said I.

"There are ways of getting unlicensed works into print," said Blackwell. "Most political pamphlets are unlicensed. A printer can be found." He gave a low laugh. "I fully intend it to be a sensation. Everyone will want to read it, but no one will admit to having a copy."

"If they find you are responsible, your head will sit next to that of Scutterfield," said I.

"That may be," said Blackwell, "but I will be able to congratulate myself that I told the truth at least once in my life. Now where is the brandy?"

"I fear you commit suicide."

"There are many ways of committing suicide," said Blackwell. "One of them is sitting still, and waiting for a tyrant to kill you."

Duisland's monarchs were in Longres for no more than two nights before a solemn three-day retreat was proclaimed by Their Majesties, and so we were all obliged to retire to the Monastery of the Footsteps of the Pilgrim to celebrate the Day of the Seven Words. I shared a monk's plain cell with two of the lord chancellor's secretaries. We diced for the one pallet, and I lost, but stretching my blanket on the rushes, I found myself more comfortable than the unfortunate victor, who tossed sleeplessly on a hard mattress intended to mortify the flesh.

Much of the day we chanted for our own enlightenment and that of the world, for Their Majesties' health, for the health of their unborn child, or for success in war—unlike the monks of Duisland, who during the war chanted for Berlauda but would not curse the rebels, the monks of Loretto had no difficulty invoking supernatural aid to drown the enemy in his own blood. I had been raised outside the community that followed the Compassionate Pilgrim, but from what little I knew, I did not believe the Pilgrim would have approved of such a sanguinary petition.

I found the chanting tedious, and the postures meant to invoke spiritual power were uncomfortable. By the end of the first day I was twitching like a man overcome by fleas. While the droning went on, I occupied my mind with plans for expanding my black empire of ink, or with the dimensions of new ships I hoped to build, or with pleasant thoughts of Elvina.

I suppose I might have damned the whole enterprise with my irreverence, for it is held that those who perform such petitionary chanting must do so with utter sincerity, and my impurity may have canceled any intervention by the divine. Yet its seems to me that nothing else could be expected from someone compelled to attend, forced into uncomfortable postures, and made to mouth the same syllables over and over for hours. These things, I feel, are best left to the professionals.

We were also blessed with homilies by the abbot, an obese bald man who dressed in brilliant satins, with gems winking on every plump finger. He discoursed on fate and chance, and the wisdom of accepting either with the proper resignation. The opinion in Loretto was that Eidrich the Pilgrim was not a man, as the Pilgrim himself claimed, but an emanation of the creator spirit of the universe, sent to the earth to bring an awakening to its miserable inhabitants. This was a view endorsed by King Henrico, and endorsed with the noose and the wheel, which were reserved for those of contrary opinions.

The Pilgrim, the abbot proclaimed, had set us each in his proper station, great and small alike, man or woman, in order to teach us the proper acceptance of our condition. Kings and paupers had their burdens alike: the first to justly rule a realm, the second to submit to those placed above them. All had an equal chance of freedom, for freedom was found only in the mind, not in things of the world. I thought it a fine philosophy for a fat man to so disparage his jewels, his satins, and the silk cushion on which he perched his buttocks, and wondered how he would fare if I dropped him naked on a wintry mountaintop, and with what resignation he would enjoy his true freedom.

I felt enlightened by this idea, though perhaps not in the way Their Majesties intended.

At this retreat I made the acquaintance of the cofferer of the royal household, Elvina's brother. Harvey Meens resembled his sister not at all, being a bluff, booming gentleman a few years my senior, tall and broad-shouldered, with long dark hair and a beard cropped very short in the Lorettan fashion. He was genial and lively, but I noticed that as he told a joke, or commented on some doings at court, his dark eyes watched me with close attention, as if judging how well I might best serve him. He was ambitious, I concluded, yet I reasoned ambition is not a sin in a courtier.

Ambition or not, he was pleasant enough and soon absorbed into Elvina's coterie, where he joined our merry-making.

Five days after the retreat, Henrico, Dom Nemorino, and Priscus were gone, to join the army forming on Thurnmark's borders. Priscus made a formal farewell to his Berlauda on the steps of the palace, and she gave him a silken banner to fly in battle, a banner stitched by her own hands, along with those of her ladies. She was visibly with child, and kissed her husband tenderly before he mounted his horse, doffed his cap, and rode away. He went with trumpets and drums and the rattling of armor, Loretto's royal guard marching in their white jerkins, and demilances trotting in advance of columns of pikemen. No soldiers of Duisland marched, for our battalions had not yet arrived, and the Queen's Own did not join the army, for they were Berlauda's personal guard, and the sight of their handsome young officers was a solace to our queen in the absence of her husband.

I wished for solace myself, but Elvina was obliged to spend the day with her husband, consoling Berlauda in her loneliness. I rode home with a reduced company of Elvina's friends, for half the gentlemen had ridden to war just that morning, and though we enjoyed a good dinner, games, drink, and song, we were more sober than usual, and wondered how many of our friends we would not see again.

One afternoon in mid-February I was lying with Elvina in my chamber. We had closed the bed curtains for warmth, and in the near darkness the bed seemed like a small boat drifting down a warm, lazy river of pleasure. Even in the dusky light I could see Elvina's body rosy with contentment, and her scent lay heavy in the air.

"Dom Petro is heartbroken," Elvina related. "Contesa Amaranta is to be married off on the orders of her father."

"You were married off," said I. "But you and I manage to find time for one another. Can't Dom Petro manage a similar arrangement with his mistress?"

"Not everyone has a husband as reasonable as mine," Elvina said. "Viconte Xabier is a haughty man, very concerned to maintain his rights. Or so Amaranta says."

"Poor Petro." Petro and Amaranta were both young members of Elvina's set, and very much in love. Amaranta's father would not permit his daughter to marry a mere knight, and had found an older, far wealthier nobleman eager for the match.

"Petro said he might go to the war, in hopes of winning a title, or at least a fortune. But even if he succeeded, it would be too late."

"We should learn from this example to make every moment count," said I, and took her in my arms. "Fate could sever us at any moment."

She received my kisses for a moment, and as I began to caress her, I sensed a shift in her mood.

"My love?" said I.

"Quillifer," said she, her tone earnest. "What do you think about our having a child?"

You might imagine that this took me by surprise. As was my custom, I had used sheaths to keep our love free of any consequences save that of pleasure, and now Elvina had raised an issue that I had never considered.

"What would my lord of Erquem say about that?" asked I.

Elvina made an equivocal sound in her throat. "Well, I think it would not so much matter. For he has three grown sons, and the continuance of his line is assured. And of course I might convince him the child is his."

"Unless the infant has the ill luck to look like me," said I.

"I would like to conceive a child in love," said Elvina, "and I do not love my husband. And if I should conceive, I think dear Blaise would not be so terribly put out."

"I should care for a little more reassurance along those lines," I said, and wondered how I felt about a child of mine being raised as a count's younger son. The idea seemed too fantastic for me to have any response beyond amusement.

I reached for her again. "For the present time, let our arrangement remain as before," said I, "and I will ponder on what you suggest."

"I should like to have your child, Quillifer," said she. "And as for my husband, he will not live forever."

I felt my ardor dissipate, and I considered how a degree of darkness might be concealed behind my lover's ingenuous manner. "Well, my dear," I began, and then there was a knock on my door.

"Dom Keely-Fay." I recognized the deep voice of Braud the steward. "*Si?*"

"You have a visitor, milord. A Lord Edevane."

"Offer him refreshment in the library," I instructed. "I will see him directly." I turned to Elvina, but she spoke before I made my apologies.

"Edevane?" she said. "Everyone is terrified of him!"

"The more reason why I should see him, then bundle him out of the house."

"But why should Edevane want to speak to you?" Then she clutched the sheets and pulled them to her neck. "Unless he's here about me!"

"I doubt it, my sweet." I kissed her on the nose. "I am after all a royal official, and he may wish to know how well I am killing monsters." I opened the bed curtains and reached for my hose. "I will return as soon as I can."

I dressed with care and brushed my hair, then went to the parlor where Lord Edevane waited. He wore his gold chain, gold-rimmed spectacles, and violet-colored velvet, and stood by the window fidgeting with a pomander. Braud had brought him a cup, a silver-gilt ewer filled with sweet sauternes, and a footman to pour it.

"Leave us alone, if you please," said I, and Braud and the footman withdrew. I bowed to Edevane.

"You are welcome, my lord," I said. "If you had let me know ahead of time, I would have been here to welcome you."

Edevane regarded me with his mild, dead eyes. "I apologize," he said. "The business is trivial, but I was in the neighborhood, and I failed at first to realize you had another guest."

He not only knew that Elvina was with me, but he wanted me to know that he knew. I decided that his omnipotence was verging on impertinence.

"The inconvenience is trivial," I assured him. "But first I should let you know that the iron birds of Inchmaden are no more. I received word this morning that my deputy has accounted for all of them."

"I heard that some days ago. The lord lieutenant wrote directly to me."

"Have you then some other task for me, my lord?"

He set his wine-cup down on an onyx table and frowned. "You failed to report to me in the matter of Wilmot's death."

I spread my hands. "I was unaware that you would have an interest in that business, my lord."

"I am bound to have an interest when the son of a duke is killed by violence," Edevane said. "His Grace of Waitstill has every reason to expect the crown to make a full report."

"Allow me to refresh your glass, my lord, and I will tell you the story."

We sat, and I related the story of Wilmot's madness, malice, and death. I stressed that his mind had been damaged in his fight with the dragon, and how I and the others aboard *Kiminge* had gone to great lengths to spare his life.

"Prince Alicio is a witness, then?" Edevane asked. "As well as Dom Nemorino and the captain?"

"Ay," said I.

"But the first two are in the army," said he. "And the last frozen in the ice of Steggerda or some such place."

I stood and went to my portable desk, which had been placed in the library, and I opened a drawer. "I have their statements already prepared. You are welcome to view them."

My experience in the law, and particularly my sanguinary appearance before the Siege Royal treason court, had recommended to me that I secure testaments from all witnesses, lest some magistrate, prompted no doubt by Orlanda, hurl me in a dungeon. "There are also testaments from Countess Marcella," said I, "as well as Elisa d'Altrey."

Edevane paged through the testaments with a frown. "I asked you also to report on those two ladies," he said.

"I discovered nothing that could not wait," said I. "Countess Marcella was furious with Wilmot because he mistook her for a courtesan, and I think she may be heartily sick of the company of humans and ready to return home. She said nothing of her origins to contradict the story she has told elsewhere."

"And Mistress d'Altrey?"

"She resents her loss of standing after the rebellion, the more so because she says that she warned her family not to underestimate Queen Berlauda, and they ignored her."

He looked up from his reading. "Do you think her loyalty is in question?"

"She plots no plots," said I. "How could she? She has no power. Yet I think the best way to secure her loyalty would be to give her something to lose. A small estate, a pension." I shrugged. "The usurper's rebellion was hardly her fault. She was raised with expectations of high estate, and now she has nothing but what Princess Floria gives her."

"I will take your suggestion under advisement," said Edevane. "Though I hardly think the crown has estates to spare." He returned the testaments to me. "These statements support one another," he said. "They are not in the same hand, nor even in the same language, and all are signed and with the appropriate seals attached. I shall write to Lord Waitstill and assure him that you did your best to preserve his son's life."

"I thank your lordship," said I. "I should also mention that both these ladies have expressed their strong reservations concerning the apartment to be offered to Princess Floria. It is but a single room, and a small one."

Edevane appeared untroubled. "The palace is old compared with Ings Magna, and filled with inconveniences. It is so crowded that there is little room for anyone."

I had heard from Countess Marcella of the luxurious apartments granted Berlauda and Priscus, filled with gold, mirror-glass, and bright hangings.

"There is no room for Floria and her ladies together."

Edevane waved a hand. "The palace has hundreds of servants. How many ladies could Her Highness need?" He touched the fingers of his left hand with those of his right. "Have you considered my suggestions for election to the House of Burgesses?"

"My lord," said I, "I could run, but I would lose."

"Perhaps in Ethlebight," said Edevane. "But your manor is in the county of Hurst Downs, is it not?"

Curses raged silently inside my skull. "That is correct, my lord."

"Hurst Downs is ably represented by Sir Silvanus Becket," he said. "But if Becket is elevated to a barony, he will support Her Majesty from his place in the peers, and the seat in the Burgesses will be open to you in a by-election."

It will cost the crown nothing, I thought. *For it all takes to make a baron is a letter patent signed by the monarch.*

"I am astounded and flattered by the attention you pay me," said I.

A smile ghosted across Edevane's lips. "I have every confidence you will serve Her Majesty well," he said, and rose. "And now I will leave you. I apologize to you and to your guest for the inconvenience."

He floated out of the room in his royal velvet, pleased with himself, and I, displeased, returned to Elvina, and found myself worried less about what might grow in Elvina's womb than what vicious, bloodthirsty beast might be engendered in Lord Edevane's mind.

The encounter with Lord Edevane made me wonder if I had tarried too long in Longres, yet I decided to remain. I didn't fancy a winter passage home, for the passage would take much longer in the teeth of the prevailing westerly winds. I was pleasantly situated with Elvina, but more importantly, I had received a report from Mountmirail and the surveyor that my plan of a canal from Ethlebight to Gannett Bay was feasible, and would require only money and the ability to obtain the right-of-way. The money I felt I could probably raise, but permission to obtain the right-of-way from those holding possession of the land would require an act of the Estates confirmed by the monarch.

I wished to consult members of the Privy Council, but I hesitated, because their number would necessarily include Lord Edevane. He might be able to pass the bill through the Estates, but I feared what he might ask in return.

Invented testimony at Princess Floria's treason trial, perhaps.

And so I remained at court and devoted myself to the pursuit of pleasure in a place devoted to little but pleasurable pursuits. There were entertainments, hunts, games, music, and plays—Blackwell's players made an enormous impression with their dragon, and followed that play with *The Kingdom of the Birds,* which enchanted everyone. After the birds came *The Red Horse, or the History of King Emelin,* which—as it explained to Loretto the magnificence and heroism of the founder of Queen Berlauda's dynasty—was out of politeness well received even by those who did not understand the Duisland tongue. The play had been altered somewhat from when I had last seen it, for new scenes were added for the boy actor Bonny Joe Webb, who played Emelin's queen, and whose performance in all three plays charmed every audience. The court went into raptures over his beauty. Blackwell paid little attention to the success of his work, for he was embroiled in writing his verses about the vicious follies of the court.

My pleasures were lessened when Elvina left Longres with her husband. As there was little need for an ambassador when queen supped with queen, and king marched with king, Erquem had received permission to leave court and visit his estates, both those in Duisland and in Loretto. So I sadly kissed Elvina good-bye, and realized that there was even less reason for me to remain in Longres.

"Your problem, Quillifer," her brother told me, "is that your office does not call attention to itself unless you turn up at court with the head of a dead monster. Whereas as cofferer, I am seen daily by the chancellor of the exchequer, and by others of importance at court. As I pay the queen's servants, I encounter them all, and I'm in a position to speak with all of them, and hear all the news, and I can place this news in the ear of anyone who might help me rise in office. Whereas you—" He waved a hand. "You are merely *here*."

There was another advantage to his office that I had worked out on my own. As Meens had access to the funds that supported the palace, he would be able to advance monies to the servants or the office-holders, or to his friends, and then charge a rate of interest that would go entirely into his pocket. The monarchy would support his money-lending, and that was a fine perquisite indeed.

The skies loured on us, rain tapped the windows, and we took our recreation indoors. We spoke in Prince Alicio's game room, and played bagatelle while our other friends occupied themselves with cards or dice. Logs snapped and popped on the hearth, and wood-smoke scented the air.

I missed my stroke, and my ball stranded itself among the pins. "Sadly, Harvey," said I, "you state the case truly."

"You must find a way to stand out."

"In Howel I was well known, I believe. A dragon-slayer, a captain of my own galley—"

"A duelist," said Meens. "It is a route to fame, but comes with a degree of hazard."

I agreed, but by this time I was growing wary of any kind of fame. The higher a man rose, it seemed, the greater his chance of meeting a scaffold.

Meens bounced his ball off one of the pins, and it dropped into a hole, scoring five points.

"Of course I am known for my gems," said I. In fact, with a single exception, I had sold every gem I had brought to Longres and now awaited the return of *Sovereign* from Tabarzam, with a new supply of stones.

"I say nothing against it," said Meens, "but some might view that as *trade*, and trade is very much looked down on here."

"Yet without trade the court would have to do without its silks and smaragds," said I.

Again he waved his hand. "I do not approve of this prejudice, but I acknowledge its existence." And then he struck the ivory ball with his cue, and it bounded from pin to pin until he won twenty points.

What Meens said was true, and I could not change the opinions of an entire country. This I took as yet another reason to leave Longres, but I thought I might stay until Berlauda gave birth, so that I could give the child a gift, the magnificent and nearly flawless sapphire I had saved from my hoard for just such a purpose.

In fact I did not stay that long, but I remained long enough for the news of King Henrico's astounding winter campaign to reach the city. For marching in February, months before the season for campaigning normally opened, he and an army crossed the frozen river on the Thurnmark border, stormed several cities, and besieged others. This notable achievement was itself more success than any reasonable person had expected, yet it was followed by wonders. For once Thurnmark had committed its own forces to shoring up its borders, Priscus, with Loretto's main army, crossed into the empire of Sélange, on Thurnmark's southern border. Despite the imperial pretensions of its monarch, Sélange is a small nation and could put up no resistance. Priscus fought no battles in Sélange, and did not attack its cities, but marched across the country to attack Thurnmark from the south, outflanking Thurnmark's fortified river lines and marching deep into the heart of the country. When Thurnmark's army under their Hogen-Mogen met Priscus at the Hill of Menne, the result was a resounding victory for Loretto, and the Hogen-Mogen's forces scattered to the winds. The forces of Loretto spent less than two weeks in Sélange before marching out again, leaving no devastation behind them.

It seemed the war was all but won. Bells of thanksgiving pealed out from every monastery, and the palace thronged with cheering courtiers. I found my sometime-companion Lord Barkin in the crowd, a professional soldier who had fought at Exton Scales and was now coronel of the Queen's Own Horse. Barkin was a bustling man, with graying hair and beard, and briskly he explained the fighting to me on a table, with cups representing enemy forts, spilled wine the rivers, and knives the thrusts into the enemy's country. He was all admiration for Henrico's cunning strategy, using his person and the royal banner to distract the Hogen-Mogen from his son's larger army.

Harvey Meens came up to me as we viewed this improvised map. "Quillifer!" he called. "You are an unprincipled, hedge-born lewdster!"

"Very possibly," I said absently, for I was absorbed in Barkin's explanation of the Hill of Menne. Then Meens seized my shoulder and pulled me around to face him, and I saw that he was red-faced and furious. The scent of brandy tainted his breath.

"I just overheard two of Elvina's friends saying that you intend to get her with child!" he shouted.

I looked at him narrowly. "In point of fact I do not," I said.

"Do you expect me to believe that they lied?" he demanded. "Or do you say that *I* lie?"

"I say that someone misunderstood what someone else said. I do not say that person was you." I looked at the hand that still clutched my shoulder. "Now kindly unfist my doublet."

Lord Barkin took a step to place himself somewhat between us. "Sir," he said to Meens, "this is not a suitable conversation for a public place. Your sister's reputation—"

"My sister's reputation is not to be ruined by this bedswerving cullion!" cried Meens.

"Instead it is to be ruined by a drunken, bellowing brother?" said I. Other people were staring, and I could imagine this scene being re-enacted in every parlor in the city by the next day. "I advise you to cease this ranting and find some quiet place where you can grow sober."

"You filth!" he said. "You break every law of decency!"

By now my own temper had snapped. I stepped close and spoke in a lowered voice. "I do not intend to be lectured on morality," said I, "by someone who pimped his sister to an old man in exchange for office."

At that point he tried to hit me, but Lord Barkin seized his arm, and together we wrestled him into immobility. "I challenge you!" he said.

"I do not fight sots," I said.

"And we'll fight fair!" he said. "Nothing to do with boats or sails or oceans—none of your tricks!"

"If you want to fight me," said I, "you'll have to sober up first."

By this point I was feeling little but disgust. Not for myself, or Meens, but for Orlanda, who must have prompted this challenge. Three duels in a row, I thought, showed a complete failure of invention.

"You'll fight me! You'll fight me!" Meens tried to throw us off and failed. He was a big man, and I think he was used to being able to manhandle people as he saw fit, and his inability to wrestle free frustrated him.

"You married your sister to an old man," I hissed into his ear. "What did you *think* was going to happen? Erquem is wiser than you, and he understands his situation full well."

"I'll tell him!" Meens said. "He'll keep Elvina away from you!"

"Cause a scandal," said I, "and see if you can keep your office. Erquem arranged for you to have it, and he can take it away." I thought that a threat to his office might give him pause, for advancement at court seemed all that he truly cared about, but instead he continued to struggle.

By and by a captain of the guard came, and we were separated. Meens was escorted to his lodgings in one of the palace buildings, and a guard placed on his door to make certain that he stayed there. I thanked Lord Barkin for his aid.

"That fellow is going to ruin himself," he said.

"I think it will still come to blows," said I. "There is a spirit of malice behind this that does not originate with Meens."

He raised a graying eyebrow. "You have been with this lady?"

"Lady Erquem is not behind this," said I, "nor is she with child." Or so I hoped.

"There were rumors about Westley," said Barkin. "That some figure at court was behind his challenge."

"I think the rumors are not wrong," said I. I turned to Barkin. "I care not what a drunken man says, but if he repeats his remarks when sober, I may be obliged to take notice. If that is the case, will you act for me?"

Barkin's upper lip twitched. "Against such an ill-sorted ephebe as this? Gladly."

"I hope I will not have to call on you."

But of course that hope would be dashed. Of that I had every confidence.

CHAPTER TWENTY-THREE

Harvey Meens's emissary arrived at Palace Ribamar the next day: Dom Emidio Custo de Fabragal, one of his sister's friends and a poor knight with fewer ducats in his pocket than letters to his name. He had frequently accepted my hospitality, and I found his appearance on this errand a trifle offensive.

He had found me in a fey mood, having meditated on Orlanda and her intrigues all night, and I made Dom Emidio's challenge more difficult by bursting into coarse laughter at several of his more florid passages.

"'Offense to his family's honor!'" I scorned. "What honor is there in selling a sister?"

"Please, Dom Keely-Fay," said Dom Emidio. "I am charged to bear this message."

"Do not then lose your bearings, for what you bear is beyond all bearing," said I. "But tell me—was Harvey drunk when he sent you?"

He hesitated. "I believe he was sober."

"Well then." I waved a hand. "Continue."

He went on for a while about my offensive conduct, and then I laughed again.

"Tell me," I said. "Has poor Harvey ever been out on the field of honor?"

Emidio stiffened. "He has not said so."

"Yet I have been out twice, and been victorious both times. Do you not think that in all fairness Harvey should challenge two other men before plaguing me with this business?"

"I have no opinion, Dom Keely-Fay."

I waved my hand again. "Continue."

I had thrown him off his stride, and he stammered as he demanded the name of my second.

"I hope you will tell Harvey that I am sorry he has agreed to be a cat's-paw in this conspiracy," I said. "He should not have listened to what other people took good care he should hear."

"I do not know what you mean."

"I mean that Harvey is being prompted by another," said I. "And so, by the way, are you. The plot may be aimed at me, or at Lord Erquem—I know not. Yet the both of you should know that if I am to fight Harvey, I will stab him in the front; but those for whom he acts may not be so nice."

"I do not understand you, Dom Keely-Fay. But I must ask you for the name of your second."

Really, I thought, this fellow was a harecop, and a thick harecop at that. There was little point in continuing.

"Lord Barkin will stand for me," said I. "You may ask for him at the stables of Queen Berlauda's guard."

"Dom Keely-Fay." He bowed, and as he left the room, I called after him.

"After this matter concludes," said I, "you should watch your back."

I doubt that Orlanda cared about these fools enough to kill them after she had used them, but I intended to sow doubt and mistrust between Meens and his emissary, and I hoped this might do the job.

Yet Meens was persistent. Emidio met with Lord Barkin on his behalf, and Lord Barkin followed my instructions and asked for the encounter to take place on a small boat on the lake at Palace Ribamar. After consultation with his principal, Emidio said that the fight should be on land, with targes and broadswords. Lord Barkin returned with my suggestion of top-mauls on the main yard of one of the ships on Alicio's lake. This was declined with scorn, Emidio saying that they would not fall for one of my infamous tricks. Rapiers and daggers were offered. I replied with the proposal that we fight with cannon at a distance of two hundred yards. I doubted that Meens would accept, but if he did I was reasonably confident that I could load a falconet more quickly, and aim it more accurately, than Meens.

The very outrageousness of this suggestion paralyzed them for two days, after which they returned to the idea of broadswords. I, through Barkin, countered with pollaxes.

I meant to mock the entire business, of course, and Meens along with it, but I meant also to delay. The longer the negotiations went on, the more time Meens would have to reconsider his position. But my main purpose in delaying was to give a messenger time to deliver my letter to Elvina.

I had written her as soon as the challenge was delivered, explaining the situation and suggesting that she show the message to her husband, and then had sent the message by mounted courier. The problem was that I knew not which of their properties Lord Erquem had chosen to visit, or even if he was in Duisland or Loretto. I asked Rufino Knott to inquire of Erquem's servants remaining in Longres Regius, but they seemed not to know either. So my messenger galloped off on his trail, and I set myself to delaying the fight as long as I could.

In the midst of the negotiations I received a note from Lord Edevane asking me to attend him. I rode to the palace on the heels of a freezing winter wind, and found him in a room adjacent to Berlauda's apartments. Windows overlooked a formal garden of winter brown, and on the opposite wall mirrors in ornate gilded frames reflected the wan sun. A draught stirred the crystals that dangled in glittering streams from the chandeliers, and Edevane's clerks wore fur-trimmed robes as they dealt with documents tied with red or blue ribbon. Edevane had no separate cabinet, but had set ornamented screens around his desk at the far end of the room, near the hearth. His little enclosure was very warm, and his face was ruddy from the heat as he rose from his desk to greet me.

"You are cold, Lord Warden," said he. "May I offer you a hot tisane?"

"I thank your lordship," said I.

We sat, and after the tisane was brought, he came to the point.

"This business with the lord cofferer has been brought to my attention," he said.

The scent of mint rose from my tisane. "This inane business is hardly worthy of your attention, my lord."

He scowled at me, his dead eyes growing hard. "An affray between Her Majesty's servants is hardly insignificant!" he snapped. "And it is made worse when those servants are guests in Loretto, and when the matter touches our ambassador's honor!" His chin gave an indignant jerk toward his shoulder. "I have spent more time trying to resolve the matter than I care to."

A warning rocket shot up my spine. "I am heartily sorry that you have gone to such effort, my lord."

In truth I had not approached him because I had not wanted to owe him any favors.

"I have interviewed the lord cofferer," Edevane said, "and I found him most intransigent. He is determined to fight you."

"I have given Meens every opportunity to withdraw his challenge," said I.

Again Edevane showed irritation. "I told him that Her Majesty would scarcely look kindly on her office-holders quarreling with one another, but he was deaf to my reasoning, and kept babbling about family honor. I think he may be mad."

"Truly," I said, "a spirit of malice seems to whisper into his ear."

Suddenly Edevane was alert. He regarded me from behind the gold-rimmed spectacles. "What do you mean?" asked he. "Is there a conspiracy behind this, as there was behind Westley?"

"Not that I know. But if there is one, it may be directed against Lord Erquem more than against me." I sipped my tisane. "But truly, I think Meens listens to the same fell spirit as Wilmot, a spirit that drives him to madness and violence."

He cocked his head. "Do you speak of an actual spirit?" he asked.

"My lord, I know nothing of spirits," said I. "But I think we have many voices in our brains, and we should take care to listen only to those that serve our true interest."

I had hoped by this an oblique warning against Orlanda, who had as much told me that she was influencing Edevane. But Edevane understood a different meaning from what I intended, and leaned forward. "And what is our true interest, then?"

"For a royal servant," said I, "that interest would be peace and prosperity for the realm, and the safety and health of the monarch."

"Peace?" Edevane said. "Does that mean you oppose our war with Thurnmark?"

"I have privateers; I hope to profit by that war," said I. "But I meant domestic peace, peace within the realm."

"Well," Edevane said. "Meens is useless to Her Majesty now. Kill him if you find it necessary. At least I will not have to write a duke to tell him how his son met with misfortune."

"I hope I will not kill him."

"Spare him, then, but Meens is hopeless either way." Edevane's eyes turned to the papers on his desk. "I hope you will forgive me,

Lord Warden, but I must return to Her Majesty's business." He picked up a paper and viewed it, then put it down. "Lord Warden," he said, "if I were to offer you advice, that advice would be to stop sleeping with the wives of the nobility."

"Truly," I said, "it seems fraught with inconvenience."

"Women may be had for a few crowns in Longres," he said. "I am informed they may be found on the Via Cocotte, and that their brothers will not intervene."

"I thank your lordship for that advice," I said.

I paid a call upon you on my way out, but you were not in your apartment. I did not visit Cocotte Street on my way home.

Negotiations with Dom Emidio continued, but after ten days or so I could tell that Lord Barkin was running out of patience. He was a martial man, and not himself inclined to mockery or foolishness, but rather accustomed on the field of battle to drawing sword and galloping straight to the fray. I did not want to earn the contempt of my second, who of course was in charge of my life during the negotiations, so when the offer of halberds was rejected in favor of falchions, I surrendered to the gods of necessity.

"If we cannot agree on weapons, then let us each have our choice," I told Barkin. "I will bring my pollaxe, and he may have whatever he pleases."

"That will not be seen as fair," said Barkin. "Weapons must be matched."

"I don't see why," I said, but then I made the suggestion I'd been pondering for some time. "Let us fight on the roof of the Monastery of the Nine Disciples in Longres. And let a variety of weapons be scattered about the roof, so that we may each take what we like when we arrive."

"Arrive?" Barkin asked. "What do you mean?"

"Let us start an equal distance from the monastery," said I. "It's as near the center of town as no matter, and we can each start from one of the gates. He may have his choice, and I will take the gate opposite."

"You mean to start the fight with a race?" Barkin was more intrigued than astonished.

"A race across the rooftops," said I. "For if anyone touches a foot to the ground, he must pay a penalty."

For the previous few days I had explored the narrow lanes of Longres, and I thought I had worked out a way to defeat Meens without being brought before a judge on a charge of homicide. For once I gained the roof of the monastery, I could hold it against Meens, and keep the man from getting a weapon at all. I might have to cut off a few fingers to keep him from getting a grip on a cornice, but I would not have to kill him.

It must be said, as you look at me in that skeptical way, that I cared not whether Meens lived or died, but I did not wish to explain to Elvina how and why I had spilled her brother's blood.

"I hardly believe that Meens or Dom Emidio will accept this," Barkin said. "They will suspect a trick, and they said they will not agree to any sort of trickery."

"You must grow very angry with Dom Emidio," I told him. "Say that his principal is delaying out of cowardice, and that if he means to fight at all, he must agree to our terms."

"If I call that gentleman a coward," Lord Barkin pointed out, "he can challenge me."

"I'm sure you will find more delicate language that amounts to the same thing. But you must be harsh with Emidio, and harry him into accepting."

"They might equally accuse you," Barkin said. "After all, you *have* delayed."

"Who will the world believe?" asked I. "A fire-eating veteran of the duello, knighted for heroism on the field of battle, or some farmer from Fornland?"

Barkin mused on this, and a smile touched his lips. "I believe I know just how to handle this," he said. "Leave the matter to me."

And so it was that three mornings later, I waited by Longres's East Gate, shivering in my leather jerkin. The sky grew pale overhead, the stars fading one by one, but down in the street it was dark, illuminated only by the fitful light of the lanterns that home-owners were required to place above their doors. The scent of their cheap lamp oil stank in the night air.

Before me was the Palace de Repos, which was not a palace but an inn handily placed for travelers arriving through the gate. When the dawn bell of the Nine Disciples began to ring, I would scale that building and begin my dash across the rooftops.

Horses stamped and steamed about me. Lord Barkin would follow my course from the street, along with a pack of Elvina's friends, who had been attracted by the novelty and excitement of the contest. Most were men, though some women had come, entranced like the men by bloodthirsty curiosity. Another pack followed Meens and included Dom Emidio, and the seconds and the witnesses would assure that the rules of engagement would be followed.

I wondered at this, that my second would be in charge of my obedience to the rules, and that Meens's own second would police his own actions. "Is there not a chance of collusion?" I asked, "May not Dom Emidio assist Meens in some way, and you me?"

"Seconds are not intended to be your friends on the day of the encounter," said Barkin. "Once the terms of the fight are agreed, we are to make certain those terms are obeyed." He favored me with a benevolent smile. "Why, Sir Quillifer, I will carry pistols, and if I observe you taking some unfair advantage, I will be obliged to shoot you down like a dog."

"I accept your rule, my lord," said I, "but do we think Dom Emidio will enforce such a stern discipline?"

"There will be a gang of your friends as observers," he said. "This encounter, illegal though it is, will have more witnesses than any crime in the history of Longres."

I feared that might be true. A group of lively volunteers had carried weapons to the roof during the dark. Others were conspicuous by their presence by gathering near the city gates on horseback. If I were the watch, I would have been interested; but the watch at Longres, like that in Selford, consisted mainly of old pensioners, and they knew better than to approach armed bravos on horseback. Instead we heard their bells and voices at a distance as they proclaimed that all was well.

It was a cold night, my breath frosting along with that of the horses, and I wore my cheviot overcoat over my shoulders, and a rabbit fur–lined leather cap with flaps pulled down over my ears. The hard leather crown I hoped might provide a degree of protection against a blade, along with the leather jerkin I wore underneath my overcoat.

The sky brightened. I bounced up and down on my toes as I tried to stay warm. My mind traveled over the route to the monastery that I had explored the previous afternoon, trotting over the thatched roofs and examining each jump and each corner for the fastest route. Some of the householders had shouted at me to get down, but none impeded my investigations.

The call of the bell came through the air, the tone echoing from each alley and building and tower, and for a moment, lost in the bell's resonant song, I could not recall why I was here, or what I intended. Then my purpose came back to me with a rush, and I shrugged the overcoat off my shoulders and launched myself onto the facade of the Palace de Repos. Using a window ledge, a pelmet, some gallets, and a corbel, I gained the roof, and with it the sun. I scrambled up the steep pitch of the thatch to the ridgepole, and from there I saw the dawn turn red the gilding on the monastery's domed belfry atop the main prayer hall. I began my run. Below, my friends yipped and whooped as if they were hunting stag, and set off in pursuit. The bell tolled a second time.

Like the houses in my home city of Ethlebight, buildings in Longres featured a first floor made of stone or brick, with upper storeys of half-timber jettied out over the street, their walls built on bressummers. The streets were so overshadowed that they remained dark even on the brightest days, but for anyone running from roof to roof, the buildings were so close together that one could easily leap the gap, which was no more than one or two yards. The thatch was soft and yielding, for the spar-coating was laid several layers deep, new thatch atop the old, sometimes six feet deep.

The air smelled of woodsmoke and old thatch, and the bell tolled again and again as I ran over ridgepoles and along gables, and hurled myself from building to building. All Lord Barkin and the others could hope was to catch glimpses of me as I leaped the gaps, and then only if they were lucky, so soon they were scattered as they hunted me down the dark streets and alleys.

On the way I crossed the Via Cocotte, the lane of public women that Lord Edevane had recommended to me a few days earlier. The name literally rendered is the Street of Cheap Perfume, but at that early hour of the morning I scented nothing more than the sharp odor of lye from large numbers of bedsheets boiling in tubs.

I paused as I came to a wider gap than usual. On either side of the lane, old buildings were dangerously leaning into one another like drunks staggering home from an inn, so stout timber braces had been added between two roofs to prevent the houses from collapsing into each other. The beams were squared off and furnished a fine foothold, so I ventured onto the nearest with the intention of crossing in only as few paces.

I had crossed on a different brace the previous afternoon, and I was unaware that this new brace was not well secured. No sooner had I put my full weight on it than it tore away from the wall behind me and swung like a pendulum into the darkness between the buildings. My courage evaporated as the brace began to drop, and without thought I fell forward onto the beam, my arms wrapping around the timber as it fell. The far end of the brace tore free for a heart-stopping instant, and then it caught in a tangle of roof-joists, ancient spar-coating, and an old lintel jutting out of the wall. The brace bucked as its downward progress was arrested, nearly throwing me free, and then with a great crash it swung into the wall. I gasped with pain as my right arm was caught between the swinging brace and the wall.

The timber had ceased to fall, but now I began to slide down the brace, and I clutched at it more desperately and wrapped my legs around the lower part, and I managed to arrest my descent.

The monastery bell tolled again. I panted for breath and looked about me. I was only three yards from the paving-stones below, but if I touched ground, I would be subject to a thirty-second penalty, and I craned my neck in hopes of finding a route back to the roof.

"Ho, Keely-Fay!" One of my friends came trotting up on horseback, a young marquess named Sansloy, who at the palace held the office of lord-in-waiting to the vice-master of ceremony, which explained why he wasn't in the army. "Have you hurt yourself?"

"Not fatally," I said.

I pushed upward with my legs, like a sailor climbing a rope, and rose a little on the beam. My right arm, which had been caught between the wall of the house and the brace when it fell, was half-numb, and I was reluctant to trust my weight to it. I reached above me with the left in hopes of finding a handhold, and then a window opened near me, and a man thrust his head out. He had a curling, graying beard, and wore a nightcap over his ears.

"What are you doing there?" he demanded. "You are destroying my house!"

"I beg your pardon, sir," I managed. "If I can get to your roof I will bother you no further." I managed to worm another foot or so up the beam.

"Damned if I'll let you on my roof!" said the man. "Get off there!"

"Mind your own business, old man!" said Sansloy from horseback.

At this point the man withdrew from his window, and a woman's head appeared. Out of modesty she had taken care to cover her head with an old-fashioned box hood, and she brandished a piece of firewood as she glared at me. "Get off my house!" she said.

"This is an affair for gentlemen!" said Sansloy. "Old woman, take yourself back to bed!"

This drew the goodwife's attention from me to him, and she hurled the firewood at him. It hit his horse on the neck, and the beast gave a shriek of fury and lashed out with its hooves, striking at nothing. My friend cursed as he tried to manage his courser, and the woman disappeared from the window only to reappear with another piece of lumber.

During this distraction I managed to creep higher along the fallen brace, and I reached out with my left hand to the protruding lintel that partly supported the tangled wreckage. The joists and beams were in such a tangle that I assumed that they included the remains of another building that had once been shoved up against this one. With the help of the lintel thrusting from the wall I managed to work my way to the upper end of the brace.

From here I looked up at a steep wall of thatch. The dark gray layers of spar-coating were at least a yard deep, and I would somehow have to clamber through them before I could get onto the pitch that led to the ridgepole.

"What are you doing there?" the woman shouted. She hurled her firewood at me, but she lacked the strength to reach me, and the log spun off into the dark lane and clattered on the cobbles.

She disappeared to get more ammunition, and during that time I got a foot onto the lintel and began to fight my way upward through the crackling, smothering thatch, all filled with centuries of straw-dust, rat droppings, and hearth-smoke. The rubbish and sweepings of the ages lay thick in my throat. So smoky was the dust that the lower levels of spar-coating must have dated from before the invention of chimneys.

I heard the monastery bell toll as I fought my way upward. Sun dazzled me as I broke through the spar-coating to gain a view of the steeply pitched roof, and then I heard the man's voice.

"By the Pilgrim's teeth, I'll pepper you!" he shouted.

"Guard you, Keely-Fay!" cried Sansloy. "He has a gun!"

Fire blazed along my nerves, and I kicked with both feet to launch myself into the thatch while I clawed with both hands to pull myself up onto the roof. My leather cap fell forward over my eyes, and my right hand and arm were nearly useless. The gun went off, and I heard a wooden crack as a bullet hit a joist.

"I'll get you next time, you damned foreigner!" cried the house-holder. "Look at you—you're wrecking my home!"

"Your home was a wreck before I arrived!" I answered.

"He's reloading!" Sansloy warned. I could hear him backing his horse down the lane as I kicked and wriggled through the thatch, and then finally managed to drag myself onto the roof, where I lay for a long moment, coughing ashes out of my lungs and wishing I'd just accepted the thirty-second penalty. Then I lurched to my feet, shifted my cap back to the top of my head, and staggered up the slope of the roof. Once I gained the ridge, I could see the golden belfry glittering just a few streets away, and I began to run. The bell itself, visible only as a silhouette beneath its dome, had ceased to toll.

As I staggered onward, the feeling returned to my right arm, so that now instead of being numb, needles of pain thrust themselves into every joint and muscle. I seemed to be unbalanced, with my right shoulder lower than my left. My vaults between houses were made more dangerous because I could count on only one arm to support me if I fell. But at length I found myself standing on the ridgepole of an inn overlooking the Monastery of the Nine Disciples.

The monastery blazed up in the sun, for the walls of its four main buildings were covered with bright tiles laid out in metaphysical designs, yellows and greens and oranges, while the roof-tiles were of terra-cotta, and the gables were edged with gold. The roof was of a lesser pitch than the thatched buildings that surrounded it, and once I had crossed to the monastery I could walk on the tiles without fear of slipping and plummeting to the streets below.

But crossing to the monastery would be difficult, and this was the one jump I had not practiced the day before. The road below was wider than any I had leaped so far, but fortunately my own building was taller. The law forbade a structure in Longres greater than three storeys, but the inn had sought a way around the law by building a gambrel roof atop their third storey, a roof tall enough to provide garret lodging. Each garret room had a dormer facing the street, and so from the ridgepole I was able to step right onto the ridge of a dormer that overlooked the roof of the monastery. I paused to catch my breath and summon my courage, my heart drumming in my chest, and then I ran along the top of the dormer and hurled myself into the abyss beyond.

The street below was so dark it looked like a chasm that led to the center of the world, but I stayed in the bright sun and landed on the main prayer hall with arms and legs splayed. I failed to sufficiently break my fall, and I knocked the breath out of myself, and I cracked my chin on terra-cotta. Tiles cracked and shifted beneath me. I lay gasping for a moment while comets chased themselves in my head, and then I painfully rose to hands and knees. There was a clatter, and I felt myself begin to slide on a river of broken tile. I clutched for a better handhold and frantically clawed my way to safer ground as broken tiles cracked to the pavement three floors below. As I paused to gasp in breath, I heard footsteps nearby, and, fearing Meens, I looked up to find Rufino Knott.

"Are you well, sir?" he asked.

"Where is the nearest blade?"

He inclined his head to my right, and I dragged myself to my feet and toward a falchion. I tried to pick it up with my right hand, but the thick cutting blade was too heavy for my weakened limb, and I shifted it to my left. I tried to comfort myself with the thought that I was inexpert with either hand, and it would not matter.

"Pollaxe?" I asked.

"By the belfry, sir."

I heard the hooves of horses as my friends filled the lane behind me. "There he is!" said a woman's voice. "Dom Keely-Fay!"

Pain chewed at my right arm and hand like a nest of rats gnawing the wainscot. I made my way toward the belfry, and a greater consciousness of my surroundings began to penetrate my awareness. In the courtyard between the monastery buildings, monks summoned by the bell walked on gravel paths toward the main prayer hall. The ordinary monks wore robes of unbleached wool, but their higher-ranking brethren wore satins and silks as bright as the sunrise. Any one of them could have glanced up to see me lurching about their roof with a sword in my hand, but their eyes were all cast down as if a view of the bright March sky would somehow diminish their sanctity.

I encountered a rapier and dagger and considered taking them, then settled for just the dagger, which was light enough for my right hand to clutch, and possibly even to wield. But I could see a pollaxe leaning against the belfry and began to hurry toward it.

"There he is! There he is!" That same excited lady sang out in a piercing alto.

I thought she was pointing me out to a new arrival, but at that point Meens ran around the belfry toward me, and I realized she was announcing the arrival of the second combatant. He was in his shirt, and his face and clothing were smeared with dust and straw.

Sweat glistened on his forehead and showed in dark patches beneath his arms and in the center of his chest. He had a rapier in one hand and a dagger in the other. One of his friends followed him, then paused at a respectful distance, ready to witness but not to interfere.

He came to a sudden stop as he saw me, surprise in his wide eyes, his chest heaving for breath. I raised the falchion above my shoulder, ready to cut, while I thrust out my useless right hand with the dagger in it. I took a breath.

"Well, Meens!" said I in a clear voice. "You do not seem happy to see me."

"I'll be happier to see you bleeding on the tiles." He gasped out the words, and I wondered if I should attack him now, while he was out of breath. Yet I was scarcely in better condition, and I had hopes that if I delayed enough, my right arm might recover its strength.

Also, we were having this conversation atop the prayer hall, and I rather hoped that some of the monks might look up and see us. I would be gratified if a few burly novices ran up to the roof to prevent us murdering one another, and decided to keep talking in hopes of spinning the matter out.

"I hope to disappoint you," said I. "But then you have disappointed yourself, have you not? For you have disgraced your sister, and insulted your father-in-law, and all for the sake of a quarrel that brings you no credit." I managed a laugh. "Will you boast of this to your friends? They will pity you."

I hoped to reach that part of Meens that had not been infected by Orlanda, and make him doubt that voice that impelled him to violence, but I misjudged, and my words had the opposite effect. "I'll kill you!" he cried, and came lunging at me with the rapier.

I danced away as I parried with the dagger. I had little strength in my arm, but it was enough to deflect the narrow stabbing blade. When I judged his hand close enough, I hacked at it with the falchion, but though I knocked down his blade, I failed to touch him, and my sword chopped instead into the terra-cotta tiles. It took so long to recover my heavy weapon that Meens came after me with the dagger. I made frantic parries with my own dagger and leaped back, gasping with the pain that shot through my arm and shoulder every time the blades made contact.

Meens's resources flagged, and he paused to gasp awhile. He was tall and broad-shouldered, with strength enough for the heavy, awkward rapier, but the run across the rooftops had drained him. I was happy to circle around him while I cocked my falchion for another blow. I saw that we had been joined on the roof by Lord Barkin and by Dom Emidio, and that monks in the courtyard, having been alerted by the clash of weapons, were pointing and running across the court. Faces appeared in the windows of neighboring buildings. *This encounter, illegal though it is, will have more witnesses than any crime in the history of Longres.* That was more true than Lord Barkin had ever intended.

"We have more spectators for your folly than Blackwell had at his last play," said I. "Yet I think you will not give such graceful speeches as those actors who died with verse on their lips, and instead babble your broken-headed nonsense to an audience mortified with embarrassment."

I had circled most of the way around him, while he shifted his stance to follow me with his blades. I saw the burning hatred in his eyes, and I remembered how coolly he had looked at me when we had first met, and how he had gazed steadily at me when he discoursed on his office and its advantages. His complete loss of reason, and his hazarding the office that was all he seemed to care about, was more evidence for the hand of Orlanda behind this affair.

It was true that she had promised not to harm those I loved. But it had to be said that I had not loved Harvey Meens, but his sister, and that if she were hurt by this business, the hurt would be indirect.

I continued to circle him, but he advanced to cut me off, his blade licking out like the tongue of a serpent. I parried with my dagger, pain blazing through my arm and shoulder. I retreated and waited for a chance to use the falchion, but my blade was shorter than his, and he was careful to stay out of range.

We separated for a brief instant as Meens tired, and then I threw the dagger at his face—throwing underarm, which was the only way my injured limb could throw at all. He uttered a breath of surprise as he took a step back and batted the weapon away with his dagger, and then I hurled the heavy falchion point-first at his belly. This time he gave a shout as he parried it away, but by the time he recovered from his surprise, I had turned and begun to run. Once he recovered, he began to lumber after me.

There were more cries of surprise from the onlookers, for they thought I was flying for my life, but in fact I was running *toward* something—the pollaxe leaning against the belfry. I snatched at it, turned, and had the pollaxe on guard before he was closer than five paces from me, which brought Meens to a sudden stop.

Pollaxes have a spike on either end, and an axe-blade on the crown, and that axe-blade has another spike growing out of the back of it. I advanced with the butt-spike foremost, the shaft supported in the middle by my weakened right hand, while the axe-blade I controlled with my left. I used my weakened right hand not as an aid to striking, but as a kind of fulcrum to aid in shifting my point either to the attack or defense.

For I was using the pollaxe not as a smashing weapon, but as a rapier, and one with greater range than that awkward length of steel in Meens's fist. With both hands controlling the weapon, I was employing Coronel Lipton's strike of the peasant.

I came straight on before Meens could work out a means of response, and now it was my weapon darting out at his face and body, while he made desperate efforts to parry. He tried knocking my point away with his dagger and then thrusting with the rapier, but the strike of the peasant was too strong, and I knocked his sword aside. He saved himself from my riposte by leaping, and I cut a piece of his shirt away, though without drawing blood.

I pressed the attack, and I saw by the growing hopelessness in my enemy's eyes that he was about to try something desperate, so when he lunged with both weapons, I took a step to the side, dropped to one knee, and swung the axe-blade at his legs. The blade itself missed, but I swept up his ankle with the haft, and he crashed heavily onto the roof-tiles.

I intended now to stab him in the leg, which would allow me to inflict an honorable wound and end the fight, but Meens's fall had shattered the terra-cotta beneath him and precipitated a slide as one tile after another disengaged from its supports, and though he'd fallen at least two paces from the edge of the roof, he found himself carried into space on a raft of clattering rubble.

I saw the fury in his dark eyes die as he went over the edge, and for a moment he looked puzzled, as if he couldn't quite remember how he had come to this fate. Orlanda's spirit of vengeance had abandoned him at the last moment, and his mind was his own as he fell three storeys into the courtyard and landed amid the watching monks. I dropped the pollaxe and, mindful not to break any tiles, made my careful way toward Lord Barkin.

"You will need to help me down," I said, "and then I need to see a surgeon."

Barkin's look was alert. "You are wounded?"

"I think I may have broken my arm."

He nodded. "Dom Emidio and I have arranged for a surgeon to stand by," he said.

"Then let us go, and quickly."

I almost fainted with pain as I clambered down the face of the prayer hall and into the lane behind the building. Barkin leaped on his horse, and Sansloy gave me his courser, and off we rode to the surgeon, leaving Harvey Meens in the care of Dom Emidio and the monks.

"No, the arm is not broken," said the surgeon. He was a charming gray-haired man with a shaven chin and curling mustaches, and he cradled my arm carefully in his two gentle hands. He spoke the tongue of Loretto slowly and clearly, so that his foreign patient would understand. "Instead there is a misalignment of the bones. I can repair it, but it will be very painful."

"What?" said I. "How do you—?"

But while I was in the midst of this civil inquiry, he took my forearm in one hand and my shoulder in the other, and gave my arm a very firm twist combined with a sharp tug. It *was* very painful, and I gasped in surprise while tears sprang to my eyes, but the extreme pain lasted only an instant, after which the sensation faded to mere agony.

"I shall make a sling for your arm, Dom Keely-Fay," said the surgeon with a smile. "You should not play tennis for a few weeks, or use a sword."

Lord Barkin arranged for a hired coach to take me to the Palace Ribamar, and accompanied me to make certain that I was comfortable. He installed me on a settee in a parlor, and had the fire built up so I would not take a chill. "If I hear of a warrant being made out," he said, "I will do my best to warn you."

"Thank you," said I. "I am very much in your debt."

"Not at all," said he. "At the palace it is all ceremony and play-soldiering. By contrast, I found this affair bracing, a pleasurable diversion."

"I am heartily glad someone enjoyed it," said I.

"Take your ease, and recover yourself," said Barkin. "I do not think justice will exert itself overmuch in the matter of Harvey Meens."

"My doctor has ordered me not to fight duels," said I, "and I will obey his instructions. But I think I will not be long in Longres—there were too many witnesses to that fight, and not all of them love me."

"I may be interviewed," said Barkin. "I will put the blame entirely on Meens, and so will Dom Emidio if he is just."

"Nevertheless," I said.

He shrugged. "You will not err by being cautious," he said.

In fact I had already decided to leave Loretto. I had been here for over two months, and had failed at everything I'd hoped to accomplish. I had thought it might be possible to achieve a reputation here as I had in Duisland, through wit and perhaps a well-chosen escapade or two, but the barriers against me were far stronger here than at home, and the reputation I'd gained had been that of a bedswerver and a quarrelsome fighter. I hadn't found Lady Westley, and I had failed to avoid Lord Edevane's conspiracies. Perhaps it was time to heed the business that was calling me elsewhere. A spring voyage to Selford was probably the best thing for me.

Lord Barkin had no sooner left for Longres Regius than Rufino Knott appeared. "Meens yet lives," he said, "but his back may be broke."

He had gained admission to the monastery's infirmary by claiming to be Meens's servant, and heard the verdict of the surgeon-monk who tended the injuries and illnesses of his brethren. Though Meens might survive, he would likely never walk again.

"Goodman Knott," I said. "I need you to arrange a carriage to take me to the western coast tomorrow. Afterward, pack my things."

"Very good, Sir Quillifer." Knott held out a letter. "The porter had this message from Prince Alicio."

I read the letter, a response to the query I had sent to him about the two ladies from Duisland and their inadequate lodging at the palace. He responded that you and Countess Marcella were welcome to stay at the Palace Ribamar, and the steward should make the arrangements.

I called for mulled cider and some bread, then went to the library, where I had the portable desk that held my correspondence. Painfully I adjusted my sling so that I could hold a quill, and put paper and ink before me. First I wrote to you, to let you know of the prince's kind offer of lodging. Then I wrote Prince Alicio, thanking him for his hospitality, and telling him that I was obliged to return to Duisland, but that I'm sure the two stranded ladies would be delighted by his offer.

Next I was obliged to write Elvina and explain the morning's events. I expressed regret for her brother's misfortune and told her that I must leave the country, and then the words seemed to drain away, and I was left staring at the half-filled page of foolscap while weariness and misery swam in my head. I remembered the look of puzzlement in Meens's eyes as he plunged over the edge, and thought how he had challenged me as the pawn of a malevolent goddess, but fallen to his fate as himself, his own master only for the length of time it took him to plunge three storeys to the ground. I wondered if I were any better, if I was blown hither and thither by some force beyond myself, and falling all the time toward some fate as calamitous as that of Meens, or Wilmot.

I could tell nothing of this to Elvina, and of course Elvina might herself be a puppet, inclined toward me by Orlanda's power. . . . *I may serve my purposes better by making the wrong people love you.* Elvina might be another of that divine lady's victims.

"Dom Keely-Fay," said Braud the steward. "There is a lady to see you."

I could imagine no lady at my door but Elvina, and so I left the library and hastened to the parlor, where I saw you on a chair by the hearth. You were wearing a blue riding dress, as if you'd just come in from a stag hunt, and your face was turned to the fire. The flames outlined your strong profile, your proud straight nose, your full lips, the noble forehead. I stopped in the doorway, surprised, and you turned your black eyes to me, and then to my arm in a sling.

"Are you injured?" you asked. "I heard you won the encounter."

"The surgeon assures me it is a trifle," I said. "At any rate I'm better off than Meens." I advanced to kiss your hand. "Mistress d'Altrey, how did you hear of the meeting's outcome?"

"Meens was hardly discreet, so the entire court knew it would take place. This morning at least a dozen witnesses galloped straight to the palace to tell everyone what had happened."

"You have come to ask about the affair?"

You dismissed the thought with a sniff. "Of course not. I received your letter when I came in from my morning ride, and I thought I'd get back on my horse and survey the accommodations."

"Let me call Braud, and explain the matter to him."

The steward seemed at first a little skeptical, as if I intended to install a mistress under his master's roof, but I had Prince Alicio's letter at hand and was able to show him His Highness's will in the matter. You chose a fine room overlooking the lake, with a mirror, a wardrobe, and a door leading to a terrace. Your bed had a canopy painted with stars, so that once the bed curtains were closed, you might fancy yourself lying beneath the open sky.

You told Braud that you would come tomorrow with your belongings and a servant, and that Countess Marcella might arrive with you. Braud said he would send servants to clean the room and withdrew, and we opened the terrace door and stepped out into the bright sun. Prince Alicio's lake stretched out before us, with a dark forest, one of King Henrico's hunting preserves, stretching out behind. The taste of spring lay in the air, a hint of things stirring under the earth. Doves from the columbarium darted through the sky in pairs. We walked along the terrace toward the lake, and the pleasure-ships that Prince Alicio had moored there.

"Now you will not be obliged to share a bed with Marcella," I said.

You waved a hand. "When she is there, she sleeps so quietly that I barely notice her," you said. "But she barely sleeps at all, and is in bed only a few hours each night. I wondered if that was normal for the Aekoi, but I've since learned they take as much sleep as we."

This I found interesting. "Where does she go at night? Does she have a lover?"

You smiled. "Do you wish to be that lover? At present you are without a paramour, I believe."

"Marcella may be a little fierce for my tastes. I think also she may not like humans."

"Certainly not those who think her no better than a courtesan. She has boxed the ears of more than one impudent rogue since we have come to Longres."

I shook my head. "She will tell sad, unflattering tales of us when she returns to her home."

"But I think she will return in something like luxury. She gambles late into the night, and she wins more than she loses. Sometimes I partner her at rentoy, and she is fair in sharing the booty." You regarded me from half-lidded eyes. "I hate the palace and its smug denizens," she said, "but I may regret losing that income. I hope also I will not regret any scandal that may attach to me for living in a man's house with one of Duisland's most notorious seducers."

I frowned. "I dispute both 'seducer' and 'notorious.' The former assumes I must employ falsity to somehow coax or trick women into my bed, and the latter term is mere sensation, completely overblown."

You laughed. "Yet you did not hear how you were characterized this morning, when word of your encounter arrived at the palace. It's generally believed that all your fights were over women."

One woman, I thought. "Well," I said. "I suppose the courtiers will find other things to talk about, by and by. And in any case, this last encounter with Meens will oblige me to leave Loretto, and you and Countess Marcella may retain your chaste reputations, an you desire them."

"You're leaving?" You seemed surprised. "When?"

"Tomorrow. You see, I sacrifice for your convenience."

We reached the corner of the terrace and paused. A formal garden stretched before us, with topiary figures in the shapes of fantastic animals, and gardeners planting the spring bulbs. The calls of geese sounded in the air as a series of V-shaped formations flew high overhead, all heading north. Sun-silver glinted from their wings. You took my left arm, and I felt a thrill run up my spine.

"I wish to applaud you," you said. "You played with Meens, and played well. You left him so frustrated that he had no choice but to join your game of roof-leaping. And then you hurled him from the monastery in front of a hundred witnesses."

"Strangely enough," said I, "Meens managed that fall on his own. If the doctors examine him for wounds, they will find none inflicted by me."

"You encompassed his ruin cleverly then," you said. "And you gave a lesson to anyone else who would challenge you."

"I have given such lessons before," said I with some bitterness. "And it did not prevent Meens from challenging."

"Your previous lessons had a limited audience. This had an absurd number of spectators, and by morning the whole city may be pondering the lesson you taught Harvey Meens." You put your hand on mine. "If your life here may be likened to a game of rentoy, you are sending the right signals. It is not enough to be clever; you mortify your enemies as well as defeat them—no one so shamed will be taken seriously again. You disregard foolish notions of honor or tradition. And you are a marvelous hypocrite, the best in the world!"

I looked at you in slow surprise. "I have not considered myself quite in that light," said I.

"Oh, I saw you a few weeks ago at the Footsteps of the Pilgrim monastery—adopting the postures, chanting with the others, putting on the most pious face imaginable! You were every inch the oblate, but I'm sure you care no more for the Pilgrim than I care for the health of the King of Josand!"

"I found that retreat inconvenient and uncomfortable," I said. "If I seemed devout, it seems I am a better hypocrite than I knew."

You leaned close. "It seems I know you better than you know yourself," you said. Your breath was sweet, with the merest suggestion of orange and clove.

"Will you accept a kiss," said I, "from the best hypocrite in the world?"

You tilted your face to mine, and I pressed my lips to yours and inhaled your scent of myrrh. The kiss went on for some while. When we paused, I discovered to my pleasure those faint freckles on the bridge of your nose, which for some reason embarrass you and which you employ your arts to obscure.

"If you are still concerned for your reputation," I said after a while, "perhaps we can continue this elsewhere, in privacy."

You favored me with a demure smile. "Is your room nearby?"

We went to my room, and I think we were both surprised by the profundity of what followed. For myself, I felt that I had found the one true woman of whom all others were a shadow, and for whom I would dare anything, and sacrifice anything, that we might only remain together. For it seemed to me that you were a supreme reality, and that all else was but contingency. In you I found a revelation of truth, fully as grand as those who suffer sudden illumination by the Pilgrim, or who claim some sudden and penetrating understanding of the universe.

I was touched, also, by your care for my wounded arm, and by your concern that I would not suffer unnecessary pain as we interlaced. By that point I cared little about how I damaged myself, so that I might grow nearer to the real and perfect eidolon that is yourself.

After this new knowledge had shaken my understanding of myself and of the world, I began to make plans to remain in Longres, but you dissuaded me.

"It is better that you leave," you said. "You will be safe from the authorities, and I don't think I'll be here much longer. Queen Berlauda has declined to intervene in order to procure better lodging for her sister, and so it seems that Floria is being slighted by deliberate policy. I do not think she will come to Longres, and I expect Marcella and I will be recalled as soon as Floria receives our letter." You kissed me. "And so we should reunite in Duisland."

"If I must leave tomorrow," said I, "I wish this day would last forever."

You gave me a wicked smile. "It won't last forever," you said, "but it need not end *now*."

And indeed the shadows grew long before we ceased our explorations and I helped you to dress. I was less dextrous than was usual, as I had the full use of only one hand, but you forgave that fault as you forgive all my faults.

And then I kissed you and returned to my library, where I looked down at my unfinished letter to Elvina, and I thought that Elvina seemed farther away than ever.

CHAPTER TWENTY-FOUR

I finished that letter to Elvina with the hope that she would not hate me forever and sent it by courier. I also wrote to Lord Barkin to thank him for representing me so well, and to Lord Edevane to inform him that I would be returning to Duisland.

Traveling in a hired carriage and changing horses at each post, Rufino Knott and I traveled to the coast on the road that had been repaired for the convenience of Queen Berlauda. I found a ship to Bretlynton Head, and from there visited my manor at Dunnock, just to make sure all was in order and to collect my rents. Less money awaited me than I had expected, for, due to the great storm, the harvest had been poor. Yet there had been enough to prevent hunger, as there was in Fornland.

One foggy morning before my departure, one of my tenants came running to me to tell me that a ship had blundered into the Races in the fog, and was now caught in one of the ferocious tidal storms that tore twice each day through those toothlike stony cays.

From Dunnock there is no way down the steep cliff, but on a neighbor's estate there was a ravine that led to the beach, and I rang the fire bell in my old tower and brought as many of my servants and tenants down that ravine as I could. By the time we gained the sand, the fog had lifted, and we saw a small galleon caught in one of the great foaming whirlpools. Even as we watched, the galleon spun away from the whirlpool, struck hard on one of the stony half-submerged ledges, and began to sink.

We had no boats, and even if we had, no boat would survive in the Races once the tide began to rage and foam. I sent men galloping to my neighbors to find any boats that could be brought to the scene when the tide slackened, and in the meantime we could do nothing but watch the ship founder.

A few of the sailors, clinging to wreckage, were carried near enough to some of the cays to clamber onto the rocks, and these were later fetched off at slack tide by some fishermen. The rest we were forced to watch as they drowned or were swept out to sea, and to hear the growling tide as it overpowered their screams and cries for help. Seven men survived out of a crew of sixty, and the ship and its cargo were strewn over the stony bottom where no salvager would dare go.

I made the survivors as comfortable as I could, had their wounds bandaged and their broken bones splinted, and then carried them to Bretlynton Head. The sailors were taken in by a monastery until they were fit to return to work, and I took ship to Selford.

Kevin Spellman was at his family's house in town, to attend the launch of our new ship to replace *Royal Stilwell*, lost on Gannet Island ten months before. I lodged with Kevin and his parents, and was present when the great 850-ton galleon shuddered down the ways into the Saelle, the water foaming beneath its tumble home as it shouldered broadside into the water and sent a great swell across the river that crashed into the wharves and piers and ships on the far side, sending out a long, shuddering echo that sent seabirds whirling into the sky.

Sea-Drake, intended for the trade to Tabarzam and back, still lacked its upper masts, many of its fittings, its guns, and its crew, and would spend at least another six weeks in Selford fitting out before taking on its cargo and beginning its long voyage abroad. I had named the ship after the great serpent I'd seen at the storm's outset the previous summer, and from one of the shipyard's expert carvers had commissioned a magnificent coiling figurehead that would soon be brilliant with rainbow paint and gold leaf.

While *Sea-Drake* fitted out, I busied myself expanding my ink empire. My self-created master ink-maker at the works in Howel, having trained his own replacement, had come to Selford and begun setting up a new factory. He had brought with him a suitable number of Mountmirail's grinding machines, and I approached the business in the same manner as I had in Howel, by securing a near monopoly on oak galls. By the time I left Selford in July, Q Sable Ink was being sold at every stationer's in the city. Since all the government ministries were headquartered in Selford, the market for ink was even greater than in the winter capital.

I began to think of red ink, blue ink, green ink, and even silver and gold ink, and sent my master inker to experimenting in order to produce these.

The Duchess of Roundsilver had given birth just before I arrived in the city, and I was able to congratulate their happy graces in a visit to the Roundsilver palace, and present to the week-old Marquess of Ethlebight the beautiful sapphire that I had originally planned to give to Berlauda's child. I also informed their graces that I planned to form a joint-stock company to build the canal from Ethlebight to Gannet Cove, and that I hoped Their Graces might subscribe, and help in attaining a monopoly from the crown.

"You must be careful who you talk to, Quillifer," said the duke. "For if the wrong person gets wind of this, he may form his own company and snatch your prize out from under you."

"That would be difficult," said I, "for last summer I took the liberty of buying the sole right to purchase Gannett Cove, and to forbid other purchases, for ten years. They may sell to me, or not at all, and there is no other deep-water harbor on that coast."

The Roundsilvers looked at each other and laughed. "That is very well!" said His Grace. "I will of course be delighted to become a subscriber! But you must go to Ethlebight and get pledges from our friends there—I will provide letters of introduction, if you like."

"I wonder if Wenlock will join?" I asked. "He may hate me, but I think he loves a good profit."

"He will try to destroy you if he can," said her grace.

"Only if Edevane lets him off the leash," said I, "for I think Wenlock is now Edevane's lap-dog."

All these developments took place to the constant drumming of rain, for the spring had turned wet and cold, and the summer that followed was no better. My crooked finger ached continually. It was obvious that the crops would drown and the harvest would fail. The previous year's harvest had resulted in hunger, but this year's would produce famine. The Spellmans and I sent orders to *Sea-Holly, Able,* and our other merchant ships to venture abroad and purchase grain for the relief of hunger at home.

In years of bad harvests some landowners came to the relief of their tenants and neighbors by employing them on building projects so they could afford to eat, so I wrote to my bailiff at Dunnock to build a watchtower overlooking the Races to alert the manor to any ships in danger, and also to investigate a limestone outcrop on a part of my property to see if stone might be quarried there for the tower, and also for paving the roads in the district.

While in Selford I received word that my privateer *Ostra* had captured two ships returning to Thurnmark from abroad, and that these were awaiting the judgment of the prize court in Ferrick. Once the court had ruled, and the crown had taken its twenty percent, the ships and their cargoes would be mine to dispose of as I liked. Without waiting for the ruling, *Ostra* had returned to the low-lying coast of Thurnmark to look for more captures.

I left Selford on *Sea-Drake*, its hold loaded with wool, ingots of tin and iron, blocks of steel suitable for turning into knives and swords, and a cargo of fine cannon made in Selford's foundries. The cannon I could sell anywhere in the world, for Duisland's cannons were prized, and the metals also. The wool would be sold in Varcellos, and exchanged for fine wines and brandies that would delight the palates of the Candara Coast. The great ship, traveling always in bad weather, made slow progress down the coast to Amberstone. As we neared the city, we could hear the thumping of guns and the chime of bells far out to sea and, as there was no enemy fleet in sight, reasoned that either we had won a great military victory, or that Queen Berlauda had delivered her child.

We did not put into Amberstone to take part in the celebrations, because the captain wanted to make some adjustments to the rigging and to re-stow the cargo in order to improve the ship's speed and handling. But as soon as we came to our mooring, the celebration surrounded us in the form of boats full of cheering, half-drunken citizens, and an anchorage heavy with gunsmoke. From the oarsmen of one of the boats we learned that Berlauda had given Duisland and Loretto a royal heir, the infant Prince Aguila.

I went onshore to toast Aguila's birth, though I wondered if I might also be toasting the death of the former heir, Princess Floria— for Lord Edevane, who had such a talent for anticipating the wishes of the monarchs, might try to rid Aguila of a rival.

These thoughts darkened my merry-making, so next day I took a coaster to Ethlebight, where, after running aground in the main channel and waiting four hours for the tide to take us off, we finally made the port.

I stayed at the Spellman house in Ethlebight, and spent the evenings with old friends, while my days were occupied in meeting the principal people of the district. Because my father had been an alderman, I already knew the other aldermen, the mayor, many of the foremost merchants, and most of the officials of the guilds; but I knew few of the gentry and none of the nobility beyond Roundsilver and Wenlock. Most proclaimed themselves willing to endorse the canal scheme, except for a few who I suspect intended to launch their own company. These I hoped would go to the expense and trouble of surveying the route, and only then discover that they could not purchase the fishing village at the terminus.

I visited Sir Cecil Greene, the member of the Burgesses who had spoken out to the displeasure of King Priscus, and found he was willing to introduce the necessarily legislation in the Burgesses to allow the canal company to purchase land and the necessary right-of-way. "Though you may wish someone else to introduce this bill," he said, "for Their Majesties love me not, and may refuse assent out of spite."

"I might introduce it myself," said I gloomily, "for Lord Edevane wishes me to run in a by-election in Hurst Downs."

"Where exactly is Hurst Downs?" Greene asked. And after I told him, he said, "At least there will be another vote for the canal scheme."

"Yet Edevane may exact a price," said I. "I fear he will wish me to perjure myself, and provide evidence against his enemies."

"Then you must refuse him," said Greene. "Once you are a member of the Burgesses, you will be immune to prosecution by the crown."

"That immunity did Sir Edmund Tryon little good," said I. "His head now ornaments a pike."

Greene was firm. "The viceroy cannot rule the Burgesses through terror. The lower house represents the people, and the people are the foundation on which stands the edifice of the nation. We are greater than the monarchy."

I hope the headsman will agree with you, I thought. Still, I thought the next session would go better without the presence of Priscus and Berlauda, and that whoever managed the Estates on behalf of the crown would prove better at negotiation than the monarchs.

Well, you know what became of *that* hope.

I enrolled a great list of subscribers in Ethlebight over the months of July and August. I did not ask for money, for as yet the project had no budget. If you rode a horse from Ethlebight to Gannet Cove, it would be about eighteen leagues, and with relays of horses you might do it in a day; but the canal necessarily had to divert around rocky hills and forests, and would be something like twenty-five leagues. It would have to be dug about two yards deep and fourteen yards wide, and there would have to be good towpaths on either side, and stables and fodder for the mules that would draw the barges. An aqueduct would be needed to carry the canal over a steep river valley, and in addition there would be ten or twelve locks to carry the barges up and down hills, and down to the final destination in the cove—and I did not know how to build a lock, nor did anyone in the kingdom. All the locks in Duisland were in Bonille, they were of ancient Aekoi manufacture, and no one had ever built a new one.

But, I thought, the first thing would be to pass the bill through the Estates, and gain royal assent. Once that was obtained, I could raise funds and find an engineer at the same time.

I received a letter from Lord Edevane that Sir Silvanus Becket had been made Baron Becket and a member of the House of Peers, and that I would be expected in Hurst Downs for the by-election to fill his seat. The election would be in mid-September, so in the middle of August I took ship to Bretlynton Head, and again I arrived to the tolling of bells. I saw moored beneath the castle the galleon *Sovereign*, just returned from the Candara Coast, and I saw that its yards were cockbilled and askew, with ropes' ends trailing, and the flag at half mast, drooping over the poop. I went at once to see Captain Gaunt, and from him learned that Queen Berlauda, weakened after childbirth, had died very suddenly of a fever that had also struck Queen Arletta, though not fatally.

This left Priscus sole monarch of Duisland, for Berlauda had crowned him her co-equal, with the infant Aguila first in line of succession. But I wondered how Duisland would accept this foreign autocrat now that he was not wedded to the rightful queen, and I wondered whether this would be good for Floria, or the reverse. For it would not be very long before some bright spark suggested to Priscus that a solution to his problems in Duisland would be to marry Floria.

Despite the mourning bells tolling in the city, I spent a pleasant night drinking wine with Captain Gaunt in his great cabin, and hearing the tales of his voyage and back. I told him that *Sea-Drake* had been launched and was already on its way to Candara. He opened his strongbox and showed me the gems he had bought on my behalf in Tabarzam, as fine as I could have wished, and when I left the ship next morning, I took that strongbox with me.

From a tailor in Bretlynton Head I ordered mourning apparel, then rode to Hurst Downs and Dunnock. I inspected the half-built watchtower overlooking the Races, and viewed the limestone outcrop, which was even now being sawn and wedged into blocks. The large slabs were used in the construction of the tower, and the smaller ones would be crushed to improve the surface of the roads on my estate, and in the district generally.

In Hurst Downs I dined with the new-made Lord Becket and the other leading men of the district. Becket, a stout, gray-haired man with a large estate and a deer park, had already informed his guests that I was the crown's choice for their representative, which made them wary, and they seemed a little startled by my youth; but I had the advantage of wealth and a royal office, and a certain reputation as a soldier and dragon-slayer, and so in the end they raised little objection to my candidacy.

They told me frankly, however, that they resented having to pay for what they called "Priscus's war." In that war they saw no advantage to themselves or to their country, and to raise more taxes in a year when the crops had failed was nothing short of madness. Their own wealth depended on the yearly harvest, and this year they would have to borrow in order to meet their obligations. To squeeze more money out of them in order to send yet another army to Thurnmark was, they thought, preposterous.

I agreed with them, but felt their cause was helpless. There was very little precedent for the Estates defying the monarch in any matter the monarch felt truly important; and I knew that Priscus and his family were in need of troops, and as they were involved wholly in killing the enemy, they would hardly trouble themselves if they had to kill a few members of the Estates. I spoke frankly of this to my hosts in Hurst Downs, and I think they appreciated my candor. At the election, I was duly elected their representative in the Burgesses.

So I, with Rufino Knott, returned to Bretlynton Head, got my mourning garb from the tailor, then took passage up the Dordelle to Howel and Rackheath House. The passage upstream was bleak, the river a gray, sullen, and torpid flood, often turned white with the impact of sudden cloudbursts. The constant summer rains had burst the banks of the Dordelle in numerous districts, and the implacable waters now carried full-grown trees with their spreading branches and entangling roots, along with derelict watercraft, wooden piers torn from their pilings, and entire houses that had been carried away from their foundations. These unusual hazards lengthened the journey and delayed my reunion with you. For we two had sent letters back and forth all summer, and I knew that you and Countess Marcella had been recalled to join Floria in Howel. Floria had declined the scant hospitality of Longres Regius, and sent instead magnificent presents to her sister and the infant Aguila.

I had barely hoisted my flag over Rackheath House when you arrived at my door in a litter. When your name was announced,

Goodman Knott was still unpacking my chests and hanging my clothes in my dressing room, a maidservant was lighting the fire in my study, and Master Stiver was in the act of presenting to me the household accounts for the months since my departure. I fear that I offended Master Stiver when I ran from his presence to your arms, and I kissed your noble brow, your cheeks, and your lips in front of half a dozen startled servants. You were dressed in deep mourning, and that perhaps made our embrace all the more surprising.

"All business is postponed till tomorrow," I proclaimed. "Bring a decanter of sauternes to my study."

The study was smoky from the fire that had just been lit, and we stayed only till Knott brought the sauternes and some glasses. We spent the next several hours on Lord Rackheath's great canopied bed, and we scarcely needed to draw the bed curtains closed, for the wine and our ardor kept us warm.

"How is Her Highness?" asked I, after we had reached a stage of temporary satiation. Your cheek rested on my shoulders, with your warm, massy, myrrh-scented hair spread across my chest.

"She mourns, I think sincerely." You reached across me to fetch your glass from the stand, and I took the opportunity to kiss your fingers. "Berlauda stood between Floria and Priscus. Now there is no defense, and the king will have his way."

"And what way is that?" I asked.

"He sent Baron Lestrange with an offer of marriage."

Mere weeks, I thought, after the death of the woman to whom he had seemed so devoted. Yet I thought this marriage might save Floria, though at the cost of being closer to Priscus and his *caw-caw-caw* than she might wish.

"In law," said I, "it is considered incest to marry your late wife's sister. And the penalty for incest is the scaffold."

"That is not the case in Loretto. And it will no longer be the case here, an Priscus wills it."

"Well then," said I. "Do you fancy waiting upon our new queen?"

"Queen she might be," you said, "but I think she will not marry Priscus. She sent Lestrange away with the message that it was improper for a person in deep mourning to receive such an offer, and also that when her mourning is over, she would not say yea or nay to a mere emissary, but that Priscus should press his suit in person."

I took your glass from your hands and tasted the honeyed-walnut flavor of the sauternes. "She delays, then. Her mourning will last—what? A year?"

"And Priscus is at the war until his father releases him. As the royal army is in some jeopardy, Priscus may not be released for some time."

I was surprised. "How in jeopardy? I thought the war with Thurnmark was nought but one triumph after another!"

Your lip curled. "The latest news is far from triumphant. The government has not seen fit to tell us that we're at war with five more countries."

"Five?"

You then told me how the despised emperor of Sélange, whose small country Priscus had crossed in order to outflank Thurnmark's defenses, had resented his cavalier treatment at the hands of Priscus and declared war on Loretto. Since his military force was negligible, this threat was viewed as risible; but the emperor, being the prudent ruler of a small country situated next to a large, aggressive neighbor, had provided himself with allies, and so in the late summer the combined armies of five nations marched on Priscus's lines of communication. There had been a ferocious battle, which seemed to have been a draw.

In the meantime, Thurnmark's Assembly of Notables had dismissed their prince—which, however startling, was allowed by the custom of the country—and anointed a new Hogen-Mogen somewhat more talented in the military sphere. This gentleman had gone on the offensive and fought a series of bloody battles, which he had not won, but which he had not lost, either.

The twenty thousand soldiers from Duisland had arrived in the field two or three regiments at a time, were thrown piecemeal into these encounters, and had suffered accordingly. They had not been assembled into that army of Duisland that Priscus had desired to command, but were brigaded haphazardly with the soldiers of Loretto. In the meantime Thurnmark had launched privateers against Loretto and Duisland, and our own commerce was now in danger.

"And how were we of Duisland meant to discover this?" I asked.

"The information is being withheld until the Estates vote more war taxes."

I laughed. "But everyone knows, I suppose."

"Floria heard from her friends returning to Howel after Berlauda's death. I imagine those same friends are telling their entire acquaintance."

I considered Floria and the strategy she had adopted, and I thought she had done well. Caught amid an abundance of hazards, she had declined to commit herself to any course of action, and awaited events. For myself, I have never been inclined to inaction; but in Floria's case it seemed the safest policy.

You were looking at me from beneath an arched eyebrow. "You should attempt a more intimate acquaintance with Floria," you said. "She asks me about you."

For a moment I was speechless, and seeing my expression, you laughed. "I did not mean the intimacy now suggesting itself to your mind. But she finds you interesting, and it is in your best interest to let her pursue her interest."

"I think she views me as an exotic form of trained monkey," I said.

You waved a hand. "And what is wrong with that?"

"Nothing," said I, "were I actually a trained monkey."

You affected great patience and sighed. "Quillifer, you are singular, like your name. No one has met anyone like you, and no one knows what to do with you."

"No one but you," I said.

"I am remarkable for my intelligence and discernment," you said. "I think you and Floria are well matched. She alone would know how to employ you."

"Her Highness," I said, "is in a precarious position. Would I not find it dangerous in her vicinity?"

Your words were scornful. "It is dangerous to be at court. It is dangerous to hold office. If you wished a life without danger, you would have stayed in your father's shop, and not chased dragons."

If I had stayed in my father's shop, I could have saved him, and saved the rest of my family. Your words were words of reproach, though you had not meant them that way.

I reached for a cup of wine. "When Her Highness asks about me," I said, "what do you tell her?"

"That you are intelligent, original, amusing, and experienced in the arts of love."

I spluttered into my cup, and then searched for words. "Did Floria ask for that last piece of intelligence?"

"No. But she is nineteen, and though she is a virgin by state policy, yet she is curious. Why should she not know what it is like between a man and a woman?"

"She knows about us?"

"Of course. There was no reason to keep it from her. I think she approves."

I sipped sauternes while futile thoughts fluttered through my head like bats about a lantern. You leaned close to me, and your warm hair brushed my shoulder. "Yet if Floria decides to take you to her bed," you confided, "you should comply."

I looked at you. "Your disinterest is alarming. Are you tired of me already, that you wish to give me away?"

"No." Your black eyes were bright. "Were you and Floria lovers, there would have to be an excuse for you to be in her company, and that excuse would be *me*. We might spend more time together than we would otherwise."

"Until I was hanged, drawn, and quartered. I don't imagine there is any mercy for the seducers of princesses."

"All the more reason to be discreet." You put an arm across my chest and laid your head on my shoulder. I inhaled the sweet myrrh-musk of your hair. "Consider," you said, "there is only one frail infant life between Floria and the throne."

"There are Priscus and Aguila both."

"Priscus is nothing. It is Aguila who is the heir of the Emelins, and he be frail, he may not live long." You kissed my throat. "Imagine being the lover of a queen."

"I already am," I said. "You are the empress of my heart."

You laughed. "I accept your homage, but I cannot give you what Floria could. Titles, offices, money, land."

"She can give little unless she is the monarch."

"That hope is not without foundation." You took the glass from my hand and drank, and I kissed your lips that tasted of honey-sweet wine.

"Enough of might-bes and amorous fantasies about princesses," said I. "You are woman, and monarch, enough for me, and you may not hand me to another."

Amusement touched the corner of your mouth. "We shall see how far the royal prerogative extends."

"I need to know what impends in Howel. What is the temper of the court?"

"Bloody and contentious. Viceroy Fosco has appointed a commission to establish regularity in religion here in Duisland. On its recommendation several abbots have lost their places, and two Retrievers have lost their heads for denying the divinity of the Pilgrim."

Surprised, I considered this development in regard to the law of the country. Duisland had no official faith, and the creed of the Pilgrim was supposed only to be the private religion of the royal family. Yet no follower of the old religion could expect to achieve high office, and so out of self-interest the nobility conformed to the beliefs of the monarch, and repeated the teachings of Eidrich the Pilgrim whether they believed them or not.

Yet I could think of no precedent that would allow the monarch, or his representative, to dismiss clerics from their appointments, let alone hack off their heads.

"Aren't the monasteries independent institutions?" I asked. "How can Fosco use force to interfere in their business? What is his justification in law?"

"It is what is done in Loretto," you said. "If he has any other justification, he has said nothing about it." You leaned close and laughed in my ear.

"You should play the hypocrite again and go on a monastic retreat," you said. "It will do you no harm, and may convince the viceroy of your orthodoxy."

I thought I'd had enough of politics, and I took you in my arms. "Purely in the interest of orthodoxy, perhaps we should then practice one or more of the postures said by initiates to bring about ecstatic spiritual fulfillment."

You laughed low, then drained your cup and let it drop from your listless fingers to fall to the soft carpet by the bed. "I shall humbly await your instruction," you said, and wrapped your arms around my neck.

When, the next day, I was able to catch up on my affairs, and at last view ten months' accounts along with Master Stiver, I read also the mail that had arrived in my absence, and found there a letter from no man other than Harvey Meens, a letter written four months before.

I own that I expected its contents to consist of little but abuse, but instead I found a graceful apology.

> *I know not what madness possessed me to make me challenge you. I thank you sincerely for the mercy you showed me, and I am heartily sorry that I so foolishly traduced you, and acted to the discredit of my sister and her husband.*

From hints given in the text I understood that in the fall he had lost the use of his legs, and with it lost his post as paymaster to the palace, and lived now in retirement on his estate in Fornland.

I put aside the letter and considered that Meens might be happier than many an ambitious courtier, caught between his own ambitions and the perfidy and suspicion of the court. Fosco was cutting off the heads of the clergy, and I could hardly imagine he would spare the Burgesses.

From Elvina I heard nothing. I began a letter to Meens, but put it aside as other business began to press.

I visited with my galley's crew. Boatswain Lepalik was keeping them in practice, but there was little reason, for the court was in mourning, and the season's regattas had been canceled along with balls, large feasts, and other great celebrations. The courtiers would have to find other ways to amuse themselves, and I would have to postpone introducing *la volta* into Duisland.

My next visitor was the poet Blackwell. He called on me that afternoon, while I was still absorbed by the household accounts. I was glad to see him and took him to the library, where he might be at home amid the sight of the gilt-edged bound volumes, with their rich scent of leather and fine paper—but he was agitated, his indigo eyes darting from one lodging to another. He asked for beer, and I asked for two to be brought. After the beer arrived in a pair of fine glass beakers, he collapsed into one of the tall, carved oaken chairs and gave me a bleak look.

"I am blockaded," he said, "and I must find a way to break free."

"Is the master of the revels refusing your plays again?"

"Ay, but that is not what is driving me mad." He looked over his shoulder at the door, which stood open, and then rose to close it before returning to his seat. He put his elbows on the table between us, leaned as close as he could, and said, "It is my satire, my *The Court of Laelius*, the petard with which I hope to blow up the administration."

"You told me of this work in Loretto. Have you been discovered as the author?"

"Nay, I am still safe. But the work itself has been shut up in a warehouse under guard, and I know not how to break it out."

"Was it stolen, then? And what was it—a manuscript?" I asked. "Or a printed copy?"

"A chest filled with the octavo edition," said he. "I had the work set in type by a fellow in Bretlynton Head who supplements his income with a clandestine press for unlicensed works. I then carried the bound volumes up the Dordelle by barge. The bale was put in a warehouse till I could bring them to the sellers of books and distributors of pamphlets, but there has been so much pamphleteering ahead of the Estates that Fosco is enraged by it all, and Edevane has put a company of the Yeoman Archers on the docks, and now everything is searched."

I sipped my beer, its tang a heady antidote to the dusty ledgers of the household accounts. "Is not bribery usually recommended in these cases?" I asked. "These guards cannot be rich men."

"Parkins tried it, and was arrested and carried off to Murkdale Hags."

"Who is Parkins?"

Blackwell gave a contemptuous wave of his hand. "A puisny little hireling, a mean, unscrupulous mercenary who writes pamphlets for any faction that pays him. The world will be a little cleaner for his imprisonment, and Murkdale Hags a little fouler, but if Parkins could not bribe his way free, it seems that I will not."

"What size is your chest?"

"About four feet long, three feet long, less than three feet high. A rounded lid, to keep off the rain."

"The chest itself must weigh forty pounds."

Blackwell shook his head. "It took three men to carry it."

"That will not be easy." I frowned into my beer a moment, and then looked up. "Have you a copy of this document? May I see it?"

Blackwell produced a copy from within his doublet, and I read it over. It purported to be a history of Laelius, one of the empire's most corrupt and invidious rulers, though it took no great discernment to read that Laelius was meant to represent Priscus, and Hortensius the lord chamberlain Scutterfield, Valerius the lord admiral, and so on. The lines were filled with rage when they were not filled with bitterness, and the whole as complete an indictment of the present government as could be made before a judge by the best attorney in the land.

"It is a fine piece of subversion, to be sure," I told Blackwell. "But how am I to aid you in setting free your octavo edition? What can I do that you can't do yourself?"

Blackwell raised his hands in a helpless gesture. "You have a boat, do you not? If you could bring it to the wharf tonight . . ."

"I have a racing galley," said I, "a lightly built vessel which has my manor's name engraved on the stern counter, just under my crest. Even if we could drop your chest of papers into the boat without sinking it, my escape would not be anonymous."

"Well then, I know not what to do."

I looked into his indigo eyes. "You could give up treason and write a play."

Anger settled onto his features. "I am determined to have the poem before the public before the opening of the Estates. I owe it to my lord Scutterfield and his family."

"Can you have the work reprinted by someone in town?"

He shook his head. "The printers here are watched."

"Well." I contemplated Blackwell from over the rim of my beaker. "I will look at this warehouse and see what may be seen."

Blackwell leaped to his feet. "Shall we go now?"

I held up a hand. "Nay, Master Blackwell. I will go tomorrow."

"But—"

"I have business to conduct. But call on me after dinner tomorrow, and I will see what can be done."

Dissatisfied, Blackwell left without finishing his beer. I returned to my ledgers and my correspondence, and just before supper received a command from Lord Edevane to report to his office in the morning.

The game of conspiracy and murder, I thought, was about to begin.

CHAPTER TWENTY-FIVE

Before supper I decided to ride into Howel and view the waterfront to see how well it was guarded. I took my palfrey, and for company's sake Rufino Knott rode behind on a cob. It was a fine autumn day, the air crisp and fine. Now that the harvest was ruined, the foul weather that had flooded the fields and pounded the grain flat had gone, and those who starved now did so in fine weather. The fine wide streets of Howel were as crowded as ever with carts, litters, and carriages, but in the alleys and greens and narrow lanes the poor now thronged. Many seemed to be country people come into the city for want of food, and there was little sign that they were being fed. I gave some money to a poor woman burdened with a pair of babes, and at once a mob of the dispossessed came boiling out at me, hands all outstretched. I had to spur my horse away or be dismembered.

I went past the Hall of Justice, where I found many more heads than when I had left, including those of Chancellor Hulme and his deputy Tryon. I gazed at the eyeless head of the chancellor and wondered if perhaps I was viewing my own future. Certainly, as a self-made man, I had more in common with Hulme than with the better-bred heads on display, and like Hulme I had less protection against my enemies. Perhaps I needed a patron to survive, and perhaps that patron was Edevane.

I was thus in a thoughtful mind when I came down to the docks. The Yeoman Archers were conspicuous in their red bonnets and black leather jerkins, and took an active interest in anything coming off the boats and barges that were sometimes moored three-deep against the quay. The Archers had long since stopped carrying bows and were here armed with halberds and steel-hilted short swords, and they wore sprigs of rosemary in their caps as tokens of mourning for Queen Berlauda. The soldiers being largely unlettered, any shipment of books or papers was set aside for an officer to view. It would be difficult, I thought, to carry a vast chest before these men.

The warehouses were narrow, deep structures of whitewashed stone or brick, two storeys tall, with simple peaked roofs and a sturdy ridgepole that thrust out over the street, with an iron hook for the tackle that would sway cargo up and down. There were one or two wide doors on the ground floor, and another door on the second storey, so that cargo could be swung from the upper floor to the quay below.

I returned to Rackheath House and ate a simple, solitary supper, after which Rufino Knott and I made music. As we played, Knott leaned close to me and said, "Sir, I have discovered one of Darnley's informers in the household."

"Who is it?"

"Parkins, the yeoman of the buttery."

He who refilled the wine-cups, and was in a position to overhear what might be said between myself and my guests.

"I hope he has reported that I instruct the servants to offer a loyalty toast before each meal."

"If he hasn't," said Knott, "I have."

"Very well then."

We played pleasantly for an hour or two, and then I went to bed. Your faint scent still lingered in the sheets, and when I fell into slumber, it brought me sweet dreams.

When I walked through the doors into the palace at Ings Magna, I saw the great marble staircase rise before me, lined on either side by the bright gilt mirrors. It seemed that ages had passed since I'd last been here, though it had been less than a year.

I followed a page up those stairs, turned, and progressed through that long anteroom dominated by shelves filled with documents wrapped in blue and red ribbon. The page took me into Edevane's office, where a fire snapped merrily in his hearth, and he sat behind his desk in a gown of green watered silk. He viewed an orrery, a mechanical model of the sun and planets, with our terraqueous globe in the center surrounded by gears and rods and whirling spheres. I wondered if Edevane was fancying himself as a god in the firmament, with all mortal life at his mercy.

"Is your lordship studying the heavens?" I asked.

"The mechanism is a gift from the grand seneschal of Loretto," Edevane said. "It is ingenious, but useless."

I thought that the same might be said of the grand seneschal, who had proven so inept at finding lodging for Princess Floria, but I did not speak the thought aloud.

"Useless?" said I. "The same might be said of many pretty things. Paintings, tapestries, centerpieces of silver. Yet we fill our houses with them."

"I know of no one, not even Roundsilver, who fills his house with orreries." His lifeless eyes rose from the mechanism to fasten on mine. "May I offer you wine or other refreshment?"

"It is a little early for wine," I said. "I will take small beer, if you have it."

"Please be seated." Edevane gave instructions to the page, then turned again to me. "Have you anything to report?" he asked.

"Ay, as the Warden in Ordinary Against Monsters," said I. "There are a pair of wyverns in the Toppings, and kitlings in Ethlebight. I shall send my deputy to deal with them."

"Wyverns?" he said in his soft, reasoned voice. "Are they not dangerous beasts, like dragons? Should you not go in person?"

"These are small. I have encountered this pair myself, when they were the pets of Sir Basil of the Heugh."

"That robber you killed."

"Ay," said I. "I intended only to capture him, so he might be tried for his crimes, but there was a fight and he died. When he and his band were in the Toppings, he raised the wyverns from eggs, but he abandoned them when he fled, and they are now plundering the cotters' geese and hens."

"And kitlings? What are they?"

"Furry, winged creatures the size of large dormice. They eat rats and other vermin, but they are growing in size and may soon be a menace. It will be a case for nets and traps, I expect."

Edevane tilted his head. "Your plans seem often to go amiss, Lord Warden," he said. "Especially where force is concerned. You wished to capture Sir Basil, but you killed him. You intended to give Sir Brynley a dunking, and instead he drowned. Harvey Meens you wished to spare, and instead he broke his back. Only Sir Edelmir seems to have escaped, and he fled as if the sheriff were after him."

"My plans were fine, I think," said I. "But I admit the failure of execution."

"I trust there will be no more wrathful husbands or brothers?" said Edevane. "At least with Mistress d'Altrey, no male relations will interfere."

I was only a little surprised that Edevane knew about you, and the surprise was only that he had found out so quickly. But then I had kissed you in front of half a dozen servants, and so the whole town had probably found out within hours.

"I am following your advice, my lord," I said.

"I advised you to buy a woman," Edevane said. "It is by far the simplest approach, and is attended by the fewest consequences. But I am glad you are involved with Mistress d'Altrey, for through her you may have access to the household of Her Highness Floria."

"You are still concerned for the princess?"

"Always." The word was very deliberate, and I detected a flash of determination in those dead-fish eyes. "I had hoped you would by this time have information concerning Her Highness."

"She foiled my best efforts by not following me to Loretto."

Edevane allowed annoyance into his soft tone. "Her Highness has left the security of Ings Magna and purchased a house on the lake. It is now more difficult to keep her safe."

I understood "safe" to mean "under Edevane's control," but responded to the more literal meaning. "Well," said I, "I will do my best to preserve her, an she permits it."

Edevane's plans, I thought, had become unmoored. With his facility for discerning in advance the wishes of his superiors, he had assumed Berlauda would view her half-sister as a threat and had been building a case against the princess that might bring her to the scaffold—but now Priscus had offered marriage, and that meant Floria's life was suddenly precious to the monarch, and worth her weight in rubies. Edevane was obliged to treat her as a potential queen while still allowing for the possibility that he might have to arrange for her indictment as a traitor.

"And Countess Marcella?" Edevane demanded. "What information have you about Marcella?"

I looked at him in surprise. The soft, precise voice had disappeared, and he had turned curt and angry.

"I have from Mistress d'Altrey that she sleeps little," I said. "Other than that, nothing."

"I believe she is a complete fraudster," Edevane said. "Over the winter she swindled over five thousand royals from Her Late Majesty."

"Swindled? Do you mean at games?"

"Ay," said Edevane, "for the countess cannot be honest and still win such sums."

"In my experience it is better to be her partner than not," said I. "But in what game did she defraud Queen Berlauda?"

"Cards and hazard both. I do not know the details." Edevane's mouth twitched in what was probably the beginnings of a snarl, but he was too disciplined to allow his anger full expression. "Marcella has notes for the money with Queen Berlauda's hand and seal," he said. "If she presents them to the treasury before the meeting of the Estates, there will be an outcry very inconvenient to the cause of His Majesty."

I recalled how the issue of royal gambling had been raised at the last Estates, and reckoned this would be worse.

"Is there some way to prove fraud?" asked I. "Were there no witnesses?"

I knew Edevane could call up all the witnesses he wanted with a wave of his hand, but they would all be professional informers and perjurers, and it would be hard to rely on such men when arraigning a noblewoman under the protection of a member of the royal family.

Edevane looked at me, and there was a calculation in those dead eyes that sent a chill up my back. "Perhaps you could buy the notes?" he said.

"To be presented to the treasury at a later date, I assume." My words floated into a great silence. I shook my head.

"I would like to oblige your lordship," I said, "but I have little ready money."

The response was quick. "Did you not just have a great ship arrive from Tabarzam?"

I was not surprised that Edevane knew of *Sovereign*'s arrival.

"*Sovereign* brought a rich cargo," said I, "but I cannot sell it for what it's worth. There is famine in the country, and all ready money is caught up in speculation in the grain markets, which drives the price of bread up and up, and the price of everything else down. My goods are intended to adorn the person and enhance the standing of the greatest in the land, but even the greatest have less money now. My own situation is now such that I must borrow to live, and borrow to warehouse my cargo until I can sell it. And of course I own *Sovereign* in partnership with another, and so the profit does not go entirely into my pocket." I waved a regretful hand. "I am sorry that I cannot oblige your lordship, but in these desperate times I am near to drowning in debt. I am living from month to month, and I fear that soon I will be unable to meet my rent on Lord Rackheath's house." I shrugged. "Yet if the prize court in Ferrick can be persuaded to rule on the two prizes taken by my ship *Ostra*, I might be able to purchase some of these notes, though hardly all."

Edevane's tone turned curt. "I trust you will soon pay a call upon the princess," he said. "And now I have other business."

"My lord." I rose, and Edevane held up a hand to prevent me leaving.

"You have a new set of gems, do you not?" he said. "Bring some to my house within the week. I would buy my lady some ornament."

"It would be my pleasure, my lord." I bowed and made my way out. Around me, clerks scribbled with Q Sable Ink and tied the documents with red and blue ribbon. *Blue ribbon is used for matters that are still in progress,* Edevane had said. *Red ribbon for those matters which have reached a happy resolution.*

Ribbon red as a condemned traitor's blood.

Blackwell came to my house after dinner, and I told him what would be required to get his octavo edition free of the warehouse, and then handed him foolscap. "I have writ lines for your crew. You may improve them, but do not lose their sense."

Blackwell scanned the pages. "How am I to find this cast of characters?"

I shrugged. "Are you not a member of an acting troupe? And surely someone in your company knows how to drive a cart."

He knit his brow. "When should this be tried? The dead of night?"

"Tomorrow afternoon, I advise just before the watches change at four. The guards will be tired and hungry and less likely to interfere."

The playwright sighed. "Must it be turnips?"

"Cabbages and neeps are also permissible," said I, "but nothing so small as celeriac or a parsnip."

Blackwell's troupe assembled the next afternoon in a former stable used for rehearsals, a large, open-beamed empty space that smelled of old dust and newly painted scenery. Mountmirail's mechanical dragon hung from the wall on pegs, its fangs bared. Waiting just outside was one of the two-wheeled carts used to shift costumes and scenery from one venue to another. The company were suitably disguised, with Blackwell in a white wig and whitened beard, and his narrow frame bulked out in a suit that made him look like an obese, jolly publican. I, as the most recognizable public figure of the company, had a vast black spade-shaped beard stuck to my face with glue, and a pair of horn spectacles perched on my nose.

We spent the morning in rehearsal, marred somewhat by the clowns, who tried to improve their lines and create new comic business. Blackwell and I both opposed this on the grounds that real laboring men do not display uproarious well-honed routines in the course of their work.

The cart was loaded with burlap bags of turnips and trotted away to the waterfront a quarter-league away. The empty cart was back in half an hour, and the company shared some cider, bread, and cheese while Blackwell sat in a corner, beneath an open window, and penned his next work, sometimes counting out the meter on his fingers—he was experimenting with trochaic tetrameter catalectic.

The guard would change at four o'clock, and so we set out at thirty minutes to the hour. I let the cart and its crew leave first, and then Rufino Knott helped me atop Phrenzy, then leaped upon his cob. I wore a leather jerkin and breeches, carried a whip in a hand marked by a gaudy signet, and affected to be a rustic member of the Burgesses come to town, with Knott my footman in a livery borrowed from the company's costumer.

We ambled through Howel's broad avenues to the docks. The poor and dispossessed were everywhere, haunting the city like a legion of ghosts. When we came to the quay, we saw the cart waiting outside the door of the warehouse, with the driver on the box. Beneath the working man's disguise I recognized Lexter, the young actor who seemed condemned to always play the male ingenue's best friend. A cool, gusting wind plucked at my beard.

The quay was filled with traffic, workers shifting cargo on and off the boats and barges that were packed along the waterfront like sardines. The red bonnets of the Yeoman Archers could be seen up and down the quay, and I saw one of the officers leaning on a bollard while a servant tended to his bay charger. I marked him to approach later and moved down the quay, feigning an inspection of the boats.

My false beard itched like a flea-infested hound, but I was afraid to scratch lest the whiskers detach themselves from my face.

Blackwell stepped out of the warehouse door in his portly-publican guise, and I knew that my little play was about to begin. I turned Phrenzy and rode to within a few paces of the officer, but reined up when Phrenzy's ears pricked up, and I sensed he might be contemplating an assault on the officer's bay charger.

"Pardon me, sir!" I waved my whip at the officer. "Have you seen the barge *Fair Maude*? Captain Whelton?"

He gave me a condescending look. He was one of the handsome

gentlemen with which the late queen liked to surround herself, a lithe, languid young fellow scarcely able to raise a respectable goatee. He clearly considered himself my superior, or at least superior to the rustic squire I was imitating.

"What boat was that?" he asked.

"Fair Maude." I spat out bits of false beard that had pasted themselves against my teeth. "My wife and her sister are aboard. Have you seen them?"

The officer indicated the crowds on the quay. "I have seen many pairs of women today." Over his shoulder I saw a net swing out from the upper storey of the warehouse, a net filled with rough hempen burlap bags. This was quickly lowered to the cart and emptied— though over the shouts and bustle of the crowd I could not hear the lines I'd written, I could nevertheless appreciate the superbly performed bit of comic business that unfolded before me, as Blackwell and another of his troupe collided, and one of the burlap bags spilled its cargo of turnips onto the quay.

There was a shout, a scramble, and laughter from spectators as turnips bounded over the cobbles. Blackwell and his actors dashed to retrieve the turnips, but some vanished beneath the cloaks or skirts of destitute men and women. The officer looked over his shoulder at the chaos, gave a condescending smile, and returned to me.

"I'm afraid I cannot help you, sir," said he.

"My wife is a tall woman," I said helpfully. "She would be wearing one of those new caps, you know, with a feather."

The net rose to the upper floor of the warehouse and was drawn inside to be refilled.

The bag that had spilled had been filled with turnips, and had been spilled deliberately in order to help convince onlookers that *all* the bags were filled with turnips, even though many of them had been stuffed with copies of Blackwell's *The Court of Laelius*, with turnips thrown on top to give the bags the proper irregular shape.

To the officer I continued to describe my supposed wife, giving her dimples, curly hair, large feet, and several chins. The officer seemed to be enjoying the description and did not notice as the net descended a second time to the cart. Blackwell and his group shifted the bags into the cart, and then the net rose again.

A member of the troupe appeared in the door with a burlap bag in his arms. "Here's the last one, sir!" he said, and let it fall.

The cart's box was surrounded by "stakes," that is, upright pieces of wood that rose from the bed and supported horizontal planks that framed the area reserved for cargo. The stakes extended well above the box itself, and could be strung with netting to restrain any large bits of scenery or wardrobes for the troupe's costumes.

No one in the cart was expecting forty pounds of contraband to be dropped on them, and Blackwell dodged the bag that seemed to be aimed for his head. It landed not on the other bags, but on one of the stakes that supported the sides of the cart. The bag burst as it was skewered by the stake, and I saw a perfect white cloud of *The Court of Laelius* rise over the vehicle.

Lexter whipped up his nag before the paper began to settle, and I knew that it was necessary to keep the officer from viewing the cascade of paper. "Now my wife's *sister*, you see," I bellowed, "*also* has large shoes, but not because her feet are big, but because she suffers from *bunions*." But my words were in vain, for the crowd had cried out at the bursting bag, and octavo pamphlets were still drifting toward the ground when the officer turned to see what was the matter. His supercilious, languid pose vanished, and he pointed at the retreating cart.

"You there! *Halt!*"

"What is it?" I cried eagerly. "Is it a thief?" I urged Phrenzy forward, blocking the officer's view—and Phrenzy muttered deep in his throat, a sound akin to the growl of a ban-dog, and then sank his teeth into the hindquarters of the officer's bay charger. The bay gave a shriek and lashed out with both hind feet, and struck Phrenzy on the chest. My steed bellowed a challenge and reared, his forefeet flashing out, and the bay snorted and shifted out of the way. This brought the officer's groom, hanging on to the bay's reins, dangerously within range of Phrenzy's hooves, and he ducked away and tried to calm his animal.

"Curb your horse, sir!" he told me sharply.

I had no chance of controlling Phrenzy whatsoever, but I did my best to imitate a proper equestrian and yanked the reins around while continuing to bellow, *"Is it a thief? Is it a thief?"*

Unfortunately, amid all the chaos, the officer kept his head. He grasped the silver whistle he bore on a chain around his neck, raised it to his lips, and blew. "Halt!" he cried again, and then in an admirably smooth motion leaped into the saddle, gathered the reins in his hands, and spun his horse around.

I kicked Phrenzy forward and blocked the obstinate soldier. "Where is the thief, sir?" I demanded. "I'll thump him for you!"

The officer blew on his whistle again and pointed. In the crowd I saw red bonnets turn, then begin to move toward the cart. The officer guided his horse around Phrenzy, and I kicked Phrenzy into motion again to keep between the officer and Blackwell's burlap bags. The soldier expertly evaded me, and we sped on. The quay was so crowded that it was impossible to gallop, or even to canter, but even at an uneven trot we were faster than the nag drawing the cart. I could hear Rufino Knott's horse clattering right behind me. Dockworkers and costermongers dodged out of our way, but workers with carts, or those hauling cargo, were not so nimble, and we had to evade them. The officer's bay made a beautiful leap clean over an oyster-seller's cart and took the lead.

The fellow was a natural horseman, damn him.

I saw the cart take a right turn toward the center of town, and then, as we approached the turn, the child actor Bonny Joe Webb kicked a football out into the road and led a pack of scrambling children directly into our path. We pulled up, Phrenzy rearing under me while I desperately tried to keep my seat, the officer's bay rearing and screaming alongside. To relieve his feelings, Phrenzy then took another bite out of the bay, which reared again. The officer shouted at the children to get out of the way, but in the end it was a pair of Yeoman Archers on foot who cleared a path, clouting the jeering tykes out of the way with the flats of their swords. I thumped Phrenzy's sides with my heels and managed to steer directly into the officer's path. "Yo-ho!" I cried. "Yoicks!" And thus did I exhaust my entire store of rural expressions.

The cart was visible only distantly, and we were off again. I tried repeatedly to run the officer into one of the trees that lined the avenue, or into one of the hawkers' carts that were set up in the shade, but he expertly avoided me. He drew his sword. "Block me again, sir," he said, "and I shall strike at you!"

I thought it was civil of him to put it that way. Though as a supposed country squire I carried a sword, I had no intention of fighting him, which would give me the choice of dying immediately by the sword, or dying later on the scaffold. Instead I beat Phrenzy's flanks with my heels and gave my charger his head. Phrenzy roared down the street like a comet, streaming his tail behind him and scattering lesser stars and planets out of his way. I spat out bits of false beard that were trying to crawl down my throat, and as I came up on the cart, I saw Blackwell in the back, sitting on burlap bags and clinging wide-eyed to one of the stakes. His white wig was askew, and its curls blew in his face. I heard the officer's horse clattering up behind me. I brandished my whip at Blackwell, as if I were about to thrash him, and said, "Hand me a turnip, for Eidrich's sake!"

He stared at me, but then rummaged into a bag and produced a large turnip, which he tossed to me. I caught it with some difficulty, then looked over my shoulder to see the officer just behind. The wind tore my beard from one cheek. I flung the turnip at the officer and struck him full in the face, knocking him back over the charger's croup, his booted legs flung high in the air. Rufino Knott, just behind, had to exert himself not to run the man over.

Not bad, I thought, for an over-the-shoulder throw.

I could see a mob of red caps running behind, and thought they might just be persistent enough to catch the cart. "More turnips!" I called. "Find a bag with nothing but turnips!"

Blackwell complied. "Free food!" I bellowed, and waved my whip. "Free food for all!"

The playwright emptied the bag onto the road, the turnips bounding in our wake. A double wave of starving people swarmed onto the pavement from both sides of the avenue. "More!" I told Blackwell.

More turnips were flung from the cart, along with one parcel of *The Court of Laelius*. The pursuing Yeoman Archers ran into the crowd of scavengers and then came to a slow halt, as if they'd sunk up to their ankles in a marsh. When the cart was out of turnips, we turned into a side street and made our way, by devious ways, to the old stable where the troupe conducted its rehearsals.

I tore my bushy disguise from my face. The octavo edition was fetched out of the remaining bags, and the sweating horses were walked until they cooled, and then given water. I tried to wash the gum off my face, with mixed success. Those left behind on the docks arrived in ones and twos, and included at the last the careless man who had flung the bag down on the stake and put us all in mortal danger. He was met with hisses and catcalls worthy of an audience of groundlings, but at least all had escaped in the confusion. Now the troupe lifted their cups of cider and rejoiced.

"We shall repaint the cart," Blackwell pronounced, "before we let it be seen again in public." He was free of his bulky costume and had resumed both his bladelike form and his youth. He turned to me and clasped my hand. "I owe you a great debt," he said. "And yet I do not know why you chose to help me. We are friends, but not companions of the heart, and you expressed little sympathy for my efforts. You are in the House of Burgesses now, and surely such an exploit put you in danger."

"I do not know that I had any reason at all," I confessed, "but that I went to the docks and saw a way to do it—and once I made that plan, I could not prevent myself from attempting it."

"Well, I owe you a great debt. I hope you will call on me if you need any help."

"You may regret that offer," said I, "for I may call on you sooner than you think."

Knott and I left after an hour and made our way by the more obscure streets to Rackheath House, where I found you waiting for me in my parlor. And so we had a merry time together, and did not part till dawn.

CHAPTER TWENTY-SIX

I t is a sensation, to be sure," said His Grace of Roundsilver. "But the hunt is up for the author, and if he has sense, he will be in hiding."

"Perhaps we will see him in the gallery of the Burgesses," said I, "making notes for a sequel."

"I hope he will not be so bold," said Roundsilver. "There have been enough men delivered to the scaffold this season."

I wondered how His Grace would react if he found out that the author of *The Court of Laelius* was a member of his own company of players.

Blackwell's satire had, as predicted, become widely read by people who could never admit to owning or seeing a copy. *Laelius* was the talk of the capital, though most of the talk took place behind closed doors.

"I have seen works purporting to be sequels," Roundsilver said. "And the original was first seen this last week."

We were in the game room of Rackheath House, my guests assembling before going to the hall for one of my Savory Dinners. Meat and fowl of high quality were now easy to find, and at low prices, but for a melancholy reason. Due to the disastrous harvest, there was not enough fodder to maintain the herds over the winter, and they were being sold off, probably at a loss.

I wondered if the poor scarecrow scavengers who thronged the city could now buy a cutlet for less money than a loaf of bread. I hoped so, for these displaced country folk were desperate. I contributed to several charities that distributed food to them, and donated as well the broken meats from my own table.

The duke sipped from his silver goblet. He had come for the Estates, and a meeting of the Great Council, and I thought he would not enjoy either. He had left behind in Selford his duchess and the infant Marquess of Ethlebight, and I imagine he hoped to return as quickly as he could. He was here for business and business only.

"The verse," said I, "was more than serviceable. Approaching genius in places, if you like invective."

"I hear enough invective at court," said the duke. "I need not read it in a pamphlet."

Sir Cecil Greene, burgess for Ethlebight, approached and bowed. "Your Grace," he said. "You are discussing *Laelius*?"

"The topic seems unavoidable," said Roundsilver.

"It is a work of the most exquisite poison," said Greene. "I hope it may set blood afire throughout the realm."

"I wish for peace and good hap," said the duke. "I hope we may avoid blood, fiery or not."

"Then we must unite," said Greene. "We must be firm about the misuse of the treason court. We must demand that the viceroy inform the Estates concerning the state of the war, including all the other nations that are leagued against us, and how our soldiers have fared in battle. And as for Edevane's extortion—I heard that Thistlegorm bought his own head for twenty-five thousand royals."

"It was thirty thousand," said the duke. "I had it from that lord's own lips."

Greene puffed out his cheeks in amazement. For thirty thousand, the attorney general had been allowed to resign rather than be condemned by the Siege Royal. He was too prominent a Retriever, walking the palace in his white doublet and trunks at a time when other Retrievers were losing their heads.

"Edevane has allowed others to purchase immunity," Greene said. "Gregory, Coleman, and Judge Hawthorne, who presided at the Siege Royal until it became dangerous for Retrievers to walk beneath the sun. But Thistlegorm . . ." He nodded at Roundsilver. "His fall is a pistol pointed at the head of all the peers."

"That pistol was Scutterfield," said I.

Though in truth the misuse of the treason court was not clear in law. Torture was illegal in Duisland, and always had been, and so was the sort of arbitrary justice produced at the Siege Royal. But it had also been accepted that, in times when the state was under threat, such practices were necessary for the salvation of the nation and its monarch. The Pilgrim knew that history provided enough examples of deep-laid conspiracy at court, and so the Siege Royal was allowed to exist, as long as it operated quietly and only in times of great danger. But once tradition accepted an institution like the Siege Royal, then who was to say how often the treason court could sit and dispense its judgment?

"And now the Commission of Inquiry," said Greene. "What right has the viceroy to regulate the Pilgrim's worship, let alone execute poor monks who preach in public squares? Who has authorized this commission, and who paid its members? It was not the Estates."

"I think—" began the duke.

But we were never to know what the duke thought, because at that moment Floria entered the room with her train of ladies. She was ablaze in that dark company, her satin gown white as that of a Retriever, for while the rest of us dressed in the black of mourning, the royal family wore white when mourning their own. White diamonds and white pearls were sewn over the gown, and over the headdress that framed her face. Her disorderly hair was caught in a white snood, and her jewelry was of silver ornamented with white gems.

We bowed, and I approached Floria's presence. "Welcome to my house, Your Highness," said I. "You honor me with your presence, and truly you thrive in shade."

I caught your haughty smirk over Floria's head, your amusement at the conventions of my obeisance.

"Thank you, Sir Quillifer," said Floria. Amusement glittered in her hazel eyes. "If you were discussing *The Court of Laelius*, pray continue, for I seek enlightenment as to some of its allegories. Am I represented in the work as Horatia, do you think, or as Primula?"

"Neither, Highness," said I. "I think you are that lady confined in the tower, struck dumb by the gods."

"Struck dumb?" Floria's eyes widened. "That hardly seems like me."

"Though if you are not in the poem at all," offered the duke, "it is the greatest compliment, for everyone else is blackguarded."

"In truth, Your Grace," said Floria, "by now I have been blackguarded often enough that I can now hope only to be blackguarded in an interesting or amusing way."

I looked up and saw the angular astronomer Edith Ransome numbered among Floria's ladies. "Mistress Ransome," I said. "Welcome to my house. I had thought by now you would be viewing the stars with your quadrant."

"The summer storms were fatal to the project," said she. "A flood swept down from the hills and destroyed the quadrant before it could be completed."

"I hope you will be able to rebuild it in a more waterless place."

Her thin lips crooked in a smile. "Her Highness very kindly assured me that this would be the case."

"I am glad you are here, for I wish to introduce you to a friend of mine, who has brought a sample of a new astronomical machine."

Mistress Ransome's brows knit. "It is not in aid of horoscopes, is it?" asked she. "Because I am merciless about horoscopes."

"It is about navigation."

Floria interrupted. "If we are going to discuss navigation," she said, "then I should like a glass of wine before we begin."

"Of course. I fear I am a lax host, Highness." I gestured to the yeoman of the buttery, who arrived at once to ask Her Highness's pleasure. Wine being fetched for Floria and her ladies, I introduced Mistress Ransome to Alaron Mountmirail, who bowed over her hand.

"Master Mountmirail has invented a new engine for use in navigation," I explained. "I thought it might be useful in astronomy as well, though I am not competent to judge."

Mountmirail's moon face split into a huge grin. "I recently had occasion to sail to and from Ethlebight," he said. "And I observed the navigator working with his cross-staff in order to determine the latitude. And the navigator was young, but going blind."

"Which is often the case," said I, "for when doing the noon sight, the cross-staff requires the navigator to stare directly into the sun."

"That is why I use a pinhole," said Edith Ransome.

"This navigator did also," said Mountmirail. "But still his vision was fading. So I had an idea—if you will forgive me, ladies—"

He went into my study to bring out his instrument. It seemed somewhat crude, for he'd made it himself, in his own workshop.

"Rather than stare into the sun," he said, "this employs the sun's *shadow*."

It was a long staff with an upright piece and a long curved scale on the end. "You hold it thus," Mountmirail said, "with the sun behind you. You sight along the horizon through the hole at the end. Then the sun casts the shadow of the upright piece—I call it a 'gnomon' onto the curved scale, and its altitude is revealed."

"May we try this out of doors?" asked Mistress Ransome.

Mountmirail, Floria, and her ladies trooped onto the lawn, which, despite the arrival of autumn, still made a carpet of unbroken green descending to the lake. A cool breeze ruffled the surface of the water. Mountmirail demonstrated his machine, and then Edith Ransome took the device and attempted to work it. "The sun is too high," she said. "We are near noon. I can't view the horizon and keep the gnomon's shadow on the scale."

"Ah. Then you must deploy the swing-arm."

I watched delight break out on Mistress Ransome's beaky face as Mountmirail demonstrated his device. Floria walked up to my elbow and spoke in a low tone. "Well, you have enchanted Mistress Ransome," she said. "And of course you have debauched another of my ladies. Have you plans for any of the others?"

I nodded. "I was going to advise Countess Marcella to bring those bills of hers to the treasury, before the government finds some way to prevent her."

"Bills?"

I explained to Floria that her sister had lost over five thousand royals to Marcella, who had her notes of hand complete with Berlauda's seal. Floria received this news without surprise.

"Or perhaps her ladyship should sell them to a broker at a small discount," said I, "and let the broker then worry about collecting—of course she must find a broker who has that sort of money on hand. In any case, it should be done soon."

"It would be a great embarrassment to the government," said Floria, her tone offhand.

"I'm afraid it would be."

Floria's countenance was inscrutable. "I shall pass your message on to the countess," said she.

"Your servant," said I.

"That leaves Mistress Tavistock." She nodded at her fourth lady, she of the charming overbite. "Have you plans for her?"

"Should I?"

"I hope you do not. She is engaged to marry Lord Mellender, which is a very good match for her. I cannot tell from your history whether marriage will make her more attractive to you or not, but in either case I urge you to refrain."

I bowed. "Chenée Tavistock I shall worship only from afar," I said.

"I am heartily glad to hear it," said she. "It is tiresome enough hearing Mistress d'Altrey forever singing your virtues, and urging me to make use of you for I know not what project."

I was very flattered that I had been hymned in this way, but I responded lightly.

"A project? I hope to build a canal from Ethlebight to another harbor on the coast."

"Ay? You have once more adopted a new occupation? Well, that will keep you out of mischief here in the capital."

I nodded at the engineer. "Master Mountmirail was supposed to be working on the canal when he decided to invent his astronomical engine. His mind flies from one thing to another like one of his mechanical birds."

"And I imagine you have found a way to profit by that astronomical engine," Floria said.

"I intend to manufacture them," I said, "and pay Mountmirail a fee for the right to do so." I shook my head. "He is brilliant, but has only a primitive idea of commerce. He would give away all his ideas if he could."

"How lucky that you are here to see to his interests."

I gave her a sharp look, and she returned a serene smile. "Tell me about this canal. But I'm not dressed for the outdoors, so let's leave our astronomers and go inside."

"Of course, Highness." We left Mountmirail chatting happily with Mistress Ransome, and as we strolled back to the house, I told her how I hoped to save my native city. "But no one knows how to build a canal," I said.

"Of course we do," Floria said. "Howel is full of canals."

"But they are ditches that connect two bodies of water that are at the same level. The Ethlebight Canal will have to go up and down hills using locks, which we don't know how to build. But Mountmirail tells me that the real problem will be the danger of the water leaking out."

Floris looked at me in surprise. "Leaking out? Water does not leak out of the canals in Howel."

"Nay," said I, "but that water is the same level as the lake, or the Dordelle, and these are the same level as the water below the soil. There is no place for the water to leak *to*, for below the ground everything is wet. Whereas if we are to build a canal where the water flows above the level of the water under the ground, the water will ooze out unless we seal the canal with some kind of impermeable substance."

I was about to step ahead to open a door for Her Highness, but my footmen were alert and swept open the doors and bowed as Floria passed. As she walked into the game room, she gestured to the yeoman of the buttery, who refilled her goblet. She took a sip, then turned again to me.

"What sort of impermeable substance?" she asked.

"The old Aekoi engineers lined their canals with a kind of mortar that repelled water," said I, "and you can see this in the old canals that survive in Bonille, but the secret of its manufacture is lost. I had thought about lining the canal with Ethlebight brick, but bricks must be fixed with mortar, and if the mortar is washed away, the canal will still fail."

"Master Mountmirail admits he has no solution?"

"The canal could be lined with clay," I said, "but the clay would have to be renewed every few years as it washed away. But Mountmirail will begin work on the problem once I have built him a lime kiln, and I'm confident he will find a solution before the first spadeful of earth is turned."

Floria smiled. "It must be useful to have such a prodigy in your service."

I waved a dismissive hand. "He is not in my service, Highness. He labors for me only so long as I provide interesting work for him. And if you look for genius, have you not Edith Ransome?"

"She is brilliant, ay. But her interests and conclusions are of little practical use to me. Whereas you will get a canal, an astronomical engine to sell to every mariner in creation, and ink in bottles." She sipped her wine again, and then the dinner gong rang. She touched my arm. "Perhaps I will sponsor this canal of yours, Quillifer. But you will have to forego your plans to name the canal after yourself, and instead name it after me."

I was so astonished that it took me a moment to recover. "Your name may grace the project, of course. Though I had no plans to name the canal after myself."

Floria's eyes widened in feigned surprise. "How unlike you, Quillifer, not to trumpet yourself. Are you sure you are feeling entirely well?"

Roundsilver approached to take Floria into dinner. She took his arm, then turned to me. "I desire immortality, Quillifer," she said. "And if it must come in the form of an astronomical observatory and a stretch of water, then I will take what I can."

Between my duties as host, the discussion of *Laelius* and politics, and the necessity of explaining the canal project to possible investors, I was unable to find a private moment with you till the afternoon was far advanced. I found you in a corner of a parlor, and I hastened to embrace you and feast upon your lips. "Can you stay the night?" I asked.

"Floria will have us all return in a body," you said. "She will not have it said that she lost one of her ladies at a gentleman's house."

"You would not be lost," said I, "for I would keep you under my eye every moment you are here."

You smiled and kissed my nose. "Yet I must attend Her Highness tonight. I might have some time free tomorrow afternoon, and I will send a message if I can call upon you." You freed yourself from my arms and adjusted your myrrh-scented hair.

I told you that Floria had offered to sponsor the canal, and you laughed. "I have been urging her to make use of you, and now you make use of her. The canal will provide your excuse to visit us, and so we two may see each other all the more."

"And without the tedious necessity of my seducing a royal princess," said I, "and as a consequence, being condemned to death."

You gestured with your fan. "We may keep that plan in reserve then," you said. "For there is no gain without risk."

CHAPTER TWENTY-SEVEN

Two days later I called upon my lord Edevane at his home and sold him some gems. I asked more money than was usual for me, and rejoiced in depriving him of some of the profits of his extortion schemes. He dressed grandly in black velvet and sat enthroned in his cabinet, surrounded by chalices of gold, mirrors framed in silver, and carvings of ivory and alabaster. Costly carpets were piled on the floor, and the impression was that his house was worth a lord's ransom—Lord Thistlegorm's, as it might be. An angry light shone behind Edevane's spectacles, for he was livid that Countess Marcella had presented her bills to the treasury, and that word of Berlauda's extravagant losses had reached the people. "This is what I most feared," he said, "that Her Highness Floria is subject to the daily influence of this creature who cheated Her Majesty."

"Her Majesty has passed from this world, along with her extravagance," I said. "There will be other issues raised by the Estates." I looked at him. "For instance, my lord—is it true that we are now at war with Sélange and its four allies?"

The light behind the spectacles faded, and I repressed a chill as those dead eyes sought mine. "Where have you heard that?" he asked.

"There is free passage between Loretto and Duisland," I said, "and news does not stop at the border."

"Floria's ladies, I'll warrant," said he. "Countess Marcella again."

"I did not have it from her," said I. "But if it were intended to be a secret, it is the worst-kept secret in the world."

Edevane pursed his lips in thought and tapped the fingers of his left hand against the fingers of his right. "The viceroy will not be pleased," he murmured.

I wondered now at the precise nature of Edevane's position. For his post was that of principal private secretary to Queen Berlauda, and Berlauda was dead. It might be argued that his position had died with her, but yet he remained in his office at Ings Magna, and continued to manage the documents wrapped in red and blue ribbon. His position depended on the continued favor of King Priscus and his viceroy, the abbot Fosco, and delivering bad news was notoriously a way to lose favor.

"I have also obtained a means to regularly access Her Highness's house," I said.

"Besides Mistress d'Altrey?" His tone was ill-tempered.

I told him of my canal project, and how Floria had suggested she might sponsor the work. "Should the bill for the canal pass the Estates, and receive the royal assent," said I, "I will be making reports to Her Highness on the progress of the work, and have every excuse to be in her household."

His ill-tempered tone did not fade with this news. "And what will the canal cost the crown?" he asked.

"Not a penny," said I. "We would not bother the government at all, if it were not for the matter of receiving permission to purchase right-of-way along the line of the canal."

He regarded me with his cold eyes. "You have not the funds to buy those notes of Marcella's," he said, "and yet you plan to build a canal."

I donned my innocent-choirboy face. "My lord," I said, "I did not say I would build it with *my* money. I propose to recruit investors, largely from those merchants of Ethlebight who will profit most from the project." I inclined my head toward Edevane. "You might consider investing yourself, my lord."

"My interests are closer to home than Ethlebight," said he.

"As you wish, my lord."

Again he tapped his fingers together. "His Majesty desires twenty-five thousand new troops," he said. "We assume the government can count on your vote."

I noted the royal "we" and replied. "I will do everything I can to oblige His Majesty. But before they send more troops, the Estates may wish a reckoning of what happened to the last batch."

Edevane chose not to respond, but instead dismissed me with the wave of a ring-bedecked hand. "Come to me when you have news."

I rose and bowed. "Your servant," I said, and made my way out. As I passed through the parlor, I found waiting the Count of Wenlock, his black mourning dress a contrast to the brilliance of Edevane's tapestries, carpets, and mirrors. His hands crumpled his cap, working at it like a baker kneading dough. I nodded.

"I believe you still owe me twenty-five royals," I said.

A cold light glittered from his blue eyes. "I spent it repairing the boat you wrecked," he said.

"Well, it would be tedious to call all the witnesses to testify to the wager," I said, and then turned my eyes deliberately to the door of Edevane's study. "Yet it would be a shame to have to inform your master that you are not a man of your word."

The red of rage filled Wenlock's face, but before he could say anything more, Edevane's page came to announce that Edevane would see him. I made my own way out.

The Estates would meet the next day, and we would see if Fosco could manage them any better than Priscus had.

The previous autumn I had ridden as part of an armored column to the House of Peers, a thousand men clad in steel thundering down the avenues of Howel as escort to King Priscus while the crowd cheered and waved banners and handkerchiefs. This year the column of riders came with Viceroy Fosco to the Estates, but I was not among them, and instead waited for them inside the House of Burgesses. The old college hall was surprisingly small, its five hundred members crowded nearly atop one another, and the old tapestries on the walls made it dark. The venerable oaken benches, carved with the initials and mottoes of long-dead Burgesses, were long and hard, and each member brought his own cushion, and some brought footstools. As a new member, my bench was high up in the chamber, where I had a very good view of the coffered ceiling, with its tessellations and gilt rosettes, and could look straight down at the wan winter light gleaming on the Speaker's bald head.

The visitors' gallery was nearly empty, for no business would be conducted in the house that day.

I had nothing to do, so I made the acquaintance of the members around me. One had a flask of brandy, which he shared, and so we passed the time pleasantly till the herald of brass pounded on the door and was turned away, to be followed by the herald of silver and the herald of gold, at which point we rose and walked in procession to the House of Peers. We walked along practically under the noses of the mounted force that had come with the viceroy, and if the purpose of those stern knights in armor was to intimidate the Burgesses, they certainly succeeded, at least in my case. They were in a bad temper, for unlike the previous year there had been no cheers from the meiny, no waving of handkerchiefs, nothing but jeers and sour looks. I remembered Greene saying that the Burgesses could not be ruled through terror, and I maintained a blithe countenance, and waved a greeting when I recognized a face beneath the visor of the helmet.

The House of Peers is a motley, shambling structure, very old and rather dirty, but it has one magnificent feature, which is the great hall in which the peers sit. The hammer-beam roof with its gilt carvings rises thirty yards or more from the paving, and frames the huge canopy of scarlet and gold that overhangs the throne. There Fosco sat, in dark, silken monk's robes, with the white rod of his office in a hand glittering with jeweled rings. He was flanked by the seated peers, two hundred or more, all wearing their coronets and their red, ermine-trimmed robes. Among them were a few in the robes of monks, for abbots of some of the oldest monasteries were ranked among the peers. The scent of olibanum wafted on the air, from a ceremony that had been performed earlier.

We Burgesses, in our black, clustered before the Bar of the House like a murder of crows. We were permitted to go no farther than the Bar, and no chairs were provided for us, so we remained on our feet for the entire ceremony.

The Speaker bowed to the viceroy as a signal that the Burgesses were prepared to hear the latter's address. Fosco rose and began to read his speech aloud.

His command of the Duisland tongue was uncertain, and he had a strong accent that at times made it impossible to make out exactly what he was saying. But most of his speech was plain enough to his listeners, for he spoke without the rhetorical flourishes that a native politician might employ, and his message was direct.

Duisland was at war, he said, and its king in the field with his army. In order to bring the war to a successful conclusion, His Majesty required twenty-five thousand more troops, plus supply and cannon and transport. The Estates were enjoined to provide these, and to make certain they were paid for.

As the previous year's taxes were in arrears, the government would introduce reforms in the collection of revenue to make certain that these new taxes would be collected.

In addition, the government intended to introduce a new bill making it treason to publish libels against the government. It was already illegal to libel the crown, of course, with the penalties ranging from fines to prison to the pillory, but the new law was clearly aimed at the author of *Laelius*, and at bringing him to the scaffold to be torn to pieces by the executioner. I worried for Blackwell, for it was clear that the government's hunt would be thorough and prolonged; but I feared also for anyone who dared to criticize Priscus or Fosco by any means whatever.

The virtue of Fosco's address was that it was short, after which Lord Chancellor Oldershaw thanked the viceroy, and the Burgesses were dismissed to return to our own chamber. After which we held our adjournment, and I went to the quay where my galley waited, and was taken to the house of Her Highness Floria, a small, shabby old palace called Wenweyn Hall, which would require a good deal of work before it was truly a suitable lodge for a member of the royal family. My crew was made welcome in the servants' hall while I told Floria about the viceroy's speech. You were present, of course, along with Mistress Tavistock and Countess Marcella, who asked a number of questions about our Estates, to compare it with the ancient senate of her own country.

"It is good that you have come, Quillifer," Floria told me. "The viceroy does not consult me on these matters, and I am as ignorant of the political life of the capital as a country squire from the West Range."

I think that was not precisely true, for I was not the only visitor. Roundsilver arrived, and that Lord Mellender who was engaged to marry Chenée Tavistock, along with a few barons, a count and countess, and a marchioness or two. Princess Floria, in her stainless white satin gown, began to look like the shining monarch at the center of a miniature court.

Floria led the party into the game room. It was then that I was finally able to speak to you alone, as we faced each other over a game of bagatelle. "You said that Her Highness didn't wish to lose a lady at the home of a gentleman," I said. "I wonder if you can contrive to lose yourself here, for the space of a few hours?"

"It would be noted if we vanished together."

"I believe our love is hardly a secret."

"Secret or not, I prefer not to behave scandalously in front of others. And I know Floria wouldn't like it."

I sighed. "What is the point of having a liaison known to everyone, if we can never actually liaise?" "Liaise" being a word I invented on the spot.

I took a shot, and my ball bounced off the pins and came to a rest more or less where it had started. Triumph glittered in your black eyes, and you readied your cue.

"Let us play another hour or so," you said, "and then I will claim fatigue and withdraw. You will play on for a while, but at five o'clock I will meet you on the quay, and then your galley may carry us to whatever pleasures the evening may offer."

And then you struck the ball with your cue, and it sank into the hole for eight points.

There were a surfeit of delights upon our return to my house, but one was unexpected, and that was a bill on the Bank of Howel from the Count of Wenlock for my twenty-five royals. His fear of Edevane had caused him to open his purse, and I began to think how we might best enjoy this unexpected bounty.

"I would like to propose to this house," said Umbrey, "that the bill under consideration be tabled for the present, until the crown answereth those questions which perplex our members."

Umbrey, the merchant from Selford, stood beneath the coffered ceiling of the House of Burgesses, prepared as he had been before to lead the opposition to the government.

"We desire to know how many nations oppose us in the field. Is it one? Six? Ten?" He made a grand gesture. "And have there not been battles? Battles at Diewil, at Monsour, at Mont Arlen, at Mennhaym, at Thurnhout? What were the results of these battles, and how many of our country were engaged, and how many were killed and wounded? Since His Majesty's glorious success in his campaign this last winter, is it true that the fortunes of war have not favored us, and that we now fight on the defensive? When does His Majesty propose to bring the war to a victorious conclusion—will there be need for more troops next year, and the year after?"

The new chancellor of the exchequer, an infestulous little man named Morley, glared at Umbrey from across the aisle. He had laid the bill for the soldiers and new taxes before the house, and now Umbrey was proposing to ignore it.

Umbrey pointedly spurned Morley, his gaze passing over him as if he were invisible, and Umbrey's voice rose to fill the great echoing space of the chamber. "Why are enemy privateers allowed to plague our coasts without opposition from the navy? Why do our naval ships remain in port while the enemy carries away our shipping from under their very noses? Why have we lost two hundred thousand in commerce to these raids, and why must our merchants bribe our naval officers in order to provide an escort for their ships?"

Some of Morley's placemen hissed and booed at this slur on the naval service, but Umbrey, sure of his facts, ignored them. Morley had been lavish with his bribes and offers of office, but there were over five hundred Burgesses, and Morley lacked the resources to bribe all of us.

"Hath His Majesty plans for relieving the tens of thousands of his subjects who stare into the face of starvation? Hath grain been purchased? Is grain being distributed?"

Then Umbrey squared his shoulders and planted his feet firmly on the floor of the chamber. He looked directly at Morley.

"And furthermore," he said, "how doth His Majesty's government justify the execution of monks for preaching the word of the Compassionate Pilgrim? Two holy men have been killed at the command of this Commission of Inquiry, a commission that has not been authorized by the Estates. And yet public money supports this commission, and this money has not been voted by the Burgesses."

Morley rose to answer. "The Commission of Inquiry it not a department of His Majesty's government. It is not a ministry. It is an organization completely its own, created by private members of the clergy who are concerned by a lack of uniformity in worship."

Morley barely got the words out before he was drowned in laughter. His claim was ludicrous.

Umbrey's body seemed to inflate, as if with triumph. He appeared to loom over Morley, though they were on opposite sides of the aisle and at least three yards apart. A wide, disdainful grin spread over Umbrey's dark face. "If His Majesty's government did not authorize the Commission of Inquiry, or the execution of those monks, then the commissioners are guilty of murder. I move that this house issue warrants for the arrest of these commissioners, so they may be brought to the bar of justice."

This was too much for Morley, and he leaped to his feet shouting, and so the day went on. The crown's proposal for more soldiers was ignored as the Burgesses wrangled over Umbrey's questions. The party of the crown had no answers, and the viceroy's partisans tried to replace answers by shouting and abuse. Witnessing the wrangles made me think of how much it was a grave mistake for the government to have executed Hulme and Tryon, as they had managed the Burgesses much better than Edevane's pitiable minions. In contrast Umbrey, along with Ethlebight's representative, Sir Cecil Greene, had their own faction well in hand.

By the end of the day, a motion had passed that the series of questions posed by Umbrey would be sent to the viceroy for his comment. Warrants would be sent to the sheriff for the arrest of the Commission of Inquiry.

I did not speak, as I was far too junior in this assembly to be taken seriously by anyone. In addition, I had no desire to argue in favor of the crown's absurdities.

Nor was I obliged to vote. No one on the government side dared to call for a division, as it would only call attention to how badly they were outnumbered, and so the Speaker—the sweat that glistened on his bald pate a clear sign of his reluctance—declared that the house was in agreement. Greene was deputed to write the inquiry that would go to the viceroy, and Umbrey himself wrote the warrants to bring the commissioners before the bar.

The Burgesses adjourned in mid-afternoon, and again I went to Her Highness's house, where others had already assembled. It was then I learned of the wrangles that had gone on in the House of Peers.

The peers had raised many of the same issues as the Burgesses, but they were also concerned with violations of what they considered to be their own privilege. For when Scutterfield, Hulme, and the lord high admiral had been found guilty by the Siege Royal, it was a violation of the traditional right of the peers to be judged by those of their own rank.

Lord Chancellor Oldershaw managed the peers better than Morley had the Burgesses, but he was even more outnumbered, for the peers were nearly unified against the crown. The attack on the government was led by Lord Scarnside, the premier baron of Bonille, with whom I'd had that disagreeable encounter the day of the horse-ballet, and by Lord Slaithstowe, who had briefly been attorney general under Queen Berlauda. Slaithstowe could dispute fine points of law with the chancellor, while Scarnside could outshine anyone in point of pride. His effortless conceit and self-regard raised the peers in defense of their dignity, tradition, and honor, while Slaithstowe demolished the government's justifications.

Not only did the peers pass a bill making the peers immune to any court but themselves, they insisted that peers not be judged, as was customary, by a jury chosen from their number by the lord chancellor, but by the entire body of the peers sitting together. Which meant of course that no peer would ever be convicted of anything, for peer families were so interconnected by marriage and interest that they would never vote to condemn one another.

As for the rest of us, apparently we could continue to be murdered by the treason court. That was none of the peers' affair.

The peers also petitioned the crown that the young Prince Aguila be raised in Duisland, and his welfare and education supervised by a board of governors chosen from the greatest men in the realm, which is to say themselves.

The peers did not offer comment on the war, which they viewed as the king's affair, or taxes, because taxes were the business of the Burgesses.

Her Highness Floria had so many callers, and their dissection of the day's events was so excited and so intricate, that I never had the opportunity to speak with you in private, but only to yearn at you from over the heads of the others.

You were amused, I think, but nevertheless I hope you appreciated the sincerity of my devotion.

When we Burgesses reported to our house the next morning, the serjeant-at-arms informed us that our sitting was delayed till noon. The reason for this was soon apparent, for a number of Burgesses had traveled to the house by way of the Hall of Justice, where they found the heads of Greene and Umbrey mounted on pikes and dripping upon the paving-stones.

I remembered Greene's words to me in Ethlebight: *The viceroy cannot rule the Burgesses through terror.* Apparently we would find out if he could.

A number of Umbrey's faction, fearing the Siege Royal, vanished into the town. The rest of us waited and watched the peers troop past in their carriages, for they were not being kept out of their own chamber.

I thought about my part in the business of *The Court of Laelius*, and I briefly considered joining the flight of Umbrey's faction, but decided that I should avoid anything like the appearance of guilt. No one had yet seen Blackwell's head on a pike. Yet fear crept on soft feet along my spine as I entered the Burgesses at noon and saw that the scarlet-and-gold royal canopy that normally graced the peers had been set up in our house, and that a throne sat beneath it.

A deadly silence filled the chamber, broken only by the shuffling of feet as the Burgesses moved to their places. I took my high seat just below the coffered ceiling, and all waited in silence.

The silence was broken by the opening of the door behind the throne and the marching in of half a dozen of the Yeoman Archers, each carrying a halberd. After they had grounded their arms, Viceroy Fosco swept in. He paused before the throne for a moment, his long white staff in his hand, his dark eyes narrowed and suspicious, his falcon nose raised high as if to sniff out subversion. Most of us took off our caps in the presence of the representative of majesty, though a few kept their caps defiantly on their heads.

I did not want to die for a cap, and so I removed my own.

Fosco continued to glare at us for a while, and then sat on the throne, his white staff draped over the crook of his elbow. The Speaker announced to us all what was perfectly obvious, that the viceroy wished to address the house, and formally invited Fosco to speak. Fosco removed papers from his robes and began his speech in a sharp, angry tone.

"It has come to the attention of the government that treason has been practiced in this house," said he. "The Siege Royal has acted to curb this danger, and now the traitors Umbrey and Greene have even been executed. Lord Slaithstowe and Lord Scarnside have been removed to Murkdale Hags for interrogation."

Fosco's fury made his hand tremble, and his papers shivered before his eyes. He flapped the pages out once or twice, then refocused his attention on his script.

"The House of Burgesses has in its insolence voted to send a list of questions to the throne. We are pleased to answer them now."

He let one of his papers drift to the floor, and he read from the next.

"The aspersions against the officers of the navy were libels," he said, "and the libelers have now been executed."

He frowned down at his pages. "It is not the business of the crown to relieve the hunger of paupers," he said. "If we purchase grain, we purchase it not for paupers, but for servants of the state. If paupers need relief, private charity, the city corporations, and the county officials are competent to execute this function."

He looked up, his dark eyes passing over the sullen faces of the members. "The war and its conduct lie within the privilege of His Majesty," he said, "and I charge the Burgesses not to meddle with it."

The viceroy smiled then, but the smile was so distorted it may as well have been a sneer. "The Burgesses have done us the inestimable favor to point out that irregularities existed in the creation of the Commission of Inquiry. We now will correct this by placing a bill before you that will regularize the commission, and grant immunity for any mistakes they may have made in the past."

He gave a nod to the Speaker. "Master Speaker, you have our leave to continue."

The Burgesses then, under the Speaker's direction, passed all the legislation the viceroy desired. The king got his twenty-five thousand soldiers—and I thought he would have little trouble recruiting

so many, for many were starving, and soldiers in the army are supposed to be fed. The law equating libel with treason was passed. The
Commission of Inquiry was officially established, and the commissioners forgiven their usurpations and murders. There was no vote
on any of these bills, for no one dared to call for a division, and the
bills were recorded as being passed by acclamation and sent on to the
peers.

After this Fosco rose and gathered his robes about him. "I leave
you to deliberate on the matter of raising taxes, for this is your business. But I charge you not to take too long about it."

As the viceroy swept from the room with his escort of halberdiers,
I felt in myself a growing fury and disgust. Fosco had determined
to rule through tyranny, and the Estates General, our chief defense
against tyranny, had submitted. I myself had done nothing and made
no protest. I heartily wished the Burgesses had risen in a mass and
torn Fosco to pieces along with anyone foolish enough to defend
him—there were five hundred of us, after all—but the two leaders of
the majority had been killed, and now there was no leader but Morley,
whose position was gained through his meek submission.

And here I was, numb and silent on my bench. I hardly needed
Orlanda to remind me that I was a mere placeman whose ambition
had now brought him to a position of utter slavery.

The Burgesses now began to consider what are called "ways and
means," exploring methods of financing the projects of the government. Morley assigned members to various committees to study
the problem, and to my surprise I found myself a member of the
Committee on Monopolies.

The Burgesses formally recessed, and the committees withdrew
to rooms elsewhere in the old college building, or to alehouses in the
vicinity. My committee was led by a justice of the peace from a county
south of the Cordillerie, a jolly fellow called Mallett with a red face
and a pointed gray beard. He led us to the Hanged Man Tavern, sat

us about a table, and produced a paper. "The viceroy wishes to raise money by selling monopolies," he said, "and desires our opinion concerning what items should be placed on offer."

"Who is to bid on these monopolies?" asked I. "And what are the terms?"

"Monopolies will be awarded based on bids submitted to our committee," he said. "They will be awarded for three years, and then bids will be submitted again."

I looked at the list and saw that it included salt, sugar, furs, indigo, cotton, silk, grain, wine, brandy, felt hats, gemstones, saltpeter, and a long list of spices. Half the list seemed to be aimed directly at my own cargoes, but I decided to begin my objections with a commodity in use by all.

"I see that salt heads the list," said I. "I am willing to wager that another committee is considering a tax on salt while we debate selling a salt monopoly."

"Ay," said Mallett. "I have no doubt. Would you pledge with me a glass of beer to the health of His Majesty?"

"Willingly," said I. "But I must say first of all that you cannot tax a thing and then sell a monopoly on that same thing."

"We are to make a report," said Mallett, "not pass a law. Someone above us will judge all these things."

"I also do not see how a monopoly given to a private entity can be enforced," said I. "Say that a monopoly is granted on brandy. How does the monopolist enforce his rights? Must he form his own customs service at his own expense? Or may he call on the resources of the state?"

"All that is yet to be decided."

I frowned down at my glass. "Say that I sail to Tabarzam to buy silk. Say I am gone a twelvemonth, and when I return, I find that a monopoly has been granted on silk, and that I must sell only to a single person at whatever that person is willing to pay."

Mallett laughed. "Then you will be in a sad state, Quillifer. Come, let me fill your boozing-can."

Over the afternoon the Committee on Monopolies managed no business whatever, which I found more comforting than not. After the meeting I took my boat to Her Highness's house, and I found you waiting for me by the boathouse.

"Her Highness is not receiving today," you said. "She heard about the executions, and decided not to let people attend her when they are angry. She does not want it said that she listens to seditious or heated talk."

"Commendable caution," said I. "I have practiced commendable caution all day, and it has made me sick of myself."

You put a hand on my arm. "What choice did you have? Your death would have meant nothing."

I looked at you. "If it did not mean leaving you behind, I would throw up my office and join my privateer."

"Then I am glad that I restrain you. For if you cannot see opportunity in this day's doings, I very much overestimate you."

This brought me up short, and I considered your words. I had not viewed the day as anything but an exercise in murderous tyranny, and had not considered the ways in which tyranny might be of use, even profitable.

You stepped close, and even in the chill wind of autumn I could scent the myrrh in your hair. "You chose the life of a courtier," you said. "Then you must be the best courtier in Howel. For are you not the great dragon-slayer of Duisland?"

"Well," said I, "that, at least, I am."

Gravely you kissed my cheek. "I must return to Her Highness," you said, "but I hope to see you again in a day or two."

I returned to my galley and sped home along the lake. On the way I encountered the galley belonging to His Grace of Roundsilver, and hailed the great lord as we drew up to him.

"I am leaving on the first boat south," he said to me. "If I can arrive in Selford ahead of the great gales of winter, I shall be the most contented man in the world."

"Please tender my very best wishes to Her Grace," said I.

"You may join me on this voyage if you are so minded," Roundsilver said. "There is nothing here but death and desolation."

"Alas, Your Grace," said I, "I hold an office."

"And now perhaps you understand why I have never held an office in my life," said he, and then he turned thoughtful. "Yet you are a monster-slayer," he added. "Perhaps a monster might be found in Fornland, that you must come away to kill, and you will be excused attending the Estates."

"If I can bring the canal into being," said I, "there may be some good come of this session."

The duke looked at me with a skeptical eye. "Well," he said, "you can but try. I will tender your greetings to my lady."

When I arrived at Rackheath House, I was told that Blackwell waited in the parlor, and that he was drunk.

"This is nothing new," said I, and walked to the parlor, where I found the poet huddled miserably on the floor by the fire. I closed the door behind me, then advanced toward Blackwell. He turned to me, his appearance wild.

"It's all my fault, isn't it?" said he. "My *Laelius* killed those men."

"Now I see why the vanity of poets and players is proverbial," said I, and as anger flashed in his indigo eyes, I added, "Umbrey and Greene did not die for writing your poem. They died because they defied the viceroy."

"Yet I made Fosco furious. They are making ballads out of some of my verses."

I had not heard this, but was not surprised. "If you wish to assign yourself blame," I said, "you can blame yourself for the new libel law. But that law has not yet been passed by the peers, or received the royal assent, and no one has been arrested on those libel charges. So when someone is convicted and executed on those charges, then you may feel wretched, but until then you may not feel any more wretched than I, who in fear of my life did vote for that very law."

He turned to the fire. "Well, we are brothers in misery, then."

I drew a chair near the hearth and sat. "Your patron Roundsilver is leaving for Selford," I said. "You might want to go with him."

"My company performs in Howel all winter," Blackwell said.

"Your whole company knows you wrote *Laelius*," said I. "If one of them has too much to drink in a tavern and speaks too freely, you may be the first victim of this new law."

The warm light of the fire danced on his face. "It may be what I deserve," said he.

"The government has not thought to offer a reward," I said. "But if they do, and one of your company decides he wishes to become rich . . ." I left the thought unfinished.

Blackwell waved a hand. "Where would I fly to?"

"I can put you on one my ships. You can learn to hand, reef, and steer, and amuse the crew with your verse."

He found this droll. "It is a salubrious life, on the sea," he said. "But as an actor, I am devoted to a malign and depraved existence."

"Go and write your verse," said I, "and leave me alone to my own misery."

Blackwell obeyed, and I ate a lonely supper of beefsteak and a little wine. I reasoned we now lived under a tyrant, and that I could not alter his tyranny by any action of mine. Therefore it was best that I provide for myself and my own safety.

Under your inspiration I considered the Committee on Monopolies, which was made up of country gentlemen chosen not for their financial acumen, but their presumed loyalty to the crown. Clearly they understood more of taverns than of business. I considered forming a company for the purpose of purchasing a monopoly, or even becoming the monopolist of canals—I could put a turnpike on every canal in the kingdom, and charge a fee for every boat, barge, or scow.

But first, I thought, I should secure the fortune that I already possessed. *Sea-Drake* was on its way to Tabarzam for silks and gems, and I should make sure my cargo did not fall foul of any monopolist granted a charter by the viceroy. By the end of my supper, I had thought of a way that might be accomplished.

CHAPTER TWENTY-EIGHT

October eased into a cold November. I built Mountmirail a small lime kiln, and he began his experiments on mortar that would be proof against water. I attended the Burgesses, I paid court to Floria and appealed to her regarding the canal project, and I met with the Committee on Monopolies. I met with you privately as often as I could, but not as often as I desired.

The two Thurnmark ships captured by my *Ostra* had been condemned by the prize court at Ferrick, and I set in motion my plans to sell the ships and their cargo. Twenty percent would go to the crown, half to the crew, and the remainder would be mine.

I wondered if Edevane had urged the court to speed the verdict, in order to provide me with funds to purchase Countess Marcella's notes. If so, both he and they acted too late.

Because my comrades on the committee knew nothing of business, I was able to unduly influence the report on monopolies. I was able to manage a vote that no ship that had left Duisland before the royal assent of any import monopoly should be subject to the monopolist on that ship's return, which I hoped would keep *Sea-Drake* and its cargoes safe. I wrote to Kevin Spellman that we might form an association of merchant adventurers to purchase one of the monopolies, and that we might seek to dominate the Tabarzam trade. To that end I began to frequent the house of the Honourable Companie of Mercers. This consisted of the greatest merchants in Howel, those who traded abroad, or bought from the guilds at fixed prices and then sold for whatever the market would bear. I was not a Mercer, but the Spellman family had introduced me to this guild, and I was registered on their books as a friend and aspirant. I began to canvass the Mercers both for the canal project and the formation of a company to bid on one of the monopolies.

The canal did not interest them, for it was far off in Fornland; but profiting from a monopoly is never far from the minds of businessmen, and here the government was preparing at a price to indulge them. They were not all merchant adventurers like myself, and so they were more interested in domestic products like salt and felt hats and fur than they were in cedarwood and cardamom. Yet I knew the competition for any salt monopoly would be considerable, and it was more than likely that the would-be monopolists would pay more for their privileges than they were worth. I knew nothing of felt hats. But my ships traveled over the world, and I knew tonnage and bottomry, respondentia and hypothecation, and I knew at least some of the principal harbors of the world, and the merchants who dwelt there.

Those who coveted monopolies viewed their privileges as the ability to place a surcharge on all suitable transactions taking place within the realm. But I had thought that a monopoly would find most of its benefits abroad. The Empire of the Aekoi, for one, was dominated on its periphery by warlords, chieftains, and pirate fleets, and lone ships under a lone master found it hard to cope on any kind of fair terms with these rapacious brigands who viewed all the world as prey. But if the ships belonged to a monopoly, they could treat with the reivers on far better terms. They could act as a state, and sign with foreign powers documents that would have the effect of treaties. Their ships could convoy together for self-protection, and play the warlords against one another in order to win privileges on foreign soil.

"If only I had money," I told you one evening, as we lay in sweet exhaustion on the Count of Rackheath's feather mattresses. "I live day to day, and at any moment may find myself at the mercy of moneylenders."

You propped yourself on one elbow and gazed at me. Soft candlelight gave your face a flickering glow, and your scent danced in my senses. "Yet one of your great ships brought in a cargo of spices and gems. And your privateer has taken two prizes."

"Yet I cannot sell either the spices or the prizes. All the money in Duisland has gone into the grain markets."

"Well," you said, "our merchants profit from starvation. You should do likewise."

I passed a hand over my forehead. "I have sent ships abroad to buy grain, but when it arrives, I must sell it to these same predatory merchants who have withheld grain from the markets while the prices rise. I myself have no means of storing grain, and I have not the resources to sell it to bakers or to the people." I sighed. "So my fine plans for a monopoly may come to nothing, because I lack the means to invest in my own scheme."

"Can you store the grain on your ships?"

"Yes, but that means the ships cannot travel. If they sit in port, they aren't making money."

"But you tell me there is no money to be had in any case."

"There is," said I, "but abroad, not here." I turned to you. "If I fly this country on my ships, will you come with me?"

A smile tugged at the corners of your mouth. Candlelight flickered in your black eyes. You lowered your head and dug your chin into my shoulder.

"Ask me on the day," you said, "and perhaps the answer will please you."

About that time the fever that had killed Queen Berlauda crept west from Loretto and began to rage in Duisland. The paupers in the streets suffered badly, for starvation had already weakened them. The theaters were closed, and large public meetings restricted. Only the meetings of the Estates went on, and our halls echoed with hacking coughs more than they did with speeches. Two Burgesses collapsed on their benches and were carried from their seats on planks. One of them died.

We had been called to the house in order to pass a new land tax. Last year's session had raised the tax from two to three crowns per royal, and now we were to raise it from three to four. The bill passed— as all the government's legislation did—by acclamation, without a vote. At least a third of the Burgesses had ceased to attend at all.

We remained after the vote because Morley wished us to pass an Act Against the Despoliation of Grain Houses, for by now the desperate public was storming granaries and carrying off the contents to feed their families. Its was already illegal to loot a granary, but now it would be even more illegal than before, with even more hideous penalties.

I sat waiting on my bench high in the room while Morley droned through the bill, and sick Burgesses coughed and rattled about me. Then a herald in a bright tabard came to Morley and handed him a paper, and when he read it, he turned pale.

"Gentlemen," he said, "we are summoned to the Bar of the House of Peers."

Which meant some great announcement, because the Burgesses still had much business, and we would not be prorogued until we had done it. I imagined there would be some proclamation about the war, perhaps the news that Priscus had taken Seaux-en-Laco, the city he and his father Henrico had been besieging for the last four months.

"I suppose it's too much to hope that it's peace," said Mallett, as we assembled for our procession.

"I fear so," said I.

We made our formal procession to the House of Peers and shuffled our way to the Bar. Coughs echoed off the great hammer-beam ceiling. Fosco sat beneath the great canopy, his white staff in a clenched, jeweled fist. His jaw worked as he watched us, as if he was grinding treason between his molars, and his glance was so fevered I wondered if he had caught the grippe that was blasting the town. Fosco presided over only a few dozen peers, for they had not been expecting any business that day. Morley bowed to the viceroy to signal that we were ready to hear his address, and Lord Chancellor Oldershaw asked Fosco to address the Estates.

"We bring melancholy news to the Estates," said the viceroy. "It has pleased the Compassionate Pilgrim to relieve the mortal suffering of King Henrico and King Priscus, and to take them into his eternal realm, where he and they will reign forever." A great murmuring began among the Burgesses, and so it was with difficulty that I heard the viceroy's next words.

"Their Majesties had decided not to retire to the capital during the winter, and were with the army at Seaux, sharing the hardship of their soldiers. Their sacrifice should serve as a glorious example to their subjects, and shows they are fully worthy of their ancestors."

He rose to his feet and thumped with his staff on his dais. "The Estates General will be prorogued for at least several days. But stray not far, for warrants will soon be sent." He raised his staff.

"The king is dead! Long live the king!"

We duly echoed that ritual phrase, but by then I was hurrying for the door. Once I was free of the House of Peers, I dashed to the river, where I found my boat and crew and had them row like madmen for Wenwyn Hall and Princess Floria. From the boat I jumped to the quay and crossed the lawn to the rear portico. I knocked, and to the footman who answered said that I urgently needed to speak to Her Highness, and then I waited while Floria was called from the company of her ladies. When she appeared, I took off my boat cloak and offered it to her.

"Highness, will you walk with me? My good woolen cloak will keep you warm."

Curiosity and calculation crossed her face, but her eyes held steady on my own, and she nodded. I draped her in the cloak, and then we walked out along the sere grass between her house and the quay.

"King Priscus has died at Seaux-en-Laco," I said. "His father is dead also, and now an infant is heir to our two realms. The Estates have been prorogued for a few days while the viceroy decides what course to adopt."

"The Pilgrim give them rest," she said in a soft voice. She kept her hazel eyes downcast on the sward ahead of her footsteps

"I think this will alter your situation, Highness," I said. "I felt I should give you as much warning as possible."

"I thank you," said she.

"If you need anything whatever," said I, "I hope you will call on me."

She paused then, and looked at me with appraising eyes, as if she were a jeweler valuing a gem. "I will find myself beset by Lorettan princes desiring marriage," she said. "May I count on you to challenge them to duels?"

"I hardly think you need my aid in fending off suitors," said I. "But you may have any help that is within my power."

"I think I will sponsor that canal of yours, Sir Quillifer," said she. "For it will furnish us opportunity to speak together." She turned and began her walk back to her house. I could see your face among others at the window, all wondering what construction to give to my unorthodox visit. "I now," she said, "must prepare my household. So I will return your cloak, and you may return to your own business."

"My business is prorogued," said I.

"I hardly think so," said she, "for you will not be satisfied until you have adopted every occupation in the world. Come tomorrow, after dinner, with news of the canal." She unclasped my cloak and handed it to me, and with a smile left me standing alone on her porch.

Floria was right, for I found employment for myself immediately. When I returned home, I found a message from the privateer pinnace *Able*, which I owned jointly with the Spellman family. *Able* had arrived in Longfirth after an unprofitable cruise, and I wrote to the captain to buy cargo he could sell in Fornland, and to wait for a passenger I would send him. I also wrote to the lank-haired gunner Peel to be ready to go to Fornland to fight kitlings and wyverns, and to visit me for instructions. His previous work for me on the dragon quest had resulted in his promotion from journeyman to master in the Loyall and Worshipfull Companie of Cannoneers, and now I would add to his fame.

In the morning I went to visit Alaron Mountmirail to see how he fared at discovering a mortar proof against the corruption of water. To my surprise I found him sharing a rose-scented tisane with Edith Ransome, Floria's astronomer, while his mechanical birds darted about the studio and an automaton of cogs and wooden rods produced some wheezing notes on an organ.

"Mistress Ransome," said I. "I hope you are enjoying the morning."

She lowered her tisane and smiled. I do not believe I had ever seen her smile, and I found the expression on her severe face more than a little eerie.

"Have you come to see Alaron's antihydraulic mortar?" said she. I could not help but notice that she and the engineer were on first-name terms.

"Antihydraulic mortar? Is that what it is called now?"

Mistress Ransome's smile sharpened. "You are not the only one who can invent new words, Master Quillifer."

"'Antihydraulic mortar' is not bad, for a beginner," said I, and turned to Mountmirail. "Have you made progress?"

"Not yet," said he. "I have barely started."

He took me past the new lime kiln to the work shed, and showed me how he had employed hammers, mortars, and his own grinding machines to create piles of powdered limestone, shale, gypsum, and clinkers, and to these he proposed to add various quantities of clay, sand, and ash, and test the result.

"It seems that you are employing anything that might repel water, and just adding it in random proportions," said I.

"Not quite random," Mountmirail said, "though you are not far wrong. There is nothing written about mortars and plasters that I can find, because all recipes are held secret by the guilds, and so I must write my own."

We discussed his experiments for a while, and then I turned to Mistress Ransome. "I was going to report this to Her Highness later today," I said, "but your account may arrive first."

"There will be little substance to it either way," she said. "Alaron's experiments have hardly begun."

"Then I shall leave him to his work."

I returned home to find Peel the cannoneer waiting for me. I gave him his instructions and some money, and told him to travel to Longfirth, where *Able* would take him to Fornland.

After dinner I took all the documents that Mountmirail had prepared for the canal project and carried them in my galley to Wenwyn Hall. In Her Highness's parlor I waited, sipping from a cup of mulled wine, while she met with Lord Chancellor Oldershaw in her cabinet. To secure both Floria's privacy and her virtue when she was closeted with a man, Chenée Tavistock acted as chaperone and viewed the meeting through a window opened into the next room.

Lord Oldershaw was the highest ranking officer of state, and had held his position since the foundation of Berlauda's reign. He had not been required to ransom himself, as Thistlegorm had, and as he was in charge of the courts, whatever irregularities had taken place at the Siege Royal must have occurred with his knowledge. I was inclined to wonder whether he had taken a portion of Thistlegorm's ransom, and of the others who had bought their lives with silver.

That he was closeted with Floria was hardly surprising. I was certain that many of the great folk of the realm were quietly conferring with one another in order to best manage the state, their lives, and, of course, their own fortunes.

The meeting went on for about an hour, and then Oldershaw withdrew. I bowed as he passed me, a stately man with a body in the shape of a hogshead of wine, and with little swinish eyes. He carried the rod of his office, and his black mourning gown was so covered with brocade that he crackled as he walked.

I was called into Floria's cabinet, a small room that smelled of cedar, with shelves of documents and books. Floria, in her white samite, glowed like a beacon in the small, dark room. She had turned her face pale with a mixture of egg white and talcum to which had been added ground pearls, which gave her skin an unearthly glow, as if she were a shimmering queen of faerie. A carcanet of emeralds enclosed her throat, and her gown was closely sewn with pearls and white diamonds. At her waist was the golden pomander mounted with the star sapphire I had sold her. She looked no longer a young, coltish girl, but every inch a monarch.

I closed the door behind me and sat at Her Highness's invitation. "I hope the meeting with his lordship went well, Your Highness," I said.

She gave me an under-eyed look. "Well enough," she said.

"He seems a portly man," said I. "Perhaps he is stuffed with ransoms."

Her hazel eyes flashed. "If he is," said she, "it is not your business."

"Truly, Highness." I looked at Mistress Tavistock through the window into the next room. "I have heard of anchorite monks who walled themselves up, but who left such a window so that they could view holy ceremonies, and receive instruction. I believe these windows are called hagioscopes."

"This is not in a monastery," said Floria, "and it is called a squint." She raised her head to scrutinize me. "Though sometimes I wish this *were* a monastery. I might better be able to preserve my ladies' virtue. You have corrupted Mistress d'Altrey, and now your engineer seems to have won the heart of Mistress Ransome." She made a scoffing sound. "Pilgrim's toes, she must be twice his age!"

"I think the gap is not so great," said I. "But in any case, I would be hard put to speak against a true meeting of mind and heart."

Floria narrowed her eyes. "If it were only minds and hearts meeting, that could more easily be borne. It is ill enough that Marcella is forever being mistaken for a courtesan—but as it now stands, I could be accused of running a bagnio."

"Highness," said I, "I would challenge anyone who made such an accusation."

"I will take in that what comfort I may," said Floria. "Still, it is my business to see my ladies well married if that is what they desire, and I will not stand in their way."

"I'm sure Mistress Tavistock is grateful."

"She will marry a rich and titled man," said Floria. "But what are Mistress d'Altrey's prospects? Will you marry her, Sir Quillifer?"

This question was so surprising that I had to take a moment to recover my wits. I had come, after all, to talk about a canal.

"You would promote the marriage of a butcher's son with the niece of a marquess?" I asked.

"That niece comes without a penny but what I give her," said Floria. "And I am surprised you disparage yourself in those terms."

"I know full well what I am," said I. "I have heard 'butcher's son' often enough from those who resent me, and no doubt I will hear it for the rest of my life."

"If Mistress d'Altrey is to marry," said Floria, "it must be to a rich man, and I believe you are wealthy. But such a marriage, Quillifer, will bring nothing to *you*, for her nearest kin are dead and cannot use their influence on your behalf, and the family money and property are gone." She lifted her chin and directed a thoughtful gaze at me. "Will your ambition permit a connection that brings so little?"

"Mistress d'Altrey is so well born that the connection cannot help but raise me in the public estimation," said I. "But such a marriage might debase her in that same estimation."

"Well," said Floria. "Any debasement is up to Mistress d'Altrey, I suppose. But what of Mistress Ransome?" Floria picked up a jeweled box and toyed with it. "Where is this Mountmirail from? What prospects has he?"

"His father is a gentleman from Dun Foss, near the border."

A dry laugh escaped Floria's lips. "Any gentleman of Dun Foss might more properly be called a sheep farmer," she said.

"And Master Mountmirail's prospects," I said, "include becoming the chief engineer of Her Royal Highness Floria's Ethlebight Canal."

Floria smiled. "That prospect may be a little premature."

"I hope not, Highness."

"Mistress Ransome tells me that he has not yet begun work on his antihydraulic mortar."

"I think that term has too many syllables, Your Highness," said I. "It is too complicated for the average investor, who prefers his information in dainty bites. May I suggest 'caement,' from the Aekoi *caementicium*, which is what the ancients called their mortar."

"That is a fine, classical name for a thing that does not yet exist," said Floria. "But I would call it 'water-proof,' which is a small enough morsel for these investors of yours, and more to the point besides."

"The royal sponsor of a canal," said I, "may call an element of that canal anything she desires."

Floria offered a thin smile. "Well," she said. "I see you have brought a folder of papers. Perhaps we should view them."

We spent a pleasant half hour discussing the canal and its prospects, and then Floria's steward said that the Marquess of Sylcaster wished to pay his respects.

"Pick up your papers, Quillifer," said Floria. "For Sylcaster is so ancient that I must see him before he drops dead."

"As you wish, Highness."

Sylcaster, I knew, had been King Stilwell's privy seal. Perhaps he was hoping to regain his office under a new administration.

I picked up my papers and made my way to the door. Floria touched my arm.

"If you see Mistress d'Altrey," she said, "you may tell her that I will not need her till tomorrow morning."

"Thank you, Highness."

I took my leave and bowed to Sylcaster as we passed each other in the parlor. He was indeed very old, and to keep himself warm wrapped himself in a robe of sable fur. He wore thick spectacles tied over his ears with black ribbon, and leaned on a stick. Yet it was ambition, I thought, that had brought him here, a decrepit half-ghost grizzlepate come to pay court to a princess.

You also I found in the parlor, garbed in splendid black satin with beads of jet, and I passed on Floria's message.

"I am dressed to entertain the highest of the realm," you said, "and may not wear these clothes in your galley. I will ride to your house in an hour."

"Mistress." I kissed your fingers and made my impatient way from Wenwyn Hall.

As we pulled away from the quay, I began to think how Floria had eased our meeting, even though she complained her ladies might bring her scandal. I thought there might be purpose behind this leniency, and that she wanted the two of us together, perhaps so that she could pass messages to the outside.

I rejoiced in this idea, for not only did I have leave to see you, but through you I might have knowledge of some of the great doings of the realm.

"The King of Loretto and Duisland is less than a year old," you said. "There will have to be a regency council in both realms, and Floria intends to have a place on that of Duisland, and make her voice heard through the realm."

"Will Fosco even allow it?"

"It may not be up to Fosco. If the peers unite, he will have no choice but to submit."

"The last time the peers tried to unite, two of them went to prison."

We were in my parlor, you leaning on my shoulder as we shared a couch before the hearth. You were dressed in the riding clothes you had worn on your horseback journey to Rackheath House, and we drank from goblets of warming hippocras that tasted of cinnamon and spice. In the kitchen, Harry Noach was making our dinner.

"Fosco cannot arrest every noble in the realm," you said. "For one thing, the nobles of Loretto would begin to wonder if they were next, and that would make trouble their realm cannot afford."

"I fear your optimism," said I. "And Floria's. Fosco and Edevane are united in their fear of her."

You raised your head to look at me, your black eyes intent. "And if Her Highness fails against Fosco? What will you do? Can you help Floria in some way?"

I waved a dismissive hand. "What can I do without money?" I turned to the fire and took a sip of the hippocras. "If only I could cash that letter of credit from the Oberlin Fraters Bank."

"You have money in that bank?"

"I do, but little. But I have a letter on that bank for a fortune, and no way to cash it."

I explained that the letter of credit was in the name of Charles Morland, which was a name used by the bandit Sir Basil of the Heugh. He had deposited his loot in that bank, which had branches abroad, and intended to carry the letter of credit to Steggerda, where he would begin his life over. But ill fortune brought him to Longfirth, where I had tried to arrest him and killed him instead. I had found the letter of credit in his boot.

"That letter is for over fourteen thousand royals!" said I. "That is enough money to build a ship of six hundred tons, or buy this house from the Count of Rackheath. But I am not Charles Morland, and I know not Morland's passwords, nor do I have his seal, and without these I cannot have the money." I looked at you. "This is exactly the sort of action that would stir you, for Sir Basil was the strong man who plundered others, and I am the stronger man who plundered him—but alas, I am thwarted by a set of clerks in a counting-house. If I only knew the bank's secrets, I could fill my pockets with gold."

I saw the deep calculation moving behind your eyes, and I knew you were contemplating some bold action, and I felt my heart throb in anticipation.

"I believe I know—a person—at that bank," you said. "He is a kinsman of mine."

I kissed your lips in gratitude and adoration. "Can you sound him out?"

You pressed your lips together in thought. "May I show him this letter of credit?"

"I don't keep it here."

You frowned a little. "He will award himself a fee, to compensate for the danger."

I waved a hand. "If the fee is not extortionate, I have no objection."

There was a soft knock on the door. You detached yourself from my person and sat up straight, so as not to shock the servants with a scene of intimacy.

"Yes?" I said.

A footman opened the door. "Supper is ready, master, an it please you."

"Thank you." I rose from the couch and helped you to your feet. I was half-dizzy with the thought of the evening to come: a fine supper, an evening of pleasure with you that might stretch on into the morning, and the possibility of riches dropping into my lap like a rain of gold from heaven.

Surely, I thought, sure in your love I was the most fortunate of men.

CHAPTER TWENTY-NINE

Again I walked through the room filled with clerks and their papers tied with blue and scarlet ribbon, and I waited by the door of Edevane's office for the page to call me in. My breath smoked in front of my face, and for warmth I wore my old cheviot overcoat with my wool boat cloak over it. A slow winter storm had crept over Howel the night before and dusted the ground with snow. The sun was now doing its best to turn the snow to mud, but the freezing temperature was obstinate and would not rise. Gems of frost spread themselves on the windows, and there had been tiny ice crystals floating on the surface of the lake.

At last the page beckoned me in, and I walked into Edevane's office, which was rosy with the blaze on the hearth. He wore a white ruff over his black velvet doublet, and gems I had sold him glittered on his fingers. His dead-fish eyes rose to mine.

"What have you to report, Lord Warden?" he said.

"My deputy Peel has reported from Longfirth, your lordship," said I. "He is aboard the pinnace *Able*, and by now will have sailed to Fornland, where he will spend the winter exterminating the kitlings."

Edevane's look betrayed his impatience. "I care not about kitlings,

Sir Quillifer," he said. "I have asked you to report on Her Highness Floria."

"Her Highness seems willing to sponsor the Ethlebight Canal." And then, seeing his frown, I added, "Though to speak truth, I know not whether in the current state of affairs this will aid the canal, or hinder it."

He tapped the fingers of his right hand against the fingers of his left. "There is only one way for this canal to be built," he said in his soft, toneless voice. "And that is if the government moves the bill through the Estates, and if the viceroy gives his assent." He nodded. "I can have this bill passed at any time, but other business must take precedence. Her Highness Floria, for example, must be secured from the influence of Duisland's enemies."

"How can I help your lordship in this matter?"

He placed his hands on his desk. "Who visits Her Highness?"

I raised my hands. "I'm sure you have a more complete list than I, my lord. But I have seen Lord Sylcaster; Lord Chancellor Oldershaw; Baron Berardinis, who held Longfirth for Queen Berlauda; the Count of Culme; and Viscount Drumforce, Lord Scutterfield's son."

"Drumforce," said Edevane. "He preaches sedition, like his father."

"He preaches it not in my hearing," said I. "They are all very grand people, and they do not speak to the likes of me."

"What matters is not what they say to you," said Edevane, "but what they say to Her Highness."

"She speaks to them privately in her study," said I. "Her ladies guarantee propriety, by watching from the next room through a hagioscope."

"You mean a squint?" Edevane's corpse eyes fixed mine, as cold as the frost on the window. "You must find me evidence of this treason, Lord Warden."

I composed myself carefully, and donned my learnèd-advocate face. "Do you wish me to perjure myself?" I said.

Contempt twitched at the corner of his mouth. "That is hardly necessary, if you are clever enough. Find me a letter. Overhear a conversation. Offer to join a conspiracy. Say you will bear messages. We know the treason exists, we need only find proof."

"Of what," said I, "does this treason consist?"

"There is a plot by powerful men," he said, "to supplant King Aguila and to place Princess Floria on the throne, then rule the realm through Floria and the Council."

This, I thought, was even possible—though if the conspiracy existed, it underestimated Floria.

"I will do my best, my lord," said I. "But, as I have said, these grand folk do not speak to me."

"You are an expert at insinuating yourself into the company of men grander than yourself," Edevane said. "Exercise your talent. And if you bring me what I need, the Ethlebight Canal will flow."

It could not be put more plainly than that. At the cost of Floria's freedom, my prostrate city of Ethlebight would rise again to prosperity.

"I am your servant," said I. "But, my lord, do you know of anyone else in Floria's household that I could trust? Two might work at this better than one."

Again that contemptuous turn of the mouth. "You whispering in corners with a servant? It would attract notice."

"I understand, my lord."

"Hold yourself ready for the Estates to meet in two days. The warrants will go out later today."

"Yes, my lord."

I made ready to leave and wrapped my boat cloak about me. Edevane raised a hand. "And if what you find for me is good," said he, "you will secure one of the monopolies."

I made my way out of Edevane's domain with my head spinning, and I found myself wandering Ings Magna half in a daze, wondering where and how to proceed from this moment. By chance I encountered Coronel Lipton, who was scowling his way down the grand marble staircase toward the palace entrance. I hailed him.

"You look not well, youngster," he said.

"I confide I am at a loss," said I.

"I will drink a glass of wine with you," said he, "and either the wine will settle your wits, or it will send them entirely astray, and either way you will be in better case than you are now. But you will have to lay down the silver for it, for the pay of my regiment is five months in arrears, and I have just applied for it to the exchequer, and been rebuffed."

We went to the officers' mess, drank hock, and enjoyed a mess of eels taken that morning from the lake. I could not speak frankly to him of my problem, for others in the mess might overhear, but from the conversation I understood that the officers of the artillery were greatly discontented. The artillery, requiring an abundance of technical skill, did not attract lords or rich men, but instead clever officers of humble backgrounds who had to live on their pay. Now they were all at the mercy of moneylenders, and the interest rates were high.

"And the Queen's Own Horse, and the Yeoman Archers? For the officers may have money, but the ordinary soldiers do not."

Lipton sighed. "They do not starve, but neither have they got new clothes or shoes, and their pay is as far in arrears as mine. Perhaps it will be better when Lord Barkin returns with his companies from Loretto. Barkin may know someone near the viceroy who can shake loose our money."

"I will be right glad to see Lord Barkin again," said I. "And we of the Burgesses are trying even now to root out your pay from wherever it lies hidden. Yet I am surprised that you are not all marching to the fighting in Thurnmark."

"We guard the monarch. But now the monarch is dead, and we guard the viceroy instead."

"The Pilgrim send you better employment."

Lipton informed me of the circumstances of King Priscus's death. He and King Henrico had determined to besiege and take Seaux-en-Laco, but the siege began late in the season, and before the city fell, it was time for the army to seek its winter quarters. But as the army was well supplied where it stood, and since the previous winter's campaign had been such a success, the decision was taken for the army's winter quarters to consist of its own siege camps. Which worked well, apparently, until the fever began to rage through the trenches.

"For siege camps are unhealthy places, youngster," said Lipton, "and we soldiers always pray to be delivered from long sieges. And now both kings are dead, and what remains of the army is dragging itself home."

"I feel as if Howel itself is under siege," said I. "And I fear that a fever may soon rise."

Lipton's face was grim. "That it may," said he, "and I hope we are both spared."

Afterward I went to the house of Her Highness, and after waiting a while in the parlor, I was called to an interview in Floria's study. She had been writing, for I saw ink on her fingers and a bottle of Q Sable on the desk. I saw your lovely face through the squint, and saw you were reading a book, or pretending to.

As briefly as possible I told Floria of my interview with Edevane. "He says that he wishes to protect you from harmful influence," said I, "but I hardly think he will stop at anything short of placing you under arrest, or possibly on the scaffold."

"This is not precisely news to me," said Floria. "Yet I do not know how to evade that gentleman's malice."

"That may not be possible, Highness, at least in Howel."

She gave me a sharp look. "You believe I should fly?"

I evaded a direct answer to the question. "It is better to fly, not away from something, but toward something else, some object," said I. "In any case the decision would be up to you. I hope you will remember that I own ships, and that I am at your service."

"That is very kind," said she.

"In the meantime," said I, "is it possible that you give me something that will satisfy Lord Edevane? Cannot you receive a letter that might cast some doubt on one of the viceroy's most loyal supporters?"

"Such ingenuity is only to be expected from you," Floria sighed. "But such a plan is more likely than not to go astray. I prefer not to be interrogated about my correspondence."

"You would know best, Highness."

She cast a glance at the squint. "You and I should only speak directly to one another. I would not compromise Mistress d'Altrey by sending messages to and fro. She is already in danger enough, in my service and also born to an attainted family."

This, I thought, reflected well on Floria's kindness, though of course I have told you everything anyway.

I said that I would make it my business to visit two or three times each week, or whenever I had news. And then she bade me good afternoon, and I bowed and made my way out, casting a glance through the squint to see you still reading your book. And then your eyes flickered upward to meet mine for the span of a heartbeat, and I read there a promise that you would fulfill later that night.

"You are in an admirable position," you told me that evening. "For if Floria ends in a position of power, you will have your canal and probably your monopoly; and if you provide Edevane with information, you will have the same."

"That information would be perjured," said I.

"What?" You laughed. "Are you the only honest man at court?" But you saw on my face the inward struggle these words had provoked, and you put a hand on my arm. "Ay," you said, "who would not prefer Floria? She has been kind to me. But the fate of my father and brothers taught me a terrible lesson, which is that we cannot save everybody. If Her Highness is doomed, then we must look out for ourselves."

We spoke in Lord Rackheath's great carved bed, with the velvet curtains drawn open to allow the flickering light of scented candles to dance in your eyes.

"We must see Floria is not doomed," I said as I gazed in futility at the dark canopy overhead. "But I know not what to do. If I had money, I could attempt something."

A glimmer of interest shone in your eyes. "I have spoken to my friend at the bank. He said he might be able to help us with the letter of credit."

In burning joy I kissed you. "I will bring you that letter tomorrow."

In joyless procession we trooped across the square to the House of Peers. The viceroy's armored escort, looking down at us from their chargers, were no less miserable, for the skies mizzled down on them, cold raindrops ringing off their steel helmets.

We Burgesses entered the House of Peers and gathered before the Bar. Collectively we smelled like a pack of wet dogs. I saw that the viceroy already sat in his throne, his hand firmly closed about his white staff. Only half the peers were present, their fine scarlet cloaks and gold coronets dull and dark on this dreary day. A storm of rain pattered on the windows as the Lord Chancellor asked Fosco to speak.

"We mourn the loss of our king and queen," Fosco said, "but we rejoice in the continued health of our new royal master, King Aguila. I am pleased to inform the Estates that the regency council has been formed in Loretto, and Her Majesty Queen Arletta has been placed at its head. The late king's brother Prince Tiburcio has been placed at the head of the army, and from his generalship much is expected."

He raised his head and favored the peers with a defiant look. "No alteration in the government of Duisland is contemplated. The arrangements made by the late king and queen will remain in force. We reserve to ourselves all the power of the Crown of Duisland, and we will continue to be advised by the Privy Council as it now stands." His glance turned to those of us mustered before the Bar.

"We again urge the Burgesses to do your business quickly, and raise the funds necessary for victory against Thurnmark and her allies. Do your duty to King Aguila, worship the Compassionate Pilgrim, and, lastly, contemplate no strife, and the blessings of peace will rain upon these houses and the realm."

Perhaps the word "rain" was ill-advised. A squall stormed in the square as we left the House of Peers, and we scurried over the cobbles in an undignified mob. The armored escort, plumes drooping, ignored us as they formed to escort Viceroy Fosco's carriage back to Ings Magna.

Back in the House of Burgesses, we threw off our dripping cloaks and spent the rest of the day trooping one by one to the Speaker's bench, and there swearing formal allegiance to an infant. I cared no more for the oath than I did for the child.

I didn't go to Floria's that day, for I was sure any number of people would flock to tell her that there would be no regency council in Duisland.

I had an unexpected visitor at Rackheath House that next day: Baron Becket, who had held my seat in the Burgesses until his elevation to the peerage. He wished me to sign a petition directed at Queen Arletta and her regency council, asking them to dismiss Fosco and set up a regency council in Duisland, headed by the great lords of the realm.

"What?" I asked. "Do you think I have a spare head?"

"I think if we stand all together—" he began.

"Loretto thinks of Duisland as a fountainhead for money and

soldiers," said I. "Neither Queen Arletta nor any other member of their council cares for Duisland's rights or privileges, and all hope that you will surrender your liberties and your fortunes and get on with the melancholy business of turning our country into a conquered province."

Perhaps I was oversharp with him, but I think I was right in not wanting my signature attached to anything like an act of subversion. I could see his face tighten in anger.

"I am sorry, my lord," I said, "but this is business for the peers. If all the peers stood together and refused Fosco's misrule, that might attract the notice and even the sympathy of the Lorettan peers; but I saw your house this morning, and it seems half the members are missing—run away, or hiding, or having already surrendered all power to the viceroy."

His lips worked, and then he shook his gray head. "Ay, you may be right," he conceded. "Yet this tyranny must be opposed."

"If the peers will not oppose Fosco, then the country must. But that opposition must be *in* the country, not in the capital, where Fosco has his power."

Becket made a disgusted noise. "Fosco is already raising his twenty-five thousand soldiers. He has the household troops. He could use them against us."

"They will be worth little if he can't pay them."

Beyond the monarch's bodyguard, and some companies of royal troops holding royal castles and the citadels of the major towns, Duisland had never had a standing army. We were proud of the Trained Bands, our militia, but these were under the orders of the city corporations or the lords lieutenants, depending on where they were raised, and they were not obliged to serve abroad. The forces of the country significantly outnumbered the forces of the king, and this had been a significant check on the monarch's power. King Stilwell had raised a large army to invade Loretto, but he had been a popular king who fought a traditional enemy, not a foreign despot intent on subduing the entire population.

"You think we must resist paying these taxes," said Becket.

"I think there are ways in which tax collectors can be convinced not to oppress their friends and neighbors," said I.

Becket rubbed his chin. "Do you think I should return to Hurst Downs? Meet with our neighbors?"

"Wait until the Burgesses vote," said I. "And then you can tell the voters of Hurst Downs just what the Crown expects of them, and let them make up their own minds what to do about it."

The next day the Burgesses met to vote on a hearth tax and a window tax, that tax that had darkened the dwellings of all Loretto. But worse than the window tax was the hearth tax, which would lie heavily even on those common people who could not afford windows, or even a chimney.

Both bills were recorded as passed by acclamation, as no one asked for a division.

It seemed that Fosco or Edevane had overheard my comment about the discretion of tax collectors in oppressing their neighbors, because the next vote was to have the taxes farmed. Instead of collections being made by local authorities or by the revenue service, the taxes would be let out to private companies, who would have the authority to invade the houses of every citizen of the realm in order to count the hearths and windows, and to make certain the land tax was properly paid. Once the tax farmers turned over to the crown those revenues that were due, they would keep any additional monies they had extorted from the people, and would live on their spoils like little kings.

Even the Burgesses that had been tamed by the executions of Greene and Umbrey raised objections to this, until Morley firmly called for a division, and we filed into the lobbies to be counted.

Though no one liked the bill, only a dozen or so defied the viceroy by voting nay. They were so few I reckoned it would hardly be worth Fosco's while to cut off their heads.

As for myself, I meekly voted with the majority, though in my defense I can say that I never once considered bidding for one of the tax farm contracts. It would have made me rich, but I would have despised myself.

From the palace, Viceroy Fosco announced that he was issuing writs quo warranto for the surrender of the charters and foundations of all the major cities in Duisland. He would "adjust," he proclaimed, these charters, removing irregularities and corruptions, and reissue them in purified form. In the meantime, legally speaking, the cities would cease to exist—and it was plain that no city would be rechartered unless their mayors and aldermen were heart and soul the viceroy's men.

Similarly, the Commission of Inquiry moved to impound the charters of all monasteries throughout the kingdom, in order to seek out what they called "irregularities." The monasteries were to be "reformed" and brought into compliance with Fosco's notion of the divinity of the Pilgrim. Abbots and other monastic officers would, no doubt, be interrogated on the validity of the Fiat of Abbot Reynardo, the Pilgrim's eternal existence before and after time, and other articles of Fosco's creed. Those who failed the test would be replaced, possibly by divines from Loretto. I wondered if dissenting monks would lose their heads, or merely be walled up in their cells.

The viceroy did not see fit to consult the Estates on these matters—and in truth, the foundation of monasteries and the granting of city charters had long been the business of the crown.

In subsequent days we of the Burgesses voted for higher taxes on wine, felt hats, and bedsheets. We voted to impose a salt tax, in which all salt was to be sold by government warehouses at a price to be determined by the crown, and every household in the nation would be obliged to buy five pounds of salt each year.

The Committee on Monopolies delivered its report, which was turned into a bill allowing the purchase of monopolies on spices, silks, foreign wines and brandies, oil, furs, sugar, saltpeter, and gemstones. I assembled such mercers as I could to bid for a monopoly on trade with the Empire, Tabarzam, and the Candara Coast, and I wrote to everyone in Ethlebight and Selford I thought might be willing to buy shares.

Only you kept me from the disgust I felt at my submission to Fosco and Lord Edevane. You reminded me that I was powerless to oppose those votes, or change the viceroy's policy, and that if there were to be monopolies anyway, I might as well profit from them. And besides, if the Ethlebight Canal were created, good would result.

And when I took you home, I found your kisses were honey and amber, your tresses myrrh and olibanum, and your body gold and ivory; and I was so besotted with thoughts of you that I walked through my miserable days in a stupor.

I met every few days with Floria, and we had private discussions in her office, or strolling on her lawn wrapped in our cloaks. In these visits I kept my eyes open, and I observed the box that Floria kept in a drawer of her desk.

I paid a call upon Lord Edevane, who received me in his warm office, with his dead eyes gazing at mine and his hands pressed together below his chin. I might have thought him praying, save that in his particular case the very thought was ludicrous.

"I believe I am now the most faithful of Her Highness Floria's visitors," said I. "Most of the others have fallen off, now there will be no regency council and Her Highness will have no hand in awarding offices."

"Who remains?"

I told him what, I am sure, he already knew. Floria had been deserted even by one of her ladies in waiting, for Lord Mellender had decided that his fiancée Chenée Tavistock's association with Floria put her in too much danger and taken her away with the excuse that wedding preparations would require her full attention.

I then added the news that had brought me to his office. "I believe I have found where Her Highness keeps her private correspondence," said I. "It is in a coffer that she keeps in a drawer of her office desk."

A gleam of interest flashed into Edevane's dead-fish eyes, then vanished. "Can you get into this coffer?"

"She keeps it locked, and the key is kept on her person." I looked at him. "Can you send someone to my house to offer instruction in picking locks?"

He nodded. "I will arrange it."

"I'm sure that I can arrange some sort of distraction that will give me a chance to get into Her Highness's office unobserved," said I, "though I may have to pick the door lock as well. But as I will have access only for a few moments, I must ask what you want me to do with the letters? Steal them? Read such of them as I can, and then return them to the coffer?"

Edevane reached for a pen and scratched himself a note. "I will give the matter thought, and send instructions."

"Very good, my lord."

I returned to Rackheath House with my mind buzzing, and I thought perhaps I had just secured my monopoly.

"You are trying to scour your freckles," said I.

"With a mixture of buttermilk and lemon juice," you said. "I have made a good start at eradicating them."

"But I love your freckles," said I. "I love each and every one."

"I do not." You touched your fan to my arm. "Now hush, for Bonny Joe is playing."

We were spending an afternoon at Wenwyn Hall, in the reduced company of Floria's remaining friends. Floria's house was in deep mourning, and so there could be no feasts or extravagant entertainments, but a banquet had been provided—no meat, but plenty of fine pastries, nuts, cheeses, and wines. Since the theater was closed, Blackwell's company provided entertainment in the great hall. The clowns knocked each other about, the orchestra played, the actors declaimed, and Blackwell read his latest verse. But the great conclusion was the company's new sensation, the young actor Bonny Joe Webb, who sang in his sweet boy's soprano and accompanied himself on the lute.

Truly he was an enchanting child, with his fine golden hair, blue eyes, snub nose, and dimples. He sang with such sentiment and feeling that he convinced me he had suffered the pangs of love, the loss of hope, and the shattering of his heart, even though my own good sense told me he could not have experienced any of these things. When he finished, he was applauded to the rafters.

"I want to take that boy home with me," you said, your black eyes shining.

"I remind you that you are already at home, mistress," said I. "And I find it intolerable to be supplanted in your affections by a suckling babe."

You leaned close to me, and whispered behind your fan. "I have heard from my banker friend. He will take forty percent of your money, but will have it ready tomorrow."

"Forty percent?" I sighed. "Worse than I'd hoped, but better than I'd feared."

"That leaves you nearly nine thousand royals—or rather, because the bank has not that much gold, a hundred and seventy-three thousand crowns, which is a great weight of silver—he said just over a ton. You will have to send a carriage for it."

We made arrangements for the delivery of the silver, and just as we finished, Viscount Drumforce entered. Drumforce was the son of Lord Scutterfield, who had been lord great chamberlain until Edevane brewed up a charge of treason against him. Scutterfield had been attainted after his death, which meant that he had lost his titles and lands, and his son was now merely Amador Wending, but everyone called him Drumforce anyway. He was a tall man with fair hair and drooping mustaches, and possessed an air of ferocity. I do not know if this was his manner before his father's execution, but now he prowled about the capital with his jaw grinding and fury blazing from his eyes, and it was hard to view him stalking through room after room without thinking that he was bent on a bloody vengeance.

Drumforce went straight to Her Highness Floria, and then the two went into her office. You cast me a resigned look and went into the next room, where you could view the meeting through the hagioscope.

I stood for a moment fingering the picklocks in my pocket. Edevane had sent a lock-maker to my house, with a selection of locks to practice on, and I was growing in confidence, though I could hardly pick the lock with so many people in the house. I had also equipped myself with a short fashion cloak to wear as a flourish, with certain pockets sewn into the lining.

Drumforce had been in Floria's cabinet no more than two minutes when she appeared at the door and beckoned me to her with an impatient flick of her fan. Drumforce bowed his way out of the room, and I closed the door behind me as I entered.

A portion of Drumforce's nervous agitation seemed to have passed to Floria, for she did not sit behind her desk, but stood in the corner, trembling like a hound straining at the leash. Cold anger burned in her eyes as she looked at me.

"Lord Drumforce just told me that my mother has been arrested at Bonherbes, along with her servant Doctor Smolt."

At the news I felt a strange rush of cold fire through my limbs. There was a rising hum in my ears. With this I felt a mental serenity, as if I had been readying for this moment all my life. *At last it begins,* I thought.

"What are the charges?" I asked.

"Practicing sorcery against Berlauda and Priscus," said Floria. "Casting horoscopes of the royal family." Her mouth twisted in anger. "They will be brought to Murkdale Hags for interrogation. My mother will defy them, I know, but they may confuse her into making some kind of admission. As for that mountebank Smolt, I trust him not at all."

She looked at me and gave a little lift to her chin, as if she were challenging me. "We have spoken of many contingencies, Sir Quillifer," said she. "Do you stand ready to fulfill your promises?"

"Highness, I am at your service." I smiled. "I have conceived this plan for you—so how can I resist putting it into execution?"

"We will speak later," she said. "For now, I must inform my household, and also my friends."

She left the room, and through the squint I saw you rise from your chair and go to attend her. I remained for a moment thinking, and then I silently closed the door. At Floria's desk I drew out a deep drawer to reveal the coffer that lay there. The lock was as easy to pick as I could have hoped, and I had the casket open in just a few moments. I took out a bundle of letters, put them in the pockets of my fashion cloak, and then held the cloak over one arm as I left the room.

I saw Floria in a circle of her shocked friends, her white gown a brand burning against their somber darkness. She held herself bravely, like a lone sentry challenging a howling, approaching darkness, and I paused for a moment of pure admiration before I slipped briefly away from Wenwyn Hall, went to my galley, and stowed the traitorous letters in the locker by the stern.

CHAPTER THIRTY

Y ou lie against me on my couch, your myrrh-scented hair draping my shoulder, the firelight dancing in your black eyes. In just a few moments, our treason will begin.

Countess Marcella has been sent to Floria's country house of Kellhurst with orders to ready it for Her Highness. This, I hope, will cause Edevane to believe Floria will travel there, perhaps with the intention of flying to Ferrick or Stanport and sailing on to a foreign country.

Meanwhile, I will in just a few moments carry you in my carriage to the Howel quay and put you onto a barge bound for Bretlynton Head, where my ship *Sovereign* is undergoing refit after its return from Tabarzam. You will carry secret orders for the captain, to ready the ship for sea and for a passenger of distinction.

In a week or so, Floria and I will take a fast boat south along the same route, and join you aboard *Sovereign*, bringing with us 175,000 crowns, less that which I have given you for your own journey. And then we will take Floria abroad, where she may begin her plans for a brave return to Duisland in circumstances very much to her liking.

I must again caution you against speaking to anyone on this

journey, or of even informing Captain Gaunt who his passenger might be. For while the government might hesitate to imprison Floria on such charges as a scoundrel like Doctor Smolt might make, they would have no choice were she to be caught in flight.

"You have just told me that you took Floria's letters," you said. "What will you do with them?"

"They are by way of insurance," I reply. "If everything goes awry, I can give them to Edevane to prove my loyalty."

"Have you looked through them?"

"I have not."

You offer a languorous laugh. "That is a strange delicacy for one so bold. I think you should look at those letters, for you never know what knowledge might be to your advantage."

Perhaps you are right. But now I see through the window that the eastern sky is growing pale and the stars are fading, and that a fine December day will soon dawn. You should have a trouble-free journey down the Dordelle, and I will soon follow. But for this next moment, let me kiss you, and lose myself in your lips, your warm breath, and your perfect dark-eyed mystery.

CHAPTER THIRTY-ONE

For these three months I have lived in terror, for I was convinced that once our plan had failed, you would find yourself in one of Edevane's dungeons, and subject to starvation, torment, and abuse. Yet here you are, newly arrived in Selford with scarcely a hair out of place.

Two days after you went down the Dordelle on your barge, I received a letter from Captain Gaunt that he had finished *Sovereign*'s refit, taken on cargo, and was about to leave Bretlynton Head for Selford. I sent one messenger galloping after you on horseback, and another by boat, but they must have failed to catch you. I pictured you lost in Bretlynton Head, terrified and alone, and pursued by the huntsmen of the crown.

Yet I had reckoned without your resourcefulness, and I had forgot that you come from the port city of Winecourt. For once you arrived at your destination and realized that *Sovereign* had sailed, you made your way to Winecourt, where you hid among friends and were eventually able to secure passage to Selford, crossing a sea filled with storm and war, and a land afire with fury and rebellion.

Come, my love, and rest you in my apartment. It is not Rackheath

House, but at least I lodge in a palace, and my rooms are large and fine, with tapestries of trees and birds and fruit, and this great bed carved with roses. I will send for wine, and honey-cakes if you want them.

I still can scarce believe my eyes, for I had thought you lost forever, and here you are before me, your lips warm from my kisses, and your myrrh scent aswim in my senses. I know not whether I wish to weep with relief and joy, or leap and cavort, or all these at once.

For once I received that message from Captain Gaunt, I knew that I had to act, and act at once. I sent those messengers after you, and then I had to attend the Burgesses, where I was expected to vote up some new taxes on wool and hides. Since there was no actual vote, and the bills were recorded as passed by acclamation, I was there only to sit upon my bench, above the members filling the room with coughs, sneezes, and sniveling, and be counted—and once the roll was taken, I slipped away and carried the package of Floria's letters to Edevane's office. As he was attending the peers, I left the package with his page, along with a note saying I had purloined them from Floria's casket but had not read them.

This, I should note, was a lie. I had looked at the letters and found they were all sent to Floria years ago by her father, King Stilwell, and concerned mainly instructions for her education, comments on her deportment, and admonitions to obey her tutors and study the words of the Pilgrim.

From the Burgesses I flew to Blackwell's rooms in the Cat and Custard Pot. Since the theaters were closed, he had turned to poetry and was buried in writing a sequel to his *Laelius* encompassing the latest crimes of the administration.

His rooms were small and filled with stray bits of furniture, piles of foolscap, stacks of books well read and scribbled in. The air reeked of mildew and spilled ale. In great surprise he looked up from his desk as I came bursting in, his pen poised above a bottle of Q Sable Ink.

"Master Blackwell," said I. "You told me once that you owed me a great debt, and that you would repay it willingly. I am here to tell you that the time has come."

From there I went to Wenwyn Hall. Since you were on your way to Bretlynton Head, Marcella had been sent to Kellhurst to open the house, and Chenée Tavistock had been carried off by her future husband, Edith Ransome was the only lady left to supervise our meeting through the hagioscope. Eventually, though, she was called into the room with us, so that she would understand her part in the play that was to follow.

That night, after the household had gone to sleep, I brought my galley to the landing and disembarked along with Blackwell, his wardrobe mistress, and the child actor Bonny Joe Webb. Mistress Ransome let us in through a side door, and from there we crept to Floria's chamber. There Bonny Joe was dressed in Floria's clothing, and a wig and a cap put on his head. The wardrobe mistress then cut Princess Floria's tight curls away, leaving her with a boy's short-cropped poll. With hose, a doublet, trunks, and cap, and any remaining appearance of femininity concealed by a hooded wool cloak, she seemed a plausible, fresh-faced young page.

I went with Blackwell, Floria, and the mistress of the tiring-house back to my galley. Blackwell and the wardrobe mistress were left at the quay in Howel, and Floria and I were carried to the northwestern corner of the lake, well past the palace of Ings Magna that crouched like a vast, savage hound on the edge of the water, its eyes glittering. We could clearly hear the calls of the sentries.

On the shore we met Rufino Knott, who had come with two horses acquired from a posting-house on the highway to Longfirth. Floria and I were in the saddle before dawn, and cantered westward down the highway.

I had decided that our only hope of escape was that my privateer

Able had not yet left Longfirth, or that if it had, we might acquire some other transport there. Longfirth possessed another advantage: In terms of days spent in travel, a journey from Howel to Longfirth was nearly the longest from the capital to anywhere in Bonille. Any rider would have to cross the high, watery plateau of Howel, with all its bridges and fords, and then climb up and down the slopes of the Cordillerie, then get down the Brood and its long firth to the city. If Floria and I could get a sufficient head start, pursuit could be days behind us, not mere hours.

And so we rode in silence along the highway. The air tasted of woodsmoke from the hearths of the city and the farms, and the trees on either side of the road were bare, their rattling, skeletal fingers reaching to the distant, cold stars. Floria was in the lead, an expert horsewoman used to the sidesaddle, and now riding astride for the first time since she was a small girl and first learned to master her pony. I lumbered along behind. We were well armed, each with a broadsword and a brace of horse pistols, and I with a pocket-pistol and a poniard besides.

As I rode, I contemplated all that I was leaving behind. My friends, Boatswain Lepalik and my galley, my Rackheath House. Rufino Knott and his music, along with my guitar. Stern Master Stiver, my cook Harry Noach and his savory feasts. My empire of ink. Alaron Mountmirail with his kiln and his experiments, which he would now continue to little purpose. The armor that I had taken from Sir Basil of the Heugh. My castle at Dunnock, my new tower over the Races, my mill.

I sacrificed my office and my obligation to battle monsters. My place in the Burgesses I threw away gladly, for there I had no voice and no power, and existed there only as a slave. But with that I threw away also my canal, which would no longer save my home city. I had abandoned also my hope for the monopoly that would make me as rich as a prince.

And most of all, I had sacrificed you. I could not know whether I would ever see you again, or whether I had sent you straight to imprisonment or death. This gnawed at my heart as I rode on through the chill night, and left me blind to the glories of the sunrise.

All this I had sacrificed for the sake of a young girl who had never ceased to view me as a source of amusement, and who greeted me with raillery whenever she saw me. Yet I had been unable to resist her.

Or perhaps it was the plan I had failed to resist. For once I had conceived the plan that would deliver Floria, I had been unable to resist carrying it out, simply to flaunt my own cleverness before the world.

Though it must also be said that I stood firmly within the compass of a recognized tradition. All know that the duty of a knight is to rescue the princess.

The day was fine and still. We changed horses at the next posting-inn, called the Bridge House, and had a breakfast of porridge, cheese, some dried plums, and small beer. While we were stretching our aching limbs and warming ourselves before the fire, Mistress Ransome would emerge from Floria's bedchamber and tell the household that the princess was feeling ill, and would not appear in public today.

Yet Bonny Joe did not remain entirely hidden. He had been instructed to show himself at intervals, looking out the window, or walking with Mistress Ransome between one room and another. We knew the house was watched, and we did not want anyone suspecting that the princess had fled.

You ask where and how we carried the silver. I regret to say that I dared not burden myself with such a great weight as 170,000 crowns, but instead carried only enough coin for our present needs, plus some gems to sell if necessary. I had left my fortune behind, as I had left everything—though I have hidden the silver well, or so I think, for I have sunk all of it in chests near one of the islands in Lake Howel. I stand a good chance of recovering it, if I ever see Howel again.

But back to the day. We changed horses every five leagues or so, which meant nearly every hour. The farther we got from the capital, the worse the roads, and this slowed our pace. There were also fewer bridges, and we were compelled to ford some of the streams, though they fortunately were not in flood and never reached the horses' knees.

Floria did well in the saddle. I did not want her to exhaust herself, but she led the brisk pace, and if she felt anything like the pain that shot through my thighs and crackled along my jouncing spine, she gave no sign.

We could see the tree-crowned mass of the Cordillerie looming dark in the west, with the pale gold sun kneeling toward the horizon. After nightfall we would come to Peckside, and I regretted that in the dark I would not be able to show the improvised entrenchments that the usurper Clayborne had built against the knight marshal, or the hillside meadow where the traitorous leaders of the rebellion had been beheaded.

Perhaps, I thought, it would be poor politics to show that meadow to Floria, for she might view it an omen of her own fate.

I was thinking of Peckside, and a warm hearth, and mulled wine with a fine hot supper, and I did not notice at first the ragged men coming like ghosts out of the trees. "Ho, Quillifer!" Floria called. "Brigands!"

I was more acquainted with brigands than she, having been held hostage by Sir Basil of the Heugh, and these seemed not to be vicious wolf's-head robbers, but half-starved cotters desperate to feed themselves and their families. Nevertheless they came on bravely, eight of them, brandishing half-pikes and swords and a blunderbuss with its match glowing cherry-red in the shadows. One youth reached for Floria's bridle while an older man menaced her with a spear.

The robbers' faces flared out of the twilight as they reflected the flame of Floria's pistol. She shot the youth in the head, and then an instant later her second pistol flashed out, and the shot knocked the spearman onto his backside. Then Floria clapped spurs to the sides of her horse and dashed right through the crowd of them, her head tucked down on her mount's shoulder.

Her actions left me as surprised as any of the robbers, and my horse reared away from the pistol shots and the grasping hands of the brigands. I felt one man clutch at my stirrup, and I kicked out and felt my boot thud into his shoulder. I managed to get out a pistol and fired into the brigands as I kicked my horse into action, and then I fumbled for my second pistol as my steed gave an unnerved shriek and galloped after Floria, who was fast vanishing into the growing night. The robbers scattered, all except the fellow with the blunderbuss, who stepped out into the road, tucked the stock under his arm, and touched off the weapon. There was a terrific blast and a belch of flame, and then a great whirring and shrieking in the air, for the blunderbuss had been loaded with a double handful of old iron. Severed twigs tumbled from the trees, and I felt invisible fingers pluck at my cloak. My horse was hit in the rump, but that only prompted the beast to run faster.

I caught up with Floria a few hundred yards farther on. She had reined up, and had her sword in her hand. She looked at me, her hazel eyes sparkling.

"Oh good," said she. "I won't have to ride back and rescue you."

"I'll let you rescue me next time." I gasped for breath while my heart hammered high in my throat.

Floria had been raised in the saddle, and had been enjoying blood sports since she was a little girl. I had seen her bring down deer and shoot pheasant from the sky, but I had not imagined that lightning-fast draw with a brace of heavy horse pistols.

We went a hundred yards farther down the track, then reloaded our weapons before going on. But there was no pursuit, and no more gangs of robbers, before we arrived in Peckside. There I told the postmaster that my horse had been shot while fleeing bandits. He gave me a look from beneath bushy gray eyebrows.

"I thought you smelled somewhat of gunpowder," he said.

"Have you had much trouble on the road?"

He waved a hand. "Now and again. The people are hungry, the viceroy does nothing, and many prefer to risk hanging than starve to death."

I thought the brigands might well be his friends and neighbors, even his family. I decided not to tell him that we had left two of them in the dust.

"Does the sheriff do nothing?" I asked.

"The sheriff does what he can. But the wood-rogues are better armed than he, for weapons were free for anyone willing to walk to the battlefield and scavenge from the dead."

I said that we would need a light carriage to take us farther into the Cordillerie, for we were bound for Mankin Clough. We supped on a pottage of lentils, salt beef from a cask that might have been filled during Clayborne's war, and raveled bread better suited for the postmaster's horses. It was the best fare to be found in a hungry, cold country, and even though it was wretched, I was amused to realize that there was no sugar or sweetness in this meal, and I had been served one of my own savory suppers.

After supper we were taken to meet our postboy, who was no boy but a lanky man of at least thirty, armored against the cold in a fur-lined leather riding coat buttoned up to the chin. "If we meet brigands," said I, "pay them no attention. For my cousin Ludovico here is a deadly shot with a pistol."

"There will be no brigands after dark," said the postboy. And then, with a meaningful look, he added, "They don't want to freeze on the road any more than I do."

I gave him a few crowns to warm him, and then Floria and I climbed into the carriage. It was a light vehicle with sides of boiled leather and window-screens of thick oiled paper, and the carriage may as well have been open, because the paper screens rattled with the frozen wind that blew into the carriage, and which caused us to pull our hoods right around our faces before our noses froze clean off. We had not even left the post-house yard, and we were already freezing. We were glad of the bearskin rug that we had been given to share, and while I was more delicate in view of our difference in rank, the princess was not shy at all and nestled against me, and I was glad of her warmth in that frozen leather box.

"Ludovico?" said Floria. "Why did you shackle me with that name?"

"It's from Erpingham's *Tales*," said I. "Remember Ludovico the Page Boy?"

She sighed. "And what name do you give yourself from that book? Andrew Littlewit? Sir Barnaby Knock-Knees?"

"Perhaps Sir Flirt Lovewell," said I.

She laughed. "If you use that name, our enemies will know you at once."

Our postboy lit the lanterns that would provide a slight illumination of the road ahead, and then climbed on the left rear horse and gave it a kick with his special wooden boot. The carriage lurched, then gravel ground beneath the wheels as we made a brief turn before pulling out onto the highway.

The summer torrents had abused the road terribly, and of repairs there had been little or none. As the water drenched the land, trickles had turned into streams, streams to rivers, and rivers to floods. Deep trenches had been scored across the roadway, and we often splashed across small ponds. As the road wound its serpentine way upward, we lurched and swayed and tipped, but somehow we remained upright as the four horses dragged the vehicle onward. We were nothing but poppets thrown about in a child's toy-box, and it would have been impossible to sleep at all were we not so exhausted.

I remember dreaming that I was back on *Royal Stilwell*, the wind shrieking through the rigging, the deck pitching under me, and the taste of salt foam on my tongue.

The horses were changed in the middle of the night, and we had a few warm moments in the post-house before we dragged our pain-racked bodies to the carriage. Shortly after dawn we came to the next posting-house, and we went inside for warmth and breakfast. To our postboy I offered more silver.

Once before the hearth, we found ourselves reluctant to leave shelter and take horse, and we dawdled over our porridge.

"You know, Ludovico," said I, "should we meet with brigands again, you should escape as best you can—and if you break free, think not of drawing sword and coming to my rescue. Too much depends on you, and you should not risk your person that way."

Floria smiled. "I have seen you ride, and I have seen you shoot," said she. "I would not leave such a helpless Andrew Littlewit in the forest to fight alone a band of outlaws."

I ventured to touch the royal arm and looked into her hazel eyes. "And yet you must," said I. "Worse things have happened to me than to be robbed by ruffians. Once they have taken my silver, they will let me go. But if you are taken, the hope of the kingdom fails."

"I think you overestimate my worth," said she in a soft voice. She looked away.

"I think I do not," I said. A flush crept across her cheeks.

Floria turned uneasily on her stool and looked at the crossed broadswords displayed over the mantel. "You fought at Exton Scales," said she.

"You know I did. You investigated the matter."

"I know what others said. But I have not heard the story from your own lips."

She had asked me for my history once before, and I had avoided an answer, for I thought she was enacting some conspiracy to disparage

Lord Utterback, my commander. But in time she had got the truth out of others, and so I saw no reason to withhold it now.

So I told her how, fleeing an enemy, I had joined the Queen's Army against the usurper Clayborne, and how I had served as secretary to the young Lord Utterback, who commanded a troop of cavalry. Through the influence of his father Lord Wenlock, Utterback was given command of a fifth of the army, and sent to guard the pass at Exton while the knight marshal with the greater part of the army moved down the Cordillerie to attack Peckside. But Clayborne had thrown the bulk of his army against Utterback, while hoping to hold off the knight marshal with his entrenchments at Peckside.

"What most surprised me was how little battles resemble ballads," I said. "For in a ballad or a poem, there are a few striking scenes, and some brave fellows storm at the enemy, and either triumph or die in some picturesque way—and then it is all over, and they celebrate with a wedding. But Exton Scales was a fight that lasted all day, with blow and counterblow, attack and counterattack, and long hours in which nothing happened at all, but men standing under bombardment and dying with no hope of striking the enemy. And I saw no weddings, but many funerals."

I related incidents of that day, which ended with Lord Utterback leading the final charge that broke the enemy, and then dying in his hour of triumph. "Just like a hero in a ballad," I said, "and there will be a statue of him in Howel, or somewhere, but neither my story nor any of the other soldiers would make a ballad of that day, for all we saw was blood and mud and murder. And afterwards, the executions."

My story had attracted an audience, the postmaster, his ostler, the girl who had brought us our breakfast, and our postboy. "May I ask your name, sir?" asked the postboy.

"Martin," said I. "Bill Martin. And this is my young cousin, Ned."

"My brother rallied to Clayborne's flag," said the postboy. "And he died on the Scales. His body was not found."

"I am sorry for it," said I.

"That boy is just as dead as Lord Utterback," said the postmaster. "But he will get no statue."

"I think Lord Utterback would rather be a living man than a statue," said I, "and this man's brother as well."

The ostler, who had delayed his message while listening to my narrative, told us that our horses were saddled and ready. We mounted and made our way into a stark dawn lit by a low, pale, chill sun. After the previous day's ride my body seemed one vast bruise punished by the saddle and the jouncing of my animal, and I was in agony the first few leagues until the pain ebbed. Because of my suffering, I did not notice Floria's pensive mood. But an hour after dawn, with invisible crows calling from the trees and the rising sun coaxing wisps of mist from the ground, Floria turned to me and spoke.

"You said that the battle at Exton Scales was not like a ballad, but murder," she said. "And here we are, on an adventure that might some day be the subject of a romance, or a play. But if we succeed, there will be more battles like Exton Scales, more blood and murder." Pale sunlight shimmered in her eyes like tears, and I felt a strong hand clamp around my heart. "Must I bring about such tragedy, Quillifer? Another civil war, with good men lying dead on the field?"

I considered the question for a moment, my thoughts whirling in my head like a gray, lightning-fletched storm. "I think the war has already begun," said I, "and began the moment Fosco became viceroy, and determined to destroy the freedoms of Duisland and subject our country to a foreign power. He murders our people at will, with Lord Edevane his accomplice." I looked at her. "He maketh war on *thee*. He will do his best to cut off your head, or see you buried so deep in prison that you will never again see the sun."

"Well," said Floria, and tossed her cropped head with the effort to return a light answer. "I am guilty. I *have* committed treason, at least these last few days."

"You were forced to it," said I. "And it is not treason, for you have not been obliged to swear allegiance to Aguila. *I* am committing treason, not thee."

"I do not imagine the Siege Royal will accept that argument," said she. She shook her head. "Now thousands may die to keep me from that court," said she. "Who am I to be the cause of such broils and slaughters?"

"You are Duisland," said I. "Or will be, once we escape and sit you firmly in your power. I think if there is a war on your account, it will be a short one. For who would fight for Fosco?"

"Soldiers who are paid to," said Floria. "He raises twenty-five thousand men."

"He has not paid the household troops in nigh on half a year, and loots the treasury to gild the banqueting hall and build his Monastery of the Holy Prophecy. Why should the army risk life and limb fighting for such a petty and ill-judging tyrant?"

"I pray you are right," said she.

"The war, as I say, has already begun," said I. "The heads in front of the Hall of Justice proclaim it. It should be our business to make certain that they who began the war should not prosper by it."

And so we rode on through that cold day, going up hill and down, through groves of tall birch, twisted oak, and spreading pine. The day began clear, with high clouds scudding in a blue sky. The sure-footed horses managed the half-ruined road better than had our little swaying carriage.

In Howel, I knew, Rufino Knott would dress in a heavy boat cloak with a hood and spend the morning exercising my galley's crew on the lake. In the afternoon, he would ride in my carriage to Floria's house, come to the door as if delivering a message, and be told by a footman that the princess was ill, and not receiving company. Knott would return home. Lacking Bonny Joe's ability at impersonation, he would make no attempt to pose as me, or ape my manner, but instead let watchers draw whatever conclusions they would. If anyone asked where I was, he was to say that I was spending the day with a lady.

As for Bonny Joe, he would remain under the care of Mistress Ransome, and let himself be seen at the window several times, or now and again in Edith Ransome's company moving silently from room to room.

Now that we were well into the Cordillerie the post-houses were farther apart, and Floria and I changed horses only twice that day. The day began to darken well before sunset, and the sun now loured blood-red in the west. A gray blanket of cloud began to creep over the pass above us, enfolding the mountain like a shroud. I did not wish to venture into its ominous darkness, but even if we retreated, the gloom would overtake us. So we climbed up toward that cold, streaming mass, and soon were enveloped in deep twilight. Dew gathered on our clothes, and the jouncing of our horses sent little showers of drops sprinkling around us. A squall brought a light rain pattering down, cleared, then pattered again. The rain turned to sleet, and the rapping of the tiny pellets of ice on my clothes and my hood quickly grew monotonous.

Relief surged through me as the next post-house appeared in a glow of lamplight, and we gladly turned our horses over to the ostler and went into the warm common room. Other guests were sheltering from the storm there, and they had eaten up all the supper but a pottage of wild pig with parsnips and onions, some raveled bread, and cheese. Yet Floria and I were so famished and exhausted that we made a merry meal of these remains, while thunder crashed overhead and talons of wind tore and rattled at the shutters.

Despite my attempts to bribe him, the postmaster refused to give us a carriage till the storm was over. The guest rooms were all taken, so he obligingly chased his daughter out of her room and offered it to us. The daughter, who was about ten years old, seemed used to this kind of treatment, and laid herself on one of the benches in the common room, wrapped herself in a blanket, and went directly to sleep.

We carried a candle into the bedroom, and the low ceiling forced me into a crouch. We were clearly meant to share the bed, which was narrow and took up most of the small chamber. Her Highness and I were forced to stand close together. I offered the bed to Floria and said I would sleep on the floor. There was an odor of lady's bedstraw, which I found comforting, because the scent repelled vermin.

"You offer the bed like a proper protective knight, Sir Quillifer," said Floria. "Though I am disappointed you do not place a sword between us."

"I might," said I, "if there were room."

Floria waved a hand. "I am sorry for the inconvenience, but as we are enacting a chapter of a romance, I suppose these sorts of trials are to be expected."

"I have slept on floors before," said I. "And this, with rushes scented with herbs, is more congenial than most."

Her Highness sat on the bed and looked up at me in the light of our single candle. "Will you help me remove my boots?"

"If there is room." I knelt and took hold of her calf and ankle, and with some effort drew off her boots. She raised one foot to the bed and rubbed her instep. "My ankles have swollen," said she. "I could not have got that boot off by myself."

"Have you experience with straw mattresses? I can see that is what you have."

She smiled. "Every day brings a new thing."

"You should shake out the mattress," I said, "for the straw has certainly shifted under that child's weight."

Floria followed my advice, and I sat on the floor and fought with my boots until I got them off, then lay panting on the rush-bundles. "This feels less like a romance," said I, "and more as if I were in one of Blackwell's comedies."

Floria settled beneath the counterpane. "If this were a play," said she, "there would be another woman disguised as a boy, and the two of us would be mistaken for one another—and you would get into a deadly quarrel with a fellow who would turn out to be your brother believed lost at sea."

I sighed at my narrow berth, which would not encompass the width of my shoulders. "I think our stage is too small for all that."

"Shall I blow out the candle?"

"In just a moment." I wrapped myself in my cloak and rolled on my side, so my shoulders should not be so constricted. "There, Your Highness. I am ready."

The wind beat about the eaves, and sleet rattled against the walls. I could hear Floria's soft breath beneath the sound of the storm howling, and then I closed my eyes and fell away into dream.

The storm had guttered out by dawn, but it left the world covered in white. Floria woke nearly as pale as the snow, but assured me she was fit to ride. We had our porridge and ale and cheese, and the ostler saddled the same horses we had ridden the previous day.

The snow was unmarked save for the paw-prints of rabbits. It was only a few inches deep, but below the snow was ice, and we rode carefully as the ice crackled beneath our beasts' iron shoes. We descended a steep slope, then climbed a steeper one, and then from the top of the pass we could look down on the next crest, and the one after that, and the horizon blue beyond. We had reached the crown of the Cordillerie, and now we had but to descend.

"Congratulations, Your Highness," said I. "For the hardest part of our journey is over, and soon enough we will be at the docks in Longfirth. The storm only delayed us one night."

Floria turned, coughed insistently into her glove, then looked down at the path ahead of us.

"How long did it take the army to march over the Cordillerie?"

"Many days, but we went on foot, and were dragging a baggage train behind."

Floria coughed again. "Let us hope they send an army after us, then. We will outpace them."

We rode down the long slope, forded a stream, then snaked up another great slablike hill. The snow faded, leaving behind patches of stone or mud. Cloudy masses of snow dropped down from the limbs of trees and landed with an audible thump. By the time we changed horses and dined at noon, the ice had turned to mud, and Floria's cough erupted continually. There was an unhealthy fever-flush to her cheeks, and I asked if she wanted to rest, but she insisted on riding the next stage.

I was uncertain about the protocol for touching a princess. "May I put a hand to your forehead?" I asked.

She laughed, but the laugh turned to a cough. "You have our permission," she said.

Her forehead was warm, but did not seem excessively feverish. She wished to ride, and I obeyed that wish.

We wound down and up hills, forded streams, leaped over gullies that rain had washed into the roadbed. Floria's cough worsened, and there was a coarse, rib-rattling quality to the sound that I did not like. The sun was touching the horizon when we came to the next post-house, and this time I did not ask permission to touch Floria's forehead. Fever blazed beneath her skin.

I suggested that we remain a night in that post-house, but the rooms were taken by travelers waiting for the snow to melt, and I thought it might be better for Floria to sleep in a carriage than on the floor of the common room, in the company of the postmaster's dogs. I hired the largest and best carriage available, with glass windows instead of paper shades, and I paid for extra blankets and some warm bricks to put in our pockets.

Two postboys managed the six horses, and it was full dark before they kicked the carriage into motion. The carriage was more stable than that which we'd ridden two nights earlier, but the road was no better, and Floria was miserable as the machine lurched from one rut to the next. Her coughing was continuous, and she began to shiver. I put my arm around her shoulders and held her close, and she managed a little sleep with her head lolling against my shoulder. Her breath was sour.

At midnight we came to the next posting-house, and I asked if there was lodging available. I looked at the room I was offered, and it did not seem insalubrious, and so I took it. From the carriage I lifted Floria in my arms and brought her to the bed. Sweat beaded her forehead, and her face was the color of slaking quicklime. I drew off her boots and made her as comfortable as I could under the rag quilt.

I went out of the room to give the postboys their vails, and the postmaster bustled up with a tisane he had brewed with willow bark, feverfew, and honey. "We have seen that fever all winter," said he, "and it is a terrible blight upon the world. After all, this sickness killed our queen, and her husband, too, I suppose."

I thanked the postmaster and took the tisane to Floria. I made her sit up, supporting her with my arm, and held the cup for her to drink. Afterward, she seemed to rest easier.

After all, this sickness killed our queen. . . . The words chilled my blood. I had brought Floria on this adventure, and the thought that I might cause her death was beyond horror. As I composed myself to sleep on the threadbare carpet, I heard the rattle of Floria's cough and could not stop contemplating that dreadful possibility, and wondering if I was destined to witness the long, dreadful decline into death of this young, vital, and completely royal woman. And I wondered what would become of me afterward—for I had staked my life and fortune on Floria, and if she died, I would be lucky to escape with my head, and then only if I fled abroad and never returned.

What drove me frantic was the thought that I had abandoned you, and that now all my hopes might come to nothing, and we would not see each other ever again.

I slept but little that night. In the morning Floria was still ablaze with fever, and her burning skin was clammy with sweat. She murmured a few words that I could not understand. I went into the common room and asked for another cup of that tisane. I had a bowl of porridge while I waited for the tisane, and then brought it to her. Again I propped her on my arm and made her drink. She complied, though she did not once open her eyes, though when she was finished she gave me a sweet smile and thanked me in a hoarse whisper.

For that long day I tended her, and I laved her face and neck with cooling cloths. Her fever burned on.

That night she shivered beneath the pile of blankets and quilts I had layered upon her, and twice she fell into convulsions so violent that she nearly flung herself from her bed. I held her in my arms to keep her from injuring herself, and afterward cooled her face and neck with a moistened handkerchief.

Yet that night was the worst, and at dawn Floria was sleeping peacefully. Her fever had not broken, but it had declined, and when I brought her some of the postmaster's tea and supported her with my arm so she could drink, her hazel eyes opened and looked into mine.

"You have adopted another new profession, Nurse Quillifer," she whispered in her new, hoarse voice. "I think I like it best of all."

"I will expect a position in your household," said I.

"It will be amusing to see you in your apron," she said, and closed her eyes, and was at once asleep.

She managed to rest that day, and at suppertime I persuaded her to take some porridge and a little wine mixed with hot water. At night her coughing was worse, and she was restless in her sleep.

Next morning she ate porridge willingly and was able to sit up in her bed. There was still no possibility of travel, but I felt as if the weight of a cannon had been lifted from my shoulders. She had passed the crisis, and I could hope only that Bonny Joe and Rufino Knott could keep Edevane's hounds off our trail until Floria was fit to travel. That night I slept soundly for the first time in days.

The following morning Floria donned her man's apparel and came down to the common room for breakfast. She was pale, and her hoarse voice acted to confirm her male identity. She thanked the postmaster for his tea and his concern, and after porridge and some bread, she returned to her bed.

The storm had nearly shut down travel over the Cordillerie, but now that the storm had passed and the snow had melted, the post-house began to receive new travelers. Those that came from Howel I questioned closely, but they had little news beyond what I already knew. Floria, I learned, was generally pitied. "They say that the vice-roy wants her head," said one traveler, "and, as he is a grasping onion-eyed foreigner devoid of decency or mercy, he will get what he wants. We all feel sorry for the princess."

"Has she no friends?" asked I.

"Nay, sir," said another. "All are too much afeared. And now some say that she is poisoned, and dying in her house."

"And I," said the first man, "am going home to Longfirth to brick up all my windows, and save paying taxes on them."

Bonny Joe, it seemed, was doing his job well.

Another storm rattled down from the sky the next day, and was accompanied by a fierce western wind that howled along the eaves and brought strong trees crashing down on the slopes of the mountains. Floria was greatly improved, and ate sparingly of such provender as the postmaster provided. The fever now touched her but lightly, though the cough had not abated. Yet she was weak, and though she said she wished to get on the highway, I decided to wait until the snow had melted. Which was wise, because the fever made another attempt to overcome her that day, and at supper she had but a few spoonfuls of a wholesome pottage made with salt pork and dried peas, and then went to bed.

No sooner had she excused herself than we heard the sound of horses in the courtyard, and two grim men entered, each in a long leather overcoat, with fur collars spangled with drops of dew. Their spurs rang on the flags, and the west wind had burned their faces. These were dispatch riders, and they called for food so they could ride the night to Mankin Clough.

"You will ride all the night?" asked I. "Is your message that urgent?"

"The storm delayed us one entire day," said one of them. "And we must ride this next stage night and day, to pass our dispatches to the next riders."

He threw on the table the black leather pannier-bags that held his dispatches.

"What is so important?" asked I, but received no answer.

While the postmaster brought bread and pottage to the new arrivals, I went to my room to find Floria already asleep. I took my old cheviot overcoat and my sword and pistols, then threw my boat cloak over all and left quietly by the back door. The ostlers were bustling in the stables, walking the riders' old horses and fetching the new, shifting saddles and bridles from one to the other. They did not see me as I moved from shadow to shadow. In the tack room I found a coil of rope, and with this over my shoulder I slipped away into the night, and hastened down the highway.

The road descended steeply from the post-house. The strong west wind threw tiny shards of ice into my face, and the trees overhead waved their surrender to the wind's fierce attack. I hurried along three hundred yards or more, then looped one end of the rope around a stout birch. I drew the rope across the road to an osier that had the stump of a limb jutting out at knee-height. Then I checked the priming on my pistols and waited.

It was no more than ten minutes before I heard the clatter of horses on the road, and I took hold of the rope and waited. When the riders appeared, I pulled the rope taut off the surface of the road, then secured it by throwing a loop around the limb-stump. When the horses, trotting abreast, crashed into the rope, they struck with such force that the trees on either end of the line bowed their rustling heads as if in salute to the doomed riders.

One of the horses made a somersault on the steep road and threw its rider into the muck. The other kept its feet, but was tangled with the rope and bucked and snorted as it tried to break free. I took a grip on my pistols and stepped out of hiding.

I own that what followed was murder. I walked up to the rider still on his horse, pressed the muzzle of the gun to his side, and pulled the trigger. The explosion and flash were somewhat muffled by his heavy overcoat, but still he pitched off his horse and fell motionless on the highway. The other rider was lying stunned in the road, and I had no trouble shooting him in the head with my second pistol.

I drew my broadsword and returned to the first rider, but the sword was unnecessary, for my bullet had struck him both in heart and lungs, and he was already dead.

The sequel was laborious. First I had to calm and restrain both horses. The one that had tumbled was lame. I tied their bridles to the osier, and then dragged their riders into the forest to where they were screened by some buckthorn shrubs. Then I had to reload my pistols and lead the horses to their execution, for I could not have them wandering home and alerting the postmaster to the fate of their riders. I shot the horses in the brains, and then, taking the pannier-bags, I panted my way uphill. I took the single dispatch I found in the bags, stuffed it in my pocket, and threw the bags into the forest.

When I came in through the back door of the post-house, I feigned having returned from a trip to the jakes, and then made my way to my room by the light of a horn lantern. The dispatch was large, of heavy crown paper, and sealed with three seals that, by the light of the lantern, I did not recognize. I broke the seals and opened the dispatch, only to discover that it was in cipher. I debated whether to try breaking the cipher, but decided against it. Reading the message would not change what I had done.

I cleaned my pistols, pulled off my boots, and took to my hard, lonely bed on the threadbare carpet. I was awake for some time, my mind returning over and again to my actions. It was possible—even likely—that I had just killed two innocent men. But that ciphered dispatch might have been to the lord lieutenant in Longfirth, ordering him to close the port and search the town for Floria, and that meant I could not take the chance the message might find its destination. Now, because the message was in cipher, I could not know whether I had acted rightly or not. In the hollow of my chest I felt a sharp pang of misery at the thought of those two strangers whose blood I had spilled, and who now lay cold on the mountainside.

I slept poorly, and in every sound, in every moan of the wind or step on the stair, I heard the tread of the bailiffs coming to take me to my cell.

In the morning Floria was much recovered and ate her breakfast with a will. Her glance was sharp and quick and clear, and there was color in her cheeks. She wanted to continue the journey, and I was myself eager to be away in case I had failed, in the dark, to properly conceal the bodies of the riders. We said farewell to the kind postmaster, and passed silver to him and to his staff, and then took a small, snug carriage to Mankin Clough. We were happy to endure the misery of that little bouncing box as it was dragged up and down the hillsides, and I managed to sleep despite the ruts and the ditches and Her Highness's continued coughing.

We reached the town as the shadows grew long. Floria wanted to ride all night, but I did not want to risk her relapsing into pneumonia— so because there was a suitable room available, I took it for the night.

Floria ate her supper with a fine appetite, and because in our room there was a little trundle bed rolled beneath the oaken frame of the guest bed, I was able to sleep on a mattress for the first time since I had left Rackheath House, though Floria laughed at the way my feet overhung the end of the little bed.

The next day we renewed our journey and came out of the Cordillerie at last to the River Brood, which led to the firth and the Sea of Duisland. The wide gray river was filled with rafts of logs destined for Longfirth, for the logging continues even in winter, and it is a great pleasure to see the loggers jump nimbly from one great bole to the next as they guide their timber rafts down the chill waters. I rejoiced in the shimmering sight and liquid chuckle and fresh cool scent of the river, and my heart lifted at the thought that we were approaching the end of our journey.

There was no way that Floria could be put aboard one of those rafts, so I went to the quay to negotiate with some of the boats I found there. And so we found ourselves aboard the barge *Cadge*, bound for Longfirth with a cargo of building stone quarried upriver. The barge was the property of the matriarch, and her son-in-law was the skipper. Her two grown granddaughters, strapping girls with callused palms and windburned cheeks, were the crew, as was her grandson, who was about ten years old, but skilled enough to rope a bollard or set a sail.

They had intended on leaving in the morning, but silver convinced them to depart sooner than planned. On our journey Floria and I seemed to specialize in evicting daughters from their beds, for we were given the daughters' little cabin, while they slept on benches in the kitchen. Lamps were lit fore and aft so that other boats would know to keep clear of us, the sail clacked up the mast, and we cast off while the matriarch and her daughter stewed a fine dish of an old rooster cooked in wine till he was tender.

I have never had trouble sleeping on the water, though in the morning Floria complained of my snoring. "You are worse than Mistress d'Altrey," said she. "Though you would know about her snoring, wouldn't you?"

I rose at once to your defense. "I am unacquainted with it," said I.

"Well," said Floria, "you must then have been doing something other than sleeping."

The river turned to face west, and we were heading directly into that hellish western wind that had by now been blowing for three days. The sail was doused, and the barge let the current take us down the river, aided by the two daughters, who, with their long sweeps, kept us clear of the log rafts and other traffic.

I went onto the foredeck to enjoy the sight of the sun on the river, and the brave sight of the rich lands on either bank, the fields and orchards and fine houses and the sheep dotting the water-meads, but I stayed on deck only a short time before the wind drove me back to the roundhouse, where I found myself under the stern eye of the matriarch. She was a straight-backed woman with a tasseled shawl over her shoulders, and possessed a hawk face and a glaring eye, and a hairy mole on one cheek.

"You had best treat that girl well and seemly," said she, "and if you abandon her, I hope the gods curse you to a cold grave."

"What girl?" said I.

Her eyes narrowed. "You take us all for fools? For plain as daylight you two are runaways, and I hope you fly with her out of love, and not with intent to use her and then abandon her among strangers."

She had penetrated Floria's disguise, sure enough, and there was no point in maintaining my pretense.

"You mistake us a little," said I. "We are not lovers."

Her mouth twisted in a snarl. "You intend to be her pander, then?"

A whole arsenal of invention whirled in my brain, while I tried to sort out which lie she might believe, and which not.

"I told you she was my cousin," said I, "and that is true. But I fly with her not to take advantage of her, but to save her from a miserable fate. Her stepfather intends to marry her to an imbecile, for there is money that comes with that slack-witted, drooling half-man, and the stepfather covets it. It is to save her from that ill fortune that I fly with her. Once we come to my house in Selford she will be safe, and may resume her woman's garb, and live free and, I hope, happy."

She looked at me with suspicion. "I hope you speak truly," said she. "Otherwise my curse will follow you."

I did not wish to be cursed by an old lady, with or without a hairy mole, and so I put on my grateful-suppliant face. "I swear to you I will not harm or debase her," said I.

The matriarch seemed not quite to believe me, but at least did not challenge my tale. I gave her a small, respectful bow, and went to our cabin, where I acquainted Floria with my new invention.

"I will play the part well," said she, "for all my suitors have thus far been imbeciles."

By mid-afternoon we drifted down into the great deep firth that led to the sea, with the city of Longfirth at its narrow western end. To continue aboard *Cadge* would be to row the heavy barge into the teeth of that western gale, which was flat impossible even if we passengers agreed to crew another pair of sweeps, so *Cadge* moored to the quay while I went ashore to find a way of getting to the city. I found a small galley that took messages and passengers back and forth along the firth and the river, and they were willing to carry us to town but would not start till the next day. So we spent a last night on the *Cadge*, and I bought some bottles of fine red wine to make the night a merry one. After a cup of the wine even the old matriarch smiled.

The galley was open-decked, and there was no place to shelter from the wind and spray, so I made certain that Floria was well wrapped against the wind, which still blew fiercely from the west. The galley did not row into the teeth of that gale, but raised its lugsail and tacked back and forth across the firth, gaining a little westering with each board. Though the width of the firth varied from half a league to a full, the galley made each board so swiftly that it seemed scarcely to have settled on its new course than it was time to come about onto the new tack. Floria and I tried to stay out of the way of the bustling sailors, but the galley was so small that we were ever in danger of being trampled. Yet by this crooked course the galley made headway, and as the burning sun settled into the west, we could see silhouetted against the scarlet horizon the towers, walls, and bastions of Longfirth.

It was dark by the time we gained the town, which lay on the north bank where the firth narrowed to the width of a river, and was called again the Brood. The quays were alive with ships, and I hailed several to discover if *Able* was still in port, but none knew. I nearly lost heart, but I bribed the galley's crew to search for the privateer, and to my surprise and delight we found her, swinging on her buoy in the midst of the Brood's swift current. I hailed her and we came aboard, to be greeted by Peel, my cannoneer, and by Captain Langsam.

I had expected that *Able* would have left a week or two before, but the pinnace had been delayed by a refit, bad weather, and by half the crew coming down with the fever. But now she was busked and boun, as the saying is, and ready to sail, and I told Langsam that I wished to depart immediately. I was told that a departure was impossible till the turn of the tide, which would be an hour or two after midnight, and that with the wind holding westerly we should not get far.

"I wish to get as far as possible," I said. In truth I wanted to get out of the range of the city's cannon.

I did not know Langsam personally, but I knew he had been employed by the Spellman family, and they trusted him as a fine sailor. He was still young, under thirty, with a clean-shaven face and a disordered tangle of sun-streaked hair. I told him also that my page was recovering from the fever, and I wished to get him into shelter as soon as possible. To accommodate owners or important passengers,

Langsam's cabin could be divided by screens, and these were brought up from the hold and set in place. To Floria I gave the deep bed built against the bulwark, and for myself I stretched out a hammock in which I slept pleasantly until I heard the vessel getting underway. I wrapped myself in my overcoat and boat cloak, and went on deck to see a longboat being lowered into the water. With the western wind heading us, we could never set a sail, but must drift with the ebbing tide, and the boat was to take our hawser, lead us out of the harbor, and keep us from swinging broadside to the wind and running onto the shore or onto another ship.

We took our pilot on board and drifted with the tide, first slowly, and then with a great rush, the lights of the city receding swiftly as we raced down the Brood, the longboat pulling to keep us in the center of the channel. There were eight leagues of low sandy hills between the city and the sea, and we made that journey in a single rush, after which the tide carried us right out into the salt water. The channel to the open sea was beset on either side by dangerous banks of sand, on one of which *Royal Stilwell* had struck before the battle in which I took her, and it required all the skill of the pilot, aided by the navigation lights on shore, to bring us safely into the deep ocean.

And there, the ebb finally failing, we had to drop anchor in eighteen fathoms of water, for still the western wind assailed us and we could not get completely clear of the land. We put off the pilot, and I returned to the cabin and my hammock until eight bells, when the crew were called to breakfast. Floria and I rose from our beds and looked aft, out the great stern windows, to see the pale sun on the eastern horizon just breaking free of the land.

For the first time in weeks, I felt my heart ease. For here, as the ship pitched at its hawser's end, was the evidence that our flight was successful, and that we had won free of Bonille.

CHAPTER THIRTY-TWO

During the morning, *Able* pitched at its anchor while the wind whistled and moaned through the rigging, but at noontide Captain Langsam thought the wind had backed a little, so when the tide began again to ebb, he set sail. Were our track southerly we would run straight onto the sandbanks, so he shaped our course a little west of north, and thus we clawed free of Bonille. Unfortunately, our course took us farther from Selford, not nearer, but Langsam intended to tack back and forth, as the galley had on the Long Firth, to come by slow degrees to our destination.

Close-hauled, the ship's motion was unsettling, the stern rising into the sky in a great swoop, then descending through a series of lurches, each violent enough to rattle the teeth and cause the crockery in the cupboard to clatter. Floria proved a good sailor and was not ill, though the lurching of the ship made it hard for her to rest. Even so she continued her recovery, and her cough faded under the influence of possets of honey-sweetened wine.

We continued northward till dawn, then wore around onto the other tack. The western wind continued to blow fierce and cold, and

Langsam proclaimed that this dry, persistent gale was the strangest, most froward wind he had ever encountered.

We tacked back and forth for another day and night, and then at dawn we saw another ship on the horizon. I recognized *Sovereign*, which had stranded you at Bretlynton Head and had then been tacking back and forth into the same western wind for days. *Sovereign* was a far larger and more comfortable vessel than *Able*, and Floria and I shifted from the privateer to the great galleon, and to the protection of its formidable guns. I now commanded a brave squadron that was small, but far stronger than any I was likely to encounter in the Sea of Duisland.

Floria and I had a large cabin all to ourselves, for *Sovereign* had quarters beneath the poop reserved for owners or distinguished passengers. At the stern was a great expanse of glass to let in the wan winter light, and we had our own private stern gallery if we wished to venture into the air. We had a large oaken table that smelled of polish, and armchairs with embroidered cushions, and deep boxlike beds to larboard and starboard.

Though the cabin was spacious, Floria found it too small for her temper. To maintain her boy's disguise and avoid the company of strangers, she pretended to be more ill than she was, and shut herself away from company. When she could not avoid speaking, she spoke in gruff whispers. But she was restless in this self-imposed confinement, and often I found her pacing back and forth by the windows, her eyes glancing out at the sea, then down at the stout timbers of the deck, then out again. Sometimes I found her on the gallery, the wind snatching at her tight short curls, her hooded cloak spangled with spray.

"Curse this perverse wind!" said she. "I wish we were in Selford, so that I could take counsel there with my friends, and choose my course of action."

"I will be your counsel," said I. "And as for your action, there is but a single course possible, and that is you should be proclaimed queen on Coronation Hill."

She gave me a dark look. "Still you counsel civil war," she said.

"I did not fly with you from Bonille to watch you surrender yourself in Fornland," said I. "And I think what follows your coronation will be less a war than a parade that will end with your triumphant installation on the throne of your ancestors."

"I hope you are right," said she. Then she approached me and put a hand on my arm. "You may be an excellent sailor, and I know you are a caring and devoted nurse, but you must leave the business of politics to me."

"As Your Highness wishes," said I.

Reflected by the waves, spots of afternoon sunlight danced on her face. Our wooden lodging creaked and groaned about us, and I heard the thud of feet on the deck above us as the hands were called to the braces. Floria's hazel eyes looked up into mine.

"I wish to thank you for your care of me," said she. "There were many times on this journey when you could have abandoned me, and run to save your own life."

"I could not do such a thing and still look at myself in a mirror," said I. "For remember—you shot down those brigands, and were willing to come rescue me sword in hand, and I could never desert one with such high spirit and courage."

"I think you are not so simple a man as that," said she. "Your motives are never so simple."

"Perhaps they are not," said I, and kissed her parted lips.

It may be that I would not have so kissed her if we had not been hanging in that strange suspended moment of time, zigzagging in that persistent westerly wind, unable to go forward or back. The hurly-burly of the world, the trumpet-cries of power, and the very judgment of the gods seemed far away, and the girl in my arms had become the only reality.

She was not surprised by my kiss, nor did she reject it, but instead accepted it gravely, and ventured, as if conducting an experiment, to brush her lips against mine. We kissed and kissed again, and her kisses grew in confidence, and her cheeks flushed with desire. I picked up her small form and carried her to her bed, and there I allowed Floria to continue her experiments.

I have some experience with women, as you know, but it must be admitted that I know little of virgins, let alone royal ones. And so I contented myself with being but a guide to the world she now chose to explore. I think she was little surprised by her own capacity for pleasure, for she was after all an Emelin and the daughter of King Stilwell; but she had not anticipated her ability to draw pleasure from another, and was a little taken aback by this revelation of her own power. But she learned soon enough to relish her dominion, and as the days went on, and *Sovereign* continued to tack back and forth in that endless, timeless, streaming wind, she became a monarch indeed, and exercised that power as she wished.

As we lay together, my mind was a whirl of sensation, of delight and laughter and joy, but yet I heard your words whispering in my inner ear: *Yet if Floria decides to take you to her bed, you should comply.*

For in this, too, as in all things, I submit to your will.

The starry night blazed above me, with Cthonius rising in the east, and *Sovereign* was close-hauled on the starboard tack. Cordage thrummed, and the bonaventure creaked overhead as I paced the poop to take the air. That beastly west wind blew my hair about my ears, and I felt my cheeks burn with the cold. I had left Floria asleep in the cabin, her slight body curled beneath the counterpane, lashes dark crescents on her cheeks, her breath sweet with wine. I spoke briefly to the mate who stood the watch, and then went aft to stand below the great stern lanterns; tall as a man, and view *Sovereign*'s silvery wake stretching out on the sea. And as I gazed on the salt-scented rolling sea, I became aware of another figure standing erect by me, her head crowned by the radiant light of Cthonius.

"My lady," said I, as I recognized Floria's lady-in-waiting, Countess Marcella. Her lithe Aekoi form advanced, and stars shimmered in her liquid eyes.

"You do not seem surprised," said she.

"I know that your ladyship is composed of miracles."

Those star-flecked eyes searched mine. "How did you guess?"

"You always were a little too extraordinary," I said, "and no one, least of all Floria, seemed to know where you came from, and so it seemed that you had some great power to influence even a princess. But it was when we were aboard *Kiminge*, and you so politely asked me to carve the ham right under Wilmot's nose, that I recognized your peculiar brand of malevolence. For you took the occasion to turn that man's mind to violence, and then let him fall into the sea to his death."

"His death was a blessing," said Marcella, "for otherwise he would have lived all his life with a disordered brain."

And then her form shifted, and the golden skin paled, the slight form grew in stature, and the dark hair turned to tongues of red flame. Her emerald eyes glowed like Horagalles in the night, and her gown of forest-green satin blazed with gems.

"Afterward," I said, "when you made such a point of introducing me to Elvina, I assumed some kind of trap, and I was on my guard. You could at least have saved Meens from that fall."

"When my instrument breaks," said Orlanda, "I blame the instrument."

"I had wondered why you inspired three men to attack me," I said. "I wondered if your invention had failed, and you could only repeat yourself. But then I realized that these threats to my life were to distract me from something else."

Maleficent mischief glowed like moonlight in her face. "Do you guess what that something else might be?"

"Something that brings me here, to this sea, this ship, this wind that keeps everything at a standstill."

"Yes," said she, "something that has caused you to abandon your fortune, your plans for advancement, and your mistress. But now you have another mistress, do you not?"

"I am most fortunate in that regard," said I.

"You have chosen a princess and the life of the court," said she, "but I tell you that you would be safer on a battlefield. For at court flattery conceals the deepest envy, the wine-cup conceals bubbling poison, and deadly ambition is hidden by fair words, Bonille lace, and perfume. And there, Quillifer, you will contend with a malice so bottomless, and so time-honored, that it is become the very ocean in which the courtiers swim."

"I believe I have encountered the malevolence of courtiers before," said I.

"But however it swelled your pride, a Lord Warden in Ordinary Against Monsters is an insignificant office. Whereas the favorite of the monarch is another species of monster entirely, and the object of the greatest hatred in the world."

I shrugged. "I am accustomed to being hated."

Orlanda favored me with a catlike smile. "I think your vanity is puffed only by the regard of others, or by their hatred, which at least assures you that you are important."

I folded my arms. "Is that all you have to say, my lady? Because the night wanes, and my bed calls me."

"*Your* bed?" She smiled. "I think you mean the bed of another. Yet soon your other mistress will appear, and you will have to decide which to betray." She leaned close, her smile glittering. "And remember, Quillifer, I know who you really love."

Orlanda vanished then, and I stood for a moment beneath the great stern lamp, contemplated the wan light of Cthonius over the eastern horizon, and then returned to the cabin. I was soon curled against Floria in her deep, narrow bed, the arc of her body a warm comfort to a man who had spent too long in the cold air conversing with a cold-hearted nymph. Yet sleep did not come, for I picked through Orlanda's words carefully, and the only thing I could understand was that soon you would return to my life, and at that I felt my heart soar.

I wonder, therefore, if Orlanda gave you aid in that journey from Winecourt to Selford, with the intention of you arriving in the palace to cause chaos and heartbreak to explode around me.

I found Orlanda's vaunting less than convincing. She knows my ambition, and intended me to betray my friends to Edevane and the viceroy, and in the eyes of the world become a mean perjured informer, basely paid for treachery. In this she failed, but of course she may have laid deeper snares against me, and I would have to beware.

She also tells me that I will betray you or Floria, but I believe I have arranged things so that we all may be happy. I shall tell you that plan later.

We tacked back and forth for another day, and then finally the wind veered to the northwest, and we were able to shape our course directly for Fornland. The wind continued to veer and to moderate its force, and after another day we reached the latitude of Selford and were able to set a course directly for the mouth of the Saelle, and in another two days we reached Selford's harbor at the Isle of Innismore. I thanked Captain Gaunt for his kind hospitality and hired a coach to take Floria and me to Mossthorpe on the left bank. Across the river I could see soldiers drilling on the Field of Mavors, some of the viceroy's new recruits. As we came closer to the royal capital, I could look across the river and see the lacy white royal castle that crowned the bluff above Selford, and I felt a surge of joy that soon Floria might lodge there, a crown shining on her short dark curls.

But I did not want to go directly to the castle, for I didn't know what news had reached the castle's warden, or the commanders of the guard companies sworn to Aguila's service. Instead, once we crossed the great bridge from Mossthorpe to Selford, we took the coach to the park on the west side of town, and to the vast Roundsilver palace, with its facade of many-colored Ethlebight brick, its battlements and towers, its twisting chimneys carved into fantastic beasts, all snarling into the sky.

I told the footman at the door that Sir Quillifer the Younger of Ethlebight needed to see His Grace on a matter of urgency. He said that the duke and duchess were riding with friends to the royal deer park south of the castle, but would be back before dinner. Roundsilver's steward knew me, and we were shown into a parlor and offered refreshment.

It was not an hour before His Grace came into the room, still in his riding clothes, and followed by his golden duchess. His dark eyes fixed mine, and he walked toward me.

"What is it, Quillifer?" he asked. "What's afoot? What is so urgent?"

But Her Grace looked from me to Floria, standing behind me in her boy's clothes, and comprehension dawned like a sunrise across her face. She made a deep curtsy.

"Your Highness," she said.

The duke paused, turned toward Floria, and comprehension entered his dark eyes. He bowed gravely, then straightened and looked at me.

"Well," he said, "I imagine this promises more unhappiness for the kingdom."

"The viceroy aimed at bringing Her Highness before the Siege Royal," said I. "I have rescued her and brought her to your house."

"Ay. My house." Weariness seemed to settle upon the duke, and all at once he seemed ten years older than he had been but a moment ago. "There is a reason I never entered public life," he said.

Her Grace walked in graceful silence to the duke and took his arm

He looked at her and sighed. "Well," he said finally, "it ill suits me, but I will do what I can do."

Roundsilver could do a great deal, not least because he could open his strongbox and send forth his gold and silver into the world to work their wonders. Within two days the castle's companies of Yeoman Archers, Horse, and Artillery had received their months of back pay and declared for Floria, and Floria and I moved into the great white castle that shone above the city. The lord mayor and the alderman came to kneel and offer their allegiance, as did the Trained Bands and the masters of the guilds. The new recruits drilling on the Field of Mavors also bent the knee and swore allegiance to Floria. Nobles and great gentlemen galloped from their estates to pledge their fealty.

Eight days after her arrival in Selford, Floria was crowned Queen of Duisland on Coronation Hill south of the city, to the acclamation of the population. Because Berlauda's crown regalia had not returned from Loretto, Floria's scepter and orb were antique pieces taken from the castle strongrooms, and the crown had last graced the brow of Emmius the Good. It was in an old style, I suppose, but it looked just like the crowns on the money. In her coronation speech, Floria said that she had come to restore the ancient liberties of Duisland, and would abolish taxes wrung unjustly from the people. Both sentiments were interrupted by wild cheers. It was my duty to lead the cheering, but the crowd was so delighted that my task required little effort.

The celebration following the coronation was far less grand than that presided over by her sister Berlauda, who had fed the entire city. In a time of hunger, and with only a few days to organize the ceremony, Floria could not find enough food to feed the population, and so the coronation was celebrated by a great show of fireworks that blazed up from the castle and showered burning stars and shining flower-petals upon the gaping citizens below.

In this great rush of events and of people I was little remarked on. The great of the land flocked about Floria, offering homage and hinting at office, and none of them looked to me for anything. As was proper, I lodged apart from Floria, for the knowledge that she had taken a butcher's son as a lover would have shocked the sensibilities of the peerage, and brought out the monks and mendicants to denounce her. Floria's manner was so brisk and businesslike that I feared she had resolved to put love firmly to the side, but the day after her coronation, she assigned me lodging in the inner ward of the castle, in a room overlooking the courtyard. The room was surprisingly dainty, for there was a bed carved with arbutus and budding roses, and brilliant tapestries embroidered with a riot of fruits and flowers, birds and animals. A fireplace of pink marble was carved with gloxinia and camellia. A motif of day lilies was carved into the crown molding, and facing the door was a life-sized portrait of King Stilwell, blond and magnificent and fingering a pomegranate. Candles, already lit, flickered on tables and on the mantel. The room bore a faint musky scent, like an old trace of perfume.

I had few possessions to move into this grand room, for I had only the clothing I'd taken with me from Howel, plus a few clothes I'd commissioned since my arrival. I had taken only a few of my rings, the rest being held in a secret place near Howel, and I had also left behind my chain of office.

In bemusement I wandered over the room, surprised at the richness of it, and then the portrait of Stilwell swung open like a door and revealed Floria. She wore a dressing gown of dark green satin, with embroidery in silver thread, and on her short hair, worn like a panache, was the crown of Emmius. At the sight my breath stopped in my throat.

Amusement shone in her eyes. "Don't look so surprised, Quillifer," she said. "My father built a number of these passages, so that he could privately visit his mistresses."

"Did they all have his portrait?" asked I. "They could not escape him even if he was away."

"I think that was the point," said she. "If the sight of my royal father makes you uncomfortable, we could replace it with a portrait of me, once I have the chance to sit for one." She swung shut the secret door.

I embraced her gratefully and kissed her. Her galbanum scent sang in my senses. "It has been a hardship these last days," said I, "to be near you always, and unable to touch you, or show myself anything but the proper, dutiful subject."

"Do you think it is any easier being a monarch?" she asked. "To have the command of half a kingdom, and to send my subjects dashing from one place to another on my errands, but to be obliged to conceal the one thing I most desire?"

"In shadow we gather power," said I. "Some day concealment may not be necessary, and in the meantime our love will thrive in the shade."

Her arms tightened about me. "But now we must be very, very careful. Kings may have lovers, but queens must be chaste in the eyes of the world."

"I shall await Your Majesty, then, every night in this chamber of flowers, and I will test your chastity to the utmost."

She looked up at me, eyes a-shimmer with candlelight. "Lay aside this 'majesty,' " she said. "At least for tonight."

"Yet I would kneel to you as my queen," said I, and fell to my knees before her. I drew back the dressing gown to reveal a translucent nightdress of sheer lawn that revealed her small form, the high breasts and narrow hips, the dark moss beneath the dimple of her navel. I laid my cheek against the soft warm flesh of her belly, and let my arms sweep around her waist.

"I wish we were back at sea," I said, "tacking back and forth in that baffling wind, back and forth forever on that sweet ship."

She caressed my hair. "We will always be able to fly on that ship," she said. "When we meet together in safety, we may set sail, and go to whatever paradise we desire."

"Let us go there now," said I.

And so I rose, and took her hand, and led her to that rose-carved bed.

So I think I may safely report that Floria loves me. And slowly I have brought her around to the idea that, so that she and I should not be suspected, I should be seen to have a lover. And that lover is—will be—you. I will be seen with you, and will be seen entering your chamber at night. We may spend together all the time we like.

Mundus vult decipi. I trust this meets with your approval.

Oh—and I should recommend that you see Blackwell's new play. It is but a single act performed as a preface to his other comedies, and it is called *The Doctor and the Fever-Struck Princess.*

It is a version—fairly accurate, he tells me—of Bonny Joe Webb's adventures impersonating Floria, with the hero playing himself. For after word reached Ings Magna that Floria was ill in her chambers, the palace began to doubt its own agents' reports that she had been seen, and insisted on sending one of the royal physicians to examine her. While Mistress Ransome—who is a servant called Goldy in the play—holds the doctor outside the door, Bonny Joe touches up his paint and tucks himself in bed with the counterpane drawn up to his chin, and with hot bricks hidden beneath the topmost mattress to give him a sweat. At length the doctor was allowed to enter the room, but could only interrogate his patient through a screen—there is some fine comedy there, with the doctor ducking and leaping to get a glimpse of the princess, and Goldy dodging about to block his view. But at length the doctor insists on seeing the patient, and Bonny Joe does a perfect imitation of Floria, and summons him into the room. He pronounces the fever dangerous and prescribes an emetic and a phlebotomy. Bonny Joe is unable to resist the doctor bleeding him, but there is more fine comic juggling as Goldy hides the emetic and replaces it with something harmless.

At length the Yeoman Archers come to arrest the princess, but Bonny Joe has only to swab off the paint, resume his boy's dress, and make his escape in the confusion. Goldy also gets away, although I understand that Mistress Ransome was, in fact, arrested.

I would not like to be the man assigned to interrogate her, for she has the sharpest tongue of anyone I know. She will berate him, and he will have to put up with it.

I understand that Bonny Joe was able to keep up the impersonation for eight days, which meant that by the time Floria's absence was discovered, she and I were in our carriage riding into Mankin Clough, and with every hope of escape.

Alas, this also means that I had killed the two messengers for nothing, for whatever their dispatch said, it had nothing to do either with me or with Floria. Their deaths weigh on me like a stone.

Blackwell's company toured the provinces six weeks after Bonny Joe's escape, as the ports were closed, but after word had come that Floria had been proclaimed in Selford, the ports of Bonille were opened to allow commerce to resume and the taxes to be collected. And so Blackwell and his troupe made their way here, and perform now in the castle, or in the courtyard of their old inn in Mossthorpe.

In the last months Floria has built a government, and is building a fleet and an army. In Selford we have the treasury and the mint, for all that little bullion remains there. The great nobles and merchants of the land have opened their purses—and it is strange, is it not, that people will give freely of their fortune more than they would under the compulsion of taxation.

All but one of the members of the new Privy Council are great nobles—Roundsilver has the exchequer, for he understands the ways of money. He has my friend Kevin Spellman to help him as cofferer. Lord Slaithstowe is chancellor, and hopes thereby to win back his thirty-thousand-royal ransom, and Waitstill is privy seal. Drumforce, that fierce man, is constable, and at the head of the army will pursue his vengeance to hell itself. And that one among these not born to the nobility is Sir Quillifer of Ethlebight, who is Her Majesty's principal private secretary.

Ay, I have Edevane's office. And I strive to fill it with what skill I can, for all that I am not a soiled soft-tongued thief and manslayer.

The viceroy must know that, come the first breath of spring, a fleet shall set sail from Selford and land an army in Bonille. What he knows not is where that army will land—and that, when it happens, will amaze him. For we will land in Longfirth, where Count de Cibel has agreed to betray the city and its citadel. Ay, I know that de Cibel has married a Lorettan woman, and is a friend of Edevane and was raised to his peerage by the viceroy. But he has approached us, and we have agreed on his price. The fleet has only to come over the horizon, and he will wave the white flag.

But enough of these developments. You are new arrived, and must be weary. Let me kiss you and take you to your lodging. I dare not dally with you here, for fear Floria will come through that portrait. Our true reunion must come later, once you have rested.

But know that you are my all, my other half. We have come through storms together, and now we shall be rewarded by our grateful and love-besotted queen, and all fine things may be ours.

CHAPTER THIRTY-THREE

Once again, my love, I welcome you to this my chamber. Your nostrils flare, I see, at the scent of galbanum, and I own frankly that Floria spent this last night here. It must chafe you, I know, to serve her every day, and to see her happiness, and to know that she comes down that hidden passage most nights to see me.

Yet rewards have come. Am I not brave in my new ribbon, as a knight of the Order of the Red Horse? The order was established by King Emelin himself, and now I may lord over lesser knights—which is to say all of them, for the Red Horse has precedence over the other orders, and of course the knights-bachelors, too.

Floria has let slip that you shall be rewarded as well, though she has not said with what. I hope it may bring you joy.

Come, sit by me in the settee, and let me take your hand. Floria is all bustle now, putting the realm in order, and so must her ladies bustle along with her. I am sorry I have visited your chambers only thrice in the twelve days since your arrival, but I have been engaged in a task of great importance, and though it has driven me half-mad, I think I have finally seen it through.

To be brief, in my capacity as private secretary I have uncovered a nest of Edevane's spies here in Selford. We have been following them for some time, and I think I now know them all.

This troupe of turncoats was led by a lawyer at the Tiltyard Moot, who was passing messages through a pawnshop on Chancellery Road, and thence to a ship-chandler in Innismore, who carried the treasonable correspondence to the captain of a crumster, who took dispatches to Bonille. They will all be in my net by midnight, all but the sea-captain, who I fear may have got away on the afternoon tide.

You tremble, mistress. I hope you have not a chill. Let me put my arm around you to warm you.

Yet still you shiver even in my arms. Have you perhaps something to say to me? No? Then I must be the one to speak.

Ay, you were followed from the moment you arrived in Selford. We noted everyone you spoke to. If I have uncovered that spider's web of intelligencers, it is because you led me to them, and I was able to follow your dispatch from one hand to the next, and onto that swift crumster that even now follows the Saelle to the sea.

That message you sent is poison, and deadly not to me or Floria, but to Edevane. For I told you that our force would strike at Longfirth, and that Count de Cibel would surrender the place to us, and this was all a flat lie. Once that dispatch comes to Howel, the viceroy will replace a loyal servant, and perhaps cut off his head, and he will rush reinforcements over the Cordillerie to the city, and once marched over the Cordillerie they are not so easily recalled.

Nay, Floria's army will land elsewhere. Where we have proven friends, who will open their gates and join our forces to theirs.

You wonder, I suppose, how I knew you to be a creature of Edevane's. Floria and I both knew that Edevane would have a spy in Floria's household, and that spy would likely be a corrupted servant. But two of Floria's ladies also were suspect.

Marcella, first of all, for no one knew where she came from, or for certain who she was. And while she proved to be a treacherous, angry, and spiteful creature, she was no pawn of Edevane.

That left you. Floria had taken you into her household on the recommendation of her sister, but why would Berlauda, who hated all Clayborne's faction, recommend the grand-niece of an attainted traitor? Only on the suggestion, I submit, of Lord Edevane

It was Floria, before I joined you on that journey to Loretto, who suggested that I get into your confidence.

But still there were doubts. True, you were always prompting me to treason, and urging plans to put Floria and myself in danger, but that might be put down to your ambition.

But we took no chances. You know that Floria and I met together, and that, for your own protection, you were not to be told the subject of our conversations. But when you and I met, out of my love for you I told you what was said between the princess and myself—and, now and then, I lied.

And that correspondence I stole from Floria's study and delivered to Edevane, and which turned out to be letters writ to her when she was a child? She had placed those letters there deliberately, knowing I would take them, and that they could do her no harm.

But that still left your own status unresolved—we knew better than to trust you, but we knew not where your true loyalties lay. What finally betrayed you was your offer to negotiate Sir Basil's bill for fourteen thousand royals. I knew full well that you, from a family of high-ranked peers, would have no relations in the Oberlin Fraters Bank. Such factors and speculators are far too common for you. So that money had to come from Edevane, and no doubt you took your share before passing it to me.

Edevane planned to have me and Floria arrested somewhere on the trip from Howel to Bretlynton Head, or even on my ship *Sovereign*. He would recover the money and have proof of treason. But it was not Marcella's journey to Kellhurst that was intended to mislead, but your voyage to Bretlynton Head. Edevane would set his trap in the wrong place. Once you were safely away, Floria and I were away on horseback to Longfirth.

It was no accident that we met *Able* there, for though I told you the pinnace was about to sail, I had secretly sent instructions for it to wait for me. And *Sovereign* did not leave Bretlynton Head by accident, for that also happened on my orders.

I knew that my letters were being read, and that meant I could post false messages with the knowledge that they would be read by Edevane, while sending my real instructions by private messengers. My groom Oscar, for one, or Boatswain Lepalik, traveling as a guest of one of the barge-captains on the Dordelle.

Nor was it an accident that *Able* met *Sovereign* in the Sea of Duisland. They were meant to convoy together, along with my privateer *Ostra*, which missed the rendezvous but joined us in Selford later. All will form part of the fleet that will soon set out for the conquest of Bonille.

And are you as amused as I at the thought of Edevane frantically searching the islands of Lake Howel for the chests of silver that I told you were sunken there, and which he foolishly let slip from his possession and which he will desperately need to pay his own troops? For I never did such a witless thing. When the chests were carried into Rackheath House, they were met by officers of the Bank of Innismore, who counted the contents and carried them away to their own strong-room. Parkins, Edevane's informer in my household, had been sent away on an errand to buy wine and was unaware of the transaction. I had the letter of credit in my doublet all the way to Selford, and as soon as I arrived here, I arranged to collect my fortune from the bank.

For you see, my poverty was a pretense. I sold my cargoes and my gems for good money, but I complained to you and to Edevane that I was without funds, all in hopes that you would cash Sir Basil's bill, provide me with money to aid Floria's cause, and thereby prove that you are false. And so it has all come about, just as I planned.

I have been accused of preening and vanity, but I think in this case the charge is justified.

Ah mistress, you are unsettled. You are pale, and your trembling has not ceased. Are you perhaps anticipating the crudities of the interrogators, the tall black candles of the Siege Royal, the grim hemp dangling from the scaffold?

I will save you all that. If you will look under the pillow to your left, you will find your passport and a little money. Two of the Yeoman Archers wait outside to take you to Innismore and a ship. There you will be held until Floria's army departs, after which the ship will take you to sun-kissed Varcellos. You will be put ashore there, and after that you may go anywhere you like.

I do not necessarily recommend that you go to Howel. By the time you arrive, the capital may have fallen, and Edevane been put to flight, or in a cell at Murkdale Hags. And even if he still inhabits that snug little office, I do not know with what charity he will view an agent who has so completely failed.

I suppose I may be criticized for this mercy. They will call me sentimental. After all, you did your best to see me hanged.

Yet despite your treachery, I do not wish you dead, only out of my sight for all time. So let me rise and open the door, and introduce you to the sentries who will see you to your new lodging.

CHAPTER THIRTY-FOUR

I returned to my apartment and sat again on the settee, musing on the candles' dancing flames while Elisa d'Altrey's myrrh scent faded from my senses. The great portrait of King Stilwell swung open on its noiseless hinges, and you stepped out. Your new ladies—for a queen must have a dozen or more—had removed your court gown and combed out your growing wiry hair. You wore your emerald dressing gown and shoes with little bows, and you glowed in the light of the candle in your hand. I rose and bowed to Your Majesty.

"Is she gone?" you asked.

"I saw her into the carriage and on her way to Innismore. I doubt that any of Edevane's party are left to rescue her."

"That is a nuisance dealt with then."

You put your candle on a table, then came to me and kissed me lightly on the lips.

"At least," I said, "I no longer have to pretend to love her. The flattery grew increasingly burdensome, for in order to please her, my praise had to grow ever more extravagant. I called her an eidolon, my second self, the true pattern from which other, inferior women were but shadows."

You gave me an artful smile. "Consider it practice for a life at court."

"I hope that sort of gross flattery will not be necessary. There is only one person now that I hope to please, and she already knows that I worship every particle of her being."

You stretched, your arms thrown wide. "My particles are on the verge of exhaustion."

"Will Your Majesty take wine?" I asked.

"No, I have had enough tonight, for that supper with the officers of guards ran late and long."

"I will have a little, with your permission." I opened the doors of the cupboard and poured myself a goblet of hock, fine and golden in the silver-gilt cup.

"Sit," you said. "And please, for tonight, forget that 'majesty.'"

I kissed your knuckles, then placed myself in the settee. In a rustle of silk, and with the grace of a panther coiling, you sat in my lap, and I put my arms around you and let you kiss the wine from my lips. The scent of galbanum whirled in my senses. I buried my head in the corner of your neck and shoulder, and felt the flush of warmth from your skin.

"Is it hard," you asked, "to be false to a woman?"

"It is harder to be true to oneself."

You gave a dry laugh. "You evade my question. I remember at that astronomy party, a year and a half ago, you said that you reserved the right to lie to others."

"I rarely lie outright," I said. "I do not feel myself to be a convincing liar. I prefer to mislead, by speaking truth in such a way as to lead another down the wrong path."

"You were false to Mistress d'Altrey."

"And she to me." I considered the matter. "Yet, however pleasing she tried to be, she could not entirely restrain her contempt for me. Out of the slant of my eye I would see her lip curling, or her eyes hardening with scorn. It was a sentiment I tried always to conquer in her, but never succeeded." I kissed your neck. "She resented having to couple with me, I think. I suppose Edevane ordered her."

"I imagine he did. But so did I."

I drew back and looked at you in surprise. You waved a dismissive hand.

"Oh, I never made it plain. But I said I wished her to become your intimate friend, to sound you out and find out how reliable I would find you in a crisis."

"What did she tell you?"

Amusement glittered in your hazel eyes. "She said you would dare anything, so long as it fed your vanity. She also gave me some particulars of your abilities in the bedchamber."

I laughed and took a sip of wine. "She told me she had. Have I fulfilled your expectations?"

"Oh yes." Your eyes were bright. "D'Altrey's reports did not do you justice."

I kissed your moist lips. "She was always trying to bring us together, I suppose to compromise you. She said I should sleep with you, if you were willing. I wonder how she feels now that she has succeeded in this, but in a way that brings us every joy and her no benefit?"

You put your arms around my neck and kissed my forehead. "She was a poisonous toadwife, and we are well rid of her."

"Our best revenge on her," said I, "is to live in perfect pleasure all our nights."

"Yes," you said, and then a pensive look crossed your face. "But some things must be said first, for I know some of what d'Altrey said to you, and I can guess the rest, for she has said some of the same things to me." Your eyes gazed into mine. "I wish to draw her poison out of you, and so I must be frank."

I looked at you in deep surprise. "Say what you will, but I have long banished that woman from my heart. After all, she had freckles on her nose, and I have always hated freckles."

You looked at me levelly. "You will not turn me from my purpose with a jest, Quillifer."

I sighed. "Then say what you must."

"Because d'Altrey praised my hypocrisy in seeming a dutiful sister to Berlauda, I know she praised your hypocrisy as well, but for what I know not."

"My piety," said I, "on Berlauda's retreat."

"Yet you made the postures, and chanted the chants, and offended no one. It is less hypocrisy than politeness."

"Though it must be admitted I only went because I thought it might earn me higher office."

"Men have done worse things for higher office, and you have not." You took a fistful of my long hair, and gave it a sharp tug. I winced.

"Now will you let me praise you?" you said.

"I will accept praise," I said. "If not from my mistress, then who else?"

You gave a little tight-lipped smile. "D'Altrey would have commended your contempt for those knights who attached themselves to your dragon hunt, and died because their vanity would not permit them to withdraw from a hopeless fight. Yet you offered to save them, and at least some became your friends—Dom Nemorino d'Ormyl, for example."

"And Westley, till he was blackmailed into challenging me."

"And Westley, too. You gain allies, and you inspire loyalty in your friends. Look at Rufino Knott, at Captain Gaunt, at Prince Alicio, at Roundsilver and his lady. You reserve contempt for the truly contemptible, but among the rest you win hearts." You looked at me close, and I could feel the power of that gaze prickle along my skin. "You won mine, Quillifer, and I have never given my heart to any man."

I sought for fine words, and settled for the truth. "I am astonished perpetually by the honor you do me, Your Majesty."

You frowned at me. "D'Altrey would also have praised your ruthlessness in humiliating your enemies rather than killing them. In dragging Westley out of the drink, or demonstrating your superiority by hurling Meens off a building in front of a crowd of witnesses. Yet—" You put your hand on my cheek. "I see a reluctance to take life. Whatever you are, you are not a killer, and you treat even your enemies with compassion."

I felt a fist close on my heart. "My lady," said I, "there is a matter of two couriers—"

"We may speak of that later. Whatever you may have done, and under what necessity, it does not alter what I see in you." You kissed me on the lips. "You are generous, you are kind, you are clever, and you rescue lost princesses. If I did not suspect you would laugh at the word, I would say you are chivalrous."

I blinked at you. "I am surprised well beyond any laughter. And even if I am not quite this person you describe, to please you I will endeavor to become that person, if it is within my power."

You put your arms around my neck and touched your cheek to mine.

"So have I drawn d'Altrey's poison, Quillifer? Have I freed you from the misapprehensions with which she tried to shackle you? The burdens she placed on your soul?"

"My soul flies free, Majesty. It circles about the room like a hawk in its gyre. And you need but to hold out your wrist, and my soul will light to feed from your hand, and you may keep it in your possession forever."

"I will keep it then, so." You kissed me fiercely, and when I began to respond, you drew back. "If I may raise one other matter . . . ?"

I tried to restrain my longing. "As you wish."

You looked at me with sober concern. "It seems to me that since you lost your family, you have been in flight. You fly from one avocation to the next—lawyer, sea-captain, soldier, jeweler, merchant adventurer, knight-errant—and perhaps that is because the memory of the night of burning Ethlebight is too painful."

I felt an ache in my throat. "That may be so, Majesty," I said.

"I cannot tell you how to grieve," said she, "for that varies from one man to another. But I know something about flight, and I will but repeat your words to me—that it is better to fly *toward* something, and not away."

"Like my soul, I fly now to you," said I. "And I will rest here with you, and shelter in your shadow, and never leave unless you send me away."

At this you began to kiss me again, and when I drew off your dressing gown, your flesh was hot and seemed to burn my palms. The rest of the night was fire and passion, and together we burned till dawn.

"I like not that lean man," said I, viewing the Marquess of Stayne from your window at Ings Magna. "Do you truly mean to make him a general?"

You were at your desk, quill in hand, applying Q Sable Ink to a document. "He raised his own regiment," you said, "which is more than most of my generals have done. Besides, he will serve under the knight marshal, and can do little harm." You signed your name with a flourish. "You only have a prejudice against him because he tried to murder you."

"That brawling touched your own safety somewhat," I reminded. "And he was exiled for it."

You looked up from your desk. "You *did* cuckold him," you said. "He had some reason for his poor temper."

"In which case, he should have challenged me, not sent his miching assassins."

You touched the quill to your chin. "Well, he is useful. I hope he teaches ambitious men to raise their own soldiers, and save me the trouble of paying for them out of the treasury."

I wondered how long Stayne could afford his soldiers. When he had been exiled, four years ago, his finances had been in ruins. Would four years on his estate, relieved of the necessity of playing a magnificent lord at court, have been sufficient to recover his fortune and buy a regiment?

I fear you will have to pay for those soldiers after all.

The march to water-girdled Howel had gone much as I had expected. We landed at Bretlynton Head, and the city and its castles were formally surrendered by the sea-consuls and the lord lieutenant. My colleague from Hurst Downs, Baron Becket, had met us with a company of foot raised from my own estate and others. You took up residence in the castle while we worked out the business of getting the army up the river.

All that was required to win the love of the people was your proclamation that all the new taxes were illegal, and would be canceled. And the love of the monasteries was assured when you announced that the Commission of Inquiry would be disbanded, and its members prosecuted for murder. Abbots rallied to you, and began preaching your cause to the people.

What followed was, as I had predicted, a parade. We sailed up the Dordelle, receiving lords and squires and officials from all over Bonille, who rode in to tender their submission. A force of militia was sent against us, but it surrendered before it came within sight, and received new standards from the new monarch.

The viceroy readied the household troops to defend Howel, but instead they rioted and demanded their back pay. When Fosco paid, the guards took the money and returned to their barracks, but then would not come out. Finally Fosco, Edevane, the monks of the Commission of Inquiry, and some of their supporters fled on wagons loaded with booty, along with a group of Lorettan ladies who had come to Duisland to find husbands and instead found only fear and rebellion. To keep them from being massacred by a mob on the road home—which would have brought our nation into dishonor—my friend Lord Barkin and some of the Queen's Own rode with them to keep them safe. Barkin took the viceroy and his party to the border, then to their vast surprise took the wagon-loads of booty, turned back to Duisland, and rode home in time to welcome you to the capital.

So now Barkin is lieutenant-general of cavalry, as my friend Lipton is lieutenant-general of artillery. You are generous to those who love you.

"For every appointment I make," you said, "I create one ingrate, and fifty envious foes."

I must admit I was a little envious of those ingrates, for my services to the crown were unrewarded except for my enlarged knighthood. Yet I could console myself with my ships, the gems and money I had recovered from the undercroft of the Howel branch of the butchers guild, my ink business, the workshop I intended to create to make Mountmirail's backstaff for mariners, and my canal—for while I was in Fornland adoring Your Majesty, Mountmirail had found a recipe for antihydraulic mortar, by cooking his powders at a much higher temperature than anyone had before attempted.

"In war there are jobs for all," said I. "Let those who want to serve you—or say they do—join the army, or the fleet."

It would be safe enough for them, for there would be little or no fighting this year. Duisland did not yet have a proper army, just those half-trained remains of Fosco's twenty-five thousand who had not deserted or been sent to Loretto, and Loretto's armies were facing the wrong way, prepared to hold off the threat from Thurnmark and its allies.

Your mother has been freed from Murkdale Hags, along with the sorcerer Doctor Smolt and Mistress Ransome. Dowager Queen Natalie is free to roam the palace, chattering out her scandalous anecdotes, and Doctor Smolt has been banished from the capital, though he has been told he may win his way into your favor by casting spells to blast your enemies.

Mistress Ransome will marry Mountmirail, providing a happy ending for any observer who wishes one.

All butcheries were postponed to next year, to grandly be called Floria Year II.

Warrants have gone out for new elections, and the subsequent meeting of the Estates. For we are at war, and wars must be paid for. New taxes will be imposed, though it is hoped they will not be so tyrannical as Fosco's, and the Burgesses will vote on them without compulsion.

We were speaking in your private office on the second floor of the palace, all gilding and mirrors. One of your ladies-in-waiting watched us from the next room, through a hagioscope. I longed to kiss you, or at least touch you, but the formal guard on your chastity was still in place, even though your virginity had long since melted away. I looked out over the bowling greens in back of the palace, toward the water gardens. The first rays of summer were warming the land; daffodils, tulips, poppies, and bluebells blazed in the gardens; and the apple trees were in blossom. The weather this year had been kind, and the wheat and rye were green in the fields. If the weather remains fair, we will have a good harvest, and the famine will be over.

Berlauda's great banqueting hall, to my right as I looked out, remained unfinished, with the gilding incomplete and the great frescos abandoned. Such an extravagance could not be borne, not in a nation straitened by famine and war.

I saw the Marquess of Stayne approach the palace as he walked down the gravel path on his way to the day's audience. He was a lean fellow, with a graying pointed beard and a small, pursed, disdainful mouth, and he was followed by a crowd of clowns and lackeys. I entertained myself with the idea of dropping a vase on his head.

"This will amuse you," you said, and reached into a drawer for a letter. I took the letter, opened it, and with a start recognized Edevane's hand.

"He offers to make his submission," you said, "if he is given a pardon for his crimes."

I considered this. "Let him confess those crimes first, to a panel of judges empowered to ferret out the truth. And let him bring his files with him, all the documents tied in red and blue ribbon. After which—" I waved a hand. "Deprived of his fortune and all the property he thieved from their rightful owners, he will be allowed to retire to his wife and the little barony he inherited."

"He will cause mischief wherever he lives."

"I will keep a better watch on him," said I, "than he kept on you. And if he conspires, he will lose his head."

"Well," you said, "that being the case, I will send him the reply he hopes for."

There was a knock on the door, and one of your ladies entered to say that the ambassador of Thurnmark awaited your pleasure in the waiting room. You looked up at me.

"The Privy Council meets at two," you said. "Don't forget."

I bowed. "Your servant," I said.

I went to my apartments, and there for my dinner I had a manchet loaf, a cup of wine, and a cold lamb pie. I remained under the eye of royalty, for my apartment has a large portrait of King Stilwell, behind which is the private passage that connects my rooms with those of Your Majesty.

After dinner Goodman Knott dressed me for the audience that would precede the Council meeting. My doublet and trunks were blue watered silk, and I wore matching sapphires on my fingers. My hose and linen were spotless white, I wore the ribbon of the Red Horse over my shoulder, and I wore a jaunty velvet bonnet with a feather and a badge.

As always, though I did my best to look well, I did not dress like a courtier, with their flounces and purfles and pearl-sewn doublets. I remained, alas, myself.

Leaving my apartment, I made my way toward the Chamber of Audience to await your appearance, but as I hastened along the second-floor corridor, I suddenly tripped, and landed on hands and knees on the marble floor. A kick lodged in my ribs and knocked the breath from my body, and then rough hands plucked me from the floor and drove me into the wall. I found myself gasping for breath and surrounded by a wall of lackeys, each with a smirk of satisfaction on his face, and then the wall parted to reveal the Count of Wenlock, his lips drawn in a smirk. Brandy fumes filled the air as he approached.

"Think you I had forgotten you, barber-monger?" He thrust his face at mine, and his hand clutched at my collar. "Do you not know that a gentleman always pays his debts?"

"A gentleman fights his own fights," said I, "and does not hire rudesbys and assassins."

"I would not soil my hands with such common blood as yours," said Wenlock. "But know that I will have my twenty-five royals back, and the cost of my sunken galley, and that the price will be carved from your flesh."

He shook me like a rat, and my head knocked into a wall-sconce. Stars exploded behind my eyes. Wenlock turned to his crew of ruffians.

"Maul him," he said, pronouncing the words with pleasure, and then I heard another voice.

"My lord of Wenlock!" said my Queen. "Kindly unhand the Count of Selford!"

You swept down the corridor toward me with your company of ladies and the surprised ambassador of Thurnmark. A look of thwarted anger crossed Wenlock's face, and he released me. His lackeys fell back in embarrassment.

"We will not have these brawls in our home!" you proclaimed, and looked Wenlock in the eye. "Now apologize to his lordship, and get you gone—you will return at once to your home in Ethlebight, and come not to court until you are summoned!"

Wenlock purpled in anger, but he did as commanded, and hastened away along with his following. I barely heard his words, for echoing through my head were those words—*Count of Selford*—and as I looked at you in rising astonishment, I saw the confirmation in your eyes.

"You had best go back to your apartment," you said, "and change your linen and hose. You are somewhat soiled, my lord."

"I obey, Your Majesty." I bowed, and waited till you and your party passed, and then, as elation blazed through my blood, I returned to my rooms—where later, in the soft silent hours of the night, I would await Your Majesty's pleasure.

ACKNOWLEDGMENTS

With thanks again to Ada Palmer, for a lucid explanation of the differences between *assurgo, cresco,* and *convalo.*